THESE BRIGHT AND LOVELY NIGHTMARES

THE SILENCE THAT ONCE WAS
BOOK 1

GIOVANNI DIAZ

GIO WRITES STUFF

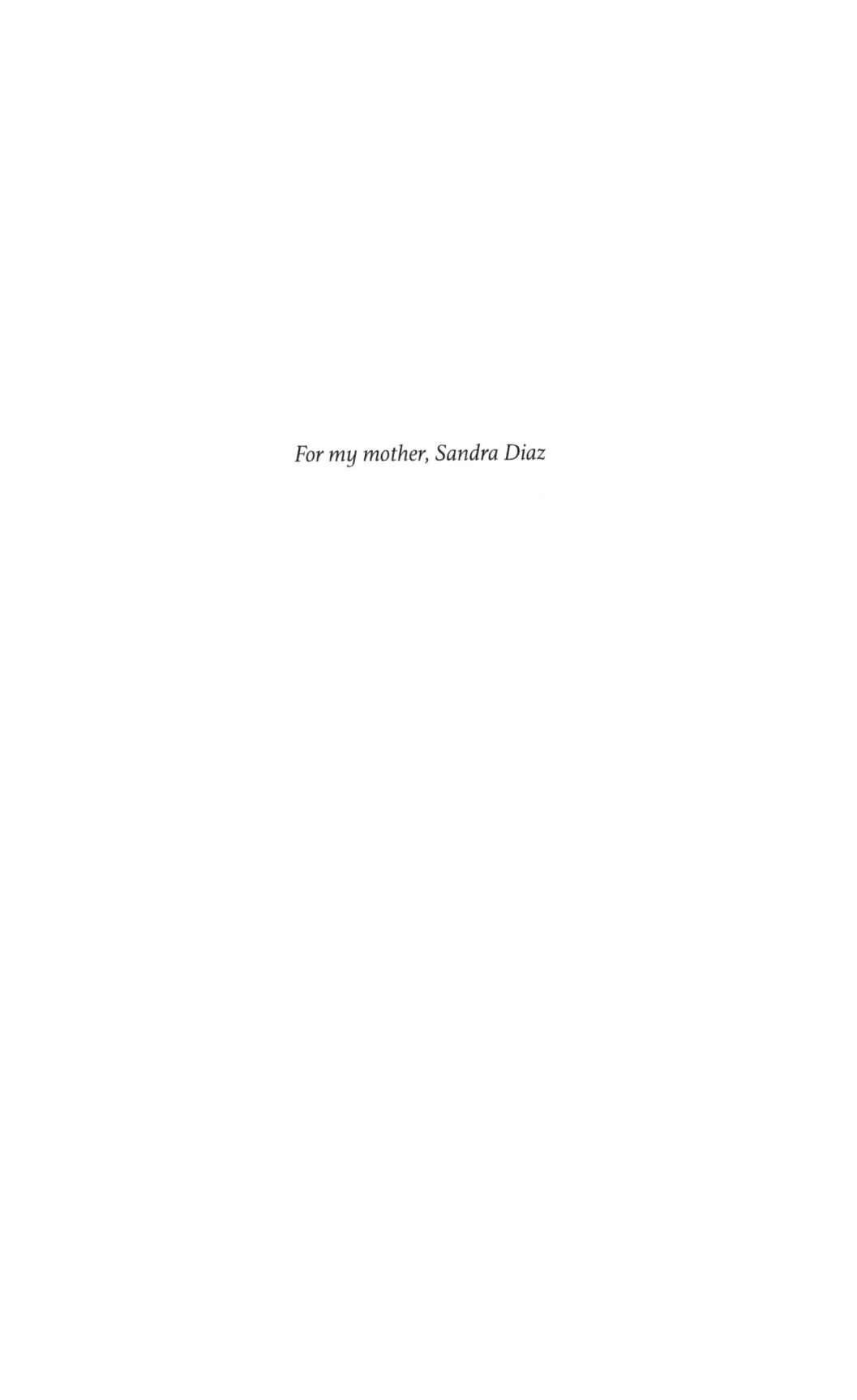

For my mother, Sandra Diaz

CONTENTS

ACT I

DEATH OF A DEAD MAN

1

Fire leapt from Eleanor's fingertips and engulfed the candlewick rising from the stone floor.

"Don't be scared," Ian said.

Eleanor glared up at him, the flame casting twin spirals in her brown eyes.

"I'm not," she replied. "Shut up."

Ian smiled and ruffled her hair. She batted his hand away, blew a strand of black curls from her face, and held her quivering fingers over the shifting candlelight. The warm glow danced on the floor and dissolved against the surrounding darkness.

Ian stood near the light's edge like a sentinel from another world, his shadow long and distorted at his feet. He smoothed his suit jacket with a few strokes of his hand, and, as he did so, his shadow bled upwards through the floor, rising as if from the netherworld. It squatted beside him, craned its head, and peered at Eleanor. Then it crawled towards her, growling.

Eleanor trembled, but held its gaze.

Ian adjusted the knot of his necktie and tapped his foot once in command. His shadow stopped, hissed, and crawled backwards, squatting at the boy's side.

Eleanor took a deep breath.

"I'm never gonna get used to that."

Ian gave his tie a final stroke.

"You know I won't let it hurt you." He gave her a searching look. "You don't have to do this yet, Sis."

"Don't start."

"Defending against possession's a serious thing, Ellie. Most magicians don't train with me until they're teenagers. Even grownups don't like it."

Eleanor frowned, the youthful contours of her face scrunched into an incredulous mask, willful intelligence alive in her dark eyes.

"Most magicians don't have know-it-all demons for brothers," she said. "I gotta get something outta that. And we could-so get attacked."

"Not here."

"Yeah it could. Pop's always saying we have to be ready for the worst, 'cause..." She cleared her throat and affected a gruff Russian accent. "'Eh, the worst is out there looking for us'. Besides, you're barely a teenager, but he lets you train with older magicians. Fair is fair, ass-face."

Ian gave a silent laugh.

"I have to help them," he said. "I'm all they have."

"Bullshit. Like you don't get something out of it."

"Okay, maybe. But I still think this is a lot for you to handle. It's way too dark in here, for one thing."

"Ian—"

"There's no shame in being afraid of the dark."

"I'm gonna fuckin' hurt you."

Candlelight flickered on Ian's cherubic face, a fourteen year old boy soon to be a child no more. His hair was parted, prim, dark. His eyes spoke of calm that many go their entire lives being unable to attain.

Eleanor flared in anger, a twelve year old girl in jeans and a red hoodie, poised to launch an attack against her big brother. She took a deep breath and stared into the candle, watching the wax pool. Then she stretched her hand over the flame and wiggled her fingers from pinkie to thumb, thumb to pinkie. The candle flame jolted and swayed like an entranced snake. She cupped her hand over the fire and snatched it back as if plucking something from the earth. Darkness saturated the room. The candlewick smoldered. She turned her fist palm side up and opened her fingers. The flame hovered there, tracing the lines of her palm as if they were canyons blazing under a merciless star. She closed her fingers over the flame, blew into her fist, and flicked her hand open. Five tethers of fire erupted from her fingertips and lassoed the wick.

She shot Ian a challenging look, daring him to say something.

He held her gaze.

"Pop warned you about showing off," he said.

Eleanor blew another strand of black curls from her pale cheek.

"Okay, then," Ian said, resigned. "Ready?"

"Ready-fuckin'-spaghetti."

"If you really want to impress me, you'd do this in the dark."

Resolve withered on Eleanor's face, and fear slithered through her insides. The surrounding darkness mirrored her fear, hungry to devour the feeble candle light. She shook her head in answer to Ian's dare, and shame flushed her cheeks.

Ian touched her shoulder and nodded, smirking as if he held to some private joke. Then he stepped backwards and was enfolded by darkness. His shadow lingered, a deformed thing squatting on legs bent backwards at the knee. It lurched towards Eleanor, hissing laughter. Then it crawled away, waving as it followed its master.

Eleanor suppressed a shudder. She folded her legs, laid her left hand into her right, and focused on the candle.

She closed her eyes. She breathed.

Calm enveloped her. Each exhale eased her heartbeat to a gentle rhythm. But tension lingered, fueled by a tumult of anxious thought.

"Your first time against a demon - Too dark! Too dark! - Wonder if Pop knows..."

Eleanor accepted these thoughts as if they were enemies wielding weapons of smoke. Anxiety faded, and peace stitched itself into a growing weave that shielded her. Memories sprung forth and rushed in blurs of color, sound, and sensation. Worry, anger, joy, and grief screamed over each other until they became a tangled cacophony vying for her attention. She trembled, breath shaking, eyelids beating, sweat glistening on her brow. A sob rose in her throat. She swallowed it, exhaled, and let stress drain into acceptance. She did not fight. She did not hold on. She let go until all that was left was stillness.

This stillness stretched, deflating anxiety and doubt, leaving her awareness floating in a warm space. The redness behind her closed eyes diminished to the texture of sleep. Ripples beat through the silence of her mind, and faint beads of iridescent light awoke like gems rising from the depths of some boundless ocean. These beads gained substance and form, and strands blossomed from them and bloomed towards each other. They fused into wires of sacred fire, sparks spiraling into geometrical patterns that beat with color and sang with many voices. Yet these voices were one. The patterns writhed until they erupted into a sheet of liquid light that carried Eleanor away from the world, away from herself, and into a place where all things were endless.

And here was magic: An inner conflagration of possibility, a force defiant against the laws of nature or perhaps evident of laws unknown, swelling and swaying with waves that traversed infinite shores, that awaited a magician to wield them upon the world.

Eleanor was enveloped, as if an all-knowing presence probed at her mind to understand her limits. She probed back. An expansive vista unfolded, taking her awareness beyond the material realm to a place where time ended in ever flowing tides of beginnings.

The vastness overwhelmed her, an ocean poured into a thimble. She cursed her youth and inexperience, wondering not for the first time if she could ever master such power.

Magic wakened and wavered.

Eleanor remembered her training and accepted frustration, allowing control to slip through her grasp so she may dissolve and once more became one with endlessness. The present drifted away, and her thoughts and feelings coalesced into a single point of light that opened and infused her with the mysteries of creation, eternal clay waiting to be molded into matter and dimension. She beheld pulsating waves of light in her mind's eye, and that light was hers to do with as she would, to create what she dared to imagine, limited only by inexperience.

She opened her eyes. The surrounding darkness throbbed as if awaiting her word to transform it into something more. The stone floor seemed malleable, something she could reshape. A smile flickered on her face. She stared into the candle flame and could make out each thread of fire, looked within the melting wax and could almost hear the buzzing of billions of particles vibrating together. Magic revealed the hidden nature of all things, a vast microcosm expanding into the greater world.

There would come a day when the great source of magic would be like air in her lungs. Then she would be a true magician. For now, she almost enjoyed the act of reaching out, of letting magic fill her, of being reminded again and again that existence was the greatest act of magic ever conjured.

Eleanor whispered her incantation.

"Everything is nothing, nothing is everything. Everything is nothing, nothing is everything…"

Her skin tingled, her muscles tensed and released.

"Everything is nothing, nothing is everything. Everything is nothing, nothing is everything. Everything is nothing, nothing is…"

Crimson eyes awoke in the darkness. They peered into Eleanor's, bloody and smoldering, freezing her breath in her throat.

"Shit."

The eyes stared, veins cruel streaks of lightning frozen in boiling blood. Their pupils were perfect points of black, as if composed out of desolation, the ending of everything, hungry to consume all that dared to exist.

They vanished into the darkness.

Eleanor swallowed, regained her breath, and went on.

"Everything is nothing, nothing is—"

A growl seethed into her left ear, undulating down her throat where she could almost taste it as a coating of rust and filth. Claws made from shadow reached from behind her and brushed her cheek. Their reek coiled just under her nostrils, rotted meat and the bowels of perdition. The claws retreated, but the stench remained, wafting from the dark as if she were being circled.

Dread engulfed Eleanor, a slow drip of fear slathering her skin. She shivered and fought to keep composure.

The crimson eyes reappeared in the shadows before her, their pupils deep and dark against frothing blood. They burned and stared. She stared back, defiant, her lips quivering.

"Everything is—"

A scream erupted and splattered her thoughts with atrocity. She cried out and fell backwards, trembling. The great flood of magic dwindled to a trickle. She composed herself, sat up, and stared hard at the burning eyes. They glared back at her, dripping long rivulets of smoldering blood.

Then they vanished once more.

Eleanor steadied her breath, stilled a sob, and again laid one hand into the other.

"Everything is nothing, nothing is everything..."

Slow footsteps crunched. Something slurped and then chuckled like a demented child with a mouthful of broken glass. A sigh crept into her ears, the voice inhuman.

Eleanor breathed, slowing with each inhale, accepting the panic seizing her.

"Everything is nothing, nothing is everything..."

Magic swelled, a stream flowing from a puddle. Her fingers tingled as waves of light coursed within until she was once more conjoined to the infinite. She breathed, control becoming hers, surety blossoming in her heart.

The shadow wrapped around her shoulders and pressed its cheek against hers. Filth dripped over her skin in inky slobber. Then the shadow spoke, a legion of whispers invading Eleanor's thoughts.

"Just let us in...

"It would be so easy...

"Give up-give up-give up...

"We'll have so much fun, so many games to play...

"Let us in...

"Or we can take you by force...

"And do very bad things to you...

"Bad-bad-bad-bad-bad-bad things...

"Let us in...

"Or you won't like us very much."

Those last words stretched into groans that summoned a tapestry of pain and suffering, despair clawed out of the depths of the demon's heart and smeared across Eleanor's imaginings. But she did not fight. She let awfulness swallow her, accepting terror and daring it to do its worst. Slowly, bit by bit, fear eased into a hum, fading beneath the steady hand of release.

"Everything is nothing, nothing is everything..."

The shadow hissed. Its tumultuous face leaned over her shoulder and peered into her eyes with its own fevered and burning. Eleanor tore her gaze from it and focused on the candle and the mantra and the acceptance of fear.

The shadow vanished, dissolving into sinews of smoke.

Relief exploded through Eleanor, and all of her skin surged as she and magic melded together into one being. Hope bloomed, and she wondered if this was the time when the full force of magic would remain with her, would be hers to wield the way her father did.

Silence fell. She scanned the space. Nothing stirred.

Cold crashed into her like a million claws piercing skin. The shadow screamed in a rabid voice, its shrieks torn from the tortures of the damned, frenzied and agonized, sadistic and weeping. Its red eyes were chaotic streaks as it mauled her, swiping and biting and pounding, hurling obscenities, grunting, crying, assaulting her with visions of dead bodies, wounded animals, and agonized faces, shattering the fortress of her mind so it could seep in, take control, possess her.

In the outer dark, Ian's eyes burned.

Eleanor screamed as the shadow burrowed into her, pulling at all of her fears as if plucking notes on a demonic violin, bombarding her with visions of dismemberment, of her family being tormented, of her loved ones turning their backs on her, of desolation and loss. She wanted to run or, worse yet, wanted to give in and allow the demon to take hold, take control—anything to still the terrible sensations.

She struggled to focus on the candle flame. Nausea ripped through her, and her senses reeled, but she held to the light. The shadow penetrated until her insides burned with cold and ruin.

The demon spoke with a caustic voice dripping hatred.

"Little girls shouldn't play with things they don't understand."

"Everything is nothing," Eleanor said through tears, "nothing is everything."

The shadow laughed. Eleanor trembled and shook, and magic faded against the shadow's presence. Panic swarmed, and for a moment she thought all was lost.

Her own voice screamed in her mind:

"Stop! Breathe!"

She went still and once more accepted terror. Crashes clanged in the darkness, accompanied by screams, the cries of some tattered militia being devoured by a battalion of abominations. Cold huffed under her skin, and fingers of shadow melted into her hands and gripped the bones beneath.

"Give up," the shadow said, "and all of this ends. Give yourself to me and you will feel no more fear. You will have so much fun, so much fun."

Tears streamed down Eleanor's cheeks. The temptation to let go swelled. Darkness thickened and trembled about her, as chaotic shapes emerged and encircled the stuttering candle flame like a menagerie of the unholy, wailing and dancing as if in reverence to slaughter and all that is paid for in blood.

Beyond them, from the depths of the dark, crimson eyes watched. Eleanor felt their heat, saw the unending streams of blood rippling over swollen veins. But despite those eyes, despite the shadow's voice, despite the assaulting visions of monstrosities, magic still glowed within, a faint point, a single star shining against a burning horizon. She breathed. Calm followed, creating a clear space in her mind.

All of her focused on the candle.

She reached out with hands that felt like they were infused with liquid metal. The demon screeched, the monstrous shapes danced, and the crimson eyes burned. Eleanor pushed them all from her mind, holding to the sliver of calm that remained, accepting pain and torment as passing things, keeping to the inner fire that blossomed within. She cupped her hands over the candle, and the flame warmed them.

The shadow screamed with sudden ferocity, the monstrosities charged, and the crimson eyes burned with the ecstasy of torment.

Magic begins with imagination. Eleanor imagined well.

"Everything," she said.

Streams of liquid light erupted through her palms and hurled into the candle flame. The tiny fire ruptured into a great bombardment of golden light that devoured the darkness. The shadow shrieked. The charging abominations dissolved into black tatters. The crimson eyes disappeared, and Ian cried out as he fell.

Eleanor fell backwards and shielded her own eyes.

All went silent.

Eleanor squinted at the afterglow lingering in gentle vortexes pale and gold, spirals of creation thrumming with beatific light. For a moment she felt as if she could give herself over to this force, this mystery, to create something beyond her understanding. The feeling washed away as she returned to herself, remembering her life, her loved ones, and all that mattered. Magic receded. The candle spat fire as if belching from the bowels of the earth, then waned into a faint lick of flame before it sputtered and died.

Eleanor sat up and groaned, her muscles aching, hollowed and worn out. She screamed as she registered darkness.

"Fuck-fuck-fuck," she said. She reached out with frantic hands and found the candle. The wick hissed against her fingers. She yelped, shook her hand, and reached out with her other. A tendril of flame flicked from her palm and doused the wick. Candlelight blossomed to life. She exhaled with relief and hunched before it.

Ian chuckled.

"Seriously?" he said. "After all that?"

Eleanor went to stand, staggered, and sat back down. Sweat oozed over her brow and the shadow's slobber stained her cheek. She rubbed it away with the back of her sleeve, grabbed hold of the mound of curls framing her face, and tucked them over her ears and into the red hood. She looked into the darkness, searching for her brother.

"You okay?" she said.

Ian emerged, blinking, soot staining his cheeks. Streams of blood faded into the whites of his eyes, the veins thinning into fine pink tributaries. He walked into the circle of light and helped his little sister up. His shadow limped into the glow a moment later. It growled at Eleanor and squatted behind Ian's legs.

Ian smiled.

"Good job, Sis."

She sighed.

"Nah, it wasn't."

"You're being hard on yourself. I've taken down grownups."

"Yeah, yeah."

He wiped the soot from his cheeks and rubbed the ash between his fingers.

"I'm serious," he said. "You did good."

She frowned, seeing behind her brother's kind eyes to the terrible visions he had launched against her.

"What the hell is wrong with you?" she said.

"I warned you."

"Seriously, I think you have some issues."

"You wanted me to try and possess you. Part of that is breaking someone down. That's not supposed to be nice."

"How would you know? You've never actually done it."

Ian stared.

"Right?" she said, her tone indicating that he better not have.

"Of course I haven't. But I am what I am. Those things you saw are a part of me. I don't like it, but what can you do? Possession comes as natural to me as magic comes to you."

"Naturally fucked up."

There was a click. Electric light erupted from ceiling fixtures. Alexander Demidov leaned against a heavy steel door at the end of the room, his finger pressed against the switch. He crossed his large arms over his broad chest, a bear of a man with thick auburn hair falling over his face. A long strand hung over his cheek and brushed his aquiline nose. He smiled beneath a heavy mustache.

"Not bad," he said.

2

Eleanor went rigid beside her brother.

"You didn't tell me Pop was gonna be here," she said.

"You didn't ask," Ian replied.

Eleanor nodded as if this was expected. Then she backhanded Ian across his chest. He smiled at her and brushed the wrinkles from his suit and tie.

Alexander sighed, shook his head, and came to kneel before his children. A silver watch chain dangled from his vest pocket, and his shirt sleeves were rolled up to expose forearms roped with muscles and old scars. He looked at Eleanor.

"Was that necessary?" he said.

"No," she replied. "But it was fun."

"What kind of answer is that?"

Eleanor thought for a moment.

"An honest one?"

"Mm. Right." Alexander looked to Ian. "Okay?"

"Right as rain, Pop."

Alexander nodded, but uncertainty furrowed his brow. He looked down at Ian's shadow. It was doing what a normal shadow would, no longer squatting in three dimensions but lying in the fluorescent light in a long blotch of darkness.

"And your other?" he said.

Ian looked at his shadow. He seemed to listen to something only he could hear.

"Nothing it won't get over."

"Good," Alexander said. The expression on his face said otherwise. "Do me a favor and wait upstairs. I want to talk to the little witch."

Ian nodded, kissed Alexander's brow, turned to Eleanor and rubbed her hair. She glared.

"You better be ready for more," she said.

"I will be," Ian replied. "Especially since I was taking it easy on you."

He strolled away, hands in his pocket, humming the chant-like melody of John Coltrane's "A Love Supreme." Eleanor charged after him, but Alexander lifted her from off of the floor. Her fists and feet flailed around his arm.

"I will conjure your fucking face off," she said.

Ian chuckled, twisted open the lock, and stepped into a torch-lit hallway beyond. His shadow stopped for a moment and then bled upwards through the floor. Its eyes flashed red. Then it melted and was gone.

Eleanor struggled for a moment longer in her father's arms. He waited with the practiced patience of a parent who has done this a thousand times before. Eleanor groaned in disappointment and collapsed against him.

"Are you finished?" he said.

"No."

"Ah, well. So we stay here then?"

"Okay."

Alexander smiled.

"Well, since we are..."

He dug his hands under her hoodie and tickled. Eleanor laughed and struggled against him.

"Okay, okay, I'm sorry!" she said.

Alexander stood her on the floor and motioned her towards the wall.

They sat together, looking over the bare room, the candle a droplet of fire muted in the electric glow.

"So," Alexander said.

"So," Eleanor replied.

"Okay. I can wait. I don't have anything better to do."

"That's not true."

"Eh? You're saying I have something more important in my life than you and your brother?"

"That's not what I—You know what I—Damn it, old man."

Alexander looked at her and waited. Eleanor sighed.

"Did you see the whole thing?" she said.

"I crept in once your brother turned the light off."

"You did? Great."

"Why is that a bad thing?"

"Because...I don't know. I shouldn't need the stupid candle in the first place."

"Eleanor, we went over this. A magician needs a starting point, something to focus on when they begin to conjure greater amounts of magic. Magic is only a small part of you right now. You have to practice over and over until you can do great things. But that takes time and patience. You're advanced for your age. I probably shouldn't be telling you that, but you already know, so...But even still, for all you could do you were struggling to hold on."

Eleanor groaned.

"No, that's fine," Alexander said. "There's a difference between conjuring a little bit of fire and conjuring that explosion of light, especially with what was happening to you. It takes effort."

"I know. It's not that, it's...I had it. I freakin' had it. But then that thing attacked me, and shit went crazy—"

"Can you please stop cursing so much."

"Shit, sorry. I mean..."

"Just like your mother."

"Things! Things went crazy. I was so scared. I thought, y'know, since he's my brother, it wouldn't have been so bad."

"But it was."

"Yeah."

Alexander thought for a moment.

"Can I tell you something?" he said.

"Do I have a choice?"

Alexander smiled.

"If you had come running and screaming out of the room, I would not have thought any less of you. I have seen grown magicians do exactly that. Ian is your brother, yes, but he is a demon. I hate that, but there it is. They feed on fear, Eleanor. If you were not afraid, I would've been worried, because that would mean there is something severely wrong with you."

"I thought there already was?"

"Oh. Well yes, quite a lot, but those things are okay."

She beamed. He threw his arm over her, and she buried her face into his chest.

"I didn't know it was so bad," she said.

Alexander sighed.

"Bad and worse. Possession is a terrible thing. Don't think any less of yourself for this, because it was your first time—but Ian was right. He was taking it easy. I've seen people—magicians, werewolves, even other demons—that were...I could no longer call them people. They were shells. Worse than those poor drug addicts or drunks you see on the streets beyond our walls. Sometimes it takes months, sometimes years, but possession can and does destroy lives. However, this was your first time and you held your own. You did better than I did when I first faced a demon. You beat him back."

"Yeah, but it was cheating."

"Cheating?"

"It was just stupid light that I can't even make on my own. I don't get it. I can make fire and a lot of other stuff. Okay, I have a lot to learn, but it's still true. But with light, it's like, I don't know, like it's too much or something."

"Light is a very difficult thing to conjure, Ellie," Alexander said. "But you did make it on your own. The fire helped, yes, but you conjured it. That's no small thing. There's a reason you get to practice with us."

"Alright, fine. I get that. But I should've thought of something else. I was too afraid to think of anything better, so I just focused on the candle and that's all I could come up with."

"What's wrong with that?"

"It was, I don't know, too simple."

"There is nothing wrong with simple," Alexander said. "In fact, simple is almost always best. The best things in life, they are simple: Time with family, a good meal, a laugh with your friends, a good book...On and on. You forced the demon from yourself. It does not matter how. What matters is that you did it. The day you have to face a demon in real life—and may that day never come—you will see there is no 'fair' with them. It's you or them, and you must use anything at your disposal to beat them."

"So, simple is best?"

"Precisely."

"Huh. Never thought of it like that."

"Well. Now you do."

"But I could've hurt him," Eleanor said. "I could've made the ground eat him, or made one of those golem-thingies like I always see you making when you're training with your guys, or, ooh, lock him in another dimension—"

Alexander shook his finger at her.

" 'Could've' does not matter, because could does not always mean should. Yes, maybe you could've summoned the earth to swallow your brother whole. And what? You'd have no more brother. Is that what you want?"

"Lemme think about that."

Alexander's expression made it clear that he was not amused. Eleanor rolled her eyes.

"Sorry," she said. "Of course not."

"Little girl, when you have to resort to hurting to someone, you've lost. Even if it is a demon. Remember, they are still people. Eh. Well. Mostly.

"What you must always remember is that the best of us get out of situations by using this." He pointed at his head. "That's what you did. Of course, in a real situation, you would do your best to make sure the demon doesn't even get close to you. But sometimes they will, without you knowing. That is why I am allowing you to practice with Ian. So you can be ready."

"Did mom possess you?"

Alexander leaned against the wall and stared into the candle flame as if seeing a thousand memories born there.

"She did," he replied. "She didn't want to, but I made her."

They sat silent. Eleanor held his hand.

"I wish I knew her," she said.

"I know, angel. I wish you did, too."

She looked up at him.

"Did you use light against her?"

"Eh. I had a couple of tricks."

"Can you show me?"

"Of course."

"Yay."

"Later."

"Aw." She frowned and pointed at him. "You lied to me, old man."

"That is the second time you've referred to me as old man. I don't appreciate it. So—"

He moved fast, wrapping his arms around her and tickling her belly. She screamed with laughter, squirming against his legs. He lifted her up and rubbed his mustache against her cheeks in a side to side motion.

"Okay, you're not old, you're not old!" she said.

He stopped and smiled with satisfaction. She huffed, shaking curls from her face.

"I guess youth can be a bit overrated, huh?" he said. Then he rested his hand on her stomach. "Do you still feel all that magic?"

"Yeah, a little," she replied, resting her hand over his. "That was the good part. It's all warm. How come it isn't always with me? I mean, it's always with me, but not like that."

"It is. It's just that magic is like a muscle. You have to work at it so it becomes strong, so you become strong. It's always outside and inside of us. You are always connected. It just doesn't seem that way to you yet. I've never asked you: How do you see it in your mind? It's different for everybody. For some its light, for others water, and so on."

"Like, uh, like a big ocean of warm light. I guess. What's it like for you?"

He smiled.

"The same. Like father like daughter, eh?"

"Cool. I still don't get it, though. I can do things like light the candle, or make things change or appear around me, and I don't have to go through all that meditation and crap. But for the big stuff—"

"Number one: Meditation is not crap," Alexander said. "Okay? Meditation leads you to understand yourself better, to get to the truth of things. A magician needs to be self-aware so they can always be calm and ready to channel their power.

"Number two: Magic is always with you, but you don't understand how to fully wield it. How do I say? It's like you own a piano, but you're just starting to learn to play it. All the keys are there, and they are capable of making incredible music. But you have to learn how. Magic is the instrument. To play it, you must understand that reality is everything and nothing combined. All things are one. It's that knowledge that allows us to shape reality, to bend the rules. Okay, it's a little more than that. But that knowledge is part of us, like something you were born with. We are like, eh, how you say, generators. We can—"

"'Create nothingness around ourselves and fill it with what we know and what we can imagine,'" Eleanor said in a sing-song mantra. Alexander gave her a flat look. She shrugged. "We used to go over this all the time in Ms. K's class."

"And it bears repeating. Or should I remind you of how much

damage you caused when you first started conjuring? Remember what you did to those eggs? Hm?"

Eleanor grinned, bashful.

"Anyway," Alexander said, "you're learning control. That's good. But to manifest great magic, you must draw power. That power must be tamed. It's almost like belief. Belief helps you accomplish things, gives you confidence. But if you believe blindly, then belief can take over and, eh, obscure things. Cloud your judgment, even in the face of facts." He sneezed into the crook of his arm and cleared his throat. "Anyway. It's a strange and dangerous balance. You follow?"

Eleanor blinked and smiled.

"What?"

Alexander growled and stared at her with playful anger. She laughed. He kissed her forehead and stood.

"Okay, I get it, it's Saturday night." he said. "Come. There's something I have to show you."

3

They walked towards the door. Eleanor turned around, looked at the candle and lifted her hand towards it. She hesitated, remembering the oppressive darkness the tiny flame had kept at bay. The ceiling lights hummed, bathing the room, but the candle's warmth was still with her. To extinguish it felt like a betrayal. She left it burning and followed her father out.

They stood in a long corridor. Torches glimmered above iron doors embedded into stone walls. A group of children ran past Alexander and Eleanor, two of them going much faster than the others, their legs pumping. The boy in the lead held a vial of dark green liquid that shone with preternatural light. Some of the children called out to Eleanor. She waved and smiled.

"I think that's Mr. Herrera's new adventure spell," she said to Alexander indicating the green vial as the children piled into an empty room. "Lucky bastards."

Alexander smiled, yet a tinge of sadness echoed through him. To see the children safe and enjoying their night made many hardships worthwhile. But he remembered what lay beyond the safety of their home. What hunted them.

Eleanor leaned against him, and her presence helped him to refocus. He looked at his watch and then replaced it in his vest pocket.

"Okay," he said, "let's go."

They turned right and walked down the corridor, when shouting erupted through a door on their left. A boy stumbled out and shut it with his full weight, huffing. His green eyes were panicked, sweat dripped over his brown skin, and his golden curls were frayed.

"What the hell is wrong with you, Aidan!?" a girl said, screaming from behind the door. Aidan Horowitz took a deep breath and gestured with his hands as if trying to weave together an answer. He let them drop and shrugged.

"Sorry," he said.

"Hey," Eleanor said to him. "Everything alright?"

Aidan nodded and smiled an uncertain smile.

"Hey, Ellie. Yeah?" He looked at the door. "Yeah. Just playing with some transformation spells." He slowly pointed at her to drive the point home. "Might've gone a little overboard."

The door banged from within.

"I better not look like this for long," the girl said.

"You should be fine," Aidan replied. He shrugged at Eleanor and looked up at Alexander. "Right, Mr. Demidov?"

Alexander wondered if he should intervene, when Mario Gonzalo came running from further down the corridor.

The door banged again. Aidan cringed.

"I would not worry," Alexander said. He gestured to Mario. "But I think maybe Mario should take a look, no?"

Mario slowed and stepped into their light, a rail thin man with dark brown skin, pockmarks on his face, and curly black hair. He wore jeans and a green soccer jersey with a thick horizontal red stripe that shimmered in the torch-glow. He grinned and nodded at Alexander, crouched before Aidan and laid a hand on his shoulder.

"Oye, papa," he said. "Everything okay?"

"Uh, I overdid a transformation spell," Aidan replied. "But Elisha should be fine. Right?"

"Elisha?" Eleanor said, barking a laugh, mockery clear in her voice.

"Whoever you're talking to out there, you better make it good, 'cause they're your last goddamn words!" Elisha said from inside the room.

She banged the door again. Mario leaned towards it.

"Elisha, it's Mario," he said. "I'm gonna come in and look."

"Just keep Gandalf there the hell away from me."

Alexander nodded at Mario.

"Okay?"

Mario waved him away.

"Si, hombre, I got this."

"Good luck," Eleanor said to Aidan.

"Thanks. See you, Ellie."

Mario motioned Aidan away, then opened the door with a flick of his fingers. He looked inside, gasped, and covered his eyes, laughing.

"Hijole," he said.

"Laugh it up," Elisha replied from inside of the room.

"You'll be fine. But better don't move for a…"

The Demidovs walked on, and the corridor flashed behind them as Mario transformed Elisha Olson to her normal self.

Three children emerged ahead of them, one holding a vial glowing shifting colors of scarlet and yellow in her hands. They followed one another into an open room and closed the door behind them.

"Another of Mr. Herrera's?" Alexander said to Eleanor as they passed the closing door.

She nodded.

"Desert adventure. The one from before is a jungle thing, I think."

Alexander smiled, remembering when he would use spells to explore imaginary worlds.

A door opened on their right. A woman with a round face framed by well-kept brown hair emerged, followed by ten children. Her features were shaped from Puerto Rican and Polish heritage, and she wore a long sleeve black shirt lined by horizontal white stripes, gray jeans, and orange high heels. The children looked up at her with reverence. She was about to speak when she noticed the Demidovs.

"Well, well, well, lookie here," she said.

"Hey, Ms. K," Eleanor said.

"Maribel," Alexander said. He kissed her cheek and then frowned at her heels. "Those aren't uncomfortable?"

Maribel rolled her eyes in mock disgust.

"Of course you had to say something. Can I tell you? They're all I can wear now." She nudged him with her elbow and then winked at Eleanor. "You're not listening to anything he says, right?

"Never do," Eleanor replied.

The children, all four or five years younger than Eleanor, looked up at Alexander with awe and amazement, or pointed at Eleanor and whispered to one another. Maribel sighed with exasperation and put her fists to her hips.

"Well, my little moofs, are you just gonna stand there and look?"

"Hi, Mr. Demidov," they all said. One, bright faced and wide eyed, with a mischievous glint in his eyes, threw up his hands, nearly slapping the girl next to him.

"Waddup, partner!" he said.

Maribel stomped, wobbled on her ankle, and regained composure.

"Lenny," she said, "you don't speak that way to Mr. Demidov. He keeps us all safe. Show some respect."

"Sorry," Lenny replied. He cleared his throat and spoke in mimicry of some Victorian gentleman. "Good evening, Mr. Demidov. Your vest is so nice. Straight gangsta."

Alexander chuckled, made a flourish with his hand, and bowed.

Maribel turned to him.

"Ugh. Lemme tell you, that one's trouble."

"So he's like how you were."

"I know, right? We don't need another me around."

Alexander turned back to the children.

"I see you're all taking extra classes. That's good. You pay extra-attention to Ms. Krauss." He leaned toward them like a conspirator. "She's the most dangerous magician in the Gardens."

Some turned to Maribel with wide eyes. Others continued to whisper about Eleanor as if she was a legend come to life.

"Thanks," Maribel said to Alexander. She turned to Eleanor. "And you, my little chickadee. Are we gonna start some private tutoring soon?"

"Fuck yeah!" Eleanor replied. The kids oohed and giggled. Alexander bopped Eleanor on her head. She frowned and rubbed the spot. "Ow. I mean, yes, Ms. K."

"Alright," Maribel said. "We'll set that up." She turned back to her students. "Okay, my little cupcakes, we'll get your coats and get you back to your parents. Take it easy tomorrow. No magic. Give yourself some time to relax. Except for you, Lenny. I'm going to ask your mother if you meditated. And if you don't—"

Lenny fell to his knees in the exaggerated manner of an over-actor. "Oh, believe in me, my wonderful, amazing, incredible, uh... what's something else I could say to make you like me more?"

Alexander grabbed Maribel's shoulder, nodded goodbye, and walked on. Eleanor lingered. The children began to babble among themselves, and she heard her name spoken with wonderment. She couldn't help but smile.

"Oh, hey, if you see Frank," Maribel said after Alexander. "Tell him I hate his guts, and that I'm in the mood for steak tonight."

Alexander saluted with a finger and waved at the children. Eleanor embraced Maribel and ran after her father.

They walked by older magicians standing outside closed doors radiating light, listening to the raucous voices of teenagers within, set to the painful task of making sure the not-yet-adults did not go too far. Further ahead, two other teenagers emerged from a door on the right, the girl adjusting her skirts, the boy smiling and dazed. They stiffened as Alexander passed. He hummed and gave them a wry look.

"Practicing, eh?"

They both nodded.

Eleanor frowned at them in confusion as she passed.

"Why are their clothes so messy?" she said.

"Eh."

It was all her father would say. Eleanor knew to not ask again.

Light pooled from an archway that opened onto black steps shimmering with liquid radiance. Alexander led Eleanor up the steps to a set of double doors gilded red and silver. Freeman Way Exit was carved into a bronze placard above.

The doors opened on their own, and father and daughter stepped onto Freeman Way, a thoroughfare filled with people bustling over cobblestone. A black street sign floated over a group standing a few yards from the double doors, some talking, others with their hands stuffed in their pockets, all parents or relatives awaiting the children of Ms. K's class. The Gardens bustled beyond. Buildings varying from two to six stories lined the sidewalks, their windows glowing warm and golden. Tall black lamps cast silver illumination over rows of storefronts. A jeweler's window glittered with necklaces, bracelets, and gems that shifted colors or changed form as if they were composed from water. Besides the jewelers, a white awning was animated with a green army firing arrows and spears at a red dragon that hurled red flames. The dragon fire painted the awning crimson, and jade letters bled from underneath to form The Standing Dragon. Steam billowed around the awning, as cooks hurried over grills, silhouettes trembling in the haze. A man with unkempt gray hair, a jean jacket, and blotchy pale skin emerged from the group of patrons awaiting their food. He dumped three dumplings into his mouth one after the other from a bowl carrying at least two-dozen more.

"Dumplings!" he said, his voice rising above the others, so people around him cringed and looked on in confusion. A man and a woman went to him. They wore black military pants and high collared blue shirts with Security stitched above their front pockets, and their last names stitched opposite. The male security officer patted the dumpling-lover on the back.

"Alright, Caleb, take it easy now," he said.

"Jamal! These are really fucking good.' He offered. "Want?"

They declined and ushered Caleb into the crowd. Jamal caught Alexander's glance and rolled his eyes. Alexander laughed.

Down the street and to the left, people came in and out of a liquor store called Professor Thirsty's. Its chalkboard floated in the air before the open door and announced Spell-Enhanced Alcohol—NOT HANGOVER FREE. Liquor bottles glowed golden, jade, amber, and deep red in their displays. Steam obscured the shimmering bottles, emerging from the slide-open window of Brothers Diner, where four cooks could be seen moving over the grill like a maestros conducting a symphony. A counter ran the length of the small restaurant, and the eldest brother stood behind it, a squat man with Mexican features, glasses, and dark hair under a chef's hat, watching with a bemused smile as his lead waitress teased a heavyset man prepping a jug of ice coffee. Customers sat the counter, or at tables, tucking into their meals. Some were piled around the register, awaiting to-go orders. The teenage couple from below emerged from behind the Demidovs and entered the restaurant. The girl leaned over the counter to see what the cooks were working on. The boy began to pile packaged muffins into his arms from a tray.

A sign before Brothers read:

Attention Werewolves–Satisfaction or your money back–Every meal will fill you up, or the next one's on the house—But you'll be tested—Think twice.

The double doors closed behind Eleanor and Alexander. They were attached to nothing, standing in an empty space on the street like portals to another world. The Dungeon–Freeman Way Entrance, was carved into a bronze placard above the doorpost, hanging in midair and casting bright green tendrils of smoke to signify that the entrance was open. The doors opened again, and the children of Ms. Krauss' class emerged in a babbling melody of excited shouts. They went to their parents and relatives, some embracing them, others ignoring them to continue talking with their friends.

Alexander watched with a satisfied smile. Then he looked about.

"See your brother?" he said to Eleanor.

"Um..."

Eleanor scanned the crowds. Ian emerged from Brothers, a cup of tea steaming in his hand, standing out in his black suit and red tie among the more casually clad people and security officers walking about. Radek Stepien was behind him, a young man with bright blonde hair brushed forward, blue eyes, and steely features. He wore a white track jacket with red and blue stripes down the sleeves, and blue jeans. He popped the last of a chicken gyro into his mouth, wiped his hands together, and nodded at Alexander.

"Look who I found," Ian said, leading Radek over.

"Shift end?" Alexander said, shaking Radek's hand.

"Just now," Radek replied, his thick Polish accent clipped and to the point. He smiled down at Eleanor, and they bumped fists. He went to say something to her, when two boys sprinted towards them. Radek reached out with fluid motion. He caught one of them, keeping his grip slack so as to not shock the boy into a sudden stop. The boy slowed, startled. Radek leaned so they were face to face.

"Slow down," he said.

"Sorry, Officer Stempian," the boy replied. Radek let him go, and he jogged on, swerving between people, going after his friend at a slower pace.

Radek stuffed his hands into his pockets and smiled at Eleanor.

"I heard you were very brave," he said.

"You shouldn't believe what he tells you," Eleanor replied, nodding to Ian.

"I believe this."

Eleanor shrugged as if it was no big deal, but looked down to hide her grin. Radek returned his attention to Alexander.

"Dr. Horowitz wants to see you," he said.

Alexander frowned.

"About what?"

"He's at the station. Important."

Alexander sighed.

"Alright." He looked to his children. "You two will be okay by yourselves?"

"You said you had something to show me," Eleanor said. Ian gave his father a curious glance. Alexander checked his watch and returned it to his pocket.

"There's time," he replied.

The wild cries of a trumpet and saxophone sang over the bustling cacophony, rising in laughing tones. The music beckoned Ian, and he walked off with an excited gait. His shadow lingered a moment, then slid across the ground after its master.

"Coming, Ellie?" Ian said, not stopping.

"Pop, can I go with you?" Eleanor said.

Alexander hesitated a moment.

"You don't want to see Junior and Lincoln?"

"I'll see them later."

"Okay. Ian, we'll meet you there!"

"You got it, Pop," Ian said. He was already halfway down the street, both relaxed and excited. His shadow glided over the ground with a strange stuttering motion. People parted before the boy, some casting wary glances, others holding their children close. Ian went by without noticing, or pretended not to notice, bringing the tea to his lips and drinking without concern over its heat.

Eleanor walked with Alexander and Radek through the crowds. They followed Freeman Way past a bodega where people sat out front playing dominoes, and rounded the corner onto Autumn Lane. The street sign was saturated by an infusion of red and golden leaves that drifted past the letters in eternal fall. Two rows of oak trees lined the street, their branches pulsating gentle light. Eleanor reached up and dragged her fingers over the crisp surfaces of leaves.

Salsa music exclaimed in the syncopated rhythm of drums and horns and piano from The Frog and The Shamrock, standing in the center of Autumn Lane between two trees and their cascading leaves. An Irish Flag and a Puerto Rican flag hung crisscrossed above the signpost. Eleanor watched people dancing like twirling ghosts through lime green shutters. Alexander waved at acquaintances drinking and smoking on a veranda shaded by amber shadows. Radek spied two women in tight dresses laughing over drinks. They caught his glance, shared a look, and smiled at him. He smiled back.

Eleanor looked up at him. He caught her stare, and she rolled her eyes. He blushed. Eleanor tsked and rubbed her index fingers together.

Two teenage girls on bicycles dinged their bells and rolled past with tires that spun long multicolored tendrils of sparks into the air. Eleanor stopped and stared.

"Cool," she said.

"Not yet," Alexander replied.

"Aw, come on."

"They're using prolonged magic, baby. That's like exercising for a long time. Eventually, you'll tire yourself out. You're not there yet."

Eleanor frowned and threw her hood over her head.

They walked on. Alexander shivered.

"Cold?" Radek said. "You should see above. Snowed again."

"No, just tired. Did Richard say what this was going to be about?"

Radek shrugged.

"Just said it's important."

Alexander grunted.

"When isn't it?"

They followed Autumn Lane where it opened into a square bereft of trees. A few park benches lined the outside of the square, giving anyone seated a perfect view of a massive translucent stone pillar, one of over half-a-dozen scattered across the Gardens, rising into the patchwork dark above. The distant pillars glowed as people rose and fell through them, carried up and down to errands, revelry, and home.

Alexander stopped and stared at the pillar. No light glowed from this one, and no one rose of fell through it. An enclosure of yellow tape reading Out of Service surrounded it. A man in black and white sweat pants and a black hooded sweater stood within the enclosure, staring up at two others in blue jumpsuits and black boots standing atop scaffolding. Carl, the one on the left, had shoulder length salt and pepper hair and an Inca warrior's features. Ray was on the right, baby faced and bearded and balding. They both had their eyes closed, their hands pressed against the pillar. Waves of soft light rippled from their fingers and over the surface. The man in the sweat pants watched, hands on his hips, his black hair hanging down the center of his back. He pursed his lips and scratched his chin.

"Everything okay, Frank?" Alexander said to him.

Frank Russo whipped around as if reacting to an explosion.

"You scared the shit outta me, man. What's up?"

"Eh, you know." Alexander shook Frank's hand and nodded at the pillar.

"I don't know what's up with it," Frank said. "It's weird when this happens. One minute she's giving everything the right amount of juice, the next..." He shrugged. "This week it's been the pillars. Last week it was the pressure at Aurora Falls." He scratched his chest under his hoodie. A dark blue maintenance shirt peeked beneath the zipper.

"You think it's serious?" Alexander asked.

"Nah, nothing like that. It's just like she forgets what she's doing for a bit. Carl and Ray are just pumping in a little know-how, getting her to remember. Carl's idea, like most good ideas. I think it's working. Can see her starting to breathe again."

"Her?" Eleanor asked.

Frank stared down at her in mock-confusion.

"Who are you?" he replied.

Eleanor smiled.

"Shut up."

Frank smiled back.

"The Gardens," he said. "It's a her. She. Whatever. She's alive, and like most women, can be a complete pain in the ass. Can I say ass? You know the word ass. You've said worse. Ass. Anyway, she drifts. That's how I think of it. It's like her mind wanders and forgets what she's supposed to be doing. Everything here is part of her, so...huh." His eyes gleamed, a great epiphany drawing near, enfolding him in some secret truth that pervaded all things. Then he blinked, smiled at Radek, and slapped him on the shoulder. "Hey, man. How the fuck are ya?"

Radek went to answer, but Frank looked back up at his men, his attention refocused at the speed of thought.

"A little more, now," he said.

The waves deepened by the slightest measure. Carl made a thin sound in his throat, and Ray sang to himself in toneless reverie. Sweat slicked their brows, their shared awareness seeping through the pillar and lighting a dull flare that beat with drowsy radiance. Within they beheld a living mechanism, a matrix of magical thought manifested upon the living world, now unfocused, dormant, drifting somewhere in the nether-space of unconsciousness. Together their thoughts sought to wake it up, and Ray's impatience surged. His magic flared in a bright flash that screamed under his fingers.

"Whoa, Ray!" Frank said. "What are you doing, you fucking moof? I said a little, follow Carl's lead."

The flash subsided. Ray took a calming breath.

"You know," he said, "this requires a lot of concentration. So you might wanna shut the hell up. Right, Carl?"

"That's good advice," Carl replied. "You should both take it."

Carl pressed his hands deeper into the pillar, as if he were melding with it. The wave of light subsided as Ray eased back, and once more their magic beat in unison.

Frank sighed.

"We'll get this done, don't worry."

"Never do," Alexander replied. They shook hands. "Oh, Maribel said something about hating you, and steak."

"Okay. Come by this week, some beer and board games, huh."

"Sounds good."

"Bye, Frankie," Eleanor said.

"Don't call me that." Frank turned back to the pillar. Alexander, Eleanor, and Radek walked on. A sudden burst of bright light erupted behind them. Frank cried out.

"Goddamn it, Ray!"

"You come up and here and help then, dick-weed, you're just standing there..."

Alexander addressed Eleanor.

"Tell me, little girl, why do spellcasters make better repairmen than conjurers?"

"Because they're better at working things from the inside out."

Alexander smiled in approval.

"Good."

They rounded the corner of Autumn Lane and entered The Palatine, a winding street that rose upwards into a paved hill. A skinny man with a hawkish face wheeled a metal cart downhill, holding onto the inner edge with the tips of his fingers. Stacks of vacuum sealed meats, fish, and vegetables lay over steaming piles of dry ice. He turned the cart into a market at the base of the Palatine.

Food stands rose with the Palatine. People milled before them, eating, talking, laughing, and arguing under the hiss of frying dough, the prolonged gasp of coffee steamers, and the wet smack of ground meat worked by busy hands. Beyond the stands, where the hill began to level, shops stood across from one another, bathing the cobblestones in ethereal hues. Purple sparks sang from a tray of Linzer Tarts placed at the window of a bakery. Lost and Found's window was plastered with classic movie posters and rock band stickers, and within, two headless mannequins stood, outfits shifting over their bodies, fading in and out of being: dresses to jeans and blouses, three-piece suits to colorful winter coats and ripped jeans. A young couple emerged, a young woman examining the sleeves of a new leather jacket, her girlfriend looking inside her bag as if divining the future from her new outfits.

A group of painters, Beto, Edwardo, and Alphonse, all emerged from Teddy's Paints just ahead, where paint canisters were stacked in silver pyramids behind the glass. The painters wore white clothes bespattered in chaotic splotches of yellows and greens. They made for the food stands further down the Palatine.

"Radek. Hey, Alex," they said.

"Gentlemen," Alexander replied, giving them each a warm smile.

"Know Spanish yet?" Alphonse said.

"Que?" Alexander replied. The painters laughed and went on,

arguing over who would be a surprise in the next World Cup Qualifiers.

"They all werewolves?" Eleanor said.

"Beto and Edwardo are. Alphonse is a magician."

"Huh. I still can't tell."

"You will in time. It's the little things that give it away. For example, look at the way Beto walks. He's graceful for a man his size. Almost like everything is light around him. His movements are quick, his eyes are always moving. How does your uncle Cedric say? 'Never sleep on a werewolf.' "

Eleanor examined Beto, his movements lithe despite a beer belly hanging over his painter's pants. She compared them to Radek who walked with the same ease. Radek sniffed, his nose twitching, his eyes darting this way and that. Eleanor hummed to herself and wondered what he smelled and saw.

Shoots of grass poked through the cobblestones, the long blades swaying, dew reflecting subtle prisms of color. Trees rose behind the shops, their leaves and tangled branches a carousel of greens. Eleanor smiled at the marriage of magic to nature, as if the street and the shops and the people had all been born out of some fairy mountain.

The skinny man with the hawkish face rolled by them again, semi-jogging the now empty cart uphill. He showed no signs of strain. He whistled Johnny Cash.

"That helps, too," Eleanor said, nodding to him.

"What?" Alexander replied.

"Being super-strong."

Alexander and Radek exchanged a look.

"That depends," Radek said.

"What do you mean?" Eleanor replied.

"Well," Alexander said, "some werewolves are very strong, but have normal sight. Others can hear very well, but are not the fastest. They're just like anyone else. Pros, cons..."

Radek smirked.

"You can be strong, but not quick," he said. "Can cause problems."

"Exactly," Alexander said. "Strength helps, but if you don't know how to wield it..." He shrugged. "Remember, being gifted in one thing doesn't make up for everything else. No one is perfect, or even close to perfect. There's no such thing. Greatness always, eh, slips before something greater. So stay humble, little girl. We all have weaknesses.

"But strength does help. And you must always remember: all werewolves -"

"'All werewolves have some kinda higher percep—uh, perception than everyone else,'" Eleanor said. "I already know ya gotta be careful what you say around them. Junior always catches me making fun of him. Anyway, you already told me about their senses and stuff."

"Am I getting repetitive?"

"Little bit. But I still love you."

Alexander beamed.

They walked on. A man emerged from a glass blower's shop called Homemade, with a milk cart full of empty glass vials of different sizes and shapes.

"What about Uncle Percy?" Eleanor said.

"What about him?" Alexander replied.

"Does he have any disadvantages? Ian told me he doesn't."

Alexander smirked as if remembering a joke he could not repeat.

"Percy's...stubborn."

"Aunt Rosie says that too."

"She would know."

"Will Uncle Percy really live forever?"

Alexander sucked at his teeth. He did not want her to think of such things. Not yet.

"I cannot say. He has lived a very long time."

"Like the vampires?" Eleanor said. Her eyes were downcast, her hands clasped together with anticipation.

Alexander and Radek both stopped. They looked down at her with a gravity that spoke of terrible knowledge, of an undead blight endured but never forgotten, of bloodshed and inhumanity and all the horrors that wait in-between.

Eleanor slouched and crossed her arms, the weight of their stares enfolding her with profound dread.

"Sorry," she said.

"Percy is nothing like those things," Alexander replied. "We don't talk about them unless we have to. Right now, we don't have to. Okay?"

"Okay."

They walked on. Radek nudged her.

"Percy is very powerful," he said, lightening the mood. Eleanor went with it, humming to herself, tapping her fingers against her lips, lost in thought. Percy's name was a clap of thunder in her mind, an evocation of a semi-deity walking among mortals. Yet she considered him family, loved him the way any child loves their favorite uncle.

"King of Beasts," she said.

"He doesn't like that," Radek replied.

"He should. It's badass."

"Eh," Alexander said.

They reached the crown of the hill. The street opened before them into a great square. The Gardens rolled behind them and glittered into the horizon, a crisscross of winding streets and avenues filled with businesses, rolling green fields, and apartment buildings whose lights shimmered with the spectral incandescence of fireflies. A great cathedral with a score of different religious symbols imprinted into the stained glass windows stood on a hill opposite the Palatine. Other hills rose in the near distance, bright tapestries against a black sky.

A walkway rimmed the outer edges of the Gardens to the east, a great curve bordering a lake that stretched into darkness. People were tiny silhouettes walking, or sitting on benches, or riding bikes. The lake beyond shimmered with smears of streetlight that frothed in electric prisms as the waters neared Aurora Falls, a great waterfall spilling from some unseen source in the darkness. Steaming mist rose from the falls and clouded a bridge that connected the mainland to an island floating at the lake's center. Green and black forests blanketed the island, concealing the rising paths and meadows beneath a swaying canopy.

Alexander took a moment to marvel at it. He remembered what it had all cost. He rested his hand on Eleanor's back, and she gave him a curious look.

"You okay, Pop?" she said.

"Yes. Come."

The square opened onto a large field of grass that surrounded a track. Security officers in shorts and t-shirts jogged, drilled, and exercised. Some moved at jarring speeds, yet their faces were calm and composed as if warming up before the real exertions began. Others grappled over black mats at the center of the track, slamming each other onto the soft rubber, writhing and twisting, legs clasping, arms barred, each warrior trying to mount and take control, fluid, graceful, and fierce.

Eleanor watched the sparring werewolves, when a bright flash caught her attention. She shifted her gaze beyond the track to a smaller square of concrete rimmed by a low wall. She tugged at Alexander's vest so she could better see.

He gave her a quizzical look.

"You're much too big for that."

"C'mon!"

He grunted and lifted her onto his shoulders, and she stared in wonderment at two opposing lines of seated magicians.

A man and woman stood at the center of the square, facing one another. Their instructor stood between them, her arm raised, a nimbus of pale smoke glowing over her hand. The man and woman bowed. The instructor brought her hand down, a bright flash exploded on the concrete, and she backed away.

The dueling magicians came to life. The woman threw her arms upward, and silver wasps blinked into being as if swarming out of some other dimension. They buzzed with metallic rage and launched at her opponent. The man pulled his hands in towards his chest, raised them against invisible strain, and shoved them downward. Smoke erupted from the ground and obscured him. Hundreds of steel hands emerged from the smoke and snatched the wasps from the air, the metallic insects burning like tracer fire as they were ripped from their flight paths.

Eleanor frowned.

"Why are they moving like that when they conjure?" she said.

"They don't have to," Alexander replied. "But it helps some magicians to, eh, express themselves. Like a dance, in a way. Makes conjuring feel more concrete. Understand?"

Eleanor twisted her mouth in thought and continued to watch the duel.

The steel hands dissolved, and a figure coalesced out of the smoke, sculpting itself into a massive armored samurai that charged the woman, its footfalls clanging against concrete. The woman did not back away, and Eleanor marveled at her calm. The woman closed her eyes, made no movement save for a faint tremor in her brow, and a snake of fire blazed from under the samurai and coiled around it in a constricting inferno. The samurai pulled a great katana from within its chest and sliced at the burning snake, severing it in half. The two halves fell, but never hit the ground. They hovered, swelled with a surge of searing light, and formed into two snakes that swirled about the samurai in a predators' dance. Both mouths struck, clamping onto its shoulder and hip.

Eleanor took it all in. She looked beyond the spectacle at the magicians themselves. Sweat poured over their faces, their necks strained, their eyes trembled. Yet calm held, guiding them through struggle.

The samurai and the snakes sliced and bit at one another until both magicians fell to knee. Their conjurations exploded into clouds of vapor that wafted upwards and dissolved into beads of matter vibrating in octagonal patterns gently fading away. The seated magicians applauded, and their instructor came forward speaking, her words inaudible.

Eleanor let out a burst of air in exclamation.

"Oh, man, that was so cool."

Radek seemed impressed.

"I think you're right."

Alexander nodded in a bemused way.

"That wasn't bad."

Eleanor thumped the top of his head with both hands.

"I know they ain't you, but c'mon."

"I said not bad. As in the opposite of bad. But they still have a long way to go."

"You're shitting me."

"Hey."

He raised a warning finger at her.

"What?" she replied. "If you're saying they're just not bad, then I must be crap."

"Little girl, you misunderstand. You, nor they, are crap. You all still have much to learn. They are only more advanced than you. That's all. You noticed how neither won, eh? They were so busy throwing their full force at each other, that neither took a moment to strategize. Neither thought to do anything else except attack. Strategy is just as important as force. And patience. Patience above all. Also, it was too much. Magic is not about grand spectacles. The best magic is subtle, something you barely notice." He cleared his throat. "In time they will both realize their mistakes, just as you will when you make mistakes. That is not a bad thing. That is how you learn. No one—no one—becomes great at anything without failing. So: It's okay to be not bad, as long as you persist in getting better.

"And not everything is about you."

Eleanor rolled her head back and groaned.

"Yes, oh wise one," she said.

Alexander grunted and set her down.

They walked on, passing a warehouse where the man with the hawkish face emerged, pushing a fresh cart of frozen meats and vegetables.

Voices hailed Radek from the track. He patted Alexander and nodded towards the werewolves grappling on the mats.

"Okay," Alexander said.

Radek jogged off.

"How come he barely talks, Pop?" Eleanor said.

Alexander shrugged.

"Some people don't have to."

They walked along a path that skirted the track and field, leading them to a building with columns shimmering black and gold in their portico, towering over wide steps that spanned the width of the structure. Security was carved into the frieze above the columns, and the stone façade watched over the hilltop and the whole of the Gardens.

They walked up the steps, passing officers who ate, talked, and smoked. Some acknowledge Alexander. Some smiled at Eleanor.

Alexander led his daughter between the center columns and over a black marble floor infused with streaks of pale gold. Officers moved about, some speaking with Gardens' residents, discussing this nuisance or that. Others in plain clothes carried their gear out of one of the three doors standing open, heading for the steps, their shifts ended. Eleanor looked at two statues that rested on pedestals on either side of the doors. One was a woman seated with her open palm holding a globe of fire that burned translucently. The other was a man with his head bowed and his stone fingers dug into the pedestal, his features chiseled into a mask of concentration, his teeth gritted. Rips were carved into his skin, revealing thick ropes of bulging muscle beneath

"Lucy, Ethel," Eleanor said to each of them respectively.

Alexander shook his head and led her inside.

4

Their steps echoed within an expansive vestibule bathed in warm light. Cream colored pillars rose to a vaulted ceiling. Two hallways opened at either side of the vestibule, the left leading to a courtroom, the right towards offices where supplies were counted, debts tallied, and expenses totaled. The center of the vestibule opened into a large space where a man's voice carried over the din of people moving about.

"I am trying to provide my patients with a calming environment. When that music starts, I can barely hear myself think, let alone pay attention to what they're telling me. Would you like it if the one time a week you had license to unburden yourself, someone decided that that would be a good time to play a trumpet?"

Hank Olson stood before the duty officer's desk where Marissa Gutierrez sat listening, her face pressed into one hand, her expression an ode to the annoyed patience of civil service. Origami sculptures sat the rim of the round desk, a series of owls, cranes, and dragons born from folded paper. A pair of security officers emerged from a doorway on the right, both smirking at the scene unfolding. Alexander waited, listening to the exchange.

"Dr. Olson," Marissa said, "it's Saturday night."

Hank sighed and bent his head as if seeking patience. He wore a tweed jacket and red bowtie, his hair was black, high, and well kept, and he bore the pensive expression of a professor. His features were sharp and elfin, but there was hollowness to his cheeks that made him seem over-tired. The first lines of gray streaked his hair, and his hands were rough and calloused with dark specks of grit dotting otherwise clean fingernails.

He composed himself, seeking compromise.

"Would it be possible to have the Freeman-corner locked off until after 9 PM?"

Marissa thought for a moment. Her hair was tied into a brown bun, and her youthful features wore a practiced mask of indifference shaped from a life of heartache. But her cheeks swelled like a child's as she smiled, revealing mischief and humor waiting just under the veneer of inconvenience.

"I mean, I hear your place is really spacious," she said. "Couldn't you just see your patients above?"

Hank went red. He folded his hands over the desk.

"Officer Gutierrez, would you like it if we locked up criminals in your home?"

"We got criminals here?"

"Of course you wouldn't. Then—do we have criminals here? I certainly hope not—then you understand that my home is my home, and my practice is my practice. I prefer to keep the two very separate."

Marissa gave him a look that said she did not appreciate the condescension. She noticed Alexander and gestured to him.

"What do you say, Alex?" she said. Hank turned around and crossed his arms. "I'm waiting" was written on his face. Alexander came forward.

"Junior and Lincoln too loud for you?" he said, shaking Hank's hand.

"The boys play beautifully. Deirdre and I love their music, as we enjoy many of the other musicians who play on Freeman. But my last client is at 8 on Saturdays, and it's the only time they're available. It's very difficult to conduct a session while music is screaming into the room."

"Not conducive to therapy, eh?"

"To say the least. These people are dealing with severe trauma. Post-Possession Therapy takes a lot of careful work." He gave Alexander a penetrating look. "I don't have to tell you. You've rescued quite a few of my patients, yourself." He turned to Marissa. "And I would think that you would know better, Officer Gutierrez."

She blew out her cheeks and let that go, a low growl rumbling in her throat.

Alexander shrugged.

"Okay," he said. "We'll keep the music from your corner until 9:30. Good?"

"Perfect." He turned to Marissa. "Forgive me for being snippy, but I can't bend on this. I know you're doing your job, and I am very grateful. Well. Thank you for your time." He turned back to Alexander, noticed Eleanor, and smiled. "Why, hello, Miss Demidova. Always good to see you."

"Yo," Eleanor replied, waving her hand in a windshield wiper motion. Alexander leveled a gentle smack upside her head.

"Ow," she said, rubbing the spot and frowning up at him.

"What kind of a way is that to greet a person?"

"Sorry. Jeez. Good evening, Dr. Olson. Fine weather we're having, would you not agree?"

"Looks like you have your work cut out for you," Hank said to Alexander.

"You have no idea."

But Alexander hugged Eleanor to him with all the pride he could muster. She rolled her eyes, but beamed.

"Well, good evening, one and all," Hank said. "I'm meeting Deirdre at Rosie's. Perhaps we'll see you there?"

"Always possible," Alexander replied. "Oh, and eh, she's okay, but Elisha had a bit of an unfortunate incident while practicing with little Aidan Horowitz in the Dungeon."

"The joys of parenthood continue."

Hank waved and walked away.

Marissa shook her head as she watched him leave.

"I would kill him if he weren't so courteous," she said.

"Separates us from the beasts," Alexander replied. His gaze caught everything but her, a strange smile touching the corners of his mouth. Marissa watched him, her lips pressed to her knuckles, her eyes daring his to meet. He wouldn't, but he ran his hand over the desk, picked up an Origami-swan and cradled the outstretched paper-sculpture between his fingers.

"Dr. Horowitz here?" he said.

"He is."

"Okay. Would you mind if Eleanor keeps you company?"

"Not at all."

Eleanor frowned at her father.

"You said I could go with you."

"And here you are," he replied. "But I must speak to Dr. Horowitz alone."

Eleanor folded her arms.

"Secrets."

Alexander lifted her up and sat her on the desk.

"When you get older you'll learn there is a difference between secrets, and things you cannot talk about. Wouldn't you agree, Officer Gutierrez?"

"He's right, cutie," Marissa said.

"There you go. If you don't believe me, believe her. She knows things."

Marissa and Alexander caught each other's gaze. He lifted the origami and arched his eyebrows in question. She nodded for him to take it. He held it up as if it were a token, something to be cherished. Then he kissed Eleanor's nose and walked away. Eleanor grumbled under her breath as she watched him go.

"Don't worry, Mami," Marissa said. "He won't be able to boss you around forever."

"I'll kick his butt one day."

"Betcha you will." She leaned forward and adjusted Eleanor's hood. "He's just trying to protect you for as long as he can. Hope you know that."

"From what?"

"From bad things, slugger. There's a lot of that out there. It's nice to not have to think about it. When you get older, that changes. You... Nah, never mind. You should be having fun." She brushed a curl from above Eleanor's eye. "I love your hair."

Eleanor frowned.

"I know you're trying to distract me"

"Yeah? Betcha it's working."

Eleanor shrugged and smiled.

"It is. Wanna see something cool?"

"Always."

Eleanor threw her hands out wide. Her hair exploded outwards, and blue sparks jolted through her curls into electrified strands.

Marissa exclaimed and clapped her hands together.

"So good," she said.

"Thanks. Have you ever kicked the crap out of someone who was trying to hurt you?"

"Oh...Uh, yeah..?"

"Sweet! Do werewolves have to pee more than other people?"

Alexander walked down the hallway. Small stone gargoyles stared down at him from atop lintels, leering, grinning, each a reminder of the ugliness sometimes necessary to protect those who could not protect themselves. Alexander frowned up at them, seeing something of himself in their contorted visages, a ferociousness he prayed his children would never have to witness.

He passed a stairwell on his left leading to cells below, bolted shut by a chain link gate. He passed three interrogation rooms and nodded with bemusement at officers standing to sudden attention away from their poker game in the last room. He gave them a sarcastic wave.

He neared a heavy steel door marked SPELLS. A young red haired officer named Donald Green stood guard, wrist clasped in his hand, chewing gum with his mouth open. Alexander slowed, tucked his fist under Green's jaw, and nudged it upwards. Green's teeth clicked shut. He narrowed his eyes, but chewed on with his mouth closed.

"Sorry, boss," he said.

Alexander came to the end of the hallway and walked by a door stenciled with black block letters. They read:

Radek Stempian - Deputy Security Chief.

His own name was stenciled into the last door, Chief of Security under it. He took a breath, turned the knob, and entered.

The room was bare, save for a single desk covered in ordered stacks of paper, a snow globe with a woman in a white gown playing piano, and a black fountain pen standing slantwise in its holder. The walls were turquoise and clean. A curtained window was opened to the rolling lights of the Gardens, and muted voices swirled in from outside. Alexander's coat, along with Eleanor's and Ian's, were thrown over his chair.

Richard Horowitz sat before the desk, a stout man with a weightlifter's build bulging through a gray sweater, waves of dirty blonde hair brushed forward, a sharp nose, and green-blue eyes. He rapped his fingers against a thick medical book—Neurological Conditions and their Treatments—but his gaze was intent on a single point upon the desk, boring through to something beyond, something within, a measure of control in a tumultuous world.

Alexander went round to his chair and gestured towards the coats. They sailed upwards, floated to the right, and hung in midair. He sat, and rested the origami beside the snow globe.

The two men regarded one another, between them a short hand, a silent understanding for when it was time to put aside small talk.

"So," Alexander said.

"I need you to hear me out," Richard replied, his words precise, his tone patient and authoritative. His fingers curled in rhythmic motion, and he leaned from one side to other as he spoke. "This is life and death."

Alexander frowned, the gravity of Richard's voice making him all too aware of the countless dangers that threatened their world. He gestured for him to go on. Richard straightened, scanning the ceiling, searching for the right string of words.

"Greg found out about a group of people being held captive not too far from here, in a warehouse south of Queens Boulevard."

Alexander raised a hand for him to stop.

"Hold on, hold on. Found out? Found out how? Greg is home, I saw him the other day."

"He stops in from time to time."

"He's been going in and out of the Gardens?"

Richard shifted uncomfortably in his seat and shrugged. Anger frothed in Alexander, threatening to bubble over. He retained composure, but could not hide his indignation.

"We voted to end our rescue operations," he said. "That hasn't changed."

Richard cleared his throat.

"Greg knows what you all voted for. But he didn't agree with the Council. So when he found out that he got in with the Nunez-Delgado crew out in Sunnyside, let's just say he saw an opportunity he couldn't pass up. One last chance to do something good before we sit on our hands."

Alexander stared, wide eyed, his thoughts colliding into a single point of rage. Greg Woodard had helped free countless people from the hands of the gangs controlling the streets beyond the Gardens: Crews of werewolves, demons, and magicians getting rich off of human lives. He had railed at Alexander when the decision came down to end their raids to save people from these gangs. But Alexander had never imagined Greg would do something like this.

"He's been going out on his own?" he said.

"I know," Richard replied. "He's taking a big risk."

"A big–He's put us all in danger."

"You're the one who first told us about Nunez and Delgado. Remember? Your undercovers gave us everything: The murders, the brutalities, all of out it in the open. Turns out it's a lot worse than we knew. Since Greg has been with them, he's seen some horrible shit. They've trafficked more people through Sunnyside than any other crew before them. They kidnap immigrants, the homeless, whoever won't be missed, turn them into werewolves, and pimp them out for possession. Oh, and the women – oh man, they get it worse: They prostitute them until they're all used up, and then let demons have their way. They got three possession parlors operating along Queens Boulevard alone. But that's not even the worst part. You know how they really make their money, everyone on the Council knows, but you all still voted to stop rescuing people from these animals."

Alexander watched and waited, allowing anger to subside so he didn't launch over the table and slam Richard's face into it. He exhaled, flexed his hand, and let his mind work.

"When did he start working with them?" he said.

Richard scratched his forehead and shifted in his seat.

"He pulled a robbery with some of their soldiers, hitting a card game out in Maspeth. That got him in. He was gonna tell you, but after you voted to pull everyone out, well, he didn't think you'd care. He couldn't let this chance go. There are too many lives at stake. He knew if he got in deep enough, he'd eventually find where Nunez and Delgado house their victims. He was hoping when that time came, you'd step up."

"So, to be clear: Greg has been going out on his own for over a month, doing god knows what to earn the trust of a couple of savages. He's been lying to us, and now he expects to us help him."

"He expects you to do the right thing."

"You're going to lecture me on what's right?"

"This is about saving lives, Alexander—"

Alexander slammed his open palm against the desk. The pen jumped out of its holder, clattered on the tabletop. Swirls of snow spun around the piano player in the globe, and the origami fell on a wing. Richard waited, stern but patient. Alexander rubbed his thumb over his palm and watched him.

"I have every reason to expel you both," he said. "You want to talk about saving lives? What about all the people already here, eh? Do you think freeing a few strangers is worth leading our enemies right to our doorstep?"

"Greg's too careful for that—"

"I'm not finished."

Richard grimaced and looked away. Alexander stood up and paced behind the desk. He grabbed the back of the chair and spun it, glaring at Richard as he did so.

"Greg is so careful, that I failed to see what he was doing right under my nose," he said. "I'll give him that. But it does not change the fact that he's taken a very stupid chance.

"I know all about Nunez and Delgado. I still have my informants, and they tell me awful things about those two. Every Possession Parlor from 49th Street to Greenpoint Avenue pays up to them. Everyone in Sunnyside is afraid of them. They go outside of their territory, go after small time crews, and no one retaliates. Even Patrick Moore, with most of North Queens under him, would prefer not to have to deal with them so long as they stay on their side of the 7 train. You know why? They feed people to werewolves, and they skin and burn people alive. They took 40th Street by having Edison Morales' legs devoured while he was still breathing. They laid him in the middle of the street for his entire crew and all of their servants to see. As long as they don't venture out to Woodside, Astoria, Flushing they have free reign. Maspeth was once no-man's land, and now it's almost theirs. Yes, I know all about them. You're acting like Greg being out there without support is not complete insanity."

"That's not fair."

"Not fair," Alexander replied, bristling. "What do you think happens if he's caught? How long can he withstand torture and possession, before he gives the Gardens away?"

"That was always a risk. Nothing's changed."

"Everything's changed! A month ago our people were out there, ready to help each other at a moment's notice. That's gone. My informants will give me information, but they won't go beyond that, and I don't blame them. So what does he do if he's found out? How would we even know?"

"He's trying to save lives," Richard said. "If you'd just hear me out—"

"I don't understand you. Okay, you voted against us, but you're a practical man. You know what's at stake. We cannot respond in time should the worst happen, and even if we could, even if we took them out, got rid of that whole crew, in a matter of weeks someone else would step in, perhaps someone worse. They would be looking for us, not out of loyalty, or vengeance, but just to make the point that they are stronger than their predecessors. No, sorry. We've done all we could. We've saved many people from the Family, but the Family is too damn strong. Nunez and Delgado are doing what they're doing because they have the support or the indifference of anyone that can stop them."

Richard tapped the book against his leg. His fingers worked over the cover, shifting in tune to the workings of his thoughts.

"Will you shut the fuck up for a second?" he said.

Alexander's jaw worked, muscles bulging through his cheeks. But he gestured for Richard to go on.

"We've made a home for ourselves, that's true. But you're forgetting how. Most of our people should be dead. Go outside. Look around. How many faces do you see that your people helped to pull out of some garage, or some low rent shithole? How many of them were on the brink of losing their minds to possession, or near collapse from overwork? You know what happens to people, especially werewolves, who can't afford to keep up in the Family. We stand against the Family. It's who we are. It's what keeps us together. We only have a home because of the people who keep it going, people just like those poor bastards Nunez and Delgado enslaved. Darius didn't build this place alone. We did it together, and the people you've saved are part of that.

"Look, I know why you voted to pull us out. I know we have to hang back and think about the Gardens and the safety of the people already here. I get that. Greg gets that. He doesn't want to be out there. But we're talking about at least fifty people, probably more that Nunez and Delgado have stashed away. You know what they're gonna do with them. A few will be thrown to demons, some will be turned and put on work details, but most will be fed alive to werewolves.

"Saving them won't solve everything. It won't stop the Family. It won't even stop Delgado and Nunez. There'll be more victims in a month's time, and yeah, that'll bother the shit out of me. But I'll let that go, because you're right: We do have to worry about us now. After everything Greg's told me...Stepping back isn't right, it's necessary. We've no choice. But here's one last chance to do something for the people beyond our walls. We can hit these assholes quick, get those people out of there, and vanish."

"We?" Alexander said, incredulous, daring Richard to claim that he had ever gone out with them on raids.

Richard raised his hands in a placating gesture.

"Greg'll be done, and it won't matter that they'll be looking for him. That's the point. You can punish him and punish me if you have to. We won't fight it. But this is the right thing to do. You know it is."

Alexander gripped the back of the chair and leaned forward, bent in thought. He shook his head after a time.

"I'm sorry, Richard, but no. I'm a wanted man, you're a wanted man. The Family has people looking for us, we have to assume, at all times. If they catch one of us, they can get to the Gardens, and everything we've worked for, all the people we've rescued and keep safe, will have been for nothing. You and Greg have put everyone in danger. The only thing that's going to happen now is Greg coming home. Tonight."

"Alex—"

"Fifty people? Let's say we did try to help them. They're going to be heavily guarded. That means violence. That means killing. I already have enough experience with that, thank you. I am very sorry, I truly, truly am, but—"

"Children, Alexander," Richard said. The rest of Alexander's words dried up on his lips. Richard stared hard at him. "Greg saw kids. A lot of them. Someone is paying good money so they can eat kids. You hear me? We're supposed to just let that go?"

Alexander stared, horrorstruck. His children's faces flashed in his mind, and he felt sick at the mere thought that the world was a place where such savagery could befall the likes of them. He crumpled back into the chair, dazed.

"Oh, it gets even worse," Richard said, gripping the book, his knuckles gone white. "Greg thinks Nunez and Delgado are backed by a vampire."

Vampire: The word slithered under Alexander's skin, as if rope-like parasites burrowed through his veins.

"How—" he said, croaking, overwhelmed. He sighed and looked away. "Is he sure?"

"Nunez name-dropped Guillermo Moreno. He didn't tell Greg anything else, but—"

"That's all he had to say," Alexander replied. "No one is stupid enough to claim connection to a vampire if they don't have it. I've been wondering how Nunez and Delgado became so strong so quickly. If they have Moreno's backing, that explains it. Dear god."

"I don't get it. I thought Moreno was tight with your former father-in-law?"

Alexander sat and sneered.

"Patrick Moore doesn't need Moreno. He has..." He began to shiver. "He has Manny Ngombe's ear. That monster offered to make Patrick into a vampire once he took over North Queens. Did you know that?"

Richard hesitated a moment. The mention of Manny Ngombe drained his confidence, paled him. He suppressed a groan and shook his head, gripping the book in his hands as if it could protect him.

"Do you have to say that name?" he said.

"Oh, scared now?" Alexander replied.

"Never said I wasn't." He collected himself and edged forward in his seat. "I know with Moreno involved, it makes things a lot more dangerous, but—"

"Do you have the address?"

Richard blinked in surprise.

"I don't have to sell this anymore?"

"Children, eh? Well, you're right: we can't let that go. Your brother-in-law already put us in the center of this. It was stupid. But, children...And besides, I'll take any opportunity to hurt Guillermo Moreno if I can get away with it. It's not like we can kill the bastard."

Richard smiled at Alexander, a glint of approval in his eyes. He opened the back of the book, pulled out a slip of yellow paper, and handed it to him. Alexander glanced at the address and slipped it into his vest pocket.

"They're holding them there through tonight," Richard said. "Beyond that, Greg doesn't know. Nunez likes to move them around, and he keeps shit quiet until the last minute. We don't know when the...feeding is supposed to happen. They may not even have buyers yet." He grimaced. "Greg's on security detail, going in with the relief shift a little after midnight. He's gonna call you so you can know when to move. Nunez and Delgado aren't expecting anyone to pull anything, with the way they've been running things. A few guys and Cedric's trucks should do it. They'll figure out Greg was involved once he vanishes, but who cares? He's definitely not poking his head back out after tonight. They'll also be wondering who helped him. Maybe this'll turn them against each other."

Alexander stroked his mustache.

"We'll make it look like a rival crew. Nunez and Delgado have made many people angry, protection from a vampire or no. People are afraid of them, but there's always someone else who wants a crown."

"That could start a war in the Family. At least in North Queens."

Alexander laughed without humor.

"They're always at war," he said. "That's all savages know how to do. It's better for us if they're at each other's throats."

Richard smiled.

"Where's this guy been?"

Alexander leaned back in his seat, incredulity warring with admiration for the doctor.

"Richard: You're an asshole. You and Greg both, very special kind of assholes. What the two of you have done is beyond stupid. It won't happen again."

Richard sighed. He had no argument to give.

54

"Are you gonna tell Percy?" he said.

Alexander stood and stretched his arm under the floating coats. They dropped down.

"We both will. We'll have no choice, since we're bringing in new people. I'll save it for when they arrive and go through safety protocol. I'll eventually have to inform Deirdre and Hank as well. They're going to have a very busy few days. Richard, you did the right thing. You have the high ground." But he threw his hands out wide, indicating what he thought of Richard and Greg. "Assholes."

Richard smiled a sardonic smile.

"There are three people I love in this world," he said. "Aidan, Viola, and Greg. For years Viola and Greg risked everything by going out onto those streets. I was sick with worry every time, and I'm sick with worry now. I think about what would happen to all of us, to my son especially, if anyone of us is caught. But this had to be done."

"Does Viola know?"

Richard shook his head. Alexander laughed, grateful he was not Richard, wishing he could be there to see the doctor tell his wife, the Garden's head librarian, all he had just told him.

"Yeah, she voted with you," Richard said. "So I'm gonna hear it from her, no doubt. But kids: I can't stomach that."

"Neither can I."

They regarded each other, conspirators joined by a common cause. Richard stood and pointed at him in an offhand way.

"You're overdue for a checkup," he said.

And he walked out. Alexander stood behind the desk with the weight of many lives pressed upon him. He looked out the window at the Gardens glittering like some sacred tapestry wrought out of the works of goodness and grace. That he would not fail it. That he would live or die so it would always be so.

5

Alexander walked out of the hallway, wearing his coat and carrying his childrens'. A flash erupted from the front desk.

"What do you think?" Eleanor said.

"I like it," Marissa replied.

"Not too much?"

"Nah, it's just right."

Alexander found Eleanor still seated on the desk. Tendrils of smoke rose from her fingertips. Marissa examined herself in a pocket mirror, golden streaks now plating her brown hair. Alexander admired her, for a moment forgetting himself. Marissa caught his gaze in the mirror and smiled a knowing smile.

Alexander looked away.

"Looks good," he said, coming around the desk.

They exchanged another glance that lingered just long enough to reveal their true feelings for each other. Alexander broke away, feigning indifference. Marissa flipped her hair and returned her attention to Eleanor.

"Want me to try something else?" Eleanor said.

"No way. I'mma tell Leon to cut it like this from now on"

"You don't have to. It's already done."

Marissa looked at her in surprise.

"It'll stay?"

"Mm-hmm," Eleanor replied, nodding. "Well, for awhile, anyway. Then you have to tell Leon. I mean, you should still tell him."

Marissa laughed, then gestured for Eleanor to come closer.

"Now remember," she said, "go for sensitive areas when someone is attacking you. Hit the joints, the neck, the eyes, the boobs, the balls—"

"Eh, okay," Alexander said. "I think that's enough."

"Dangerous world, Alex," Marissa said. "Your daughter's gotta learn how to handle it. I ain't worried, though. She's something else."

Alexander lifted Eleanor up into his arms.

"Don't remind me," he said. Eleanor tugged at his mustache. He widened his eyes in mock surprise. She giggled. Marissa put the mirror away and admired father and daughter, the closeness between them. Then she cleared her throat, going serious as she remembered the way Richard had seemed upon leaving the station.

"Dr. Horowitz didn't look too good," she said.

"I know," Alexander replied.

"May I ask what happened?"

"Mm, not a good idea."

"I'm just saying, you tell me and I can help."

"I don't doubt it. Are you here the rest of the night?"

"Till 1 in the AM."

She reached out and plucked lint from his sleeve.

"Okay," he said. He knocked on the desk and led Eleanor out. She waved at Marissa. Marissa waved back, leaned in the chair, and took a bag of chocolate cupcakes from her drawer where an ordered regiment of them waited surrounded by packages of unwrapped colored paper. She opened the cupcakes and burped like a yawning bear. A few swift bites and she threw the wrapper into a trashcan littered with others. Then she took one of the packages of paper, slit it open with her thumbnail, slid a red sheet out, tossed the opened package onto her desk, and began folding origami into being.

Alexander and Eleanor went back down the Palatine, walked

Autumn Lane where Ray and Carl were closer to repairing the pillar, and rounded the corner onto Freeman Way.

Music led them to a crowd surrounding two boys. The older, Cedric McGill Jr., was dapper in a dark blue jacket with a light blue shirt opened at the collar, and the younger, Lincoln Ray McGill, was neat and crisp in a gray jacket and white shirt and well-pressed tie. Junior danced with his trumpet, swirling from side to side as if the brass in his hands guided his movements. Lincoln cradled his saxophone, his fingers precise, nothing wasted, his brow gently furrowed as if piecing together a mathematical equation. The music soared like audio fire, clean and clear notes piercing, tumbling over one another, falling and rising in celebration. The crowd bobbed their heads and clapped along. Some couples danced: Spinning, hooting, and smiling ear to ear.

Ian stood at the head of the crowd, his cup of tea discarded in a nearby trashcan. Empty space surrounded him, people keeping their distance and watching him with distrust and even anger. A woman with her two children eyed him the way people do when standing too close to a supposedly tamed predator. Ian ignored them all. He smiled with the music and watched the brothers McGill, his hands in his pockets, his toes tapping. Junior went to him, bowing close as he sustained an undulating note. Ian bowed with him, his head wiggling in time to the music. The trumpet whooped, and both arched backwards, caught upon the note as if carried high by a swing.

Alexander and Eleanor moved through the crowd and joined Ian. Eleanor clamored for Alexander to lift her up. He gestured at his back and at her size, but she persisted, and he sat her on his shoulders, and laid a hand on his son. Eleanor gyrated with the music, her curls arcing from side to side.

The boys played until their last harmonious note melted into the crowd's uproar. They bowed. Ian clapped and whistled. His shadow was stretched over the ground, its hands stuffed into impossible pockets.

Junior flourished as he bowed, smiling brightly.

"Thank you, gracias, and arigato, all you kind, cool, citizens," he said.

Lincoln nodded and waved a modest hand.

The Demidovs approached them as the crowd dispersed.

"If I did not know any better, I'd think I was listening to Davis and Coltrane," Alexander said.

"Aw, come on Uncle Alex, we ain't there yet," Junior replied.

"Maybe not, but it's a good start."

"Thanks. You should bring your piano down here. Then we'd really have something."

"Eh, I'm afraid Classical is more, how you say, my thing. I could not keep up."

Junior waved that away.

"Yeah you could."

"Coltrane and Davis had a lot of control," Lincoln said. His brother gave him a flat look. "Their talent was in making it look otherwise. We're nowhere near that kind of skill."

Junior groaned.

"Ladies and Gentlemen, jazz made boring by Lincoln Ray McGill. He's here all night."

"Wanting to master something does not make me boring."

"Doesn't make you fun either."

"Fun?"

Cedric McGill Sr. weaved through the dispersing crowd, a large man in a black leather jacket and dark blue jeans. Snow shone on his well kept hair, flakes glistening over his smooth black forehead and dampening the wire-rimmed glasses that hung from green yarn around his neck. His ears were swollen and scarred, evidence of a history of landed blows, and his eyes darted all about, taking in much. He moved with grace and strength, walking on legs that seemed to dance as easy as they could crush.

"And he's late again," Junior said.

"Nice timing, dad" Lincoln said.

Their father huffed and laid his hands on both of their shoulders.

"Ain't on me," he said. "Some cameras froze above, so I had to restart the server. Snow's messing with everything. Yeah, I know, Junior, it's always me. Maybe if you were tech savvy, you could help me out."

Junior raised his trumpet.

"Occupied," he said, grinning as if the trumpet were the key to everything he wanted in life.

"Then quit yelling at me," Cedric replied. "Shoot. Too damn cold outside. Alex, what's happening, fam."

He and Alexander embraced, slapping each other's backs. Eleanor wobbled on Alexander's shoulders and balanced herself by laying her hands on Cedric's head. Cedric looked up at her with mock suspicion, rubbed frost off of his jacket, and flicked icy water at her. She squealed. Alexander set her down, wiping dripping ice from his own forehead.

Cedric wiped his hands on his jeans and addressed his sons.

"Knock 'em dead?"

"Always do," Junior replied.

"They enjoyed it," Lincoln said. "But I'm still worried about how we come together in the end. I can tell they hear it coming."

"Oh god," Junior said.

"Boy, you are too young to be worrying about that," Cedric said.

"That's what I'm saying."

"If I don't worry now, I'm going to have to worry later," Lincoln said. Cedric opened his mouth to respond, but no response came. He shrugged. Lincoln sniffed, put the saxophone to his lips, and walked off fingering the keys, trying to divine their secret language.

Cedric glared at Ian.

"Where in the hell have you been?"

"Sorry, Uncle Cedric," Ian replied. "Been busy helping magicians not be afraid of me."

"That's no excuse. You always seem to have time to fool and fuss with this one." He pointed at Junior. "I expect you to make time for your training."

"You boxing, Ian?" Junior said. "You didn't tell me."

Cedric scoffed.

"He ain't boxing 'till he gets his little ass to the gym for more practice."

"I'll be there," Ian said.

"Good. And if you think I'm upset, wait till you see Eitan. He's ready to kick seven shades of shit outta you."

"Watch your mouth, mister," Eleanor said.

Cedric raised his fists in a mock fighter's stance. Eleanor did the same and punched his knee. He flailed backwards and fell on his ass. All the children but Ian laughed. Even Lincoln giggled, but Ian was passive and calm. Alexander saw this, noting the too-adult smile and posture his son held.

Cedric threw himself upright in a dancer's fluid motion.

"Damn, got me again," he said. He turned to Alexander. "Y'all good?"

Alexander shrugged, nodded away from the children, and led Cedric off. Eleanor watched them go. She frowned and blew a curl from her eye.

"I just had a chat with the good doctor," Alexander said. He nodded at two passing security officers, coughed, and then went on. "He told me Greg has reliable information that a group of people have been kidnapped and are being held in a warehouse right on the Woodside/Sunnyside border."

Cedric reared back in surprise.

"Whoa, hold up, how does he know?"

Alexander told. Cedric remained silent throughout, his brown eyes still and thoughtful. He rubbed his chin when Alexander finished.

"Shit," he said.

"We cannot let this happen."

Cedric fixed him with a hard look.

"You actually wanna go out."

Alexander gestured as if to say it were inevitable.

"Just like that?" Cedric said. "If Moreno's involved—I mean what if that malignant motherfucker's there? We ain't gonna be able to do a goddamn thing then."

"There's no reason for him to be. That does not mean we don't be cautious, but still."

"You can't know that."

"I do. So do you. Think about it—Nunez and Delgado wouldn't be using their people otherwise."

"Hm," Cedric said, considering. "Wouldn't need 'em. A'ight, I see that. But what about the Council?"

"Didn't think that'd be a problem for you."

"I don't like how we voted, but rules are rules. We should let them know."

"How long will that take? Greg says there's a limited window. Nunez and Delgado can move their victims at anytime. We have a chance to stop this right now."

"What makes this so different, though?" Cedric said. "Look, I'm all for helping people, but, I mean, shoot, you wanna risk our lives and then get everyone riled up at us if we make it back. This is exactly the kinda shit we decided to walk away from. It's been over a month since we stopped. People have already died. We weren't saving a whole lot of them in the first place."

"Children are involved."

Cedric tensed.

"They're selling kids?"

Alexander nodded. Cedric spat, pressed his lips together, and growled.

"Motherfuckers," he said. "That's a new low."

"I know this is a lot to ask, but—"

"I'm there."

Alexander nodded, filled with a deep sense of affection at seeing the resolute anger in his friend.

"I think I'll let Radek and Eitan know," he said. "See where they stand. We could use the muscle."

"Radek'll come. He's not too thrilled about our new isolation policy. Eitan, well, he might take some convincing. You gotta tell Percy, though."

Alexander took a deep breath and sighed. He stroked his mustache.

"I'll be seeing Percy in a bit," he said. "I'll, eh, broach the subject and gauge his reaction."

"Broach, nothing. The big man needs to be there. He might as well be. Not like we can hide it from him. We pull this off, there's gonna be a few new faces around here."

Alexander smiled.

"Won't that make him so angry."

"Hey, quit being a jerk. Convince him. Please. For me. Motherfuckin' cherry on top." He looked away, going grave as he considered what they would soon be doing. The violence necessary to save human lives. "Same as always?"

"That goes without saying. Two trucks should be enough. We hit them, and load the people in fast. If there are not too many guards, I may be able to take care of them myself. But we need guns."

"I'm on it. Let me get that address."

Alexander gave it to him.

They watched the passing crowds.

"This has to be the last time," Alexander said. "We have to play deaf and dumb after this."

"That's what you said before. Man, don't give me that look. I'm with you. I'm just saying. If they're eating and possessing children now, they're not gonna stop just because they lost a shipment. You gonna be able to live with that?"

Alexander looked at him.

"We'll have to."

Both went silent.

"You know, I've heard some nasty shit about Nunez," Cedric said. "He'd benefit from a bullet to the dome. This might work out for the best. If he's there, we can end him. Delgado too. That'll stop the problem, at least for awhile."

"Maybe." Doubt dripped from Alexander's voice. He shook his head. "But then again, you kill one savage—"

"I know. Someone else always comes along. Still, we pull this off we'll be doing the world a favor."

Alexander watched the people about them.

"The truth is, I wish I'd never heard any of this," he said. "I don't want to risk losing you, or any of our people." He smiled. "My kids need their godfather."

"Of course they do. Not like they're learning a damn thing from you."

"Idiot."

"Immigrant."

They chuckled.

"Well," Alexander said, "There's no other way around it, I suppose. I'm going to hear from Greg sometime around midnight."

"I'll have the trucks ready."

"Good. And you said you can let Radek know, right? Okay. I'll handle Eitan. I need to talk to him about something else anyway. I'm, eh— I'll tell you about that later. I'll call you when we're set to go."

"Go where?" Eleanor said. She stood near, wringing her hands together, concern etched on her face. Alexander and Cedric both shot her a look fathers master when dealing with nosy children. She took a step back, hesitated, and crossed her arms. "Going where?"

Ian, Junior, and Lincoln all turned at her voice. They joined her in crowding their fathers.

Alexander crossed his arms and stared down his daughter.

"Little girl, did you see us step away?"

"Don't change the subject."

"Hey." He pointed at her. "Don't speak to me that way. Your godfather and I stepped away, which means we wanted privacy, which means I don't want you listening. Little girls who overhear things don't have the full story."

Eleanor reddened. She held her father's gaze, defiant.

"You're gonna do something dangerous," she said.

Junior and Lincoln both went taut with worry. Ian was still, betraying no emotion. His shadow circled him, stretched and misshapen on the ground.

Alexander searched for resolve through the storm of guilt Eleanor's words wrought. Cedric growled and scratched the back of his head, his sons' expressions feeding an already rabid doubt.

"What is she talking about, Dad?" Junior said.

"You better not be doing anything stupid," Lincoln said.

Cedric went to his boys and pulled them aside.

Alexander paused for a moment. The fear in his daughter's voice withered all of the reasons he had for putting himself at risk. He longed to still her fear, to stay beside her and leave the sorrows of the world beyond their walls. He armored himself with the righteous indignation he knew he would later question and perhaps even mock. For now, he needed to believe himself on the side of goodness, a man saving the innocent from the maws of monsters.

He went to his children and knelt before them.

"There are some things that I cannot help," he said. "You know I have responsibilities to this place and its people. That means, sometimes, I have to do dangerous things. But I swear I will do everything I can to stay safe for you two. You do not ever have to worry. Your father's strong. Okay?"

"I trust you, Pop," Ian replied.

Eleanor stared at the ground. She would not look at him.

"I'm gonna go see Lily," she said. She walked off and merged with the crowd, a growing girl in a red hood, hands stuffed into its pockets, trying not to imagine what life would be like without her father, the last half of an already incomplete whole.

Alexander watched, his heart breaking at her diminishing figure. He called after her, his words rushed.

"Come—come back in 20 minutes. I still have to show you something."

She waved acknowledgement without turning around. He sighed and ran a hand through his hair.

"I'll talk to her," Ian said.

Alexander looked at his son and saw calm, the stillness of undisturbed waters.

"No," he replied. "It's okay."

"What are you showing her?"

"I'm showing you both something important. You'll see."

Ian smiled.

"Okay."

Alexander almost frowned. His daughter's concern hobbled him, but his son's calm left a perplexing weight within.

Cedric and the boys returned.

"Why don't the three of you go have some fun, eh?" Alexander said.

"Yeah," Cedric said. "Go on and see Eitan at the gym." He looked at Ian. "I know he's dying to see you."

"We'll meet you there," Alexander said.

Ian patted Junior on the back and walked away. Junior looked once at his father, and then went after, tapping his horn against his leg. Lincoln frowned, cradled his saxophone, and followed his big brother.

Alexander watched after them, as if he could see their childhoods ending with every step. Cedric grimaced and scratched the back of his neck, seeing the same thing.

"Ellie ain't stupid," he said.

Alexander shifted somewhere between pride and regret.

"No." He whirled on Cedric. "How come you didn't hear her coming?"

"Don't put that on me. I was a little distracted by some horrible fuckin'-prospects."

Alexander looked about the people seated on the curb, at bicyclists wheeling past, at steam rising from food stands. Each person carried a life full of memories, hopes, and heartaches. Each was someone weighing the world against their own experiences. They were mysteries, whole universes unto themselves, a brew of being shifting across time. Alexander felt responsible for all of them and remembered that many had been in the exact situation they now had to rescue others from.

How many had been left unsaved?

"You know, we're lucky," he said. "We have a real family here, people who care about each other."

They watched the passing throngs. A mother and father lifted their laughing child.

Cedric looked at Alexander, remembering all he had lost and all he had regained.

"Y'all did this, you know, you and Darius," he said. "We founded the Gardens together, but it was the two of you that made it possible."

Darius: The name made Alexander's throat constrict.

"We all made this possible," he replied. "We still do."

Cedric nodded. He spat and rubbed his massive knuckles.

"I miss him," he said.

Alexander took out a silver cigarette case inlaid with black vines that shifted underneath the metal. He opened it and took a rolled joint from a row of them and placed it to his lips. He replaced the cigarette box in his coat pocket, snapped a flame to life from between his fingers, and lit the joint. He inhaled and passed the joint to Cedric. The flame hovered in the air before them, imploded, and fizzled out. Cedric puffed and passed.

"I miss him, too," Alexander said. His eyes glistened. The people passing in their reflection could not mask what was lost.

6

Eleanor threaded through the crowds, excusing herself, sidestepping and spinning out of the way of an oncoming magician riding a horse made of water. She marveled for a moment, watching the writhing liquid muscles tense and release as the horse galloped by. Then she stepped onto the corner and followed the sidewalk away from Freeman towards Higgs Street.

Dreams and Things, the Gardens' toy store, stood on her left, the window displaying candy colored blocks, air planes flying together in concentric spirals, a family of stuffed animals—their plush bodies begging to be cuddled—and a great centerpiece of two clashing armies battling on a field of grass that swayed under tiny footfalls and falling bodies. The soldiers swung their weapons or raised their · shields with the frantic desperation of bloodletting, fluid and seemingly alive in their black or white armor.

Eleanor whistled and nodded in approval.

"Damn, Benny, not bad," she said, speaking of the toy shop's owner.

She walked on, passing a massage chair where a maintenance worker sat and groaned with contentment under the elbows of a masseuse. A hot towel hovered above the maintenance worker's head, wringing out warm citrus mist. Eleanor breathed deep, taking in the pleasant aroma, letting it, for a moment, blot out the lead weight of worry she bore for her father and the secret thing he was going to do.

The love she felt for him was always undercut by fear. That he should risk his life for the safety of others. But the life she knew and loved had been built upon selflessness. Such was their world, the actions of good people ever harried by the threats of monsters and murderers. What it was all for surrounded her, a home where the hunted and unaccepted could be at peace. The cost was danger to her loved ones, those who fended for the persecuted. To begrudge her father his secrets, to break his heart before he set out on a dangerous task, was to be the worst kind of child—selfish, clinging, and all the things she knew she could not be if she was to one day carry on his work. These things did not go through her mind as clear thoughts, but as feelings manifesting into waves of aggravation for turning away from him the way she had.

She would be stronger, she told herself, for his sake and the sake of their people. But the worry remained, a cinder block carved out of her heart.

She sighed and promised she would not let him leave thinking she was angry. She would bear the weight of worry, until the moment of his safe return.

If he returned.

She walked on.

Pepe's Pizza was further down the block. Through the open window Eleanor could see the owners arguing behind the counter, variations of pizza steaming its glass surface. The younger, Julio Hernandez, a stout Mexican, waved his blue baseball cap in frustration while the older, Dominic Masoni, middle aged, Italian, and wearing a black armband around his left bicep, held an open newspaper and stabbed his finger at the Sport's Page. Both ignored Eric Park, a young Korean man in a dark blue jean jacket and gray hoodie with a basketball logo on its front, standing before the counter, his hands raised in an irritated gesture, as if to say "Seriously?" Julio laughed with astonishment and slapped his baseball cap over his thick black hair. Dominic exclaimed and ran his finger along lines of stats on the paper. Julio leaned towards it as if considering a great truth. Eric Park slapped the countertop and hollered for service, and both owners started, gestured at him, and yelled as one:

"Take it easy!"

Eleanor walked on by, rounded the corner, and turned onto Cauldron Avenue.

She passed a red bricked apartment building with a stoop where teenagers sat and carried on. A café-restaurant stood next door, with people seated in plush red chairs, eating, drinking, and smoking from hookahs resting on round black tables. The musk of marijuana melded with fragrant tobaccos you could taste in the back of your throat. A man in a gray maintenance shirt walked along the street, stopped before the smoke clouded tables, and raised his hands. The smoke spun into funnels absorbed by his fingers.

"Pardon me," he said to everyone and no one, and walked on.

Drinks glowed in their mugs and glasses, not with the gaudiness of neon, but with preternatural warmth. Forks, knives, and spoons were worked over entrees and desserts, and people ate with relish, or absentmindedly, or didn't touch their food at all. Eleanor walked between the rows of diners and smokers over a purple carpet trimmed with gold, and stared up at the flowing golden letters embroidered into the café-restaurant's main window.

Rosie's

She went inside.

Crimson and shadow painted the interior. Waiters moved around, their trays hovering inches above upturned hands, laden with steaming food, glowing drinks, and hookah pipes wafting red, green, or silver smoke. A singer leaned against a piano on a stage and crooned as the accompanist swayed from side to side in reverie to the ballad flowing through his fingers. Families and couples and groups of friends sat around tables, eating, talking, listening. A few loners sat with drinks or lit pipes, watching the stage, seeing beyond it and to wherever the music transported them.

Eleanor went right. She moved between waiters and glided

around patrons milling before a blacktop bar. She passed them and entered a corridor beyond the dining room, moving into the glow of electric torches casting blue light against black walls. She walked by the bathrooms and reached a closed door with a window of clouded glass. SPELLS was stenciled on the glass in black lettering. She opened the door and walked in.

The Spells Room had a long glass counter filled with glowing spells in vials labeled to their purpose. Four tall wooden cabinets stood behind the counter, their drawers labeled and set with keyholes. A rolling stepladder rested against the leftmost shelf.

Lily Amaya sat behind the counter, a girl draped in a gray shawl covering her long sleeved blue blouse. A key dangled from a chain around her neck. She brushed purple and brown strands of hair from her face and focused deep brown eyes on Martin Gleason. Martin stood before the counter, wearing a Nirvana t-shirt that was pressed and neat, the tour dates scrawled in aged yellow print on its back. He cradled a jean jacket in the crook of his arm, emanating a youthful energy. Yet his hair was graying, his eyes were haggard, and scars crisscrossed his left cheek.

Lily handed him a brown paper bag beating with an amber glow from within, and he took it and smiled with warmth that filled the room.

"Thanks a million," Martin said.

"Anytime, Marty," Lily replied. She leaned on her elbows and tried her hand at a cool smile, and then flailed as the stool underneath almost tipped over. She caught herself, cleared her throat, and pushed a strand of purple from her forehead. Pink flushed her round cheeks. "Rosie says same as before: Take a spoonful every night before bed. But this one's a little different. You won't just be dreaming anymore, now you'll know that you're dreaming. It'll help you take control of the bad memories. It's actually pretty cool, once you get past all the scary shit."

"Grand."

Martin looked at the bag, shifting his feet as something else weighed on his mind. A slight flinch creased his cheek. He shook his

GIOVANNI DIAZ

head. He needed to be sure before he brought up what he wanted to ask. So instead he hinted.

"Rosie didn't say anything about side effects or nothin'? Nothin' unexpected-like?"

Lily shook her head, her expression leaving no room for misinterpretation. Martin sucked at his teeth and hummed to himself, something weighing on his mind.

"Alright then," he said. "I thought there may be."

Lily frowned.

"Why?"

He shrugged.

"No reason. Just wondering."

He hesitated. A mischievous grin broke his pensive expression, masking the nagging question in his eyes. He reached over and pinched Lily's cheek. She glared.

"You keep doing that, and I'm gonna conjure your next spell by myself," she said. "You'll have dreams of crabs coming after your balls."

Martin reared back.

"Jesus Christ. That's fecking terrible. You Gardens kids are too mature for your own good."

"I know."

"Your ma raised you with a wicked tongue. You cherish that now, love. Don't take any shite when you can help it." He raised the bag in a gesture of thanks. "Give Rosie my best. Tell her, ehm...well, I'll be seeing her myself."

He turned and feigned fright at seeing Eleanor, raising his hands as if he were being robbed.

"I'm just a poor werewolf," he said. "Have mercy."

Eleanor made a gun of her finger-and-thumb and aimed. Martin yelped. Lily laughed, but hid her smile under her hair. Eleanor held her "gun" on Martin until he reached the door. He blew them both kisses and was gone.

"Stupid," Lily said.

"You know you love it," Eleanor replied.

"It's that Irish accent. Mm. Hope he's still single when I'm older."

"Dude, he's 40, or something weird like that. And he's married. To Mr. Ruiz."

"So? If anyone can change him, it's me."

"You can't change that!"

"I know! Can a girl dream? Anyway, guys look better when they age. And I'm only six years away from eighteen."

"That's weird. This is weird."

"I'm playing, god. He's mad cute though, right? Tell me I'm right."

Eleanor rolled her eyes, lifted herself onto the counter, crossed her legs, and fell into Lily's embrace. Lily pulled back with excitement.

"How was it?" she said.

"How was what?"

Lily gave her an incredulous look. Eleanor bobbed her head from side to side, knowing Lily wanted to talk about her experience training against Ian. A few hours ago she would have been just as curious.

Now...

"It was, uh," Eleanor said, "would you believe me if I said it was great?"

"Nope."

"Good. 'Cause it sucked."

"Was it so scary?" Lily said, leaning forward.

"You're a little too excited about this."

Lily made an impatient gesture. Eleanor looked to see if anyone else was coming in the door. There was no one.

"I don't know how he controls that thing," she said.

"His shadow?"

Eleanor nodded.

"It felt so...cold. There was all this hate in it. Like it wanted to hurt me, but at the same time it felt like I would feel really good if I let it in. It was so fucking weird. I was...I don't know. There's not a good word for how it felt. Definitely scary, but, still, I'm glad I did it." She frowned. "I hate that that thing is part of him. But I don't care what anyone says, he's my brother. The shadow ain't who he really is. Ian's a butt-face, but he's a good person. If he wanted to hurt anyone, he would've done it already. Trust me. He really could with that thing."

"Well, I mean, I don't know. The shadow's kinda who he is. My mom told me demon's shadows are like their darkest thoughts made into a kinda-living thing, or something. It sucks, but it's part of their personalities or whatever. Anyway, guess this is what happens when you have a demon for a brother."

"Thank you, Ms. Sensitivity."

"You'd rather I lie?"

Eleanor looked at the ceiling.

"I think it's trickier than that. Yeah, he's a demon. Fine, fuck it. But he held back with me. If he really wanted to hurt me, he could've. He didn't. That says a lot. I mean, I know what people say when I'm not around: 'Oh, we love Ian, but we don't trust him'. That's bullshit. They're just afraid of him. How can you love someone if you're afraid of them? They shouldn't be, though, 'cause he does keep that thing in check, and he's always so nice and calm. I beat him up, and he just laughs. It's so annoying."

"Yeah, that's true. Know what? Fuck what the others say. Ian is who he is. I know we can trust him."

"Thanks. Glad someone does."

"So what else?" Lily said. "C'mon, I wanna know what I'm in for."

"Fuck that, I'm not gonna ruin the surprise. All I'm gonna say is, my pop was right about meditating helping out. That shit saved my ass in there."

"Really?"

"Yep. Helped me to not to freak out. Don't know how else I would've gotten through it. Remember that rhyme Ms. K used to sing us? 'Don't reject it, best accept it'?"

"I always hated that," Lily said.

"Yeah, but I get what she's saying, now. It doesn't mean give up, it means accept the situation. That way you stay calm. And how could you hate it? Ms. K is the best."

"I don't hate her, just the rhyme. It's for kids."

"We are kids."

"No, we're young magicians. That's different."

"Still kids."

"Oh my god, I'm the only one who gets it."

"Wow, really?"

Lily laughed to herself.

"So you saw some crazy shit though, right?" she said.

"I told you, not telling."

Lily smacked Eleanor on the shoulder.

"Mentirosa. You said you were gonna tell me everything."

"It would just freak you out. Trust me." She raised her hand against Lily's coming protest. "You get mad nervous, and you know it. I'm not gonna make it worse for you. It's probably different for every-body anyway. All you gotta know is that it's scary, but if you stay calm you'll get through it."

"So tell the demon to fuck its mom?"

"Uh, yeah. Or...something else? Y'know, whatever works."

Eleanor looked down at the counter. The vials glimmered beneath her, each a spell tailored for a specific person, to help them through trauma or sleeplessness, anxiety and depression. There were many empty spaces where spells once lay.

"Busy day?" she said.

"Yep. Saturday's are like that. People get some free time, and all the shit pops back into their heads. Craziness. Martin's probably the last one for the night."

"I'm surprised he was even here."

"You don't know? I'm not supposed to say too much, so keep this between us. Some really bad shit happened to him. Rosie won't tell me what, but I know he hasn't been dreaming. That's something you see a lot in people who were possessed a bunch. They get too many nightmares, and their brains say fuck it and turns them off. But not being able to dream can mess you up after a while, so Rosie made him a spell so he could again. It worked, but now he's back to an ass-ton of nightmares. Rosie put him on a new spell, one where he'll be able to control his dreams, so he can finally deal with everything. Hopefully that'll make him better."

Lily paused, twisting her mouth as if puzzling odd memories together.

"He's actually been kinda weird lately," she said, musing. "But maybe it's just reliving all those bad memories? Anyway, that's the way it is for a lot of possession survivors, especially when they're werewolves."

"Mr. Gleason," Eleanor replied, her voice resounding with pity. Lily nodded.

"Yeah. He hides it, but Rosie told me when he first came here he was really fucked up. Almost crazy—like actually crazy. She won't say, but I think he kept turning, over and over again. I bet they had to keep him in the Den for a long time, until he got that shit under control. Can you imagine? I hear turning is bad enough already, but doing it a bunch of times in a row has to make you just wanna die."

"Same thing happened to Uncle Radek," Eleanor said. "He told me he was in the Den for months before he got on a normal cycle. But I never thought Mr. Gleason was messed up like that. He's always so happy."

"You gotta give it to him. My mom, like, loves the Frog and Shamrock, so he must be doing something right. It's not easy to run a bar. I mean, it's him and his husband together, but still."

"I hope he's okay."

"Better be. I helped Rosie with his spell, and my shit's good."

Eleanor cocked her eyebrow in an incredulous gesture. Lily waved her off.

"I work every day with Rosie, no matter what," she said. "I know what I'm doing. I'm already practicing making my own spells. I love it. I get to this place where I'm, like, in the moment, where all I feel is this one emotion, and I can see this vision of how the spell is supposed to affect people. I become the emotion, and then the spell just pours out of me. It's so cool."

Eleanor frowned.

"What?" she said, sarcasm a flat timbre in her voice.

"Oh, come on, it can't be so different from conjuring."

"Maybe. I don't know."

"Well, Rosie says it ain't, and that I'm getting there. So ha! Oh shit, that reminds me, she wants to see you."

"She here?"

"Yep, down in the Brew."

"'Kay. Wanna hang out after?"

"I do, but I can't. Gonna surprise my mom with breakfast in the morning, so I gotta be up early. It's her birthday."

"Oh, cool. Is she in the kitchen? I'll say hello."

"Yep."

They hugged again. Eleanor twirled on the counter and jumped off. Lily smiled as she watched her leave, believing in that moment that they would always be friends.

ELEANOR WALKED THROUGH THE HALL, reentered the main dining room, and turned right, passing between tables and the stage where the singer shimmied her hips and reached her hands above her head as if pointing the way to a world beyond. Eleanor made another right and dodged a waiter emerging from double doors encased in black padding. She skirted through the closing doors and entered the clank, clatter, and hiss of the kitchen.

Steam billowed from a long grill as a group of chefs hurried about. Across from them, water sighed into a basin filled with mountains of soap. A man stood over the suds, raising his hands and yelling high-pitched battle cries like some Kung Fu legend, manipulating three sponges with a weave of magic over plates, pots, and glasses. He bobbed side to side as he did this, listening to the mad sway of James Brown thundering through his headphones.

Waiters moved about, taking up trays, dropping off dishes. A cook opened a large silver door and emerged holding a stack of packaged steaks in his hands, cold mist rolling over him from the freezer. Another cook stood by the open pantry, and someone within threw two bags of red and green peppers at him.

Belinda Amaya, a stout woman in a white chef's uniform, moved up and down the grill, inspecting chefs oiling pans, tossing seasoning and diced vegetables into the air, and stirring rich sauces. Her lower lip drooped as if perpetually unsatisfied. Eleanor jumped her from behind. Belinda screamed and whirled around in near-fury. She saw Eleanor, put her hand to her chest, and gave the child a good-natured frown.

"Feliz, uh, cumple-anos, mama," Eleanor said.

"You trying to make this my last birthday?" Belinda replied, grinning. She placed fists against her hips and glared. "You here to cause trouble?"

"Uh, what do you want me to answer first?"

"Get the hell out of here."

Eleanor smiled and then ran, dodging a half-hearted swat from Belinda's wooden spoon. She hurried deeper into the kitchen, past racks of clean dishes and glasses, past Belinda's office, and towards a doorway with a multicolored beaded curtain. She parted the curtain, the beads clattering behind her, and entered a large room.

It was dark compared to the bright kitchen, filled with shelves lined by liquor bottles glowing yellow, crimson, sapphire, and emerald. Eleanor gazed in open wonderment at the combined colors pulsating over stalks of marijuana plants and pots filled with dried mushrooms seated on long wooden tables. Men and women in yellow aprons went around the plants with trimmers, cutting vagrant stems. Others weighed buds in baggies, or placed bricks of the drug wrapped in plastic into black duffle bags presided over by three security officers, one of whom threw a full duffle bag over her shoulder and walked out of the room, passing Eleanor with a questioning glance. Waiters picked amongst the bottles, some reaching out and lassoing them from high shelves so they floated into their waiting hands.

Eleanor ran through the center aisle and stopped before a door at the far end of the room. She pulled it once, twice, and fell backwards as it opened. She got up and slid through as the door drifted shut.

Black marble stairs greeted her. She walked down, and vines

laden with purple flowers blossomed within the steps at her every footfall. She reached the bottom and stood before two rows of cauldrons lining both sides of a cavernous space. Flames roared under them, bubbling with spells poured from effervescent ropes of liquid-smoke that flowed through the air, stemming from a lone figure.

Rosie St. John sat cross-legged on a raised pedestal of black stone, the many colored spells emanating from her, pulsating, rippling as they spilled into the cauldrons. Serenity etched her brow, her face intelligent and kind, her golden hair rolled into a bun, and her big ears sticking out among vagrant strands.

She breathed, and an otherworldly aura shimmered in and out of being around her, as if traversing between this world and another.

Eleanor sat the floor before the pedestal and waited.

In time the spells thinned and faded. The cauldrons gurgled a bubbling lullaby. Rosie opened eyes the color of moss, let loose a long exhale, and smiled at Eleanor.

"How long have you been sitting there?" she said, her voice a song from storybook Texas.

"Like you don't know," Eleanor replied.

"I surely don't. You're too quiet, girl. 'Cept when we need you to be, of course." She yawned and stretched her arms. "Dear lord, I am tuckered out."

"Long night?"

"Uh-huh, but a good one. I believe I've outdone myself." Rosie slid off of the pedestal and knelt. "You just gonna sit there?"

Eleanor smiled and flung her arms open. Rosie embraced her and kissed her forehead. Eleanor looked around at the cauldrons. They bubbled.

"Wha'cha making?" Eleanor said.

"Oh, this and that. A lot of different spells."

"I just saw Lily give one to Mr. Gleason, for his dreams."

"How'd you know about that?"

"Eh..." Eleanor shrugged and smiled like the picture of innocence. Rosie chuckled.

"The two of you," she said. "Lily's not supposed to be telling you these things, and you shouldn't be spilling the beans on your friend. Well, it makes no never mind. Martin doesn't hide what happened to him. That poor man." She sighed. Her eyes took a faraway look. "I don't know how he's carried on to this point. Happy he has. The good lord blessed him with a strong will."

Eleanor threw up her hands in exaggerated praise.

"Hallelujah!"

"I'll slap the sarcasm out your mouth."

Eleanor raised her fists for a fight. Rosie shook her head, scooted Eleanor away, and stood. She stretched and yawned again, then cracked her lower back. Eleanor walked over to the nearest cauldron and peered inside. Pink liquid bubbled and frothed, and streaks of crimson rose to the surface. For a moment, Eleanor saw her brother's burning eyes in the bright red ribbons. Bubbles stretched and popped into sparks of amber, snapping her from the terrible vision.

"What kinda spell is this?" Eleanor said, hugging herself.

Rosie cracked her neck and looked.

"Oh. That one's for adults, honey."

Eleanor gave her a look that asked for more. Rosie knew there was no getting out of it and searched for the best way to answer.

"Makes kissing a little more fun," she said.

"Huh?" Eleanor replied. She turned back to the boiling spell and understood. "Oh. Ew."

"You asked."

"You made all these today?"

"Had to. These people are taking them faster than I can spit."

"Wish I could make spells. Then I could help."

"You're sweet, baby. Lily's plenty help. Besides, if you were a spell-caster, you wouldn't be the hardest working conjurer around here."

"It'd be so cool if I could do both," Eleanor said.

Rosie bent down to touch her toes, curled upwards, and shook herself out.

"Don't go wanting too much, now," she replied. "That way leads to trouble."

"But could you imagine how much I could do if I could make

spells and conjure?" Eleanor turned and bounced from foot to foot, as if seeing new paths opening before her. "It's happened before, right? Maybe if I work really hard at it..?"

"Well, that's a good attitude to have, darling. You understand you have to work for what you want. But what you're talking about is rare."

"Like impossible."

"Well," Rosie said, stretching her elbow behind her back. "Not much is impossible, but I've only known one magician who could conjure and cast spells. And you know who he was."

"Do you miss Mr. Bardales? My dad talks about him all the time."

"Of course I do, darling. Darius was a good friend. We have him to thank for all this. He didn't do it by himself, but he played a big part in us finding a home. On top of that, he taught us magic." She went silent. "But most of all, he was a good friend. A damned good friend."

Eleanor caught a note of sadness on her face. She turned back to the spell roiling and crashing within the cauldron, seeking to change the subject.

"Isn't kissing already fun?" she said.

Rosie suppressed a laugh, went to Eleanor, and put her hand on her shoulder.

"Come sit awhile."

"Uh oh."

Eleanor allowed Rosie to lead her to the pedestal. Rosie gestured, a flick of her fingers, and a second pedestal emerged, rising from the floor gone momentarily liquid, summoned by Rosie's will that she had infused into the space when she had created it. The pedestal set in place, the floor solidified, and Rosie and Eleanor sat facing one another.

"Well," Rosie said. "How was it?"

"How was what?"

Rosie gave her a look that said "This is not the time."

Eleanor fidgeted.

"Does everyone know?"

"Everyone who matters. That's only everyone."

"Fine. You know how it was. He's a demon. He didn't take me out for ice cream."

"Was he hard on you?"

"Uh-uh. He said he was taking it easy, the jerk."

Rosie sighed with visible relief.

"That's good," she said.

"No! How can I fight demons if Ian takes it easy on me?"

"How do you expect to do anything if you spend your days trying to bite off your own tongue? Because had he done what he's capable of, that's how you would've ended up."

Eleanor stared in defiance. But the mental image held, making her look away, filling her with long fingers of dread. She thought of Ian, his kind face, and wondered at what lay beneath.

Rosie leaned forward and took her hand.

"I'm sorry, baby," she said, "but I am trying to scare you. I want you good and goddamned terrified. The world outside the Gardens is a hard place, and demons ain't even the worst of it."

"You mean vampires."

Eleanor's gaze was much too adult, much too full of weariness. Rosie hated to see it. She leaned back and shook her head.

"No," she replied. "We ain't talkin' about that."

"Not you too."

"I said no."

"Why? It's not fair. Y'all want us ready for demons and were-wolves and the bad magicians, but you won't help us with vamp— with the worst."

"You can defend yourselves against demons, and maybe even a turned werewolf, if you're strong enough. You can fight other magicians. They're all dangerous. I hope you never have to deal with any of 'em, but you can, if and when the time comes.

"But there ain't no preparing for a vampire—might as well prepare for hellfire. If you're faced with a vampire, all you can do is pray and run. And I wouldn't waste any time praying."

"But if you use a burst of sunlight that you absorbed, you can—"

"That does absolutely nothing. You hear me? Not a damn thing. It ain't enough. The only thing you need to know about vampires is you have no business being near one. Ever. You're only safe if you keep away from them, and you hope to hell they don't know where you are. Why do you think we're all hiding here? We can't fight them, Eleanor. They're...they're worse than dying."

"But there's only a few of them, right?"

"One's too many." Rosie sighed. "Hell, I guess we can't hide this from you forever. There are nine of them: eight 'children' and their creator. You've heard of Father Manny." Her voice trembled with equal measures of hatred, terror, and mockery. "Lily asked me about him the other day, so, of course, now you know too. His real name is Manny Ngombe. He's the first vampire, the oldest, and the only one who can turn anyone else into a vampire. There ain't much else I can say 'cept he's one of the reasons we live the way we do. Meaning he's... bad, baby. Very, very bad. Make no mistake, darling, we're hiding from some terrible things. I hate to put it like that, but there it is."

"It's all their fault," Eleanor said. "All the sad people you have to help, all the people y'all try to save. It's all because the vampires let the bad guys do whatever they want."

"That's true," Rosie replied. She hiked up her purple dress and folded a boot under her leg, weighing the importance of Eleanor's innocence against the cruel but necessary knowledge of their world. She grimaced, knowing another chunk of childhood needed to be removed. "But they can't be killed. That's that. It's our job to protect you, but one day you'll be a woman, and you'll have to look out for yourself. So you have to understand that there's no time for bravery against a vampire. There ain't no way you can stop them, and yes, that's awful. But that's life. You help where you can, and run when you have to.

"So if you ever see a vampire, you run, run, and run. You hear me?"

"Bullshit."

Rosie tensed.

"What was that?"

Eleanor sighed.

"Okay."

"Repeat it."

"I said I'll run. Jesus."

Rosie stared at her for a moment, stern, watchful. Her green eyes softened. She brushed back curls from Eleanor's face and held her chin.

"You're brave, you're smart, and you're a hard worker," she said. "That's all real good. But bravery borders on foolishness. And intelligence can lead to arrogance and a special kind of stupidity, the kind that makes you think you know everything worth knowing. Hard work, well, there ain't nothing bad I can say about that 'cept you can get lost in it and forget what it is you're working so hard for. All good things have their flaws, darling. That's okay. You do your best to stay kind, you learn from your mistakes. You fix what you can. That's good living.

"But you have to know your limits. Otherwise you may meet something worse than you ever imagined."

Eleanor heard every word, but louder was the sense of doom resounding in the following silence. The darkness beyond the cauldrons seemed to whine with a legion of ravenous insects, a chorus of evil infecting the child's imaginings, conducted by the pure and desperate fear in Rosie's eyes.

Eleanor went quiet with fearful respect. Vampires took the form of a curse in her mind, an evocation of terror that whispered with abominable possibility. She swallowed, nodded, and whispered in reply:

"Okay. I get it."

Rosie kissed her brow and stroked the back of her head.

"Good girl." She pulled back and smiled. "Now, back to your brother."

Relief was fresh air rising out of Eleanor's chest.

"Uh, it was so scary," she said. "But I did okay."

"I see that. He didn't push too hard?"

Eleanor shook her head.

"Nah. I hate to say it, but I'm glad he didn't."

"Me too. Goodness, you have no idea how much. You weren't too harsh on him, now?"

Eleanor frowned.

"Whose side are you on?"

"I can't care for both of y'all?"

"Yeah, yeah."

Rosie cleared her throat. Eleanor read hesitation on her face, something uncomfortable wanting to come out.

"What?" she said.

Rosie fiddled with her earlobe.

"Well, it ain't no secret how folks 'round here feel about your brother. Not me." Rosie raised her hands against Eleanor's coming protest. "He's a Demidov, and that's good enough. But others, they only see the demon. You can't blame them. You know where these people come from. Demons damn near ruined their lives."

"Ian didn't do it."

"That's right, he didn't. He takes after your mother. But she had it hard, too. Shoot, you should've seen the time she had with some of the people here once they found out she was a demon. On top of that, they knew who her father was. A lot of people here hate your grand-daddy. He's given them plenty of cause." Rosie opened and closed her fist, wriggling her fingers around in thought. "Not to mention...nah, best not dwell on that."

"Uncle Matt?" Eleanor said, curiosity dripping from her voice about the man who had hurt her brother years ago, who shared their blood and yet had done a horrible thing. Something so horrible that he was no longer here.

Rosie pointed at her.

"Don't you ever let your father hear you call that man your uncle."

"But he was, like, my actual uncle. Mom's brother equals uncle. Pop never talks about him. He gets really pissed off if I even ask—"

"He has all the reason in the world to get upset," Rosie said. "Matt hurt your brother. He hurt him real bad. It's a miracle Ian's still functioning. Matt fooled us all into thinking he was a good man. We thought because he was your uncle, that he would be like your mama. Then he..." She shook her head, regret in her eyes. "He set your family back, is what I'm saying. Your mother had to earn everyone's trust all over again after what he did. She managed, and that's one of the reasons people tolerate Ian being here. But eventually he's gonna have to do the same, because he is a demon. And because of what Matt did."

"You hate him, huh?"

Rosie thought for a time, a panoply of memories pulling at her emotions. She remembered a crude but well intentioned man who both mocked people yet sought their companionship. She remembered his humor, his love of heavy metal and football, and his hard drinking. Most of all she remembered the way he looked at her, and how it had saddened her.

She shook her head.

"I don't hate him, darling. I pity him. Matt was the type of person who couldn't leave things alone."

Eleanor frowned.

"What do you mean?"

"I mean he locked onto things. Obsessed over them. Once he had an idea, there was no talking him out of it. I still think he didn't mean to hurt anyone, he just...didn't know how to be a person."

"I—I don't understand."

"Not sure I do either. He did a very bad thing because he thought we all hated him. That wasn't the truth at all, but in his mind, I think, if people weren't nice to him all the time, he thought something was wrong. Which is strange, because your mother was the opposite— she was thicker skinned, she understood everything wasn't about her. It's funny how people in the same family can be so different, especially siblings." She shrugged. "Anyway, I tried to be Matt's friend. He wanted something more. Something that wasn't there."

She stared off into some inner distance, remembering desperation and longing in Matt's eyes as he had touched her hand and professed his love. Pity swelled, but nothing more. She looked at

Eleanor and saw her wrestling with a question that she then voiced with something close to fear.

"Is it true that–did my father kill him?

Rosie blinked with surprise.

"Who told you that?"

Eleanor shrugged.

"No," Rosie said. "I ain't answering."

"Please."

Rosie looked at her for a time, seeing past the child to the intelligence that grew everyday in Eleanor's eyes. She sighed.

"Look, Matt paid for what he did. He was...put down. It don't matter by who. It was an ugly thing, but it had to be done. That's... that's our world, darling. I wish it weren't."

Eleanor let that sink in, took a breath, and nodded. It was enough for the moment.

"Uncle Asshole," she said, mumbling under her breath.

Rosie gave a tired laugh.

"Alright, enough of that. Back to your brother."

Eleanor nodded.

"People need to see that he ain't fixin' to possess them or their children," Rosie said. "That they can trust him the way they trusted your mother. I believe they can. But I need to be sure. So..." She stroked the folds of her dress. "I'd like you to keep an eye on him."

Eleanor stared as if she had been slapped.

"I'm not gonna tattle on my brother," she replied. "I ain't a rat."

"Not tattling, baby, no. I don't want you spying on him. You don't need to tell me about everything he does. I trust him. I do. But if you see something that don't sit right with you, something you know is wrong, that's a different story. He has the ability to cause a lot of harm. You saw so yourself. If he ever uses his powers to hurt someone, even just as a joke, it could end real bad. Not just for him, but for your whole family. I don't want that to happen, so if you do see him doing something wrong, hell, you don't even have to tell me. You can tell your father, or Percy, Cedric....any of us. That way, if there's ever a problem, we can deal with it quietly. You'll feel bad, but, really, you'll be protecting Ian."

"Did you and my dad talk about this?"

"No. Your father has a very soft spot when it comes to you two. We worry he might let something slip, so I'd feel safer knowing you were both watching out for your brother."

"We? You and Uncle Percy?"

Rosie smiled.

"Yes. Percy and me."

Eleanor made mock kissing noises.

"Uh-huh, I love my husband," Rosie said. "That okay with you?"

"That reminds me—"

"Don't change the subject."

Eleanor gave her a look that begged just one more question.

"Alright," Rosie said.

"Well, is he really gonna live forever?"

Rosie bit her lip.

"I don't know about forever, but he's been alive nearly two hundred years."

"So...doesn't that mean he'll still be young when we all get old?"

"That's something I'd rather not talk about," Rosie said. "Percy and I love each other. For now, that's enough. You through distracting me? 'Cause I need to know if you're gonna help me keep Ian safe."

Eleanor fiddled with her fingers. The demon sneered from her memory, a waking darkness hateful and hungry. Ian's face parted its black curtain and shone with love she was reluctant to admit that she could not do without. Both warred: the image of her brother, the darkness that lived within. There was no winner.

She looked up at Rosie and nodded.

"I promise that if he ever does something I think is wrong, I'll stop him," she said. "And if I can't, I'll tell you or dad. But I ain't gonna spy on him."

"Alright, then. That's how it is."

Rosie offered her hand. They shook. The woman held the girl's gaze with a look that spoke of respect. Eleanor allowed a blush to come.

"Now, you get," Rosie said. "Your father has something he wants to show you."

Eleanor tilted her head in question.

"Jesus, does he tell you everything? What is it?"

Rosie stood and rolled her head from side to side.

"If he wanted me to tell you, he wouldn't be showing you, now would he?"

Eleanor stuck her tongue out, dodged when Rosie grabbed at it, and ran back towards the door. She blew a kiss while still running.

Rosie watched her, a deep current of love taking hold, both for the girl she saw, and the woman she hoped she would become. Eleanor clamored up the stairs, and Rosie sent a silent prayer after her. That goodness would guide her. That she would always be kept safe.

The cauldrons bubbled. Rosie faced them, her work. Her creations. Spells she hoped would mend the remains of shattered lives.

7

Eleanor ran by Alexander and Cedric, doubled back, and bounced to a stop in front of them. Alexander blew a plume of smoke from the side of his mouth and waited.

"Can I try some?" Eleanor said, pointing at the joint. Cedric chuckled.

"Not mad at me anymore?" Alexander replied.

"I wasn't mad. I–ugh. I just want you to be safe."

"I know, baby."

"Let me try some, and I really won't be mad."

"Sure."

"Really?"

"When you're much older."

Eleanor groaned. Alexander held the joint between his thumb and forefinger, let go, and closed his hand before it dropped. He wiggled his fingers open and revealed an empty palm. Then he smiled and revealed the joint dead between his teeth.

"Alright, not bad, old man," Eleanor said, crossing her arms. Alexander tossed the joint into a trashcan and led his daughter away.

"We go to find your brother. Afterwards, I will show you."

"Show us what?"

"I said I will show you."

The three walked down Freeman, past the Autumn Lane intersection, and rounded the corner onto Gold Street, crossing under blue light spilling through the gated windows of Greg's Security. Alexander and Cedric both looked at the white awning advertising cameras, locks, defensive spells, and golems. A red and white closed sign was visible over a black gate. Alexander and Cedric exchanged a look that shared the same worry over their friend.

They followed the sidewalk beneath a red bricked archway, "Library" etched into its peak in white lettering. The arch served as the base of a catwalk connecting the library's two buildings, both of white marble streaked red, powerful and squat structures that seemed shaped out of the earth itself. People milled in the square, or walked the catwalk carrying books. The entrances to both buildings stood on either side of the square, brass double doors set above wide steps, opening and closing against the flow of steady traffic.

Alexander, Cedric, and Eleanor walked through the square, under another archway, and continued down Gold Street.

They went further down the block, passing the Blue & Green Coffee Shop. The air dripped with languid music and the sultry aroma of coffee. Eleanor watched the animated faces of people within: the entranced expressions of those reading, the closeness of couples or groups in conversation, the profound stillness of solitude.

They turned left onto Sunset Hill.

Cobblestones and concrete gave way to rich earth and green fields. Tall oak trees and Japanese maples bloomed on either side of the lane and came together in a crush of leaves above the rising ground, shading passersby under deep green and fiery orange. A crew of four maintenance workers stood around one of the trees, their hands linked, goggles over their eyes.

"Cover 'em up, people," one of them said. Everyone on the path shielded their eyes. The air rippled between the workers, and a bright explosion of light flashed on the tree, saturating it in a silvery substance that was absorbed by the bark. The crew dropped their hands. "Thank you."

They encircled the next tree.

Alexander and Cedric led Eleanor beneath the long parade of intermingled leaves.

They came out from under the trees and stepped once more onto cobblestone. A playground sang under the joyous feet of dozens of children, swings creaking, monkey bars clattering, seesaws whining. Sparks sailed from magician children's hands, bright sprinkles of color launched at werewolf children who dodged them with fluid ease, jumping, running, or sliding out of the way.

They passed the playground and turned onto Packing Street, a long and winding block lined with garages and men and women loading the contents of boxes onto a waiting armada of pushcarts. A forklift emerged from a pillar wider than the other pillars scattered around the Gardens, carrying a large crate. Workers unloaded the boxes, opened them, and sorted their contents. Eleanor spied slabs of meat in vacuum sealed packages, avalanches of potatoes, twelve-packs of toilet paper, and a myriad of other supplies stacked into the pushcarts.

Some of the loaders greeted Alexander and Cedric. They answered in kind and walked on beyond the workers and the garages towards a rundown gymnasium with a damaged sign hanging above a cracked stoop. No name was writ upon it. Cedric opened the door, let the others in, and followed.

They stepped into a wide space tinted yellow by hanging lamps. Weights, jump ropes, heavy bags, and speed bags were everywhere. Fighters stood akimbo around the center ring where two men boxed. Eitan Vered was tanned and bald and bearded like some pirate of old, and Shine Morris bore long black dreadlocks that were tied behind mountainous shoulders. Both danced about each other, their arms rocking this way and that, their hands pumping, their eyes searching.

Ian, Junior, and Lincoln stood nearest to the ring. The brothers held their instruments close as if they were extensions of themselves. Junior hollered with the other onlookers. Lincoln stroked his chin like a philosopher pondering the mystery of combat. Ian watched, hands in his pockets, eyes cool and bouncing between fighters.

Cedric parted through the crowd and placed his arms around his boys. Alexander and Eleanor joined them beside Ian.

"Again?" Alexander said, nodding to the fighters.

Cedric blew air through his lips.

"They'll be at this when they're using walkers."

Shine jabbed. Eitan dodged and crashed a hook into his right side. The crowd oohed and ahed as one. Eleanor cringed. Ian smiled. Shine bounced back, shook himself off, and went towards his opponent.

"They should just get a room," Eleanor said. Alexander slowly looked at her, aghast. She shrugged. "What? They should."

"They're brothers," Ian said. He nodded at the ring. "Watch their expressions. They love each other. See how Shine is smiling?" Shine grinned over his gloves, his forehead dripping sweat. "How focused Eitan is?" Eitan's eyes were wide and flowing, moving as Shine moved.

Ian nodded with appreciation.

"They fight because they love each other," he said. "Because they know they can. This is what they live for."

Junior flashed Ian a look.

"Damn," he said.

Cedric nodded, impressed, himself the participant of many bouts that formed an unspeakable bond between him and his opponent.

Shine and Eitan caught each other with simultaneous jabs, sweat exploding in silver halos above their heads, and then Shine crashed a left hook into Eitan's ribs. Eitan cringed, stomped his foot, and charged. Shine shimmied and cocked his right fist, as Eitan was about to throw his left. The bell dinged. Their punches broke mid swing. Eitan and Shine hugged, whispered to one another, and laughed. The crowd cheered and clapped and whistled, and then murmured as they dispersed and went back to their training.

The fighters saw the Demidovs and the McGills, and came towards the ropes.

"Yo, lady, gentlemen, did y'all enjoy watching me whoop Shine's ass?" Eitan said, rubbing his gloves together.

"What fight were you in?" Shine replied, wiping his forehead.

"Looked pretty even to me," Eleanor said.

Shine bowed to her.

"Thank you, beautiful."

" 'Thank you, beautiful,' " Eitan said, his voice pitched in mockery. "Why you gotta go there for? What, because she's a girl you immediately have to comment on her looks? That's motherfuckin' objectification, kid.

"What in the shit are you on about? I was just appreciating the compliment."

"See, that's your problem right there, kid, you care too much about what others think."

"Nigga, you were the one who just asked them—" Shine replied before being cut off.

"Hold up, hold up. I didn't ask. I just said what they were all thinking."

"Yeah, whatever."

"Y'all were both terrible, don't worry," Cedric said.

"That a fact, coach?" Shine replied.

"Oh, here he comes," Eitan said. "Mr. I-Taught-You-Everything. Pay attention, kids, this is how to spot the Bullshit. The Bullshit is even worse than normal bullshit. That's why it's called 'the Bullshit'."

Cedric scoffed.

"I think you're forgetting all the times I whooped your scrawny ass," he said. "How afterwards you were all 'How'd you do that, coach? How'd you move like that?' "

"No."

"Yeah."

"No, no, that's not true. How you gonna say some shit like that in front of my students?"

"They don't listen to you, ya stupid heeb," Cedric said. "They always come to me after, so I could show 'em where you fucked up."

Eitan looked at Ian.

"That true?"

Ian smirked in response. Eitan threw up his hands.

"Wow," he said. "Y'all a bunch of traitors, kid. Wow."

Shine laughed, shook his head, patted Eitan's shoulder, and walked off to his corner, ripping tape from around his wrists with his teeth. Eitan draped his arms over the ropes and glared at Ian.

"Where the fuck you been?" he said.

"Providing a very useful service to our people," Ian replied.

"Useful service. If you're not here Monday, I'm gonna usefully drag your ass outta whatever hole you're hiding at." He turned to Alexander. "What up, Big Chief? What brings you into the realm of men?"

"Come down," Alexander replied.

Eitan leapt over the ropes and landed before Alexander without a sound.

"Excuse us," Alexander said to the others. He threw his arm around Eitan, flinched, wiped the sweat from his sleeve onto the front of his coat, and led him away. They stopped a few feet from two men training on a heavy bag, one punching, one holding.

"Something's going down tonight," Alexander said.

"Okay?" Eitan replied.

"We're taking two trucks. We could use you with us. Understand?"

Eitan leaned back with a scrutinizing glint in his eyes.

"We bringing people back?"

"If all goes well."

Eitan blew air through his lips.

"Thought we was done," he said.

"It's a long story. Trust me when I say we need to do this. One last time."

"I don't know, kid. We voted on it. What, that means nothing..?"

Cedric and Shine spoke in the ring. Shine focused as Cedric reenacted the hook that Eitan used to catch him off-guard. Outside of the ring, Eleanor and Junior play-boxed, while Lincoln cradled his saxophone and pressed the keys in rhythm to a song only he heard. Ian watched his father and Eitan suddenly become animated, moving their hands as if trying to drive a point home, speaking over one another. Eleanor noticed after a moment and joined her brother.

"I ain't fucking with no vampires, boss," Eitan said.

"Moreno's name was just mentioned, there's no guarantee—"

"That ain't enough for you?"

"We're talking about children. Vampire or no, that's not something we can just look away from."

Eitan crossed his arms and gazed at the floor.

"This is mad stupid." He shrugged. "Yeah, a'ight. I just...fuck, Alex."

"I know. I would not ask if I didn't need you."

"Bunch of heroic motherfuckers. Percy ain't gonna like this."

Alexander raised his hands as if to say "what can you do?" Eitan shook his head.

"Something else," Alexander said. He looked over to his children, spotted them watching, and led Eitan further away. "I was going to come here anyway to give you a heads up. I'm bringing my children into the Den tonight."

Eitan shot him an exasperated look.

"One minute you wanna save children, the next you wanna traumatize 'em?"

"Children go into the Den all the time."

"Yeah: werewolves. 'Cause they got to."

"Don't give me that. I just saw my daughter handle a possession. And Ian...he hasn't been young for a very long time. Not since what that animal did to him. They need to see firsthand what this is all for."

"Yeah, a'ight, but it's not like going to the Den is gonna make any difference," Eitan said. He took a moment to scrutinize Alexander. "It ain't gonna change what Matt did to your boy."

Alexander bristled, the mention of Matt casting bile in the back of his throat. Memories of a man he had once regarded as family, as a brother, froze the warmth in his blood. Eitan laid a comforting hand on his shoulder, the boxing glove glistening.

"I know," he said. "It was fucked up. Matt tricked us, and your family paid for it. What he did to Ian wasn't right. But what's past is past, homie. Ian's still standing. Going to the Den right now ain't gonna make any difference."

Alexander just stared, a stubborn glint in his eyes.

Eitan threw up his hands.

"I'm saying, the Den ain't going anywhere. They know where it is. They know what it's for. That ain't enough?"

"Eitan, I'm telling you as a courtesy. I appreciate your concern, but I'm not asking your permission."

Eitan sighed and bowed his head. He looked over at Ian, spied both children watching, and sighed again.

"They're your kids, brother. Whatever. But when Percy ain't around, I'm in charge down there, and I think they're too young."

"That's kind of you. But there's no such thing as too young in our world. Too young means easy prey."

"Ian, then," Eitan said. "He might get tempted."

"All the more reason to bring him down there. If he tries anything, we'll be able to see it and then work with him. He can't hide from temptation his whole life."

"Hey, like I said, they're yours. But Percy's gonna have a titty-attack. He's down there right now."

Alexander smiled.

"I know."

Eitan shook his head.

"Wow, kid."

"As for later on..."

They went over the plan, and then rejoined the others.

Junior and Lincoln stood in the ring, their instruments lying on a table within sight. Junior shadow boxed. Lincoln stared at the ropes and touched one as if trying to divine its secrets.

Ian and Eleanor stood outside of the ring. They looked up at their father.

"Are you taking us to the Den?" Ian said. Eleanor gasped, wide-eyed, and thought back to what Rosie had hinted at.

Both Alexander and Eitan gave Ian a suspicious look.

"What made you ask that?" Alexander said, glancing at Ian's shadow.

"It was here the whole time," Eleanor replied, nodding to it. "You're taking us to the Den?"

"What else would you want to show us?" Ian said.

Cedric and his boys overheard. Junior frowned. He knew the Den all too well.

Alexander stood over his children.

"I am," he said. "But—" He raised his hand against Eleanor's sudden burst of jubilation, Ian's look of vindication. "We are going because I want you to understand the responsibility everyone in the Gardens carries. This is not a game, or meant to be fun. You will never leave my side down there. Yasno?"

Alexander emphasized the Russian word, the one he used when he wanted to make clear the seriousness of the situation.

"Da, Papa," Ian said, a solemn look on his face.

"You got it, homie," Eleanor said, saluting.

Alexander nodded. He caught Cedric's eye. Cedric shrugged as if to say it were his decision. His sons looked at Ian and Eleanor, awe on Lincoln's face, pity on Junior's.

Alexander nodded to Cedric and Eitan.

"See you later then," he said.

"A'ight," Eitan replied.

Alexander led the children away. Eleanor turned and stuck her tongue out at Eitan. Eitan hissed in self-depreciation and gestured at Cedric.

"Where's the love?" he said.

Cedric raised two middle fingers.

"You mean this love? Right here?"

Eitan nodded after the Demidovs.

"What you think?"

Cedric shrugged.

"He feels the time's right."

"Do you?"

"Eitan," Cedric said, indicating Junior. Junior stared at the ring's canvas floor and seemed to see beyond to a terrible place no one could follow. Eitan rubbed a gloved hand over his head.

"My fault. You ain't alone, Junior."

"I know," Junior replied. The look on his face said otherwise.

Eitan nodded to Cedric.

"Tonight?"

"Stay here, boys," Cedric said to his sons. He led Eitan away, the two speaking of bloodshed and liberation.

8

Alexander held Eleanor's hand. Ian strolled beside them, hands in his pockets, a young gentleman walking beloved streets without a care.

"We're going to leave our coats at Aunt Rosie's," Alexander said. "I'm too warm in this thing."

"I was just there," Eleanor replied.

"Aren't you lucky?" Alexander said. Eleanor frowned at the sarcasm.

"Will we be in the Den long, Pop?" Ian said.

"No."

They entered Rosie's. Ian smiled at the redness in the air, as if he saw himself reflected within the layers of crimson. His shadow mimicked him on the floor, hands in pockets, relaxed. But it moved its head from side to side, catching subtleties in the air no one else did— emotions, thoughts, and feelings buzzing in a babbling swarm. Alexander grimaced at the shadow. He saw others at tables doing the same and glared at them. They caught his gaze and looked away. He had done just as they had done, and that was not lost upon him. But where he worried, he suspected that others feared and hated. That he would not abide.

He spotted Rosie standing before a corner booth where Hank Olson was seated with his wife, Deirdre Torres-Olson, a woman with black hair and a regal bearing, her jaw strong, her eyes sharp and watchful, a cream colored shawl draped over her dark blouse and white slacks. The Olson's daughters were with them. Janet was tall and skinny and blue eyed, her long blonde hair a fall of waves over her shoulders, her nose long and sharp like Hank's, adolescence carving the last vestiges of childhood from her features. Elisha sat across from her father, her annoyed gaze looking everywhere but the chessboard placed before her, her hair dark and curled at the ends, her skin dark like her mother's, and her expression mirroring Deirdre's watchful nature. Janet wore a blue dress with a pattern of white anchors, and Elisha wore jeans and a baseball jersey. A journal rested by Janet's hand.

Alexander led his children over to them.

"...our responsibility to open their minds to different things at their age," Hank said to Rosie. "It's difficult for them to find themselves, with Janet a teenager now, Elisha not far behind, surrounded by all this magic, all this wonder—"

Elisha groaned, embarrassed. Hank smiled at her, went to continue with Rosie, and then spied Alexander.

"Ah, Alexander," he said. "I was just telling Rosie the importance of exposing one's children to different experiences." Hank beamed and spread his arms to indicate the chessboard. He flicked his finger, and the black Bishop moved on its own into white territory. "Chess teaches patience, advanced thinking, and strategy. When we play, we're sharpening our minds without even realizing it."

Elisha rolled her eyes and caught Eleanor's. She narrowed them, jealousy and dislike clear. Eleanor stifled a laugh and flipped her off, her middle finger raised by her hip so the adults would not see. Elisha bristled, but turned away, not daring to challenge the girl famed in the Gardens for being so ahead of the curve.

"I agree," Alexander said, throwing his arm over Rosie's shoulder in a warm and familiar gesture. "But I'm not ambitious. My children have a more, how you say, go with the flow education."

Eleanor flashed her lower teeth at Hank, mimicking an ape. Ian pretended to eye the chessboard, but sidled next to Janet. Janet looked at him, looked away, and blushed. Ian turned to her.

"Hi," he said.

"Hey."

They locked eyes. Ian waved at Elisha without looking away from Janet.

"Hey, Elisha."

Elisha grunted in reply.

A silent weight pressed against Ian. He broke from Janet's gaze and spied Deirdre watching him over her martini. He smiled at her.

"Dr. Olson. You look very elegant in that outfit. Cream is a good color for you. I see where your daughters get their grace from." He looked at Hank. "I hope you don't mind, sir."

Hank made an impressed gesture that said he did not.

"You'll go far like that, young man."

Eleanor turned to Ian with "what in the hell did I just hear?" plastered on her face. Elisha again rolled her eyes. Janet pretended to focus on the chess match, but was ever cognizant of Ian standing near her. She flipped her hair, and the slightest shimmer ran through the strands, a conjurer's trick deepening her golden waves.

Deirdre Torres-Olson regarded Ian the way a bird of prey spies a potential threat.

"Bueno, Alexander," she said, "your son is as charming as ever."

"Hell if he ain't," Rosie said, elbowing Ian playfully.

"It's all a lie, I assure you," Alexander said to Deidre, sensing her distrust and not hiding his sarcasm.

Ian refocused on Janet. Deirdre watched them and crossed her legs. Alexander saw the suspicion on her face and held back a wave of resentment.

"I hope the night is treating you all very well," he said.

"Nothing better than to sit with one's family," Hank replied. He looked up at Alexander with deep appreciation on his face, gratitude for the man who had saved his and Deidre's lives years ago, allowing them this chance to be here now. "That's something I'm always grateful for."

Alexander nodded, humbled yet proud that he had helped these people find their way. Deirdre slid her hand into Hank's, their thumbs nuzzling. But still she watched as her daughter slid closer in her seat to Ian.

"It would be better if we didn't have to play this dumbass game," Elisha said.

"Oh, come on, dude, give it a chance," Janet replied.

"Janet's right, Elisha," Ian said. "Chess can be a lot of fun. Your father had a good point, too. You'd be surprised how it can help you think."

"Jesus, what are you, like, forty?" Elisha said.

"Manners," Deirdre said.

"Its fine, doctor," Ian said. "Chess isn't for everyone."

"Can it help me conjure?" Elisha said. "No? Then I don't give a shit."

Deirdre turned to her with that nameless authority mothers wield. Elisha stiffened, muttered an apology, and tried to focus on the chessboard while testing the muscles of her face, flexing her cheeks, stretching her mouth wide, still adjusting to being herself after being whatever Aidan Horowitz had transformed her into in the Dungeon.

Eleanor reached over Elisha, moved a Knight to take Hank's Bishop. Hank responded by using his Queen to take the Knight, placing Elisha in check.

Elisha threw up her hands.

"Did I ask for your help?" she said to Eleanor.

"Better than just sitting on your ass," Eleanor replied.

They glared at each other.

"Elisha, I heard you giving Aidan a good scare," Alexander said, aware that Elisha's animosity towards his daughter was born out of frustration at not being as advanced as she was at magic. He wanted to remind her of her strengths, and made a mental note to again tell Eleanor to ease up on her. "I'm impressed. Takes courage to let a novice spellcaster practice on you."

"He's lucky I didn't raise a golem on his ass," Elisha replied, staring at the chessboard as if it owed her money.

"Doesn't Ms. K want me to help you with conjuring golems on Tuesday?" Eleanor said, smiling sweetly, mischief vibrant fire in her eyes. Alexander nudged her, but she ignored him.

Elisha would have shot her if she could.

"Yeah," she said through her teeth. "Thanks for the reminder."

Alexander shook his head and laid his hand on Eleanor's shoulder.

"Don't be so hard on Aidan," he said to Elisha. "It's difficult for spell-casters."

"It's gonna be even harder now that he's pissed me off."

Alexander motioned to her parents.

"She'll have no problem fending for herself," he said.

Hank chuckled.

Janet leaned over to Ian, her lips nearly touching his ear. She whispered something, and they both giggled.

Deirdre watched them

Alexander turned to Rosie.

"May we leave our coats with you?"

"Sure thing."

Alexander gave her their coats. Rosie looked from Ian to Eleanor. Eleanor caught her glance and remembered the conversation about her brother. She looked away, guilt and concern playing tug of war with her conscience.

Rosie turned to Alexander, the knowledge of why he came almost making the question unnecessary.

"Time?" she said.

"That it is."

"He told us," Eleanor said, excitement ringing in her voice.

Rosie nodded and leaned towards Eleanor and Ian.

"You're going to hear awful things down there," she said. "But don't fret. You'll be alright. Hopefully it'll give y'all a better understanding of why we do what we do."

Janet whirled in a breathless rush.

"Are you going to the Den?" she said.

Hank looked surprise. Deirdre's eyebrows shot up. Elisha gaped, an expression that screamed envy. She crossed her arms, growled, and pouted. Deirdre laid a hand on her shoulder. Elisha bowed her head, her lips becoming a hard white line.

"Yep," Eleanor said.

Hank seemed to wrestle with this, wondering what every parent wonders when the children of another undertakes a big step.

Deirdre rose and motioned Alexander aside. He hesitated, then followed. Hank watched. Elisha slid under the table, slapped at Ian and Janet's hands so Janet scooted closer to Ian, and reappeared beside her father. He threw his arm over her, and though her face was a mask of apathy, love gleamed in her eyes. Janet watched her mother retreating and turned to Ian with a rush of excitement. Their hands met again under the table, brushing, stroking, as if making love through caressing fingers. Rosie took the coats, went behind the bar, and hung them on a coat rack. Eleanor watched Janet and Ian, leaned for a quick peek under the table, and felt strange warmth spread through her stomach as she glimpsed their entangled hands. As if she stumbled on a beautiful secret she was still too young to understand.

Deirdre and Alexander stopped near the empty stage. She crossed her arms.

"I suppose you know what I'm going to say?" she said.

"Ian will be fine."

"It's not your son I'm worried about."

Alexander took a deep breath and looked upwards, as if asking the divine for strength. He stroked his mustache. A call for patience echoed through his mind. He nodded and addressed Deirdre.

"You have good reasons to be concerned, Dr. Olson. But Ian is my son. That means something. I will not allow him to cause any harm."

"Maybe. Your boy is a gentleman." She glanced at Ian. "But temptation is temptation, and taking him down there will be like leading a starving man to a meal and telling him not to eat. It's a demon's nature to possess, and that goes double for the possession of turned werewolves. I've treated—or attempted to treat—a number of demons. I know what they're like, and that gives me cause for concern."

"Deidre, with all due respect, you aren't like the rest of us. You don't know what it's like to...manage abilities. People like me, like my son, we have to test ourselves if we want to gain control of our powers. I have no doubt you've worked very hard at becoming a psychiatrist, but it's not the same. You wouldn't understand."

"I've managed countless sessions with demons. Doing so gave me a profound understanding of their behavior. So believe me when I say that demons are not known for their self-control."

"You don't think Ian can control himself?"

"I know he can't."

"Okay," Alexander said. "Say you're right. Say he will allow instinct to take over. If that's the case, it is all the more reason to test him early. He must learn the importance of control while he's still young."

"Fair enough. Let's say I'm wrong, then." She smiled to reveal how certain she was of that. "Doesn't it bother you that he's so well mannered? After what was done to him—and I don't say this to hurt you, Alexander."

He raised a hand to show it was okay, but his breath caught, and rage trembled.

"You also trusted Matt," Deirdre said. "We all did. We all knew what he was capable of, but we thought he would be like Phoebe."

Grief twisted Alexander. Phoebe: His wife, the woman with whom he had made a life with, who had been his partner through the dark road that had led them to a home. He gazed at her through the veil of memory, her hair a replica of Eleanor's, her eyes as deep and dark as Ian's.

But Matt's face shattered Phoebe's visage, sending a pang of hatred bubbling beneath Alexander's skull.

"He wasn't," Deirdre said, continuing to discuss Matt. "Phoebe was one thing. Her brother was something else entirely, and your son caught the full force of that. Matt possessed many people. He broke them, turned them into werewolves, or into slobbering lunatics. Yet he possessed your son when the boy was barely six years old, and not only does Ian survive with his sanity, he goes on as if nothing happened. He shouldn't even be functioning, let alone be so well behaved."

She looked over at Ian. The boy turned to her with a polite smile, leaning against the table to conceal his hand holding Janet's underneath.

Alexander said nothing. No anger showed on his face. Deirdre sighed.

"I'm overstepping my bounds," she said. "But it's only because I'm concerned for his wellbeing."

"Spare me," Alexander replied. "We both know what this is."

They looked over at their children. Ian and Janet leaned closer together. He brushed a strand of hair from her forehead, a soft smile on his face. Janet threw her hair back and pressed her lips together.

"Okay," Deirdre said. "My child comes first, I won't apologize for that. Look at them. He seems so taken with her."

"Seems?"

"Yes, Alexander, seems. If he were not your son, you would agree. Demons are master manipulators. We can't know what goes on in his mind. So—"

"You want to analyze him. That's what this is about. You want him in your office so you can toy with his brain—"

"Treatment, Alexander. Believe it or not, I had some success treating demons in the Family. I kept a good deal of them under control. So I know what I'm talking about. Put aside your preconceptions. Either your boy is lying about who he is and playing us all for fools, or he's carrying a great deal of pain, pretending that everything is fine. Or maybe I'm wrong. Maybe he found a way to be well adjusted, despite what happened. If that's so, if your boy is what he appears to be—and I want that to be the case, despite what you may think—then a word from me will go a long way into dispelling the fears of everyone here.

"Phoebe destroyed many of our notions of what a demon is

supposed to be. Matt undid all that goodwill in a single night. Even if Ian has taken after his mother, and his intentions are pure, I'm still concerned. No one survives possession without some level of damage. He needs help, before that pain becomes too great. He could be dealing with trauma, and goodness knows what else. You know that. I know you know that."

Alexander looked away from her and at the faces peering through the smoky haze. Some looked over at Ian and muttered. Others glanced at Alexander as though he were someone to be pitied. A poor fool with his evil child.

"My son is not a monster," he said. "He is kind, intelligent, already he helps my officers with mock possessions, and never have any of them felt threatened. Show me one person here who Ian has attempted to possess, eh? No. He has been through hell, this is true. Matt—" He said the name as if it were the vilest curse ever conjured in any tongue. "Hurt him in a way no one, let alone a young boy, should ever be hurt, and I will not have anyone drag it up again. He has earned everyone's trust many times over, and until I see otherwise, I have no reason to doubt it. Thank you, doctor, but I don't think my son needs your services."

Deidre looked at him for a long time.

"I hope you're right," she replied. "Just remember who your friends are. You may not believe it, but I honestly have your best interest at heart. So, for the sake of all of us, keep an eye on your son."

Alexander laughed without mirth and walked away. Deidre watched him with something akin to greed, the look of someone who has come close to what they desire. She arched her head back, smoothed her blouse, and almost smiled. There would be other times. She looked over at Ian. She was certain of that.

They both returned to the table, one after the other.

Hank puffed gray plumes of tobacco from his pipe and poured over the chessboard. Eleanor was his opponent. She stared straight at him. He looked at her and smiled.

"Are you trying to intimidate me?" he said.

"Yep," she replied. "Is it working?"

"A good adversary never reveals their true feelings."

Alexander laid his hand on Eleanor. She scooted out of the booth, and Deidre reclaimed her seat. Elisha slid back under the table and rejoined her mother.

"Can we go with them?" Janet said to Hank. He laughed as if she had asked if the world was flat. Elisha groaned in disappointment and threw a crumpled straw cover onto the table.

"I promise you, Elisha," Alexander said. "You're not missing much. I'm sure my children will tell you the same."

Eleanor nodded in solemn agreement. When Alexander turned away, she threw up her hands with forefingers and pinkies sticking out—the universal sign for rock and roll—gave a silent jubilant scream, and stuck her tongue out. Alexander gently slapped her upside the head without looking. She grimaced and rubbed the spot.

"Good evening," Alexander said. He led Eleanor away. She waved at Janet, gave a snide look to Elisha, and followed after her father.

"Dr. and Dr. Olson," Ian said, bowing. He caught Deirdre's eyes. Something unspoken lived between them. His smile widened as he addressed her. "If you don't mind me saying so, doctor, I've always been very impressed by you. It must be strange for a normal human to be surrounded by all of this. You've helped a lot of people here. I admire your open mindedness."

She gave a slight nod, but did not reply.

Ian smiled again. His shadow stretched on the wall above the booth, betraying no movements save for a single wave of its fingers. Ian shared a meaningful glance with Janet and walked away.

Janet watched him leave. Deirdre placed her hand over hers. Janet shuddered, but did not look at her mother. Deirdre leaned back and watched the Demidovs depart from the crimson shadows.

"No?" Hank said to her, nodding towards Ian.

Deirdre reached for his hand with her other.

"Not yet," she replied.

"Give it time."

Deirdre smiled.

"I know, mi amor. It won't be long."

They sat in comfortable silence, waiting with patient anticipation. Janet and Elisha shared a look that spoke of the strangeness of their parents, these people they loved beyond all others, people who cared for them, raised them, and yet seemed like outsiders from another place, mystics keeping terrible secrets. Janet shrugged, unclasped her journal, and began to write in it. Elisha crossed her arms and frowned in frustration.

Deirdre beckoned a waiter and ordered hot chocolates for their girls, and Hank took in the most important women in his life. They were a family. Whatever lingered beneath would wait. Their time would come.

Rosie saluted Alexander as they walked out. Eleanor looked back at her, still remembering their conversation. Rosie nodded, and Eleanor felt somehow older, as if their agreement was the first glimpse into what it was like to be a woman instead of a girl.

9

They went from Cauldron Avenue, wound their way through Freeman, and walked until the bustle of stores and eateries were behind them. The street slanted downhill towards the southeast, and all about them were low walls that seemed to rise out of the ground like knife blades. A low rumble thrummed through the air as the street leveled out, and they reached a great granite wall at the base of the hill. It stood three stories above the ground, a structure of sinuous black marble that spanned the southern end of the Gardens, multiple streets and avenues descending towards it. Eleanor had seen it before, from a distance. She, Lily, Aidan, and Lincoln had dared each other to go near it, but they had never gone all the way for it had seemed aware somehow, as if admonishing them for coming too close.

Now she felt that awareness considering her.

Liquid movements rippled across its surface, layers of granite undulating as an archway opened. Alexander led them through it, and Eleanor realized that the archway's ceiling was only an inch over her father's head. He caught her noticing, smiled, and bent lower. The ceiling sank, acclimating to his height. He straightened slowly, and it rose again. Then he pointed backwards. Eleanor looked. The wall had filled in behind them, solidifying with their every step in a silent and controlled landslide, so it seemed as if it were hurrying them out.

"Pop?" Eleanor said.

Alexander smiled.

"Good," he replied. "Now I know that you've never been here."

She frowned up at him.

"The wall adjusts to the people going through it," he said. "So, eh, nothing tries to escape behind you, or in front of you. If something were to try to come at us from ahead, the ceiling would collapse on them and leave us with just enough room. It's for safety. Just in case."

They came out from within the wall, and the archway closed. The surface rippled and then fell still.

They stood before a maze constructed of iron walls. Two of these shifted into an entrance, and Eleanor could see other openings in the distance to the east and west, where figures were going in or coming out.

Alexander led them in.

They followed the maze to the left, walked down a straightaway, turned right, and then a low rumbling reverberated under their feet. The dividers before and behind them shifted at 90 degree angles. A path was formed for them to follow, and the path they had taken was blocked off.

"Uh?" Eleanor said.

"The walls are always changing," Alexander replied. "Again, for protection."

Eleanor marveled, and then started with a realization.

"Does this mean werewolves can escape?" she said, nearly squeaking.

"No," Alexander replied. He bounced his head from side to side, deliberating. "At least, it is very, very unlikely. But you want to be cautious, so we built a maze around the entrances to the Den, one that always moves. That way, if a werewolf escapes–which it won't– but if it does, it'll be lost." He scrutinized the walls. "I say we, but, mostly, it was your Aunt Rosie's creation. Even if werewolves would try to climb over these walls, they would...well, there are measures in place. And the main wall, it wouldn't let them through. It can tell turned werewolves from us. So I don't want you to worry."

"Won't we get lost, too?" Eleanor said.

"No. The Gardens is making a path, leading us to the nearest entrance. Like I said, it knows we're not werewolves."

Ian brushed aside pebbles with his foot, looking at the ground as if trying to peer through it to something deeper within.

"Is the Gardens alive, Pop?" he said.

Alexander hesitated.

"In a way," he replied. He looked at his watch. Satisfied with the time, he hurried onward before either of his children could ask another question. They followed, turning as the walls about them shifted.

They went right and came upon a young woman leaning against her boyfriend. The young woman's eyes drooped, and her head lulled as her boyfriend helped her to walk. Buttons of cutesy animated characters adorned her denim jacket. Her boyfriend stroked her hair and pressed her close, heavy silver rings shaped into butterflies adorning his hands.

"It's okay, baby," he said. "It's okay."

"Mm," she replied, unable to say more. Her eyes caught Eleanor's as they passed, and she frowned in confusion. Eleanor stared back, watching the way the woman stumbled. Fear heightened her senses, making her aware of a bite in the air, and of the near hopeless exhaustion in the woman's eyes.

Walls shifted, and the couple was gone.

The Demidovs went on.

They came out of the maze and into an oval, where four security officers stood guard before a towering vault door built into a slab of rock that rose high above them. Steel ropes were connected to the top of the door. They rose into the air and there drifted, connected to nothing, sighing melodiously in the breeze.

"Chief," one guard said, nodding. The others came to attention. They looked down at the children, their faces blank. A hint of incredulity and doubt shifted between them. Alexander motioned towards the vault door. The officers exchanged a look, shrugged, and turned to it. Two of them raised their hands and conjured. The steel ropes coiled into a pulley that pulled the ropes taut. The vault slid upwards, revealing torchlight dancing within.

Alexander nodded thanks and led the children inside.

"Thank you," Ian said to the guards. His shadow trailed after him on the ground, mimicking its master, innocent save for the inverted curve of its knees.

They stood on a stone landing before stairs that spiraled down into the unknown. The vault door groaned shut behind them, clanging as it touched the ground, leaving them in the trembling glow of semi-darkness. Eleanor tiptoed and stared over the balustrade into the depths and saw all things formless and nameless from her nightmares waiting. The darkness seeped inside and fed her fears. She clutched her father's hand and shivered.

"Are you okay?" he said. She nodded. Ian threw his arm over her. The warmth of him undid the sudden paralysis. She loved him then. She knew she always would.

Alexander led them down. Their steps echoed. Their shadows spread across the walls, Ian's darting its head from side to side as if suppressing excitement.

"Be still," Ian said under his breath, his voice strained. The shadow slowed the movements of its head, but it stood rigid with anticipation, taller than its master. Eleanor and Alexander exchanged a glance that spoke of their mutual hope that the boy they loved would not be a slave to the thing he carried.

They descended. Each landing, though bathed in torchlight, was permeated by ribbons of darkness that swelled and receded and swelled again. The fires flickered and sighed. A deep silence held.

A roar ripped apart the silence, exploding from the agonized bowels of some ravaged beast, rising into a shriek that pierced the walls. Eleanor froze. Ian held his father's arm as if hearing music for the first time. His shadow swelled into a jagged smear of blackness against the wall. Its eyes flashed crimson. Ian quivered, unable to contain an ecstatic smile. He closed his eyes, breathed deep, and let go of his father. Other roars followed, screaming atrocity, tempting the inner maw within the demon-child.

Eleanor's heart thundered.

"Holy shit," she said, marveling with perfect dread at the unrestrained power and demented savagery rising out of the werewolves waiting below.

Alexander watched Ian.

The boy clenched his eyes shut. Sweat beaded his brow, day and night warring within. He longed to crash down the steps and answer those screams. But he held. His shadow was a tumor against the wall, sharp tendrils of darkness constrained only by its master's will, by a morality it was not conceived to understand.

Alexander waited. He fought the impulse to snatch Ian up and return to the safety and warmth above. No parent wishes to see their child struggle. But the struggle would test Ian and answer a long avoided question.

So Alexander waited.

Ian opened his eyes. His shadow bled from the wall and collapsed into its master's form, falling on its haunches, hissing and panting, petulant. Ian breathed hard, jaw muscles flexing, eyes wide with silent command. His shadow whined, but flattened into a pool of blackness on the landing, and the boy looked at his father and nodded.

"It's okay," he said. "I'm okay."

Alexander nodded as if this were obvious, but inwardly sighed with relief.

"Good," he said. He looked to his daughter. Her hands trembled, and her eyes were wide. But she gave a shivering thumbs up.

They went on, pushing against the howls of werewolves.

They reached the bottom, a long corridor of stone stretching into darkness. The air was made of screams, intertwining space with rage and agony. Eleanor imagined at any moment the walls themselves would bare teeth.

"We can wait for another time," Alexander said, seeing her distress.

She balled her hands into fists.

"C'mon, old man," she replied, shooting forward.

They walked the long corridor and came upon a steel door guarded by two security officers with earplugs in their ears. They nodded grimly to Alexander. One stared at the children, conflicted sorrow in his eyes. The other opened her palm. White matter danced in a spiral like some tiny galaxy and coalesced into six earplugs. She offered them. Alexander took his and inserted them into his ears. Eleanor watched him and then did the same.

"Can you hear me?" Alexander said.

His voice came clear through the earplugs. Yet the blood curdling screams of werewolves was muted to distant thunder.

"Yeah," she said, smiling with astonishment, a brief respite from the cacophony beyond the door, a reminder of the magic they carried.

Ian hesitated, the earplugs lying in his open palm. He licked his lips and swallowed as a scream ripped through the door. Then he grimaced with resolve and pushed the earplugs into his ears. The guard who had stared at the children turned towards the door, spun a valve, and pulled it open. They stepped aside and let the Demidovs pass, their faces stoic, sentinels attending their task. Alexander made no acknowledgement of them, for to do so would be akin to ripping them from whatever shelter they created in themselves against the barrage of howls. He led his children through and heard the muted crash of metal behind them as the door was sealed.

They stood a small landing. Three steps down led them into the Den.

Massive steel vaults filled the space, rows of them stretching into the outer dark. Stairs leading to exits were spaced every thirty to forty vaults, each leading to different exits in the ever changing maze above. The werewolves howled as if mauling the air, their violent shrieks threatening to rip everything apart. Vault doors shuddered and rocked, struck from within by rampaging monsters unable to contain their frenzy. Eleanor marveled that anything that strong could shake so. She again clutched her father's hand as she imagined what raged behind the steel. Ian panted, taking heavy breaths, trying to slow his breathing. His shadow screeched, dancing around him, goading him into giving in.

"Ian," Alexander said. Ian raised his hand to show he was okay.

"Away," he said through gritted teeth. The shadow growled, tiny compared to the onslaught of roars, and vanished into the floor. Ian spat and stood erect. His eyes were calm as he scanned the vaults, and he smoothed his tie and looked up at his father.

Alexander nodded and led his children deeper into the Den.

Security officers patrolled, inspecting unoccupied vaults, checking vault doors to ensure their sturdiness. Spellcasters sat cross-legged before some occupied vaults, their eyes closed, their faces passive, streams of calming magic emanating from their bodies and pouring through the steel in soft tints of blue. Muted groans came from within these vaults, the sounds of savagery quieted to whimpers as the spells did their work.

How many vaults were occupied? To Eleanor it seemed like hundreds.

They walked, watching in silence as a group of maintenance workers entered the deep and wide space of an unoccupied vault. Eleanor watched. Streaks of blood splattered the inside of the vault's door. A crisscross of jagged claw marks eviscerated the walls and ceiling, deep, ragged, and cruel. Masses of crumbled stone littered the floor or dangled in shredded ropes from the ceiling, and a discarded sheath of skin lay black and twisted at the far left corner of the vault. Eleanor had heard that werewolves discarded their human skin every time they changed, but to see it firsthand...

She shuddered.

Two of the maintenance workers raised their hands and lifted the debris on strands of black light. The stone melted in midair into a haze of particles. The other maintenance workers laid their hands against the wall, closed their eyes, and channeled the hovering clouds of deconstructed matter through themselves and into the walls. The claw marks smoothed into solid wall. A lone maintenance worker stood before the molted skin, grimaced, and snapped her fingers. The blackened flesh burst into flames, the smoke rising in acrid plumes into the maintenance worker's outstretched hand.

Eleanor jumped as a barrage of howls tore her from her reverie.

"Eleanor," Alexander said. He walked ahead. She ran after.

They came to a four-way intersection that stretched into other corridors all identical. A stairway door opened ahead, and a man lumbered out, his head lulling, bracing the railing as he descended the steps. His friend followed behind, keeping a hand on the man's shoulder.

"I think it's time, guys," the lulling man said, as two officers came and gently threw their arms over him. They led him to an open vault and began to strip him of his clothes. His friend stood for a moment on the landing, grimaced, and went back the way he came.

The children watched. Alexander watched them.

"He's about to turn," Eleanor said.

"Mm," Alexander replied.

"It's true," Ian said. "They feel really good first. Junior told me he likes that part, that you can't help it."

"It's always like that," Alexander said, squatting. "We think it's a way for them to deal with the terrible stress they're about to endure. It's like they're on a strong drug. That way, they don't feel the change before they go unconscious. It's a mercy."

"Have you seen a werewolf change, Pop?" Ian said.

"Yes."

They waited for more. He did not give it. He remembered something that did not need to be repeated. His eyes did all the telling. Cold boiled Eleanor's heart.

"But they don't remember it?" Eleanor said.

"No. Thank goodness, no."

Four security officers, a Latina woman who held a canvas bag filled with clothes, and her daughter, all stood by a closed vault a few yards away from the lulling man. The officers listened and waited to the quiet within the vault. They knocked on the door. A muted voice answered, human and tired. They looked at each other and nodded. Three of them took a step back and spread their hands and arms above their heads. The fourth waited to the side of the fault, her arms taut. Red fire streamed over her fingertips, a blast of cruel force waiting to be unleashed should a werewolf come marauding out. The vault slid outwards and then upwards from the pull of the three officers, rising until it hovered high above.

A lithe and naked Indian man lay on the floor within, dried blood caking his body. He struggled to look up and smiled.

"Fancy seeing you here," he said. The officers came forward and draped a blanket over his shoulders. His daughter rushed forward and threw her arms around him. His wife smiled with relief. The fourth magician absorbed the fierce light back into her hands. She seemed to glow for a moment. She grimaced, took a deep breath, and exhaled.

Alexander motioned for his children to see.

"In the Family," he said, gesturing vaguely above as if to a bad dream, "there are people just like that, trying to live honestly, trying to survive in the best possible way they can. But because they are werewolves—something they have no say in, or, worse, something that was forced on them—their lives are ruined. A lucky few can afford their own vaults where they can turn in safety and in the care of loved ones or paid magicians. But most are herded into places where they are possessed against their will. Those are called Possession Parlors, or Communes." He spat. "There, demons and even other werewolves prostitute their victims to other demons who wish to possess them. A werewolf is a great source of pain and rage, things demons feed on. The werewolves cannot say no to this deal, because the alternative is not an option. It is the price they pay, since they do not have the money to stay in their own vaults.

"And possession is addictive. Demons know how to release pleasure in their victims, while at the same time feeding on the suffering that pleasure is masking. After a few possessions, many werewolves grow dependent. They give in to it. They wither away. They die. Entire families. Like them."

The children looked on. The mother and daughter helped the man limp out of the vault. The officers waited, giving him warm clasps on his shoulders, looking on with understanding. Eleanor felt suffocated by the weight of sadness, knowledge that there were those who suffered that were out of her reach, who she could do nothing for. When a child learns of torment, something becomes lost, innocence never reclaimed. Eleanor learned something of the world that night, something cruel and heartless. She pressed close to her father, feeling in him the antithesis to such darkness. She understood the need for love and kindness and all the things that give life light.

Ian seethed. His eyes widened in an unblinking stare. The heat of longing that first filled him when he had entered was now lost to frigid rage, quiet and coiled, hissing to strike at those whom made such tragedies so. His shadow looked at him as though coming to a realization. He felt its reptilian voice whispering what he now knew: That a special kind of darkness can serve the light to the benefit of both. That there were those who deserved to suffer.

"I know you know all these things," Alexander said. "But to see it, to breathe it, makes it real. Life is hard. It is our task to make it a little easier for people like them." He looked at his son. "Do you understand?"

"Da," Ian replied, the word springing from his lips without hesitation.

Alexander once more breathed an inward sigh of relief. He spied anger in his son's eyes, something akin to indignation—something he dared to hope was righteous.

"Good," he said. "That's good."

"And it's all because of the vampires, right, Pop?" Eleanor said.

He said nothing, lost in memories of terrors he prayed his children would never experience. But he nodded, his expression grave and heartbroken.

Eleanor and Ian let the pieces fall together in their own way.

Quiet seized the air, each roar vanishing as if bidden to silence. Roars thundered in the distance like the echoes of bombs, but nothing raged around the Demidovs. Alexander knew why. He knew who had come. He smiled a sardonic smile, stood, and turned around.

Percy Bowles stood at the center of the crossroads, tall, strong, and blue eyed. The boyishness of his features and smoothness of his light skin was contrasted by the depth of those eyes, as if currents of ancient waters swelled within them. He wore gray baggy jeans and a white T-shirt printed with a great curved W standing for the Wu Tang Clan. A tan driver's cap with blue and red checkers was fitted on his blonde head, and a black canvas bag dangled from the belt loop of his jeans, swollen with food. He reached into it, took an apple, and finished it in three bites.

He wore no earplugs.

Eleanor fidgeted. Something about his presence always made her do so, yet she was happy to see him.

"Hi, Uncle Percy," she said, smiling a genuine smile.

"Hello, love," Percy replied, bending low and beaming in kind, his voice a remnant of London streets long lost to time. "Hasn't been too frightening, has it?"

She shook her head.

"More educational," Ian said.

Percy regarded him as if he were a docile predator, the demon-child acting against nearly everything Percy knew of their kind.

"I imagine it has," he said. "This must be difficult for you."

Ian was silent. Percy kept his gaze on him.

"You're composing yourself well," he said, "I'm glad to see that. Proud even." He regarded the boy for a time, then without taking his eyes from him: "Alex. A word."

Eleanor and Ian watched Percy stride away, his every movement like that of some royal beast, fluid and deadly.

Alexander joined him, stopping a healthy distance away from the children. Percy took a candy bar from the bag and unwrapped it. His watch glowed with cool green light, binary zeroes and ones lit on the screen instead of a regular clock face.

Percy broke the candy bar in half and popped it into his mouth. Harsh groans seeped through the vault nearest him, rising into undulating pants like the barking of a mad man on the verge of frenzy. Percy turned towards the vault and growled. A deep rumble boomed from his chest and sent waves through Alexander's shoes. The werewolf within the vault fell silent.

Alexander cleared his throat and stilled the automatic tension raised by the force of Percy's growl. Percy ate the rest of the candy bar and stared him in the eyes, waiting. Alexander sighed.

"It was time for them to see this," he said.

"Sure of that, are we?"

"Yes. I am."

Percy was silent for a moment. Then:

"I agree."

"Really? So, you're not going to lecture me about my son?"

Percy smirked.

"You were being watched before you even came in."

"So Rosie told you."

" 'Course she did. Why else do you think he was allowed inside?"

Alexander looked away.

"I don't appreciate that," he said.

"Steady on, mate. I don't care what you appreciate, not when it comes to this. If your boy gets it into his head to attempt a possession, that's something I have to be ready to deal with. Be angry. Go on. Give us a hard stare. The fact remains, he is what he is. I'm not going to risk my people on your whim."

Alexander scoffed.

"Your people?"

"Our people, then. That includes you as well, you twat."

He jabbed a finger into Alexander's chest. Alexander grunted and was rocked backwards. Percy winced, forgetting his strength.

"Hey!" Eleanor said.

"Sorry," Percy said to her, gesturing for peace. He turned to Alexander. "Sorry."

"It's okay," Alexander replied, rubbing his chest, grimacing. "Look, I'm not being, eh, how you say, obtuse. I know what people say about me. I know they think I'm soft on Ian. But time and time again he has shown that he is good. If you've been watching him, then you saw how he controlled himself." A swelling of pride made Alexander smile. "He did not let that thing win. We just have to help him face what he is so he can deal with it. That is all I'm doing, and it's working."

"You didn't think he would control himself, but you brought him down here anyway."

Alexander looked away, putting his hands to his hips, containing his frustration.

"I would've stopped him," he said.

"Would you have? Really?"

Alexander frowned in response.

"Alright then," Percy said. "These vaults are all protected by spells, so the fact is your boy wouldn't have been able to cause much harm. I reckon it would've been a minor thing, 'cept, of course, all the goodwill he would've lost once word got out. Remember how long it took to undo the hurt Matt caused?"

Alexander bristled.

"You too?" he replied. "Have you all suddenly decided that tonight would be the night to bring all this up again? You know how sick I am of hearing that name—"

"Come off it, mate. It happened. Your anger isn't going to change what that bloody fool did, and you—"

"Oh, I wasn't aware."

The sarcasm was clear. Percy took off his cap and scratched his head.

"Alright," he said. "That was uncalled for, I'm sorry. You're right. Your boy handled himself well.

"But what I want to know is what you'll do should the day ever comes that he can't control himself. If he succumbs to what he is... should he ever indulge his darker half in a situation where we're vulnerable, where he can really hurt us, what then?"

Alexander said nothing.

"See, I can't let you make that decision. He's your son. You can't hurt him. So, even if it means you hating me for the rest of your days, that responsibility falls on my shoulders. I don't want to have to hurt your boy. But I have to think about all of our people, not just those dearest to me. That leaves me in a very troubling position. Bit of a dilemma, yeah?"

Alexander took a deep breath.

"He will never give you cause," he said.

Percy looked over at the children. Ian stared back, innocent, curious. His shadow was invisible on the ground, but Percy felt it there, a blotch of cold darkness ever waiting.

"I hope so," he replied, looking at Alexander. "He has you as a father, and Phoebe, well...So I can trust you. But let's be clear: If I suspect, and I mean even for just one bloody moment, that he's going to hurt anyone, I won't hesitate. I'll do what I have to."

They stared at each other. Alexander took a measured breath, stilling the anger threatening to unleash a torrent of vengeful magic. Beyond the threat to his child, he saw in Percy, in the man he regarded as a brother, the weight of the entire Gardens. Despite the instinct to throttle him, he had no choice but to understand. He extended his hand. Percy's face was still, but a measure of relief lightened his eyes. They shook, and the tension between them resolved into familiarity.

"Thought you were going to thrash me there," Percy said. "Send me right up to the infirmary."

"I don't feel like breaking my hand today, thank you."

"It would've been very emotional for me, mate."

"You have feelings?"

Percy gave him a flat look. Alexander smirked, but Percy noticed the slightest agitation in him, a slight tremble around his eyes.

"I have to be harsh, Alex."

"I understand."

"Then what's wrong?"

Alexander shrugged. Percy narrowed his eyes, unable to do away with a sense that his friend was holding something back.

"Anything you want to tell me?" he said.

Alexander opened his mouth to speak, paused, and smiled. He heard Cedric and Eitan screaming in his mind for him to do what was right. But Percy had agitated him just enough that an old rebellious spirit took control. He now wanted nothing more than to see the look of surprise on Percy's face when he returned with the people he was to save that night from the Family.

"No," he replied. "I have everything under control."

Percy nodded, unconvinced. He glanced over at the children and waved. Then he gave Alexander one final searching look.

"Come over for dinner tomorrow night" he said. "Rosie and I are making ribs."

Percy walked off through the center path. He pulled a bag of almonds out of the plastic bag, picked one between his thumb and forefinger, flicked the almond into the air, and caught it between his teeth. He moved with ease, existing somewhere outside and inside of time, an immortal on a stroll.

The werewolves crashed into hearing the moment he was gone. Alexander frowned. He returned to his children.

They watched him, Eleanor braced against the screams, yet still curious, still a child but only just, Ian patient and knowing, his expression filling Alexander with a longing for the boy to remain just a boy.

He knelt before them. "What do you think of this place?"

"It's—" Eleanor looked around. "Sad."

Ian nodded agreement.

"Come on, Ian, but what do you think?" Alexander said.

"Things I don't want to say out loud," he replied. He looked around as if he could see the screams. A hollow clanging resounded as werewolves crashed against the vault doors, abominations attacking steel.

"I feel guilty," he said. "I feel like this is my fault."

Alexander was floored by a sudden wave of relief. He held it back and gripped Ian by both arms.

"You didn't do this," he said. "Okay? You did not hurt these people. You are one of us, just like everyone else. We help each other. When you get older, you will help, too."

Ian smiled.

"Thanks, Pop. I will. I promise."

He held his son for a moment longer. Ian was his boy and would be good. He would be good

Alexander searched for something more to say, but quit. He saw his children as lives planted within the earth, necessitating time and patience to grow. For now, they had seen enough.

"Okay," he said, rubbing his mustache. "I don't have to tell you what will happen if either of you come down here without me?"

"Nah," Eleanor said.

"No, sir," Ian said.

"Good."

"Everything okay with Uncle Percy?" Eleanor said, pointing at her earplug, confused as to why her or Ian had not been able to hear their conversation.

Alexander nodded. He spied the nearest exit and then smiled at his children.

"I think there are still some Blinis left in the fridge. Want to help me finish them?"

Eleanor threw her hands up, froze, and squinted at her father with suspicion.

"You're trying to distract us, old man."

Alexander was the picture of innocence. Eleanor shrugged.

"Okay," she said. "We still have the real maple syrup, right?"

"Always. I know how much you hate the other stuff—which is not so bad, by the way."

"Ew."

Alexander looked to his son. Ian stared in silence at the vaults.

"Ian?"

They locked eyes, and something indefinable lingered in Ian's gaze, a thing not yet named, for the boy did not understand it. Werewolves shrieked. Ian seemed beyond them.

A cold knot pressed within Alexander, and for a moment his son seemed wholly alien and unknowable. He patted the boy's head, not for Ian's comfort but for his own, as if to remind himself that the child were of his flesh and blood.

"Let's go and get some jam," he said.

"May I have strawberry, Pop?" Ian replied.

The simplicity of the question released the knot. Alexander smiled and nodded.

"I hope Mrs. Wood has that mixed berry-thingy again," Eleanor said. "It's so good with the real syrup."

"I think the two of you will have to fight it out," Alexander said, standing. "I can't afford all these sweets."

Eleanor gave him an indignant stare.

"Yes you can," she said. "People are always giving you free stuff."

"I earn that. What have you done around here, other than drive me crazy?"

"Mean. Mean, old man."

"Ellie, Pop's kidding," Ian said.

She groaned.

"Oh my god, I know. You take everything so seriously."

"I don't want you to think he's mad at you."

"Aw, so sweet."

"I think I'm leaning towards strawberry," Alexander said.

"Aw!"

They walked down the corridor to an exit ahead. The screams of werewolves followed them out.

10

They waited in line before the repaired pillar. Golden light undulated within the stone surface as a young couple was lifted upwards like divers ascending through sun streaked waters. Eleanor bobbed from side to side in tune with a song in her head and struggled into her coat. Alexander swung a canvas bag carrying mason jars full of jam, occupying himself with the back and forth motion to still his trepidation over the coming mission. Ian glanced around, watching people come and go, feeling at ease despite the glances sent his way.

Their turn came. They walked together into the pillar, the stone molding over their bodies and pulling them within. A gentle current took hold and carried them upwards. Eleanor watched the Gardens fall away until the streets and buildings dissolved into strands of bright lights beaded over rolling shadows.

Darkness swallowed everything.

Eleanor whined in her throat and threw her hand out to channel flame, but Alexander snapped his fingers ahead of her, giving life to a warm sphere of luminescence that covered them in a crenelated glow.

"I was gonna do it," Eleanor said, sheepishly.

"Oh, sorry, baby," Alexander replied. "I did not see. Next time, eh."

"Yeah, yeah."

But she exhaled with relief, grateful to him for reacting first, a secret part of her fearing that she would have struggled. She did not understand why the dark affected her so, why, despite her abilities, it made her afraid. At times she felt something waiting unseen, a presence she could not name that robbed her of courage. Grateful for the light, she took her father's hand. He stroked her fingers in kind.

They ascended.

The air melted into iridescent folds that consumed the Demidovs. For a moment they felt themselves dissolving into greater essence, each becoming one with the weightless ocean of magic. Eleanor wondered if this was the Gardens' beating heart, the same endlessness that poured through her as she conjured. The answer came at once. Here all things were known, the secrets of creation revealed in stunning symmetry and holy mystery. She felt the truths of existence and exalted for she would carry them with her into—

They stood on earth marbled by tree roots. Eleanor blinked at hollowness echoing across her heart, as if something magnificent had been forgotten. Then familiarity took hold, filling the emptiness with the comforting routines of home.

The shadows of trees jostled, and dried grass whipped under a swaying canopy of whispering branches. Cold wind whistled. Patches of snow glistened beneath shafts of orange streetlight that bathed a winding trail. The couple who had been ahead of them were now vague shapes seen through tree-fingers. Others passed them in the opposite direction, stepped off the path, rested their hands against trees, and dematerialized into soil that rained upon the ground. Eleanor knew it to be an illusion, knew those same people were now making their way down the pillar. But the sudden dissolution of the human form sent waves of disquiet up her spine.

Alexander led the children out of the tangle of branches and roots and onto the trail. The trees stood silent, obscured by a border of darkness. Eleanor could almost hear the howls of werewolves between the twisted trunks, and their memory evoked the possibility of something dark and hateful waiting in the nether-reaches of creation. She shook the strangeness away and thought about food and rest. But the comforts of home were now tinged with the intimate knowledge of those who suffered in the Den. She knew her father and others were doing right by them, had given them safety. But the agony and rage of their howling had broken a piece of her, had made her all too aware of a malignancy at the edges of being.

She took a deep breath and walked on.

They came to a black metal gate built into a fence that enclosed the trees. Alexander placed his hand on the knob. It molded and interlocked with his fingers, becoming an exact replica of his hand, the gate verifying the resident. Alexander pulled the metallic hand free and let it fall to the earth where it liquefied and snaked back into the fence. The gate clicked. Alexander pushed it open and led them out from under the trees.

They stood on a concrete path that wound under the gaze of windows shinning from dozens of nine-story white-brick buildings scattered about a sprawling apartment complex. Fenced meadows encrusted with frost shimmered under street lamps. People bundled in coats dipped in and out of amber light, their shadows twisted over waist-high chainlink fences. A security jeep crept in patrol, the ember of a cigarette burning within the darkened interior, illuminating a gloved hand hovering over the wheel and a stuffed elephant hanging from the rearview. Domed security cameras watched from the door-ways of buildings, and from the tops of emergency call boxes stamped by blue light. A high red brick wall could be seen in the distance, surrounding the entire complex. Between the rooftops to the west, the Manhattan skyline towered like pyres of steel and glass burning in tribute to electric gods.

A security officer in a heavy black coat and round glasses stood guard beside the gate's entrance, a diamond stud in his left ear. Alexander patted him on the shoulder and led his children on. Eleanor pouted and looked up at the ocean of gray clouds reflecting New York City's light.

"Where's the snow?" she said.

"Just look around you," Alexander replied.

"Not the same. I like watching it fall."

They turned right, away from the gated trees. Their footfalls crunched on the ground, and the mason jars clinked in the bag.

Other paths branched from theirs, leading to buildings, or the main entrance of the Gardens to the south, or the other gated trees that led to the Gardens-below. The Gardens-above was an active winter's night—children sledded down hills, as parents watched or spoke to each other or even joined in. Trees reached their gnarled branches to the sky, casting drifts of snow over residents carrying shopping bags. The main path wound by a fountain, its water falling in small arcs that rippled within a wavering pool tinted blue and green by electric lights. People sat benches encircling the fountain, couples sharing hot drinks, loners seeking solitude or chancing solitude's end.

The Demidovs followed the path around the fountain and merged with a lesser path that curved on their right. They followed this tributary to building 717. A siren screamed in the distance, a crier to some calamity out there beyond their borders. Eleanor looked through a space between buildings and gazed at the Manhattan skyline. She wondered much.

They climbed the red brick steps of 717 and stood before a black door. Warm light spilled from the vestibule and through the paneled windows. Ian looked out over the lawn and watched younger children in their bubble coats grunting and giggling as they made snow angels in the frost.

Keys materialized out of Alexander's outstretched hand. He opened the door and looked at his children.

"Hot chocolate, too?"

Eleanor let out a jubilant cry. Ian looked away from the children and nodded, the image of the snow angels burned into his mind.

They passed Alexander into the vestibule. He closed the door and jiggled the lock to his satisfaction. They walked by the elevator and opened the door to the stairwell and walked up to the third floor.

Eleanor dragged her fingers over the banister, tracing lines of dust in the black paint. They exited the stairwell and went left, their shoes and sneakers falling on a black and white checkered floor. They stopped before apartment 36, a black door like the others in the hall, the bronze numbers reflecting the honey glow of the walls. Alexander slid the apartment key into the catch, turned it, and opened the door.

The Demidovs were home.

ELEANOR HUMMED THE BEATLES' "Here Comes the Sun", rinsed the last dish, and placed it into the dishwasher. She turned it on, wiped her hands on her red and green checkered pajama pants, walked out of the kitchen and through a hallway, and stopped at an archway opening onto the living room.

Lamplight spilled over the pale green walls from bay windows overlooking the paths and the fountain. A candelabra chandelier of wrought iron hung from the ceiling, illuminating the room. Pictures of the children at varying ages hung across from Eleanor, a diagonal line of them sharing the wall with photos of their grandmother with her short gray hair, hawkish features, and knowing smile. The bottom photo was of a younger Alexander, without mustache, hair lighter, seated with her at a piano.

Alexander and Ian sat a petite grand piano beneath that photo, the bay windows peering into the night before them. Ian narrowed his eyes at the sheet music and played six ascending notes with his left hand and the wrong note with his right, shattering the slow moving spell of Chopin's "Nocturne No.9 Op.1."

Alexander rested his hand over his son's.

"Sl-ow-ly," he said, dragging the word over three syllables. "Take your time. It's better to be slow than to be wrong."

Ian nodded and began again. Eleanor came over and frowned at the sheet music.

Alexander looked at her sideways.

"If you let me teach you, it will not be such a mystery," he said.

She continued to frown.

"Nah. I wouldn't know what to do with it. Chopin is serious business."

"No one is saying you have to play professionally. Learning an instrument is just a nice skill to have."

Ian played on.

"He's right, Ellie," he said. "Helps you think."

"Nah," she said. "Listening to music helps me think. Trying to play makes me want smash my head against stuff. Anyway, the piano and I talk all the time, and it told me the other day that we have a perfectly good relationship. I stay away from it, and it stays away from me."

"Little girl," Alexander said, "sometimes you worry me."

"That's my job."

She smacked a fat kiss on his cheek, pulled on Ian's ear, and walked out of the living room, her bare feet slapping against the hardwood floor. She passed shelves with sheet music and ordered rows of books on every subject imaginable alongside stacks of fiction. She entered the hallway, carpeted and soft against her feet, passed Ian's room and went into her bedroom. Moments later "Helter Skelter" blared muffled from behind her door. Her bouncing footfalls made the photos tremble on the walls.

Ian's fingers stumbled as he played a dissonant chord.

"Eleanor!" Alexander said.

"Sorry, sorry," she replied, her voice muffled through the door. The music shrank to a hum.

Ian returned to playing. Alexander gave him a curious glance, watching for some sign of displeasure. There was none.

"You're not annoyed?" he said.

"At what, Pop?"

"Your sister."

Ian played on.

"No," he said. "Why?"

Alexander rubbed his mustache, shrugged, and pursed his lips in thought. "She was being loud. I thought, maybe—"

"It's no big deal. She doesn't mean anything by it."

"No. No, of course not. It's only—stop for a moment, eh."

Ian released the keys. The music dissolved.

"I don't ever see you get angry," Alexander said.

"I don't feel angry," Ian replied.

"Never?"

Ian shook his head. Alexander thought for a moment. Then he smacked Ian across his neck. Ian flinched.

"Why?" he said.

"Anything?" Alexander replied.

Ian rubbed his neck, looked at his father, and laughed.

"That was funny?" Alexander said.

"A little bit."

Alexander stared with open concern. Ian turned on the bench to face him.

"Pop, I don't have anything to be angry about. There are so many people who have terrible lives. You reminded us of that tonight. I have a home, a family...I have no reason to be angry."

"Even...even after what happened to you?"

Alexander hated the words as they spilled out of his mouth. They carried him back to the sound of his little boy screaming, to the twisted expression of pain on his face as he writhed in his bed, contrasted by the gluttonous desire on the face of the man standing over him. That man Alexander had once accepted as a brother. A real monster had stolen into Ian's room and had done the unspeakable, and here the boy sat, years on, without sign or scar of the torment the elder demon, his uncle, had inflicted upon him.

Deirdre's words came back to him. He pushed them away.

There was a liquid sound from Ian's shadow, like blood oozing through clenched teeth. Ian looked at it for a moment, and then looked at the piano, staring as if he were divining some ancient truth about order and chaos from the white and black keys.

"Do you want to know what it was like," he said, "when Uncle Matt possessed me?"

Failure and anger conspired within Alexander, the part of him that still blamed himself for what had happened to his son, giving way to searing hatred for the man who had done it. He swallowed and whispered:

"Do not call that animal your uncle—"

"You should know. I saw what it did to you and mom. You blamed yourselves. You shouldn't have, but you did. You still do."

Alexander looked at his son as if he were seeing the crime repeated, still helpless to stop it.

"If I tell you," Ian said, "maybe you'll finally understand that there was nothing you could've done." He cocked his head to the right in a birdlike movement. "Should I tell you?"

Alexander closed his eyes and shook his head.

Ian searched the piano keys, seeing something in the shadowed spaces between them.

"Can I tell you something else, then?" he said. Alexander waited. Ian stared into his eyes. "I'm still here. Uncle Matt isn't."

"I said don't—"

"But he was my uncle. It's funny: I feel like I know him better than anyone because of what he did. I understand him, who he really was. He was sad, you know? I think the word is 'desperate'. He just wanted to be loved, and that made him crazy because no matter what mom, or you, or anyone did for him, it was never enough. He always wanted more. When he used to play with me, he always wanted to keep going, longer than I did. He'd get mad when I wanted to stop. I never understood that. But then he possessed me, and even...even with all the pain...it made me understand him."

He drifted for a moment. Alexander wanted to say something, but could only listen.

"When he possessed me, it was bad. It was...horrible." Ian spoke the word as if not fully comprehending its meaning. "But it made me stronger. I understand now what real pain is. So it takes a lot to bother me. I see the little things in life, the moments that so many people ignore. I see them and they make me happy. None of it is small. You know? Yeah, you know. It's all part of something really, really big. It's beautiful. Bad or good, it's life. And things are good for us. We have each other. I miss mom. I always will. But we have each other."

Alexander kissed the top of his head, knew the boy to be his son and knew his son to be beautiful, not detached, not damaged. He smiled, and they looked at each other, each of the other, separated by what was past and what was to come, but united by what was here and now.

"If you ever need to talk," Alexander said, "about anything."

"Can I ask you something?"

"Of course."

"You promise to tell the truth?"

Alexander hesitated. The question tightened his chest. Ian stared with placid expectation, but something in his eyes was unwavering. Alexander nodded.

"Did you kill Uncle Matt?" Ian said.

Alexander stared at the piano keys without seeing, absently brushed dust from them without feeling.

"He's dead. Isn't that enough?"

"I'd like to know."

Alexander closed his eyes. His hands rested on his thighs, twitching as he relived the weight of a gun in his hand. He saw the man who had hurt his son, Matthew Moore blubbering on his knees in a vault within the Den. He felt his wife, Phoebe, beside him as she had been that night, fury and betrayal livid within her, the same curls that framed their daughter's face a tangled mass over hers. He felt her fingers as she ripped the gun from his hand, walked over to her brother, and unleashed her judgment with resounding finality. He remembered the faces watching: Rosie, Cedric, Percy, Richard... others, all with the grim expressions of those who understand that there was nothing more to be done, no other answer to be found, no mercy save for the swift end of a wretched life.

Most of all he remembered the way he had not stopped his wife from doing the unthinkable. He had watched with horrible satisfaction the horror on Matt's face as he realized whom it was that was ending his life.

Alexander opened his eyes and looked at his son.

"Your mother killed him," he said.

Ian was expressionless. He said nothing. Then he looked at his father, that much-too-adult glint in his eyes.

"Pop," he said. "I'm still here. He didn't break me."

"I know." Alexander held him close. "I know."

They stayed that way, father and son, each a reflection of the other. There was nothing more to be said.

Alexander gestured at the keys. Ian squinted at the sheet music, at Chopin climbing up and down across the page.

He played.

His shadow watched them from the wall.

11

Alexander walked through the hall and knocked on Eleanor's door. It opened on its own, Eleanor gesturing to it from her bed. The Beatles crooned through speakers mounted at two corners of the room, black cubes against white molding and dark blue walls. A digital stereo system sat a bookshelf set into the wall above the bed. The MP3 player streaming to it lay among books that fought for space on the lower shelves. Action figures were posed around the books as if frozen in a game of hide and seek. Night was painted in soft hues beyond a window at the foot of the bed, the shadows of trees dancing on the window seat.

Alexander leaned against the door and watched his daughter streak red pencil on paper, her tongue clamped between her lips as she colored. A white teddy bear rested against her legs, its black-button eyes watching him with friendly expectation.

He entered and tripped over a stack of coloring books and adventure novels and frowned at a poster of the Beatles' "Abbey Road" on the wall across from the bed, edges burnt and curled from some mishap he didn't know about. He cleared his throat and walked over a carpet strewn with drawings of people in familiar scenes, the Gardens interpreted through Eleanor's hand. Thick smears of crayon and curved pencil strokes revealed familiar faces transposed into caricatures, Eleanor's work pleasing to look upon, but not that of a great artist in the making.

Alexander leaned over the bed to see what she was drawing.

"Not finished yet," she said.

But she let him see.

Two figures sat a green bench before a pond, the smaller in a bright red hoodie still being colored in, the other in a dark coat and purple scarf. Leafless branches reached from a tree on their left, as if shielding them from the world beyond the page. The water before them shifted from lighter blue at the shore to darker at its center, inviting you to dip your fingers within.

The unfinished drawing reached into Alexander's heart and unlocked a door. He remembered this place, their hideaway on the Island in the Gardens-below, where people went to wander among trees and hills unimpeded by the bustle of their world. The Demidovs had always gone together. Alexander and Ian walked the trails and climbed rocky outcrops to watch the lights of the Gardens waver on the black lake. Phoebe and Eleanor secluded themselves in their special place before the pond, where they spoke and shared silence, the world passing between them. Easy days and nights had drifted with the hush of wind, the crunch of leaves, their reflections rippling in clean and clear water.

So many moments relegated backwards through time, a parade of ghosts ever marching behind the living.

They had not been back to the Island, as a family, since Phoebe died.

Alexander swallowed back a knot in his throat.

"That's not bad," he said.

Eleanor twisted her lips, removed the drawing from its neon green clipboard, crumpled it, and threw it among the crayons and pencils spilled over her blanket.

"That ain't it," she replied

"Eleanor, wait." He picked up the crumpled drawing and opened it. Eleanor laid her hands over his to stop him. He pulled them away. "You have to finish this."

"It's not good."

"Okay, so you finish it anyway. You do it again and again until it is good. Otherwise it will never be good."

She sighed, but reached for the drawing. He handed it back. She flattened the paper and stared at it with her fists planted in her cheeks. Alexander sat beside her and nestled his chin on her head, her curls tangled around his nose.

"I have a hard time seeing her face," Eleanor said.

"Your mother's? Ellie, anytime you want to see pictures—"

"I know. But I wanna remember her. I wanna see her the way I saw her when she was alive, like in my own head. Is that weird?"

"No. Not at all."

They sat. Wind howled against the window.

"I remember her hands," Eleanor said, examining her own. "They were long and skinny. Not like mine."

"You're still growing."

"Maybe a little like mine. You think?"

"I think."

She smiled.

"And that coat, the long one with the purple squares," she said.

"That was, how you say, more like a sweater cape."

"Yeah. She loved that thing."

"She only wore it around here," Alexander said. "Never outside. She thought it looked silly, but I knew she loved it. I think it made her feel at home."

Eleanor thought.

"I like that," she replied. "That's like Ringo for me."

She reached for Ringo, the teddy bear leaning against her, and cradled him in her arms. Alexander grabbed one of the bear's soft paws.

"You're not too old for him?" he said.

"I will never be too old for him."

Alexander smiled.

"You have a lot of her in you," he said. "She was as stubborn as you are. She had your same sewer mouth, god help us. But she was also kind, funny, and determined. Yes, you have a lot of her in you. In more ways than you know."

Eleanor smiled. Alexander made to say more, and then noticed an empty vial peeking out from under her pillow. Eleanor followed his gaze to the vial and cringed.

"What's that?" he said.

"Eh," she replied. "Would you believe...drugs?"

"Actually, I would."

"Hey!"

He took the empty vial and examined it. Eleanor sat up on her knees, brushed curls from her forehead, and placed the drawing into the middle shelf. She bunched the crayons and colored pencils in both hands and laid them on the shelf above. Then she took the clipboard, searched for a space to fit it in, shrugged, and threw it on the floor.

Alexander looked from the vial to her.

"Little girl. How many times have I told you? You cannot use illusions in your room. That is what the Dungeon is for."

"I need to practice, Pop."

"You don't get enough of that?"

"I—" She growled and hung her head back, blew out her cheeks, and looked at him. "You're gonna make me sound like a jerk."

He gestured for her to go on. She sighed.

"It's just most of the other kids can't keep up with me."

Alexander stroked his mustache.

"I know," he said. "That can be frustrating." He twirled the vial between his fingers. "But that does not mean you're ready to handle an illusion all by yourself."

"It's from Dreams and Things. Benny makes toys, not dangerous stuff."

Alexander's face twisted with incredulity, and he was glad she didn't notice. Benny Aguilar was a man of many talents, some quite unfortunate for their enemies. Best she didn't know that yet.

"They're just fun," Eleanor said. She flashed a grin. "And safe."

"Eh, nothing is safe, especially when you're involved." He looked at the vial and saw the past unfold within the slender glass. "Did I ever tell you about the first time that Darius and I almost killed ourselves?"

"Uh-oh."

"Yes, that's right, it's a story. So shut it."

"Wait, first time? How many—"

"I said—"

She slapped her hands over her mouth. He focused on the vial.

"It was still so new to us," he said. "Magic."

"Mr. Bardales created it when he was a teenager, right?"

"Eleanor, once again, he didn't create magic, he discovered it. He was about sixteen or so when he fell into his coma—you should already know this."

"I do!"

"Well?"

"He, uh," Eleanor frowned, dragging up an oft repeated story. "His mother was a demon, his father was a werewolf, and he was supposed to be one of those. But he fought that off somehow. I know meditation was a big part of it. He—he was able to stop the demon and werewolf parts of him from taking over, that made him sick, and he almost died. But...but then...shit. Wait, hold on! He went into a coma, and he was all knocked out, but really he was having one of those super-real dreams people sometimes have. And in that dream, I guess, he discovered all these things about, well, everything, life and stuff, and he found magic hiding from the evil power that turns people into werewolves and demons and, you know, the ones I'm not supposed to talk about. He was able to take magic into him, and he woke up and learned how to use it and how to teach everyone. Yeah? I got it, right?"

She offered a placating grin.

"Eh, so-so," Alexander said. "You'll understand more when you get older."

"There's a lot more to it, huh?"

Alexander shrugged, but his gaze was far within, replaying moment after moment of the time he shared with his old friend, as if stitching the past into a mosaic to be examined, to be understood.

"The way you put it is the simple version. He learned how to reach magic, how to wield it. He taught me. We taught others, for better...and for worse. That's enough for now. You'll learn more in time.

"Magic was new to both of us. Even though he learned it first, he had a long way to go before mastering it. Eh, we both did. Not that you can master it, not really, but then it was...alien. A new way of affecting the world. It's different now. Now there's structure. But then, we didn't understand it. Well, I didn't understand it. Darius was Darius. I'm not sure if he ever fully understood it, but he could do things more advanced than I could."

"Don't be hard on yourself," Eleanor said. "If he was the first magician, that makes you the second. You guys had a lot of stuff to figure out."

"This is true. We wanted to push it, to see how far we could go. We would practice all the time in your grandmother's basement, in her apartment on 64th Street, not too far from here. Darius conjured a fake, how you say, one of those city permits that said something about inspection or cockroach extermination, something to keep people out. Not that that was so important, we usually worked late at night. I think he was showing off. But it was good to be cautious.

"We started a little competition to see who could conjure the best illusions." He scratched his temple. "Eh, we went back and forth, hours every night. I remember—" he laughed, "I remember, once, I wanted to see if I could scare him. So I conjured this monster, this thing I had read about in a short story. I told him to close his eyes, that I was going to surprise him. And then—" He slapped the back of one hand into his palm. "It appears right in front of him, this awful looking creature with these long arms that were slimy, a mouth full of teeth that went all the way around inside its mouth, and these horrible black eyes."

"Jesus."

"I know," Alexander said. "Even I was startled. Darius, he screamed and fell, and I laughed, even though I was also scared. I thought it was funny because I was in control. I wasn't going to let it hurt anyone."

Eleanor beamed. Alexander waved a finger to make the point.

"But then it turned on me," he said. "No problem, right? I just let the illusion fade. Let it go, allow magic to recede into me and watch as what I conjured disappears. I do just that. I feel the connection release...but the monster stayed. It stared at me with dozens of black eyes and breathed through its teeth and began to make these noises that I can't even describe, this piercing sound that hurt my ears, and oh shit."

Eleanor giggled. Alexander smiled and shook his head.

"So, of course, it starts chasing us all around the basement. It tore holes into the walls, and Darius is cursing in English and Spanish, yelling at me to 'stop it, stop it, you jerk, this isn't funny,' and I'm trying, but it's gone beyond me. I lost control, and now this thing is trying to kill us."

"You made it real."

"Exactly. Here was this impossible creature, this monster from a scary story, something that shouldn't have had any real effect on the world. I thought I had control over it, but I wasn't strong enough. I realized the story it came from had disturbed me, and because I conjured this thing to life without taking the time to realize how afraid I really was, I lost control. Magic starts here, baby." He pointed at his temple. "You must understand what you're creating, as much as you can—the way it makes you feel, makes you think, all of that. Otherwise the thing you make may go against you in ways you're not prepared to deal with. Of course you push yourself, but you also have to know when something is too much for you. That doesn't always mean it will stay that way. It's just a reminder that mastering anything, especially your own mind, takes patience."

He went silent, rubbing his thumb against the vial. Eleanor watched and waited.

"This went on, eh, I couldn't even tell you," he said. "The thing was slow, but persistent, chasing us nonstop. But then Darius did something. I was distracting the beast, screaming at it to get its attention, and he—he conjured a jungle. Out of nowhere all these trees and bushes and vines appeared, right there in the basement. One moment we are surrounded by dirty walls, pipes, and exercise equipment, the next I could feel heat, hear insects, animals...It was like something from that movie you like so much, the one with the explorer."

"He's an archaeologist."

"Whatever. Anyway, something screamed from far off in the jungle, and the beast lost interest in us and ran after it. Once it did that, once I saw it go away, I felt something in my mind loosen. I realized it was fear. My fear of the thing was strong enough that I was still connected to it, still giving it life. Seeing it disappear made it unreal again. I could let go. I did. I came to understand that I hadn't truly processed the story it had come from. But it wasn't that the story was a bad thing, or that I shouldn't have read it. It was that I needed to accept my fear, to let it become a part of me. That way I could understand it. And by understanding it, I could control it.

"It also helped that I stopped thinking about it as soon as I realized what Darius had done. We both looked around, completely in awe, because up till then we didn't know that we could alter our surroundings that way. He said later that he had been watching a documentary about the rainforest, and it was the first thing that came to his mind. He said he felt magic pour through him in such a large amount that he forgot who he was for a moment. He just felt the jungle come alive through him. Which was also stupid and dangerous, and he couldn't conjure for a few days afterwards. But we got lucky. And he opened a new door.

"So, that's what it took to save us. If he had not done that...do you see what I'm saying?"

Eleanor looked at the vial in his hand.

"We know so much more now, though," she said.

"We do. But magic is unpredictable. If you let it, an illusion, even a nice one—" He waved the vial. "Can become real. You may not be ready to handle something like that on your own. But that's okay. It takes time."

"We're always using Benny's illusions in the Dungeon."

"Because the Dungeon is a safe place. It was built to intervene if things get a little out of control. You don't think we'd allow you kids to do anything without some precautions? And Benny designs his illusions to be safe."

"So, see! Then I could use them here—"

"They can still be dangerous outside of the Dungeon because you can conjure something of your own within the illusion. The Dungeon can help keep that in control. And even that is no guarantee. You saw what happened with Elisha and Aidan tonight. But the Dungeon is the safest place to practice. Besides, most of you go in as a group when you use Benny's illusions. That helps to remind you it's just a game. Puts you at ease."

Eleanor nodded.

"So?" Alexander said.

"I won't do it again."

"I just want you to promise me that you'll be responsible. I don't want to have to deal with a werewolf of whatever other craziness you can conjure, running around in my own home."

"I promise, Pop."

"Good." He fell silent, a tiny smile on his face. "That's good."

"You miss him a lot, huh?"

"Who? Darius?" He reached behind her and laid the vial on the bottom shelf. "Every day. He was like my brother. He was my brother."

"Is it...is it true that he became a vampire?"

Alexander flashed a look that said she was on dangerous ground.

"I heard it the other day," she said, "from stupid Elisha. It isn't true, is it?"

Alexander thought, stroking his mustache.

"It's true," he replied.

"Why? I thought they were all bad."

"Darius was a good man, even after he became one of those... things. It's complicated."

She frowned. Then her eyes darted towards him with a question.

"So, wait, how did he die? I heard from Junior that sunlight can kill a vampire, but Aunt Rosie says conjuring sunlight and using it against them does nothing. I don't get it."

Alexander leaned forward and rubbed his hand over his face.

"When we conjure sunlight," he said, "we are using less than a fraction of its true power. It's a very difficult thing to do, and you can only do it so much before you need a rest. You always see maintenance crews working in groups when they shower sunlight on the trees below, yes? What they're doing is enough for the trees. But it's still not even close to what the Sun can do.

"Sunlight does kill vampires, but it has to be direct. If you took all the magicians in New York City, had them conjure sunlight and use it against the vampires, it would do nothing. And it gets even worse. There's no hope of getting a vampire near sunlight. When the sun is rising, a vampire can sink deep into the earth, wherever they are. Darius, he told me that it's not only being underground that shields them, it's—it's a very horrible darkness, something he couldn't really describe. He called it evil protecting evil."

Eleanor was silent. The shadows of tree branches swayed through her window. She thought on the streets beyond the Gardens, how at any moment in the daylight, someone could be walking over a sleeping vampire.

She bit her lip in thought and dared a glance at her father.

"So if it's so hard to get them in the sunlight, then...how did he die?"

Alexander crunched his eyes shut, deep furrows running along his forehead. He sighed and looked at his daughter, remembering how he had admonished her for asking before. But another part of him understood that if she was old enough to question, then she was old enough to know the answers.

"Darius was turned into a vampire by Manny Ngombe."

"The first vampire. There are eight others."

"Who told you this?"

Eleanor shrugged. Alexander grunted with paternal frustration. Protecting your child from the harsh realities of the world was like using an umbrella against a hurricane.

"Well, whoever told you...I hope they had sense enough to scare the hell out of you. Vampires are..." He trailed off, his eyes heavy with great sorrow, as if he pitied the whole world for having to exist along such creatures. "Darius was turned as a reward for bringing magic to the Family. That's another story, but keep in mind Darius was born into the Family. So was your mother. For a time it was all he—all we —knew. He thought by accepting, he could use his new powers to fight Manny and the other vampires, to change things. He led a sort of rebellion. We thought we had a chance because—has Ian ever told you about the first demon?"

"No, but I've heard...things..."

"Like?"

"Like he's the Devil."

"Yes," Alexander said. "In a way, he is. His name is Abebe Ngombe, and he is Manny's brother. He is the father of all demons...look, there is too much to get into, but the simple version is he pretended to help us to try and find another way to kill the vampires, and then he betrayed Darius. He tortured him, possessed him, and forced him to burn in sunlight. You understand? He hurt Darius so badly that he made him give up control of his free will. He took control of Darius, like a puppet. That's what a truly powerful demon can do, that is why they are so dangerous. They hurt you until you give up, and then they can make you do anything. No other demon would have been able to hurt Darius that way, but Abebe..."

The saliva dried on his tongue. A great weight seized his limbs, and he knew the terrible power of fear, the awesome helplessness that comes when faced with even just the memory of a power beyond the elements, beyond the rules laid down by creation. Such things lingered in impossible chasms, chaos once unclaimed now mastered by creatures risen out of the well of nightmares.

The Brothers Ngombe.

"I don't want to talk about this anymore," Alexander said. "Okay?"

Eleanor took his hand in hers. Whispers had passed about the Brothers Ngombe to her from other children, but to hear it from her father solidified them beyond fearful myths and into real threats. She had asked, and he had answered, and now she wished she hadn't. So she nodded vigorously and clutched his fingers, reminding herself that they were beyond their reach.

A voice in the back of her mind hissed that there was no way to know that. She shouted it down and shook her head.

"I'm sorry, Pop," she said. "I'm sorry your friend died...like that."

He looked at her for a moment, as if she weren't his daughter but a cruel trick played upon him by the universe, an illusion of love and light that would one day be snatched by the true and dark nature of things. But the warmth of her hand awakened him to the magic residing between them, to love and all its mysteries. He held her close, and the shadow no longer held sway.

He took a deep breath.

"Thank you, baby," he said. "He was a good man. Your mother and I loved him very much."

Eleanor scoured her memory for her mother.

"I don't remember the sound of her voice," she said.

Alexander kissed her.

"She loved you."

Eleanor smiled at him not for her sake but for his, so he would not see the longing in her heart for what could not be.

He stroked her cheeks.

"You okay?"

"Yeah," she replied. "Even though, you know, I'm scared, but... We're here now. That's all that matters. I'm okay."

"Good. Now, I think, it's time for bed. If you have any nightmares, well, you asked."

Eleanor grabbed Ringo, put its mouth to her ear, acted as though she were listening, and shook her head.

"Ringo says not yet."

"Does he? Hm. May I have him for a moment?"

She handed the bear over. Alexander put its black nose to his ear, listened, nodded, laid him gently aside, wrapped his daughter in his arms, and tickled. She exploded into laughter, squirming under his large hands.

"He told me if you want to stay awake, I get to tickle you."

"No. That's not what he said! That's not what he said!"

She reached her hand to the right. The blanket soared upwards like a wave and crashed over her, burying Alexander's arms. She scurried underneath, poked her head out from the other end, blew curls from her face, and glared. Alexander chuckled and tucked Ringo beside her.

"See? Isn't that better?"

"I'll get you for that, old man."

He stood, tucked her in, turned off the music, and kissed her forehead.

"Pop?"

"Hm?"

"Are you still going out?"

Alexander hesitated. Then he nodded. Eleanor looked away in thought. She looked back at him wide eyed and seemed very much a child.

"Is it for a good reason?" she said.

"I would not go otherwise."

"Can you let me know when you get back? Please?"

"Okay."

He walked to the door and flicked off the light.

"Uh," Eleanor said.

Alexander remembered her sacred rule. He knelt down and turned on a nightlight. The warm orange glow reflected off of the Beatle's poster.

Eleanor blushed, but thanked him with grateful eyes.

"Goodnight, my darling," Alexander said.

"Night, Papa." She replied. She lifted Ringo's paw. "Say goodnight, Ringo." She waved the paw and deepened her voice into a terrible British accent. " 'Goodnight, Ringo.' "

He smiled and closed the door.

She rested in the semi-dark. The shadows of the room threatened with the imagined leers of vampires, of Father Manny and his brood. She focused on the nightlight, letting its glow make her aware of the warmth of her blanket, the knowledge that her brother was in the next room, and the safety of their home.

She lay that way, listening to the wind cry the passage of night. She was awake, but not restless, alert, but not tense. Sleep began to draw her into its arms, but she gazed out of the window at the foot of her bed and wanted one more thing before she succumbed.

She threw the covers off, crawled to the window, and sat on the window seat. Lamplight glistened over a frost encrusted world. She closed her eyes and pressed her hand to the window. Blue tendrils of mist flowed from her fingertips and through the glass. She opened her eyes. Snowflakes drifted down, dissolving into the night air beyond.

She curled up, hugging her knees, and drifted to sleep watching the snow fall.

12

Alexander walked over to the piano bench, lifted the padded cover, rifled through books of sheet music, and pulled out a photo album.

He carried it across the living room and sat in a chair facing the bay window. The phone sat beside him on a table, a reminder of what was to come. He checked his watch. Satisfied that there was still time, he replaced the watch into his vest and ran his fingers over the photo album.

He opened it.

Pictures of the children as babies stared up at him: Eleanor wide eyed and surprised in the bathtub, Ian nestled in Phoebe's arms, peering straight into the camera. Alexander flipped the pages, watching his children grow with every turn: Eleanor surrounded by food and drinks and condiments yanked out of the refrigerator, triumphant with a piece of chocolate in her hands. Ian seated on Alexander's lap, his tiny fingers touching piano keys as if they were relics. Sled racing and birthdays, Ian boxing with Uncle Cedric, Eleanor frowning in a dress while seated on the sofa. Every page found them a touch older, a bit more the people they were to become.

He turned the page.

There was Phoebe seated in her wedding dress at Rosie's, a

cigarette lit in her hand, a beer half-finished on the bar. Her smile was half-cocked and knowing like Ian's and her hair was a reflection of Eleanor's, as if molded in the past to be fitted into the future.

Alexander stroked her face, wishing to feel the weight of her beside him, to hear her whistle in the offhand way she had while occupied with a task, to sit with her in this very room, enjoying the silence of their sleeping children. Their life together had not been misspent. Of that, Alexander was certain. But she had left a vacancy, an aching hole no photograph could fill.

He turned the page. He had to.

On and on, the past unveiling itself, brief moments of lightheartedness with friends (Percy's eyes wide and bright as he gazed at a laptop, a close up of Cedric with one eyebrow cocked as Eitan playfully punched his chin, Rosie and Phoebe glaring at the camera, their hair matted and wet from rain...), interspersed with the family Alexander loved beyond all things.

He turned the page.

He landed on a photo he had not seen for some time. There he was, younger, hair cropped short, his nose sharper and more prominent for the lack of mustache. He stood in a basketball court, a chainlink fence behind him. Phoebe was beside him, clad in the black leather jacket she had loved so much. She leaned against a slender young man in a blue hoodie. His hair was golden brown, his features dark and lean, and his eyes a striking gray-green.

Darius.

"Yo, D," Alexander said.

He saw beyond the photo to the stream of memories that flow into the past irrevocable, silent, and sacred. There where his wife and his friend (brother) still lived. There where they smiled at a camera with the shared knowledge that they were among those who could be depended upon. A long road was before them, waiting to be shaped into the whole of their lives.

Staring at the photo, Alexander wondered at how such lives could be cut short.

He rubbed his mustache and turned the page.

A single photo stared up at him. It was ripped in half, and what remained of it revealed Phoebe seated at a table strewn with empty beer cans in a concrete yard. An arm was draped over her shoulders, a meaty hand throwing up the peace sign near her face. She smiled, but looked annoyed, as if she were tolerating someone.

Anger morphed Alexander's expression. He remembered who that hand had belonged to. He had ripped the photo in half and destroyed any others containing Matt as its subject. Then, in a fit of further rage, he had retrieved these torn images from the trash and burned them. There was no satisfaction in the act. It was the same lack of feeling as when he had watched the man die. Nothing solved. The ending of a misspent life brought no catharsis. Only anger, regret, and nothing changed. Watching Matt's blood pool onto the floor had not erased the damage done to Ian, and had not stilled Alexander's hatred.

Ian still called him Uncle Matt.

A muted pounding reverberated through the ceiling, troublesome pipes or perhaps something falling over in the apartment above. Cold wafted over Alexander, and he whipped around, certain someone had been standing behind him. There was no one. All was still.

Alexander closed the album and laid it on the floor.

A wave of snowflakes curled past the window. He frowned with confusion, and then looked with a suspicious eye towards Eleanor's room. He smiled, knowing he should admonish her, but the building was deep enough within the Gardens that outside eyes would not see, and he was proud that the snow she conjured reached around the building to the living room window, evidence of her growing power.

The swirl of snow trailed on the wind like falling stars. Alexander closed his eyes, letting his emotions come to rest, letting each thought rise and fall, becoming one with the magic within.

Peace before action. Minutes stretched into the stillness of infinity. The magician vanished into the confines of silence and there found respite.

The phone rang. He answered.

"Big man," Greg said, his voice confident, certain, and tinged with regret. Between them a history of action against traffickers and the liberation of their victims. Alexander had schooled the younger man in the ways of magic, seeing in Greg Woodard the values and courage necessary to risk his life for others. And Greg had been more than up to the task.

"You okay?" Alexander replied.

"You know. I'm guessing you're pissed at me and whatever—"

"Later."

"Rich told you everything?"

"Oh, I'm very aware."

"A'ight, then, listen: Plan's changed. I ain't gonna be there."

"Why not?"

"Nunez and Delgado are having a big meet with Maspeth, and Delgado wants me with them. I can't get out of it. I'm driving out there right now."

"You're sure it's safe to talk?"

"C'mon, fam, gimme some credit."

Alexander leaned forward in the chair.

"The people are still at the location you gave Richard?" he said.

"They're there. I saw them myself last night. But not for much longer. They got a buyer. Some assholes out of Brooklyn are coming through tomorrow to take them. I thought about asking you to wait, but now—"

"No," Alexander said. He gripped the bridge of his nose. "We have to act fast. They'll still be changing guards, yes?"

"The next shift's already there, all hitters. Nunez is bringing his best muscle to this meet, but anyone who works for him doesn't fuck around. Still, these pricks think they got the whole world by the ass. They're comfortable. They ain't gonna see you coming."

"How many?"

"Six, all carrying."

"Any magicians?"

"Nah," Greg said. "Two demons, though. They run regular patrols, but they're a little undisciplined. Delgado bitched one of them out last night for getting too familiar with one of the captives.

Alex...none of these cats are victims, feel me? These assholes enjoy their work. They gotta go. Wish there was some other way, but, if it helps, they have it coming."

"You know it doesn't."

"...I know."

Alexander paused a moment. He looked out the window. The trail of snow was gone.

"It's a warehouse," Greg said, guilt replaced by resolve. "One main gate and two side doors on either side of it, plus an alley, also gated. They got the back door sealed off. They're keeping their victims in the basement, under this trapdoor hidden by the last storage shelf on the right—your right, when you're facing inside. They're frontin' like they're housing industrial parts and shit, but most of those boxes are empty, far as I can tell. They got one camera out front, and three inside. I'll let you figure that out."

"Anything else?"

"There's an office building right next door, but they own that too. Ain't shit in there worth anything, just a whole lot of bullshit. 48th Street's a few blocks up, and some of those apartments got a decent view from their windows, so you should work fast."

"Okay," Alexander said. "You're coming home. Now."

"Yeah, about that—"

"There's no 'about' anything. You're coming home."

Greg paused.

"No," he said.

"Excuse me?"

"Alex, I'm really in with these cats. They trust me. Some of those tricks Ian taught me, about fooling a demon, that shit works. And now they're looking to me to handle the takeover of a demon-run apartment building near the L.I.C border—"

"Greg, you're the first person they're going to look at once we pull those people out."

"That's exactly what I want. I conjured some fake memories, and I'm gonna let them get at them when they question me. Make it look like a struggle and everything. After that, they'll trust me even more."

Alexander began to protest. "Nah, Alex, listen: I got a chance to get into a room with some bigger players, maybe even heads from out the City. You know that's where a lot of the Family's money is coming from. Time comes, I can learn enough and hit the right people, cause some real damage, stop these motherfuckers from ever being able to hurt anyone again."

"It won't change anything. The Family will still be the Family."

Greg sighed.

"You know," he said, "I remember when you first took me on a raid with you. You told me to look at everyone we freed and burn all their faces into memory, so I could remember that each one of them was a life. Now, what, you want me to forget that? We got a chance to save some lives down the road. I can't just let that go."

"This is not a discussion," Alexander replied, clenching his fist against his knee. "If they find you out—"

"They find me out, I'm killing myself."

"You think we want that?"

"Ain't about what anybody wants. It's about what's right."

"It's not that simple, and you know it."

"I'm sorry. Next time you see me, I'll be home for real. Until then...Good luck tonight, big man. I'll get at you through Rich."

"Greg!"

The dial tone answered. Alexander shot up, nearly slamming the phone against the floor. He steadied himself and placed it back into its base. Breathing deep, calm brought him back to where he knew he needed to be, and he picked up the phone again to dial Cedric. The line was answered before the first ring was out.

"We on?" Cedric said.

"Yes. Everything set?"

"We're by the garage right now. I got the hardware all set up. Anyone who causes us problems is gonna encounter some severe motherfuckin' disagreement."

"Greg won't be there."

"The fuck? Why not?"

"I'll see you in a minute."

"Shit. Fine."

Alexander hung up. He took a final steadying breath, flexed his hands, went to the sofa, took his coat, threw it on, and walked to the hallway.

He peeked into Ian's room. The boy slept on his back, chest rising and falling. Alexander entered and gently nudged him. Ian's eyes flew open, and he immediately sat up without complaint.

"I'm sorry, baby," Alexander said.

"It's fine, Pop. I'll keep watch until you get back."

Alexander kissed his forehead, and then stepped back to look at him, trying to discern any emotion from his son. Ian stared back, calm, controlled.

Alexander nodded and walked out.

Ian reached for something under his mattress and stepped off of the bed. The orderliness of his room was evident even in the shadows. He sat on the floor, a poster of John Coltrane staring down at him from the opposite wall. He folded his legs, opened his hands, and stared at the torn half of the photo he had saved from being burned. Uncle Matt was smug in it, eyes swollen with alcohol, jowls heavy, his smile almost a sneer. Blood swirled into Ian's eyes, black rivulets swelling into crimson. His shadow rose behind him and perched itself on his shoulders, and both boy and shadow stared red eyed and malevolently at the visage of the man they hated.

Alexander walked down the hall and peeked into Eleanor's room. She slept against the window, her breath rising and falling in perfect rhythm. He walked in, lifted her up, and laid her on the bed. She twitched, grumbled, and smacked her lips.

Alexander pressed his nose against her cheek and wished to whatever goodness there was in creation that he would return.

He left.

13

Wind shrieked, cut through fences, and barraged the sleeping buildings with snow. The fountain gurgled, the water black and churning, reflecting the onslaught of white clouds in the glowing night sky. A few figures trudged across the dark. Many windows in the buildings were blackened, portals to sleep.

Alexander followed the path around white fields. Frost bit his forehead and cheeks and fell slantwise through the air. He went west, looking up as he walked. Through the white haze he spied the brief flicker of silhouettes on rooftops, security officers at their posts. He walked until the path led him to the western wall surrounding the complex. It was bordered by a strip of soil and grass buried in white. A hanging chain fence separated the strip from the path, its black links dangling over concrete and earth. Alexander followed the fence from post to post until he reached two trees standing a few yards opposite one another. He stepped over the chain, walked between the trees, reached the wall, and walked through it without stopping. Bricks softened around him into a cloak of liquid light, and he emerged within an underground parking garage.

The floor slanted beneath rows of fluorescent light blaring over cars dormant between padded pillars. Alexander walked by them, passing yellow emergency phone boxes attached to every third pillar. Voices echoed from the right. He looked and saw men and women emptying vans with the last of the week's provisions. They locked the doors and wheeled carts filled with food and supplies into the wide glowing pillar built into the far wall, leading to the Gardens-below.

Alexander watched them for a moment, and then went on ahead.

His shadow was split in two on the floor, leading and following. The brightly lit garage left no dark corners, save those created by cars at the end of their rows. He passed two guard booths on his right standing across from each other by the rise leading to the garage gate, silent and secure against the outer cold, and walked on until he heard the rhythmic popping of a truck door opening.

Cedric and Eitan stood before two large black box trucks, their windshields sheets of radiance beneath the bright lights. Radek emerged from the passenger seat of the truck on the right. Alexander went to speak to them, when he was interrupted by the clatter and crash of the left truck's rollup rear door being closed.

Percy emerged from between both trucks, wiping his hands together. He stood beside Cedric, a reproachful look on his face.

Alexander froze. He looked at his fellow conspirators. Cedric responded with a shrug. Radek twisted his mouth and raised his eyebrows. Eitan scratched the back of his head, discomfort clear on his face.

Alexander focused on Eitan.

"He had to know, brother," Eitan said. "Can't fuck around."

Alexander sighed. He looked at Percy and waited for the lecture he knew was coming.

"The cargo ropes are set," Percy said. He turned to Cedric. "We'll follow you three, then?"

"Yeah," Cedric replied, glancing from Percy to Alexander. He pulled out a printed map and laid it on the left truck's hood. "The warehouse is right by Calvary Cemetery. There's a big furniture store up the block, and an empty lot across from it, so the only civilians I'd be worried about are kids messing around. That's unlikely. If we stop right here at this corner, that'll give the three of us time to load up, while y'all—"

"Alex," Percy said, "You should really look this over, mate."

Percy's eyes glinted with sardonic light, daring Alexander to contradict him. There was nothing the magician could say. He joined them, and together they formed their plan.

The garage door opened, one out of a long row of garages that comprised the block across the street from the western wall of the Gardens. The headlights of the lead truck washed the frosted concrete in pale yellow. Eitan led them out, turning his truck right and down the sloping two-way street split further ahead by a traffic median. Radek and Cedric sat beside him, jostling against the wall separating the cab from the cargo area. Percy and Alexander followed in the second truck, a network of yellow ropes set behind them in the cargo space, awaiting hands to grab hold and be carried off to a new life.

Alexander watched the outside world unveil itself from the passenger seat. Parked cars lined the sidewalks, surrounded by mounds of ice stained gray and black from car exhaust. Trees reached outward with gnarled branches. Street lamps marched through the winter haze, illuminating rows of storage garages that were shuttered and silent. Far and to the west, Manhattan was veiled in a whirlwind of clouds, casting a rebellious aura of light within the mounting storm.

The Gardens flew past on their left. Every man was silent as they neared the intersection. The stop light turned green before they reached it, and they drove on into the snow.

Queens rolled by: the Woodside Projects standing high and forlorn, pizzerias with their names scrawled over inviting awnings, corner bodegas shuttered and painted with street art, discount stores, chain pharmacies, delis and Chinese restaurants, houses and small apartment buildings, subway entrances with their shimmering green orbs heralding the city's underworld. The streets rose and fell and glowed under an empire electric.

They stopped at Northern Boulevard, a four lane artery that

flowed from Queens to Long Island. Cars drove up and down like lonely ghosts. The silhouette of a public elementary school was visible to the east. A fast food restaurant stood surrounded by dormant car dealerships. A gas station blared light, and the glass façade of its adjoining convenience store revealed a clerk in a yellow shirt, transfixed by the swirling snow.

Alexander cast a glance at Percy.

"You're a bloody idiot," Percy said, not taking his eyes from the road or his hands from the wheel.

Alexander nodded as if this had been expected.

"Why did you not stop us, then?" he replied.

Percy looked at him for a moment.

"For the same reason you couldn't stop yourself." They waited on the traffic light. "But you should've come to me with this straight away. When Greg comes back, we're all going to have a good long chat."

"That, eh, might be awhile."

"Meaning what?"

"He told me he wasn't coming back in yet. He thinks he can get good intelligence out of the Nunez-Delgado crew."

The steering wheel whined under Percy's grip, and his jaw muscles flexed.

"He's coming back home if I have to get him myself," he said. He glared at Alexander. "This can't happen again."

"I know."

The light turned green. Eitan led, and they followed.

They curved along Woodside Avenue, passing under an elevated train track bearing the Long Island Rail Road, passing a gated shoe factory standing across from brick homes and a Korean church, passing through the heart of Woodside huddled against the breath of winter. They turned from one street to the next, navigating a grid of homes, commerce, and worship, arriving at 58th Street and Roosevelt Avenue. The 7 Train thundered above, the silver cars beating their way to Manhattan along tracks that left the streets in a perpetual grid of shadow. St. Sebastian's Church, its name emblazoned in golden letters above three arched doors, glowed from flood lights bathing its golden bricks. People huddled on the corner across from it, before Donnelley's Pub, smoking cigarettes, flirting, or lost in deep conversation. Others walked from block to block: revelers from bars laughing and yelling, drunks shuffling on unbalanced feet, late night workers returning home.

They drove on, following 58th through a silent stretch that rose into a hill leading to Queens Boulevard. The twelve lanes of the thoroughfare were almost deserted, stretching east and west, a great river of concrete connecting neighborhood to neighborhood. Calvary Cemetery loomed on the southwest corner of 58th. A great crucifix stood upon the hill, looming over the stone wall surrounding the grounds. Carved saints wept beneath it, their unmoving forms seeming to drift in and out of being.

The trucks turned right, following the middle lane, passing automotive repair shops, condos, a mosque. They turned left onto 50th Street, leaving the boulevard. A few houses slept on their right, vagrant lights on here and there, and then 50th opened into an unused lot barricaded by a wall of faded green boards. A furniture store took up the entirety of the sidewalk on the left, a large rectangular structure painted white and red, and ahead, across from the intersection of 50th and 47th Avenue, the end of the street was marked by a black gate standing upon the stone wall surrounding the cemetery.

The trucks drifted to a stop at the edge of 50th. 48th Street stood two blocks away on their right, five-story brick buildings encompassing three square blocks. The warehouse was around the corner on their left, a small industrial space besides a two-story office building. Ahead were tombstones beyond the cemetery gates, silhouettes stretching into darkness.

A dead end sign wobbled on the corner of 47th and 50th.

Percy listened, his ears picking through the whisper of thousands of snowflakes falling, the many tones of the wind, the purring of their own engines. He heard no voices, no footsteps, no sign that anyone was coming outside.

He flashed the lights of his truck.

In the truck ahead, Radek pushed open the door in the wall of the cab and entered the cargo area. The walls were lined with racks of guns, assorted tools of death hanging oiled, loaded, and ready. Cedric followed after, and they each draped bandoliers loaded with rifle magazines or shotgun shells over their heads and around their shoulders. Radek lifted a shotgun from its rack, extra shells lining the stock, and passed it to Cedric. Then he took an assault rifle and passed it to Eitan in the cab, took another and strapped it around his shoulders.

Percy gripped the door handle in his truck and waited.

Alexander stared into the street, his eyes drifting, seeing beyond the confines of reality to the ever present confluence of magic that was within him. His mind worked, conjuring a great sphere of unreality that swallowed both trucks, shaping the snow that fell within its range into strange shapes and making the air oscillate with bright colors that shimmered in an out of existence. See a momentary aurora, a stream of eerie lights that disappeared instantaneously. But to the men within the trucks, the world seemed to soften and bend, the air itself malleable, as if they were drifting into a world not of matter but of thought and form. They each took a moment, adjusting to the sense of impossibility permeating around them. Alexander felt each of them as if they were created from his own mind, and they in turn felt each other, the magician the relay, his magic carrying their location to one another. He conjured, wrapping them in undulating fingers of fog that expanded out of nothingness, bathing the trucks. Where they moved, the fog followed, leaving them veiled. Yet the mist was translucent to their eyes, ropes of ethereal vapor.

The fog expanded beyond the trucks, engulfing the empty lot and the trees and the furniture store, exhaling up 50th and around both corners of 47th in a long river that overtook the warehouse.

Eitan released the brake and let the truck drift into the intersection, blocking the dead end street. He reengaged the brake, rolled down the window and leaned out of it so he was seated on the door, raised the rifle, and aimed in the direction of the warehouse, covering the gate and the door on its right. His hands were steady. His lower eyelid twitched.

Cedric opened the rolling door, holding it so it wouldn't clatter. Radek gripped the edge of the truck's roof, pulled himself up, and moved to the center, the fog a great wave moving with him. He went prone, his rifle trained on the warehouse and a smaller gate that guarded the alleyway separating the office from the warehouse. He squinted, seeing nothing and no one on the rooftop.

"Clear," he said, whispering. The fog carried his voice to the others.

Cedric bounded out, running towards the corner of the office building. He reached a streetlight and grabbed hold, his fingers denting the gray metal. He climbed, wrapping around the lamp post as he shimmied up, every muscle flexing, keeping him steady. He reached the top, pulled himself up, and caught his balance. Then he placed one graceful foot before the other, silent and steady. The curving metal creaked, but held, and he followed it down until he was in range. He squatted low and jumped, landing on the rooftop with a soft scraping sound. He hurried, jumping over the alleyway and landing on the warehouse roof. He scanned the alley with his shotgun and found no one. Then he went to the edge above the main gate, spying the camera just below. Waves of mist battered it. He stood on the ledge, aimed downward, and placed his finger on the trigger of the shotgun.

"Ready," he said.

Percy opened the door and ran to an iron grate in the street. He grabbed hold and waited.

Alexander slid into the driver's seat, released the brake, and turned the truck right, onto 47th. He shifted into park, got out, and opened the rolling door. The ropes shone yellow and bright through the fog. He walked to within a few yards of Eitan's truck, his fingers dancing up and down, his mind working, spreading the seeds of magic across the ground before the gate, ready to conjure death on the men inside of the warehouse.

Percy waited until Alexander was set. Then he pulled the grating, ripping it off with a guttural whine that was muted by the mist, spraying bits of concrete into the falling snow. Coils of black wires waited within. He laid the grating down and stripped off his clothes, revealing four great diagonal scars twisted over his torso. He laid his sweater, sneakers, jeans, and underwear in a pile and rested his driver's cap on top of them. Then he jumped into the hole. Sparks flew about him, a violent show of electricity flashing blue and gold within the mist. The current rampaged through him, and his hair began to smolder. He moved fast, grabbing hold of the wires and ripping them in half. Smoke and fire belched, scouring him, his nerves dulled but still awake to the pain. He cringed and ripped.

The streetlights over 47th and 50th flared and died, leaving nothing but mist and darkness and the screaming of tattered wires.

Percy lifted himself out, battered his scorched hair with his hands, dressed, ran towards the warehouse, and stopped a few yards away from Alexander.

They waited, each man knowing what was to come, each man dreading the sound of the doors or the gate whining open. The torn wires fumed in seizure, belching blue sparks, a furnace in the concrete. Snow sailed on the screaming wind. Lights from distant streets bled across the air, casting an amber glow over everything.

They waited.

They waited.

Nothing happened.

Alexander frowned, a seed of dread budding in his chest.

Percy stiffened, the stillness awakening urgency, a need to hurry and be done.

Cedric tightened his grip over the shotgun, remaining focused, allowing no fear to distract him.

Eitan's nose twitched, but his face was set, hiding a sudden falling sensation deep in the pit of his stomach.

Radek licked his lips and tried to see everywhere at once, his eyes darting this way and that, uneasy.

Nothing stirred.

"Do it, Alex," Percy said.

Cedric braced himself on the ledge.

Alexander grimaced, but set to work. He focused on the sidewalk before the gate, feeling it in his mind, seeing the inner workings of concrete like a network of atoms he could command. He conjured, reordering them, straining against an invisible barrier, as if the ground did not want to be shaped by his will. But magic broke through, and the sidewalk erupted in a wave that crashed into the gate, ripping it apart and inward with a screech and roar.

They all readied for the shouts, for the streaming of flashlights, for the flash and concussive boom of gunfire.

There was only silence.

Dust showered the air and was lost in the snow and wind. Darkness within. Percy stepped forward, his vision illuminated as if by moonlight. Aisles of tall shelves revealed themselves. They were stacked with pallets of sheetrock, drums of plaster, paint cans, and boxes. There was no movement, no sound.

He sniffed the air: The crisp scent of winter, the saturating stench of rabid electricity, the mustiness of dust. No miasma of flesh, no hint of sweat or blood or even cologne. He growled in his throat and ran, lithe and fast, into the warehouse.

Alexander followed after.

Cedric watched them both climb over the rubble, one after the other. He frowned, but held fast.

Alexander stopped beside Percy in the center aisle. Silence and stillness held sway, dampening the wind. Percy stepped forward, and his steps made no sound. He scanned the shelves, sniffed again.

"There's no one here," he said.

An orb of light came alive in Alexander's hand. Long shadows spread from the stacks, revealing the mechanical shapes of hand trucks and stackers below the shelves. Alexander took a few steps forward. The orb rose above his head, casting sheets of light, revealing gray brick walls and a darkened ceiling.

Percy threw a hand on his shoulder and stepped ahead of him, looking from right to left. Despite the tall shelves and their items, a great sense of emptiness pervaded the space, as if the warehouse had never known the living to pass within its walls.

The light revealed the last two shelves, and both men saw that the one on the right was skewed. Alexander nodded to it, remembering what Greg told him about where the victims were supposed to be. They walked over to it and stood above a trap door opened to steps leading below.

They waited. Silence and darkness answered.

"Are we too late?" Alexander said, staring into the black space.

Percy grabbed the opened trapdoor and ripped it off, the hinges shrieking as they snapped, the wood cracking. He put himself in front of Alexander and threw the door down the steps. It crashed, clattered, and landed with a resounding thud.

All was still.

And then a child's scream pierced the silence, rising from confused groans into long wails that knew no comfort.

Cedric and the others gasped under their breath, listening through the mist. Percy hissed for silence.

Alexander threw himself forward, but Percy grabbed him. Alexander gave him an indignant look. Percy lifted a hand for calm.

"Behind me," he said. Then he went down. Alexander followed, and the orb of light descended behind them.

They stepped into the basement, and the carnage waiting there revealed the fate of the prisoners and the guards.

Corpses littered the floor of the cramped space, pale things bonewhite, their flesh withered, their eyes dried into putrefied sacks. They were posed like penitents beseeching a merciless god, their hands and arms thrown up in futile defense, their mouths frozen open in silent and unending screams. Their hair was brittle and faded, their clothing dangling from their emaciated forms. Guns lay before the dead guards, their lot thrown in with the very people they had enslaved and sold.

The children were among them. They had not been spared.

Alexander and Percy looked on in horror. Alexander's heart thundered, and Percy's senses careened out of control, overwhelming him so he nearly stumbled. They grabbed onto each other, for both knew exactly what had happened here.

Every corpse bore the vampire's bite, terrible gashes on their necks, forearms, and thighs. The wounds gaped wider as their withered flesh was sucked into the bites like matter being pulled into a black hole. Skeletons revealed themselves beneath the failing folds of skin and muscle. Necks vanished, collapsing, leaving heads trembling on shrinking shoulders. Legs and arms bent in on themselves, and the snapping of bones echoed. One by one, the corpses crumpled into disappearing mounds of death, trembling like marionettes caught in seizure.

Surrounding them was a livid darkness, thick, almost moving, and ever after would this space be cursed, warped by the frenzy of an eldritch predator. All who entered would feel the wrongness, the sense of things unclean waiting in the brooding black.

These things Alexander and Percy had seen before. They knew enough to run, to scream for the others to start the trucks and race away.

But the screaming child held their focus, the one left alive.

He rocked back and forth on his knees at the center of the basement. His black hair was plastered to his brown cheeks by tears and sweat and long streams of blood spilling from the mash that had once been his eyes. Blood and eye matter gored his fingertips and dripped over Wile E. Coyote smirking from a once white T-shirt. The child screamed and screamed, and Alexander knew he was past pain, past reason, the remaining witness to an orgy of bloodletting and horror that had left him no other recourse but to gouge out his instruments of sight.

But it was not enough. It would never be enough. The child was broken, a frenzied creature without hope. All memory of love and light, of laughter, was now devoured by the terrors he had witnessed. He would remain alone in the basement, ever watching as a vampire drained the lives of every person around him, some whom he had loved. He would always see madness reflected in their dying eyes, and hear their wails of unendurable agony.

As long as he lived, this would be the only world he would know.

Percy's mouth trembled. He forced it into a hard line and stepped towards the child, knowing what he had to do.

Alexander stopped him with a hand on his arm. Percy turned to him. Alexander shook his head without taking his eyes from the child. Every piece of him screamed to not do the thing he knew he must.

"What's happening?" Eitan said, his voice coming through the fog.

Percy stared at his friend, knowing he should stop him, knowing he could not. Alexander went ahead, his eyes full of sorrow, his hand trembling. He knelt and reached out to the child, offering a soft touch to his cheek. The child cried out harder, falling backwards on the floor and banging his head against it. Alexander stood. Regret was already taking hold. But he could wait no longer.

Particles of matter shimmered into being beneath his hand. They swirled and coalesced into a snubnosed revolver. He gripped the black handle and stared at the child a moment longer. Then he took aim and fired. The violent report crashed through the basement, and the child's screaming was ripped into silence.

The bullet did its work, leaving the child dead on his back. Blood leaked from his head, bubbled around his lips, and flooded the floor. Alexander couldn't move, couldn't look away. A fine mist of blood painted his sleeves.

"What the fuck!?" Eitan said, and the others echoed him.

Percy grabbed Alexander. The corpses imploded around them. Alexander stepped backwards, seeing the dead child, seeing blood, seeing the smoke rise from the bullet wound. Percy shook him. Alexander blinked, groaning with animal fear. Percy yanked him, and they ran upstairs.

Cedric and Radek were standing by the broken gate.

"Vampire!" Percy said, screaming as soon as he emerged from the steps.

Their reaction was immediate. They turned and ran, and already they heard the rumble of a truck as Eitan started it.

Eitan threw open the passenger door, and Alexander and Percy hurried inside. The truck they had originally driven, that had been meant to carry people away, was rushing off, Cedric driving, Radek rolling the back door shut.

Eitan threw the gear shift into reverse, braked, threw it back into drive, turned, and raced after them.

Alexander sat dazed in the cab, the gun still dangling in his hand.

The corpses in the basement imploded. The child's body lay there, and his blood spread to the corpses, rippled, and was sucked into the emptiness the dead left behind, winding through the air in crimson vortexes. The wounds left by the vampire devoured everything, leaving no trace of its victims. Only the dead child remained, surrounded by an ancient darkness, the oldest kind, whispered about by children, scoffed at by adults who secretly feared it in their hearts, for somewhere deep down they knew it waited, hungry and hateful, in the nameless places of all things.

14

They drove through Queens and Brooklyn. Percy and Eitan continually checked the side view mirrors, their senses alert to every pedestrian, every car that followed, every shift in the surrounding shadows. Alexander sat between them, despondent, lost, the gun limp in his hand. He registered its weight, looked at it with disgust, and unleashed his connection to it, allowing magic to fade and entropy to take its course. The cylinder, barrel, handle, and remaining bullets separated and dissolved into a cube of spheres. Gunpowder swirled within the latticework of molecules. Then there was a flash, and the structure was no more.

They stopped at a safe house in Greenpoint, a three-story multi-family home with a brick stoop no different from others on its block. They stopped at a garage by Astoria Park—desolate, bordering the East River that wound black and bright beneath smears of city light. Both times they got out and pretended to be home, waiting, preparing for the worst. Both times nothing happened.

They pulled over beneath the Brooklyn-Queens Expressway on Laurel Hill Boulevard. The road split Calvary Cemetery in half, and the cemetery gates spread serrated shadows over the snow-encrusted sidewalks. A ghostly wail emanated from cars driving the expressway above them, as if heralding the passing of souls from one world to the next.

Alexander stepped out and paced before the cemetery. The others waited. He hung his head, and then forced himself to hurry, conjuring, changing the trucks from black to white and switching the license plate numbers to match others of a set that were registered to false identities under the Gardens' control.

He returned to the truck. No one spoke. They drove home.

They pulled into the garage and waited as the attendant leaned into their windows. Caleb greeted them from his booth, his long white hair tied into a ponytail, food stains adorning the white collar under his uniform. He locked eyes with Alexander and then waved them on, distressed at the hurt he saw in the magician, knowing not to ask.

They parked the trucks.

Eitan hesitated, and then stepped out of the driver's seat. Alexander sat in silence. Percy took off his cap and ran his hand through his hair. Patches scoured by the electrical currents were already growing back. The doors of the other truck popped open, followed by sounds of movement. Alexander leaned forward, dazed, long strands of auburn hair obscuring his eyes.

Percy searched for words, but found none. He reached out and laid his hand on Alexander's shoulder. Alexander took a shuddering breath, turned to him with a look of utter sorrow, and let himself out of the truck.

The others watched him emerge, each of them wishing they could say something, anything. He stared at them for a moment.

"I'm sorry," he said, his eyes downcast. It was all he could say. His thoughts were muddled, his mind an exhausted engine trying to piece together all that had happened. There were no answers to be found. The garage loomed like a vast prison separating him from his children, his home. He longed to see them safe, to shield them from a world that considered the killing of a child an act of mercy.

He made to speak again, feeling as if he was trying to call out to his friends across an immeasurable distance. No words came. He bowed his head, stuffed his hands into his pockets, and walked away.

Percy stood with the others. No one spoke until the magician was out of sight.

"Why did Ngombe leave the boy alive?" Cedric said.

Radek's jaw muscles tensed. Eitan spat.

Percy replaced the cap on his head. He knew the answer, and one look at Cedric told him that he knew as well. Cedric had spoken only so a voice would cut the silence and remind them that they were once more among the living.

They had all recognized the work of the monster who had authored those deaths. They all knew of Manny Ngombe, and his megalomaniacal desire to be worshiped and feared. His vanity had been placated by leaving a sole witness, a living testament to his power. It was a calling card they knew well. The whys and the what - fors were for later. For now, the corpses in the basement were all the understanding any of them needed.

Percy looked at the men, at the terror seething in their eyes. They needed to refocus, to remember who they were and what they stood for.

He nodded to the trucks.

They moved without protest, checking the weapons, searching underneath the trucks for any stowaways, cleaning the seats, working to push the thought of vampires from their minds. They left the ropes for last. These they took down as if lowering a once proud and heroic flag that would never be raised again.

15

Alexander found Ian nodding off in the entranceway.

The boy was huddled against the wall between bedrooms, his eyes fluttering, fighting against sleep. Relief surged through Alexander, coupled with a great geyser of love that blotted out the rest of the world. He went to his son, lifted him into his arms, and carried him into the boy's bedroom. Ian muttered something about keeping watch. Alexander kissed his brow.

"You did good, baby," he said.

Alexander laid Ian on the bed and stroked strands of dark hair from his eyes. He caught a glimmer of crimson on the back of his own fingers and discovered a speckling of blood printed on his knuckles. He stared, horrorstruck. A whisper of movement caught his attention, and he found Ian looking up at him, smiling. The boy laid a hand over his bloodstained fingers, and then drifted off to sleep.

Alexander pulled away from Ian, left the room, and hurried to the bathroom. He turned the hot water on and used half a bottle of soap in scouring his hands clean, keeping them under the steaming faucet until he could no longer endure the pain. He searched them over until he was certain that no blood remained, and then he looked over his clothing. Islands of blood dotted his right sleeve. He raised his hand over the stains, sought them out with invisible threads that worked from his mind and through the fabric, and pulled them from the sleeve. The blood floated in viscous globules and splattered into the sink, swirling in the steaming water.

The mirror clouded over. He wiped it down for one final appraisal, caught his reflection, and tensed against waves of sickness.

He threw open the toilet seat and vomited.

He remained huddled by the toilet, the stench of sick and the acid in his throat muted against the desolation rending his heart. Every time he closed his eyes he saw the boy lying in his own blood. He wondered who the child had been. The boy's screams answered from memory, as if to remind him that it did not matter. The child had been worse than dead before the bullet tore away his life, lost in a maze of atrocity. Alexander understood this. There had been no choice but to end his suffering.

But guilt remained. He did not fight it. He couldn't.

He brushed his teeth until his gums bled, and washed his hands again in searing water. He did not see the splatter of blood drying on his forearms, under his sleeves.

He stood in Eleanor's doorway.

She was curled in the blanket, Ringo dangling from her hand by his back leg over the side of the bed. Alexander took Ringo and slid him gingerly under the blanket with her. She stirred, looked up at him through half-lidded eyes, smiled, and fell back to sleep. He went to stroke her face, but pulled away, unable to do so.

He watched her sleep, sorrow crushed under the weight of unending love. Despite his guilt, despite the horrors he had seen, to be near his little girl, warm and safe in her bed, filled him with a sense of grace, something ineffable, evidence of a universe that forgives and understands. Perhaps it was selfish. So many lying dead, one by his own hand, and yet here he was rewarded with this his greatest treasure. But at that moment it did not matter. It needed no explanation. Here was his child, all that was good and right. Whatever was to come, whatever sins he would pay for, he knew without question that he needed to exist for her sake. He would carry the world bloodstained and screaming on his shoulders, if only to see her grow into a woman of character, goodness, and strength.

But when he reached out to touch her again, his hand failed. He let it drop, unable to allow himself to stroke his daughter's cheek after what he had done.

He walked out of the room, closing the door behind him.

He sat in the living room, facing the bay window. Snow gently fell through the streetlight, the brunt of the storm now passed. He took a joint from the case, snapped a flame into existence, and smoked, blowing pale blue tendrils through his nose. He went to take another hit, grimaced, and crushed the joint into an ashtray on the wooden table beside his chair.

He remembered the boy's face. He remembered blood.

He shook himself into the present and focused on the mirror still-ness of the late night. Dawn was still hours away, and darkness held. He focused on the last of the falling snow, the warmth of the drug easing tension from his body. His fingers twitched. His head sank into the cushion. Sleep came warm and welcome, blotting out all memory of a necessary killing. Of the innocent who had nothing left to gain from life. Of a mercy Alexander had no right to give. With his last spark of cognition, the magician prayed for forgiveness.

He awoke to silence. Sitting up in the chair, he ran his hand over his face. Layers of streetlight infused the night beyond the window, yet the living room was completely dark. Stillness held sway, not even the wind stirring. The profound quiet instilled a sense of calm in Alexander, a moment of respite from the fear and heartache of the previous hours. He leaned back in the chair and examined the subtle hues of soft light, teetering upon clarity. A broader world seemed close to unveiling itself, a perspective that would help him under-stand all that had happened. Perhaps it was a trick of his mind to help him cope. Perhaps it was something more, a divine power he had not dared to seek, but that had sought him. Whatever it was, he opened himself to it, allowing quiet to delve into his heart and unearth something greater there, something powerful, an inner voice that understood his crimes and still urged him to go on, to live, to atone through purpose, through goodness, through—

Abebe Ngombe emerged from the darkness beside the window, strolling as if out of oblivion, his hands clasped behind his back. He stared at Alexander, a tall man in a fine gray coat, dark blue suit with light blue shirt, and matching tie. Orange streetlight painted his smooth black skin, shimmering over his goatee. The brown irises of his eyes were flecked with gold and surrounded large round pupils that then narrowed into vertical slits, splitting each eye in two. He went to the window and looked out. Then he turned around, smiling, and bowed to Alexander.

Alexander fought not to hyperventilate. He dug his fingers into the chair, his eyes wide, revealing unrepentant terror that he desperately tried to suppress. His shoulders rose and fell, and his neck and jaw muscles trembled. The dead boy, the factory, guilt, all was forgotten. Animal fear took hold, fed by a frenzied mind that understood without doubt that he was face to face with the Devil.

Abebe Ngombe hummed in his throat and sat on the sofa.

Alexander struggled against his unresponsive body, willing himself to stand and fight for his children's sake, for the Gardens. But all he could do was cast his eyes in the direction of the intruder, knowing that no power he conjured would do anything to save them from the evil seated across from him.

They were found. And all was lost.

Abebe undid the buttons of his coat, reached into his pocket, and pulled out a Moleskin sketchpad. He rummaged through crinkling candy wrappers in his side pockets and pulled out a black pencil half-worn to the nub. He opened the Moleskin, stared at Alexander for a moment, and then ran the pencil over the page, drawing Alexander as he saw him.

"15,136 souls," Abebe said, the lyrical drumbeat of the Congo accenting his voice. "That is how many lives you keep safe every single day. Nearly all of them you've stolen—forgive me—liberated from us." He chuckled and wagged the pencil at Alexander like a bemused parent. "My brother has some choice words for you, Magician. He thinks of you from time to time. I would say you should consider that a compliment, but of course you fear him more than you fear me. Oh, I am not insulted. I prefer not to deal with simpletons."

He paused, stretched out his hand to frame Alexander with his thumb and forefinger, and then returned to drawing.

"You've done heroic things: a true force for good, so to speak," he said. "So then, considering the people you protect in this fortress of yours—which is quite beautiful, I must say—considering that, may we agree that the killing of a child..."

Hatred alighted in Alexander's wide eyes. Abebe continued to draw, but his eyes were locked onto Alexander's, playful, amused, a gentle smile on his face. The vertical black lines of his pupils widened back into dark circles rimmed by brown flecked with gold.

"A child who could no longer sense anything but pain, and terror, and loss...a child who was beyond all hope—may we agree that it was a necessary killing? And that, perhaps, you should weigh this tragedy against all the lives you've saved. How brightly you shine, Magician. I see it. Of course, you should feel guilt. Guilt can be useful in bettering yourself, in learning to not repeat erroneous and hurtful acts. But must you let it consume you? Where is the sense in eternally paying for your sins? See, I am much more forgiving. I understand that it is our imperfections and how we overcome them that define us. I am a realist, but an optimist.

"Come, Magician, there is no sense in self-hatred. Nothing can be gained on that path. You did a hard thing, an ugly thing, but yours may be one of the rare instances where such an action was warranted. This was not the deed of some debased murderer, some lowly sadist incapable of recognizing their own faults. How dull they are, Magician. How they justify barbarities, over and again, petty tyrants who like the stench of blood, who find any excuse to feed their fantasies of playing God. They bore me to tears. No...No, that is not you. You are just unlucky. You are a good man who was forced to do a hideous thing. But you shouldn't be condemned for that, least of all from yourself. What? Should you have left little..." His pupils narrowed into catlike slits once more. "...Pablo..." They rounded again. "...the way he was?"

Alexander flinched. The dead boy was named Pablo. That was his name.

Abebe went on.

"Would that not have been cruel? After all he had seen." He pursed his lips with distaste. "Vampires are awful creatures, aren't they? The way they kill...I have seen it too many times. Even after all these centuries, it's...." He drifted and shook his head. "Worse when it's my own brother. He likes to toy with his victims." He stared at Alexander and didn't speak, his silence chattering with nearly inaudible voices. When he spoke again, all fell still, as if these voices were within a vacuum. "Pablo saw his parents die last. My brother saved them for last. Why? Why does he do anything, Alexander? He is a monster."

"Like you," Alexander replied, his voice barely a croak.

"Ah."

Abebe stopped drawing, set the pencil between the pages, closed the book, and returned the Moleskin to his inner pocket.

"So we come to it," he said. "Of course you think so. You blame me for Darius' death. How could you not? So you call me 'monster.' You know, very few people understand what that word means. They confuse monsters with evil. But evil is a dull thing, Magician. Too many think otherwise, that it is some profound truth. No. Evil is merely rampant ego. It is animal. It is base. Yet so many aspire to it. They behold the infinite cosmos and declare all things null and void, or, even more tiresome, they try and claim the world for themselves: In their own name, or in the name of a false idol. Both are merely mindless drives to power. A lack of vision. A simple minded existence. They are no different from single-celled life forms, and I promise you, Magician, there is nothing profound about them, save that they exist at all. Tyrants do not understand as we do—trying to capture power is like trying to shepherd a storm. The universe laughs at the rulers of the earth. To me, evil isn't just selfish, greedy, and cruel. Evil is boring. Genghis Kahn did not conquer the East out of ambition, or the will to spread a new ideology. He cared not about what he could call his own, or whom he could force to bow to his will. He brought murder and rape across the world for no other reason than boredom. Millions died because a barbarian could not find a hobby. There is your evil: An ape too stupid to marvel at the mysteries of existence, ruining life for the rest of us.

"Tell me, do you believe the stars can conceive of themselves? Perhaps in some way, but I doubt it. I believe they need us to do that for them. Creation is nothing without the created. We are here to experience, to be. But here we return to the dilemma of monsters. For, in existence, you invariably come up against them. It's easy to consider them evil. But monsters are not evil. They supersede the word. They are the antithesis of creation. How is that different from the brutal dullard torturing women in his basement, or the pathetic bureaucrat ordering the death of millions? Simple: Evil causes harm because it has nothing better to do. Monsters destroy because it is what they are born to do. They are the incarnation of all that is destructive to existence. They are the argument. They look upon the children of the stars and behold not creation, but that which they are meant to devour. Yet they are also a product of that very same creation, and so are grateful to the thing they are meant to tear down. They love and value existence. They find joy in it. They don't want to see it end. They even love their victims. The dragon adores its gold. Isn't that strange? Destruction worships at the altar of creation, but praises creation by tearing it apart. So you see? Monsters are natural. That is not evil. That is something far worse."

The deep dark of Abebe's pupils pulled Alexander away from himself and into the chaos of shapes and sounds hovering within a vastness that thundered, as if a cosmos teeming with leviathans unfolded in his mind. As quickly as the vision came, it went, and once more Alexander beheld the demon seated before him.

"I tend to ramble," Abebe said, sighing. "It's a habit of mine, whenever I'm in good company. Whatever you may think of me, I hope you have listened to what I said about Pablo. There was no hope for him. And you are a good man." He smiled with such warmth, that it was as if they were old friends meeting after a long period of absence. "I enjoy you, Magician. You are always the best of company."

He leaned forward, a subtle movement that made the shadows against the walls shift with him.

"So, this is what's going to happen: You are going to leave the Gardens and enter a van that is waiting out front. Do not worry about your security cameras. I understand Cedric has been having...issues...with them for the last two weeks. That should not be a problem after this morning. Your people and your guards will all be distracted by very pleasant thoughts. They will not see you leaving. We are going to take a drive. Do not worry, you will not be alone. My son and that clever wife of his are already waiting. I would have come to you sooner, but Percy and Ms. St. John were not very receptive. But they had no say in the matter. Nor do you. You must accept my invitation. There is someone you all must meet."

Abebe stood and adjusted his tie. Alexander's face was a mask of rage. He rose, every part of him shivering.

"I'm not going anywhere with you," he said.

Abebe stared at him. He took three steps, stopped, and leaned close. Shrieks wailed through Alexander's mind, a brief flash of incomprehensible hatred manifested in an orgy of tangled shadows. He tried to break away from Abebe's gaze, but could not.

"What do you think of my drawings?" Abebe said.

He stepped back and looked around the room. Alexander warred with himself, not wanting to look. But he had to.

The walls were papered with hundreds of drawings displaying different versions of Eleanor and Ian committing violence on each other, on themselves, bloodied and ripped apart, their visages adorned with crazed smiles, or howling in pain, or raving with lunatic rage. Other drawings revealed the Gardens burning, familiar figures falling from buildings, or people withered and starved in the fields, wallowing in excrement, every face frenzied beyond recognition, a twisted promise of what was to come if Alexander did not comply.

Alexander's own face made up the top row of drawings, each version a mask of supreme grief.

"15,136 souls," Abebe said. "What a stench they would make. You will do exactly as I say. You would not want to leave your children waiting in the van without you."

He snatched Alexander's coat and threw it at him. Alexander nearly fumbled it, caught it, and then Abebe was gone, the drawings vanished with him. There was no movement, no rustle of air, no sudden burst of shadows. Abebe Ngombe simply disappeared.

Alexander ran to Ian's bedroom, and then Eleanor's. Both were empty, the beds rumpled, the covers tossed aside. He checked the closets, under their beds, but even as he did so he knew it was futile. He came out of Eleanor's room and punched the wall four times, cracking it. He panted like a cornered beast. There was nothing else for it. He threw his coat on and hurried out of the apartment.

He followed the path towards the main entrance, passing a security jeep. The guard within focused glazed eyes on the twinkling lights of the dashboard. Alexander stopped and stared for a moment, recognizing the manipulation of the great demon—not possession, but suggestion, the way he nudged people's perception so their attention was enticed by things once considered trivial. To the security guard, the bright lights were suddenly works of art, a hypnotic stitching of luminescence he could not look away from. It was, in his mind, an innocent distraction, an appreciation for beauty in a surprising moment. Such a thing was not inherently evil. In fact the opposite. But here and now it revealed the ease with which Abebe Ngombe had slipped through their defenses.

Alexander wondered about the guards on the rooftops, or in the surveillance room, about how many were now distracted by the tiniest of things. He could do nothing for them but hurry and hope that by complying with Ngombe, they would all be spared.

He came to the main entrance, the arched opening of a brick tunnel leading to an ornate black gate. His steps echoed within the corridor, and the gate whined as he turned the knob and pushed it open. He hurried past a colonnade of white pillars and stood atop wide red brick steps leading down to 31st Avenue.

A brown minivan waited before the sidewalk.

Alexander's heart pounded. He went down the steps, kicking up drifts of snow, and crossed the sidewalk to the van. The dome light flashed within, revealing three rows of seats. Percy and Rosie sat the second row, both looking at Alexander with expressions of defeat. Eleanor and Ian sat in the back, Eleanor breathing hard. Ian maintained a mask of calm, but his eyes were over-wide, almost excited. Both wore coats over their pajamas. Eleanor clutched Ringo in her arms, her knuckles white on the bear's soft body. The van's automatic door hummed open. Alexander squeezed inside and took his children into his arms. Eleanor embraced him. Ian pressed close, but kept his eyes on the passenger seat where Abebe sat.

"Are you okay?" Alexander said, looking from one child to the next.

Eleanor nodded, angrily wiping tears from her eyes, not wanting to give in to the disquiet assaulting her. Ian looked from his father and Abebe and back again, a strange expression on his face.

"You have incredible children, Magician," Abebe said. "Your daughter is very brave, and your son is quite intuitive. I know what it's like to be proud of your children."

He turned and looked at Percy. Percy glared back, doing nothing to hide the hatred burning cold and complete in his eyes. Abebe reached out and stroked his face. Percy flinched, trembling with fruitless rage, but did not stop him. Rosie reached out and pushed Abebe's hand away.

Abebe looked at her, nodded, and returned his gaze to Percy.

"Of course, they do not always understand that a good parent must sometimes be the villain," he said. Longing took hold as he gazed at Percy. "I know you do not believe this, but I have missed you."

Percy ground his teeth until they cracked in the quiet of the van. Abebe's voice summoned memories of decades spent together as father and son, when Abebe had saved Percy from death and drudgery, being the parent his birth parents had never been. They had spent long years together. But those years were meaningless in the face of the monstrous acts Percy had seen the demon perform, and his memories crashed against a wall of hatred.

He looked away from Abebe.

"Alex, are you alright?" he said.

"What the hell is going on?" Alexander replied.

"I told you, Magician," Abebe said. "There is someone I want you to meet. I apologize for visiting you last and taking liberties with your children, but I knew you would not listen otherwise. You can be quite stubborn. But you have nothing to fear. Ask your boy."

Ian focused his gaze on the Father of Demons. Their eyes locked, and a silent understanding passed between them, something unknowable to the others in the van. Ian's shadow sighed somewhere below the seats, a sound full of reverence. Abebe nodded, and the boy nodded back.

Alexander seized Ian by the shoulders and turned him around.

"What did he do to you?" Alexander said.

"It's okay, Pop," Ian replied. "Trust me."

Alexander gaped, unsure what to do or say. He wrapped both of his children in his arms and pressed them close.

"Why don't you leave the kids out of this," Rosie said. Her words shook. "Whatever this is, it can't involve them. Let them go, and...and we'll do whatever you want."

"Ah, Ms. St. John," Abebe replied. "I believe you. Of course then they would raise the alarm, and all of your people would flee. They would not get far, but you hope to buy enough time so at least some may escape. You were always clever. But, I'm sorry to say that I require their presence as much as I require yours."

"Goddamn you," Percy said.

Abebe sighed. He turned to the driver, a stout man with curly gelled hair, thick eyeglasses, and a white guayabera shirt free of wrinkles or stains. He wore no coat or sweater. He had acknowledged none of what was said, his focus on a bible open in his hands. A pale blue rosary dangled from the rearview mirror.

"Well, Jairo," Abebe said. "Shall we?"

Jairo closed the bible and slid it into the space between the dash and the windshield. The gearshift clunked under his hand, and the van pulled away from the Gardens and drove on into the waning night.

16

Despite being so near the creature who had inspired fearful whispers from her friends and loved ones, Eleanor could not help but wonder at the world beyond the Gardens—at the network of streets, homes, businesses, neon lights, and the scant traces of life still wandering through the predawn chill. A part of her was thrilled to venture from home, to be led by a legend come to life to some unknown destination. But when she looked at her father, Aunt Rosie, and Uncle Percy, she saw despair drawn deep on their faces. She wrestled with tentacles of fear that struck from some boundless center, reminding her that they had been taken against their will by a monster.

Ian paid no heed to the outside world. He looked over his father's arm at the figure seated in the passenger seat. From time to time Abebe's eyes flitted to the rearview mirror, and their gazes met. Understanding passed between them, blooming in a dark space within Ian, the first demon whispering that this moment was one of a series in a scheme that Ian was now a part of. The boy was calm. But his shadow knelt at his feet, rocking with anticipation.

Percy would not look at Abebe. He would not look at anybody for the shame that weighed him down. It was his duty to protect the Gardens from the likes Abebe Ngombe, and yet the demon had taken them all with ease. He would not have admitted it, but he felt the jealousy natural to the son of an accomplished father. But worse than that was the understanding that this dread being before them could be leading them to the bitterest of ends, and there was nothing he could do to stop it.

Rosie's fingers ticked on her knee, her eyes bouncing from side to side, her mind piecing together Abebe's words. He wanted them to meet someone, them and the children. Was he lying? Was the Gardens burning at this very moment? If so, why was he sparing them? Questions fired in quick succession, each one leading her deeper into a puzzle she could not piece together.

Alexander held both of his children close, but shifted his attention from Abebe to the driver. Jairo itched something in his mind, a warning he could not place. An avalanche of frustration overwhelmed his morbid curiosity. Abebe Ngombe was right there, but he could do nothing to hurt him, do nothing to protect his children. Any action would lead to torment not only for them, but for everyone in the Gardens. All he could do was glare, maintaining a brave face before hopelessness.

They drove on.

THEY CAME within sight of Elmhurst Hospital. A row of international flags hung from the gray brick façade, outstretched over Broadway and crackling in the wind. The van slowed to a stop before the entrance. A nurse sat beyond the sliding glass doors, filling out paperwork at a U-shaped desk. Two orderlies smoked cigarettes just beyond the entrance, shivering in the cold.

Jairo slid the gearshift into park and waited. Abebe stepped out of the van. Percy shared confused looks with the others. Jairo pressed the door's release, and the van's rear passenger door slid open. He said nothing. Rosie laughed bitterly and stepped out. Percy followed. Alexander hesitated a moment, grunted, and led his children into the cold.

The passenger door groaned shut. Abebe walked around to the

driver's window where he and Jairo exchanged a glance. Jairo's eyes flared with blood. Then he slid the gearshift and drove away.

Abebe turned to the others and read the expressions on their faces as they watched the van roll past an apartment building on the corner of Broadway and Woodside Avenue.

"Don't worry," he said, even looking to Eleanor and Ian. "Jairo will never say a word about your home. Even if he wanted to, I would sear every nerve in his body before he got the chance. Shall we?"

He walked towards the hospital entrance.

Eleanor hesitated, shivering in the cold and clutching Ringo. She stared at a darkened park across the street. Swings, playgrounds, and trees stood like inarticulate dreams. As if they were not of this world. A single burst of wind whipped through the swings' chains, carrying their metallic and discordant song over the slumbering playground. Their shadows flickered upon the mats, snow spiraled from the ground, and for a moment it looked as if a pale figure danced.

Eleanor blinked with confusion. Her father pulled her. The others followed Abebe, and she and Alexander joined them. She looked back once. The swings dangled, silent, alone.

"Why are we doing this?" Alexander said to Percy and Rosie. Eleanor looked up as he spoke.

"Don't have a choice, do we?" Percy replied.

"We don't," Rosie said. "But I reckon he ain't gonna hurt us."

"You're sure?" Alexander said.

"Look where we are, out in public like this. He needs something from us. He wouldn't have gone through all this trouble otherwise. I hope."

"That's not much better, love," Percy said.

"Better than the alternative."

Alexander sighed. There was little comfort in her words.

The glass doors slid open, and they entered Elmhurst Hospital.

The nurse at the welcome desk shivered and clutched a green and white hoodie around her. A pendant of two crossed tennis rackets was pinned to her scrubs. Her face was kindly, Italian heritage prominent in her strong nose. Her eyes were dark, and her hair was dyed a deep shade of red-gold. She looked up, saw Abebe and was about to tell him and the others that it was way past visiting hours. Abebe reached the desk, smiled, and stared into her eyes. She froze, blinked, and smiled back with such warmth that it was as if her own child had surprised her.

"Go ahead, Mr. Nelson," she said. She reached under her desk and pulled out three laminated guest passes. Abebe took one, handed another to Rosie, and the last to Alexander. He smiled at Percy.

"You'll make due, I'm sure," he said.

They all frowned at the passes, but before they could ask, Abebe went towards the elevator bank standing across from a shuttered gift shop. A police officer stood guard before a stanchion, wiping fog from his eyeglasses. Abebe flashed his pass. The officer seemed confused, but shrugged and stepped aside.

The elevator doors parted with a hushed gasp. They went inside, the doors closed, and a melodic hum beat through the walls as the elevator climbed. Lights flickered. Eleanor clutched her father's hand.

The doors opened to fluorescent light, beeps, murmuring, the squeak of rolling wheels, and the hiss of breathing machines. The stringent smell of antiseptic melded with excrement, the stench of sweat, and the disheartening sting of too much disinfectant. Two nurses peered into monitors at their station before the elevators, one young, blonde, and chewing gum, the other Filipino, older, a gold crucifix dangling from her neck. A cardboard partition was erected between them, born from years of mutual dislike. They looked up and frowned. Abebe caught their gazes. They smiled and returned to their work, both seemingly confused as if all of a sudden happy for no reason they could explain. The blonde one pulled the partition aside and offered some gum to her desk mate.

Another nurse came by, pushing a cart full of vials, pills, and a computer that monitored which patient received what drug, yawning as he did so.

Three lines were painted onto the linoleum floor. The green line led left where the hall stretched away until it crossed into a T-intersection, one side leading to the Intensive Care Unit, the other to the Emergency Room. The purple line led straight past the nurse's station and around a corner on the left, to a waiting room for patients' families. The orange line led to a pair of double doors on the right, where one word was written in block letters muted and faded over milky glass:

Hospice.

Abebe followed the orange line.

The hallway lights dimmed. Both nurses frowned, and a young Indian doctor came from around the corner and looked up.

"What is going on?" she said.

"All night," the blonde nurse replied.

"You should call maintenance."

The blonde nurse gave her a flat look.

"What a great idea."

The doctor frowned at the nurse's sarcasm.

Alexander paid no notice to the lights. He glared after Abebe as if expecting some hateful trick.

Percy sniffed the air, sorting through the miasma. Something underneath the shit and Lysol struck him, awakening a host of memories that caused him to stop mid-stride. He stared after Abebe, incredulous, the scent familiar and impossible, reaching from the past to take hold of the present.

"What?" Rosie said, catching the look on her husband's face.

Abebe waited by the Hospice doors. Percy shook his head at him.

"It can't be," he said.

Abebe pushed the door open.

"Go see," he replied.

But Percy did not move. Rosie looked from him to Abebe, cursed, and hurried into the Hospice ward. Eleanor ran after her, slipping from her father's grasp, and Ian followed. Alexander chased after them, eyeing Abebe as he passed.

Abebe and Percy were left alone.

"What have you done?" Percy said.

"What I had to," Abebe replied. Remorse shaped his expression, the look of a father who knows his boy has reason to hate him. "I never wanted to hurt any of you. I hope this will prove that."

A hornet's nest of emotions stormed Percy. The scent he caught could only belong to one person, and it held the potential to upend everything he thought he understood about the world. So it had to be some trick. The creature before him was a master of lies, but in Abebe's eyes he beheld something of the man he had once thought him, a loving heart veiled by impenetrable shadows, someone who had taught Percy how to use darkness as a shield, who always seemed to have the best intentions for others.

But there had been other things Abebe Ngombe had done, horrific things...

Percy growled deep in his chest, at war with himself. The nurses looked up at him with sudden and primal unease. He sneered and walked into the Hospice ward.

The walls were painted a warm shade of beige, and the lights in the hall were dim. Percy walked by a room with a middle aged woman lying on her bed in the semi-dark. She played Solitaire, the rows of cards laid shakily on the tray. She watched Percy with sunken eyes and offered a wave. Percy paused and waved back. Despite his urgency, he could give a dying woman that much.

But the scent hurried him on.

He found Alexander standing before the doorway three rooms down, blood drained from his face. Rosie knelt on the floor inside the room, her dress spilled around her in a great fan. Eleanor stared at the figure on the bed, as if seeing a myth come to life. Ian bore a rare expression of surprise, his head cocked to one side, his eyes wide, almost offended. Percy stepped inside and saw what he had sensed to be true confirmed.

Darius Bardales lay withered and unconscious on the bed. His once thick golden-brown hair was limp and gray. His strong shoulders were now curved, as if unable to bear their own weight. His breath gurgled, his facial muscles twitched, and death loomed near. A sickly sweetness clung to the air, emanating from his failing body.

But he was there. He was alive.

Alexander remembered the boyish features of the man who had been his best friend. The face on the pillow was older, shrunken. But even with his eyes closed, something of the man he had known remained.

Alexander looked at Percy. They shared the memory of watching Darius burn to ash on a sun drenched beach, his blood tainting the waves, swirling in and out of the surf until the redness had vanished into the deep gray-blue of the Atlantic.

It couldn't be, Alexander thought. His fists shook, a sudden frenzy awakened by the certainty that they had been fooled.

Abebe came to the doorway. Alexander ripped him by the lapels of his coat and slammed him into the wall.

"Pop!" Eleanor said. Ian took a step towards them, unsure of what to do.

"You animal," Alexander said to Abebe. "It wasn't enough that you killed him? That you took him from us? Now you do this. You show us this thing—"

"Alex," Percy said.

"This abomination. You ruin the only thing we have left of him." His knuckles went white over Abebe's collar. "You better kill me. You better end me right now, or I swear there will be no end to the misery I will cause you. I will find a way to make you suffer. I will make it my life's work. I don't care what you do to me, I don't—"

"It's him, Alex," Percy said.

Pity softened Abebe's eyes. Alexander saw his face reflected in those deep dark pools, the hateful mask it had become. Percy's words clicked. Alexander turned and saw bafflement on Percy's face.

"It's Darius," Percy said.

Alexander let go of Abebe and looked about as if searching for anything to prove that it was all a lie. Eleanor and Ian watched him in shocked silence as he snatched the medical chart hanging from the foot of the bed. The name on the chart read Daniel Escoto. Alexander waved it at Abebe in accusation.

Abebe raised both hands like a patient teacher dealing with an angry child.

"He changed his name," he said. "Prudent, would you not agree?"

Alexander flipped through the chart, glanced over terms and numbers he did not understand, and tossed it clattering to the floor.

Rosie blinked and cradled her hands against her chest, her eyes and mouth working in silent argument. She stood, went to Darius, and laid her hand on his brow. His skin was frail and dry, but she could feel the murmur of veins pulsing against the warmth of her palm.

Alexander joined her by the bed and stared into the face of his long dead friend, now dying once more.

Abebe adjusted his coat and collar. Percy went to him.

"How?" he said, the weight of that one word carrying through the room. Rosie looked up, her gaze as forceful as Percy's voice.

Abebe shook his head.

"I wish I could answer that. The truth—" He looked at Alexander. "The only truth, is that he found me over a year ago. He was older, different...he was dying. But it was him."

He looked at everyone in the room, holding each of their gazes.

"You had every reason to hate me. But now I can tell you, and now you will believe once and for all: I did not betray Darius. He asked me to help him die. He wanted my brother to think that I had betrayed him and your rebellion. He wanted the other vampires to trust me. I did not see to what end. I do now."

"What the hell does that mean?" Rosie said. She spoke as if from a distance, the world a haze between what she had known and what now was.

"It means," Abebe replied, "that he wanted to protect you. That was the bargain. By sacrificing himself, he would take full responsibility for the war. He would stop Manny from finding your home. He laid everything that happened on his shoulders. It worked. I regained my brother's confidence, but I earned your hate. I did it because Darius would not see your home or your dream fail. That is why I possessed him and let him burn in the sun."

"You faked that somehow," Rosie said. "You—hell, I don't know, the two of you figured out some way to break him free of being a vampire and—"

"I assure you, Ms. St. John, Darius burned." He nodded to Percy and Alexander. "Ask them."

The grim shadow that follows those who have witnessed atrocity fell over both men.

"I can still smell it," Percy said.

Alexander said nothing. But he watched Abebe, his gaze pregnant with the memory of screams and charred flesh.

"You hated to see it," Abebe said to him. "I hated to do it. However, Darius told me that it was for a good reason. He promised it was not the end. I thought he was mad, but I knew that killing him would satisfy my brother. I am sorry that you both had to watch him die. But it was necessary. And it was not just about saving the Gardens." He looked each of them in the eyes. He met Alexander's and held it. "Darius is not the reason I brought you here."

He walked out of the room.

They each took a moment, staring at their old friend, at his frail hands, his wheezing chest rising and falling. Then they filed out. Alexander was last, the love he felt for Darius tinged with something close to revulsion. This was not supposed to be. His children watched him from the door. He broke away and led them out.

Abebe stood near the nurses' station, watching Percy question the Indian doctor. She stared at him from over a computer screen, a bored expression on her face. The lights flickered above them.

"Sir, I'm sorry, but his body is failing him," she said. "He was septic when he was admitted. Sometimes we know the cause, and sometimes it's just...it's not cut and dry, is what I'm saying, especially with infections. They can be very hard to trace. We've done everything we can, but in all honesty, I'm amazed that he's still breathing." She blinked. "How did you get passes this late? You're not family."

Abebe leaned towards her, his expression knit into that of a bereaved wise man suppressing emotions so he could be soothing and strong for others. He smiled, staring long into her eyes. She stiffened, blinked again, shrugged, and looked back at the computer screen.

"Take all the time you need," she said, frowning as she spoke, as if catching herself sleep talking. She typed something into a chart on her screen and did not look up again.

Abebe urged Percy to follow him with a touch of the elbow. The others were close behind. They followed the purple line around the nurses' station and down a long hallway.

"Satisfied?" Abebe said to Percy.

Percy frowned. Alexander spoke up behind them.

"We have to assume everyone here is compromised."

Abebe nodded.

"A safe assumption."

Alexander shook his head, muttering under his breath.

"Son?" Abebe said to Percy.

Percy grimaced. He smelled the fine particles in the air, each unveiling the life of the hospital ward: the sick and dying, the exhausted staff and their constant struggle against death. The air buzzed and hummed and prickled his skin, as if placing a robe over his body that revealed all of the comings and goings of this place. In none of these things did he feel Abebe's influence, save for the demon himself walking beside him. He had manipulated the staff, yes, had searched out their emotions and brought other things into focus so they would ignore the strangers here at this late hour. But they were still of their own minds.

"These people have not been possessed," he said. "That's Darius back there, not some imitation." He turned to Abebe. "But I still don't trust you."

"Satisfied, Magician?" Abebe said, not looking back.

"No," Alexander replied.

They walked on.

Eleanor tugged at Alexander's sleeve, urging him to hang back.

"That's Darius Bardales?" she said.

"I—yes, it seems so.

"The Darius Bardales."

Alexander nodded.

"I thought he was a vampire," Eleanor said.

"He was."

"And that he died."

"He did."

"But, Pop—"

"Please, baby—"

"How's he alive? Why isn't he a vampire anymore?"

Alexander sighed. He wanted to know that himself.

"I don't know, okay. I know nothing right now."

She frowned. He hurried her on.

Ian walked beside Abebe. Abebe glanced at him.

"You want to ask," he said.

"You made the doctor forget what she was talking about without possessing her. And you made the nurse give you passes in the same way. The other nurses, they barely noticed us. You did that."

"I did."

"How?"

Abebe smiled.

"Perhaps one day I will show you."

"Ian," Alexander said, taking his arm and pulling him back.

"You'll come to trust me, Magician," Abebe said. "You may even ask that I help your boy understand his power. I doubt there will be many volunteers."

Alexander ignored him, smoldering at the thought, more so because there was some truth to the demon's words. The boy's mother was gone, taking with her a vast understanding of a dark nature she had learned to control. Could his son learn such things without a teacher?

Ian looked from Abebe to his father and back again, a sly smile on his face.

They came to the waiting room at the end of the hall, its door closed. Wind howled. The doorknob of a medical closet rattled on their left. The ceiling thumped, and pipes dinged. Ian's shadow went rigid on the floor, craning its head from left to right. Ian tensed with it, sensing a presence he could not place.

The ceiling lights dimmed to near darkness, and then swelled back to life. Rosie frowned up at them. Abebe leaned towards the door, peering through the narrow window and into the waiting room.

"Would you give me a moment?" he said to them.

"Why?" Alexander replied.

Abebe saw Alexander's doubt reflected in the others.

"Very well."

He opened the door for them to enter.

They walked into the waiting room and stood in shocked silence. Rosie covered her mouth. Percy snatched his cap from his head and twisted it into a rope. Alexander gasped, all mistrust dissolved into amazement. Eleanor and Ian squeezed between them and gazed with open confusion. Ian blinked once, twice, and then bewilderment took hold. He had seen enough of Darius' pictures to understand. Eleanor stared at him, confused, and then looked back at their shared point of focus with open question.

A boy sat before them. A mop of wavy black hair hung in tangles over his brow, unkempt, crazed, and streaked with strands of white. Latino heritage was evident in his skin, but his eyes were slate gray growing pale near their pupils, evidence of his mother's ethnicity and his mixed roots. He sat on a battered red chair, his head bowed and half-buried in a black hood. The other chairs stretched away from him in a V, one overturned, a crack in the wall above it. A painting of a yew tree hung behind the boy, its expansive leaves a blaze of green fire over crisscrossing branches. A book bag rested at his feet, along with a black rolling suitcase. Dried rock salt stained his boots, and a gray coat rested on his lap. He held a photo in his hands that he quickly tucked it into his jeans' pocket. Then he looked up to scan the people before him. The dark circles under his eyes spoke of loss and exhaustion beyond what a child should know.

Abebe knelt by his side and laid a hand on his arm.

"Was I too long?" he said. The boy shook his head. Abebe turned to the others. "I would like for you all to meet Jason."

They knew who he was. They saw it in the curve of his nose, in the gentle sadness that furrowed his brow. There was someone else in the boy's features, the mother they had never met evident in his eyes and the deep darkness of his hair. But there was no doubting who the father was.

Alexander felt it in his skin, in long ripples of cold that exploded through him. Shock gave way to benevolence. He spoke without thinking.

"Hi, Jason," he said, all suspicion forgotten for a moment. "I'm Alexander. I was—I'm...well..."

"I know who you are, Mr. Demidov," Jason replied, his voice raspy, soft, every word drawn out as if he were not used to speaking to others. Alexander arched his eyebrows in surprise. Jason looked at Rosie. "You too, Ms. St. John. And you're Percy, right? You're—you're like Uncle Abe."

"How's that?" Percy said, breathless.

Jason twisted his mouth to the side and looked at Abebe.

"I don't think I'm supposed to say it out loud."

Abebe nodded to him that it was okay.

Jason frowned, a keen awareness active in his gray eyes. He muttered to himself, seeming to argue with multiple ideas flung at once from an overactive mind. His head bounced from side to side, and his eyes ticked along. A consensus was made, and he looked up at Percy with an alert gaze, almost too wide, brimming with a strangely humorous glint.

"You both look really good for you age," he said. He paused for a moment, and then a slow and melodic laugh emanated from deep inside. For a moment the sadness in his eyes disappeared beneath a crazed glint.

Eleanor snorted, laughing in kind.

Denial screamed through Percy, promising him that this was some deranged dream, or the last movement of a grand deception perpetrated on them by his father. But the boy was here, alive, a participant of the world. He could hear his heartbeat, could smell the myriad of scents that were unique to the child, along with those he shared with his father.

"You're Darius' son," he said.

Numbness took hold of the boy, silencing his laughter and sending an onslaught of sorrow over his perplexed features. He shrugged and fell silent.

Eleanor looked in wonderment.

"Holy shit," she said, whispering.

Jason found her gaze, and each stared at the other with open curiosity. The boy broke away and turned to Abebe.

"Can I see him now?" he said.

Abebe smiled a sad smile.

"Not yet," he replied. "Your father just wants to speak to his friends for a moment. Then you can be with him."

Jason looked at the empty seats surrounding him, and his gaze fell on the fallen chair. He shuddered and looked away. Uncertainty spun his thoughts into knots, and a question he did not want to ask threatened to rip them apart and leave him mired in grief.

Abebe read his fear.

"He is not going anywhere. Not yet."

"But what if he wakes up, and I'm not there, and—"

"He is not awake. Remember, he does not want you with him until he is. We are going to rouse him, and we're going to speak for a little while. That is all."

Jason nodded, took a shaky breath, and stared at the floor. A part of him did not want to see his father. A part of him understood that it would be the last time that he did.

Abebe turned to Eleanor and Ian.

"Would you mind keeping Jason company?" he said.

Eleanor blinked with surprise.

"O-okay," she replied.

Ian was silent. He remained by the door, staring at Jason, his skin alive with some silent warning. The shadow hissed and growled in his mind, seizing on his apprehension, awake to the fact that here they were faced with a powerful unknown.

Abebe looked at the others, his eyes pregnant with meaning. Without a word, he stood and walked out of the room. The others hesitated, each watching the boy in their own way, wrapped in strange thoughts. Percy grabbed Rosie's hand. She took a shuddering breath, turned, and followed him out. Alexander remained, looking from the boy to his children. How to make sense of this? He sighed, regarded his daughter and son, and walked out, hoping answers waited.

The children remained, alone together, a deep quiet taking hold. Between them waited mysteries, questions that they did not yet know to ask, and answers that were veiled in their future. A strange tide was coming to pull them in, to carry them into a deep dark ocean where their destinies were written in currents of unknowable truths. Here they were, the demon, the magician, and the son of a dead man, and none could think of anything to say.

The lights flickered.

17

They stood around Darius. Abebe was at the foot of the bed, hands clasped, eyes closed. A swarm of sensations were fed to him by those he possessed, by his far reaching shadows lurking in dark spaces, watching, listening, each one playing some part in his machinations. Beyond them was Darius, a fading awareness veiled in warmth, a fantasyland Abebe had concocted so the dying man would be shielded from agony.

Abebe reached out to him, stirring Darius as if he were stoking a fire. Darkness erupted in ropes of vicious light that brought him all of Darius, fusing their perceptions together.

Pain and nausea flooded through the demon. He groaned and clutched the bedpost.

Darius came awake with a harsh inhalation.

He wheezed, clenching his eyes against the bright light, his back arched as he cried out through gritted teeth.

Blood surged over Abebe's eyes, and sweat slicked his brow as he absorbed Darius' pain. He groaned again and backed away, crossing his arms over his stomach.

Alexander went to one side of Darius, Rosie to the other. Percy looked with true concern at Abebe. The demon waved him away, but Percy joined him at the foot of the bed.

Darius opened one eye against the light, and then the other, letting vision adjust as pain diminished. The green of them was faded, nearly brown at the pupils, but the borders around the irises shone like circles of jade fire. They locked onto Alexander, and the dying man moaned and would have wept if he could have produced the tears. He stretched trembling arms, and Alexander embraced him, flinching at how frail he was. Then Darius found Rosie standing to his right, and he almost laughed with relief as he reached out to her. She took his hand in both of hers, troubled by the papery feel of his skin, but amazed and grateful to see him alive.

Darius looked at Percy. He smiled a sardonic smile.

"You still look like a dick in that hat," he said, his voice thin, rattling.

Percy's mouth was a hard line, but the flesh about his eyes trembled, as if they were restraining long buried grief.

Rosie sat the edge of the bed. Darius strained to sit up, and Alexander helped him. Darius swallowed and let another wave of sickness pass. He felt Abebe in his mind, an overarching presence carrying the burden of his failing body.

"I—" Darius said. He licked his lips and almost laughed to himself. "I don't know where to begin. It's so good to see all of you. I'm sorry it's like this. I wanted it to be another way, but I...I couldn't—"

He groaned. Abebe grunted behind the others. Darius blinked hard and this time did laugh. Even with Abebe carrying him, the pain was great.

"This is insane," he said. "I'm supposed to be dead, I know that. It has to be a lot for y'all to take in, and you deserve answers. But I can't give them to you. It's too dangerous.

"My son, though...he'll be able to explain all of it. When the time's right, he'll tell you everything you need to know. You got my word on that. For now, I need y'all to listen—"

"Are you mad?" Percy said, incredulous. "You can't just leave it at that. We watched you die! Yet here you are, with a bloody child, no less. Are we supposed to just accept that? 'Right, hello, old chap, fancy seeing you here after you burned to bloody death, bit of a strange thing, that, but you know how it is, swings and fucking roundabouts.' That's not going to fly, D. You better give us some answers. I need more than fucking riddles from you, mate."

Darius smirked.

"I'm sorry. I take back what I said. I think it's a great hat."

Percy turned away, disgusted. Abebe stepped in his place, looking hard at Darius, eyes brimming with pain.

"Answer what you can," he said. "You owe them that."

"Please," Rosie said.

Darius turned to her and clutched her hand tighter.

"I'm sorry," he replied. "It's just...I don't know how to explain it. It's—fuck, man, I just...I guess...there's something bigger going on." He looked at them with urgency, wrestling with all of the things he wanted to say but couldn't. "Something involving all of us: Everything, everyone. When I became a vampire, I found out things about existence itself, things that we all need to be saved from."

The ceiling lights dimmed, and the window rattled against a gust of wind.

"What things?" Alexander said. "D, this is...I don't understand."

"Can you slow down," Rosie said. "Just tell us how you're still alive? How is that possible?"

"I can't," Darius replied. "I know. But you gotta trust me. All I can say is that I—I was brought back so I could have my son. So he can save us."

"Brought back?" Alexander said.

"Save us from what?" Rosie said.

They spoke as one, filling the room with questions.

"Please," Darius said, a sliver of his old strength silencing them. "I need y'all to trust me. If I tell you everything, you'll be in the worst kind of danger."

"But it's fine for your son to tell us?" Percy said.

"By then he'll be ready to keep you safe. Just...shut the fuck up and listen. I've been on borrowed time for a long time, and I ain't got much longer."

He looked at Alexander. The long years of their friendship forged into an unbreakable bond—adventures, risks taken, secrets shared, hurts mended. Their footfalls echoed in memory, always in sync, always side by side. As if each were part of the other, a link forever conjoined.

Alexander nodded.

Darius turned to Rosie. The hardships of their pasts had opened understanding between them. Tragedy had shaped them, had taught them to endure, to overcome, to think, to keep moving. They shared a strange sort of ambition, the kind that forced their hands into the act of creation. Their bond was cemented by the Gardens, their experiment, their child. In each other they saw evidence that they were not alone, that there were friends in the world who looked upon your work and understood.

Rosie nodded.

Darius looked to Percy.

Between them was the animosity of brothers. Love was there, an honest love, the kind that brokered no hesitation when one needed the other. But there lingered a hint of dislike, just enough for them to be constantly annoyed with each other. The secret, however, was that they enjoyed it, this mutual need to make the other appear an ass. What went unspoken, but was known, was the fact that they didn't have to worry about offending one another. There could never be true discord between them, for every insult was a veiled message promising unending loyalty and friendship. Each saw what was broken in the other and mocked the hurts of their pasts, deflating painful memories of their power.

Percy adjusted the driver's cap, as if to say he knew it looked good on him.

Darius smirked again, then coughed and clutched his chest. Abebe groaned, a harvest of knives scattered through his insides.

Darius collected himself.

"First," he said, "I need you to take my boy in. Raise him. I know that's a lot to spring on y'all, but it has to be done. Jason's a good kid. He's kind, and smart...real smart. Things have been hard on him. He lost his mother, and now...he needs a home. A safe place to grow. He knows a lot about the Gardens—magic, all of it. So you can be open with him. But people can't know he's my son. Not yet. That's why I didn't come to you before. There'd be too much expectation, too many questions." He went silent for a moment, doubt contorting his features. "It ain't just that. Truth is, I wanted him to have some kind of normal life, at least for a little while. Maybe that was stupid. Doesn't matter now. I know I'm asking a lot, but there's no one else. It's too dangerous for him to stay with Abebe."

"Darius—" Percy said.

"Second: I asked Abebe to kill me. I needed him to. My death was enough to satisfy Father Manny, and to keep all y'all safe. Abebe's been protecting you for a long time. He's been watching over the Gardens, and he's gonna keep protecting you. But you need to trust him. Jason does. Abebe's gonna be a big help when the time comes."

"For what?" Rosie said. "Darius, of course we'll take care of your son. And, ah, hell..." She looked over at Abebe. "We misjudged you. You can't blame us, but this makes at least that much clear." She turned back to Darius. "But it don't change the fact that none of this makes a lick of sense. You're talking about your boy like he's some kind of, I don't know, savior or some such. Darius, I don't doubt he's a special kid, especially not after this, but you gotta give us something more. Help us understand."

A faraway look took hold Darius. Guilt gnawed, deeper than the pain of his dying. But there was also determination fueled by a fearful knowledge of things he knew they could not yet understand.

"Jason," he said, "has business with the vampires. Deadass, when the time comes, when he's ready, he's gonna end them."

Rosie froze. Alexander shot up from the bed. Percy tensed, gripping the bed post, cracking it.

Darius looked each of them in the eye.

"He's gonna kill them."

. . .

JASON MUTTERED TO HIMSELF, blinking rapidly, his eyes ticking left to right. His legs shook up and down, and his fingers bounced against his knees, as if his movements were being conducted by uncertainty.

"They'll think it's weird," he said, mumbling louder, caught in some self-contained argument.

Eleanor looked to her brother, questioning. Ian ignored her, watching Jason with clinical fascination.

Jason nodded to himself, and then fell still. He looked up and seemed to see the siblings for the first time.

He smiled, a cocked grin that was awkward but genuine.

"Hey," he said, his voice rising with unexpected enthusiasm, his eyes reveling with devil-may-care light. He stood, cracked his knuckles, and gestured at the chairs. "You guys can sit down. Not that you have to. I mean, it's okay if you don't want to, I don't own these chairs or anything. So you can do whatever you want with them." An errant thought gave him pause. He pointed slowly, as if nearing a realization. "Not whatever you want. They belong to someone, so— wait, who owns a hospital? I don't know. Anyway, you can still sit on 'em, 'cause that's what chairs are for."

Eleanor frowned, caught between confusion, apprehension, and a strange sense of ease. The near-crazy glint in the boy's eyes didn't seem malicious. There was warmth to them. His murmuring and twitching revealed a mind in constant motion, and while it made him odd, there seemed no anger to any of it. But there was something else about him, an air of dread that he seemed to struggle with, as if at any moment he expected the world to be torn apart.

His mother was not here, and a suitcase rested by his feet. Eleanor put together that he had already suffered a major loss, one she understood well. Another was waiting a few rooms away. His world was ending. Eleanor shuddered to think what life without her father would be like, but she did not have to imagine what the death of Jason's mother had done to him.

She hesitated a moment, hugging Ringo. Jason looked at her and looked away, resignation clear on his face, as if he were long familiar with rejection. Then Eleanor strode forward and chose the chair next to him. He looked on with surprise. She smiled.

"Hey," she said. "I'm Eleanor."

"I'm Jason" he replied, sitting back down. Questions dogpiled in his mind, leaving him to strain against the cataclysm of internal noise. He noticed Ringo. The stuffed animal cut through the discord and triggered a clear and honest thought. "Cool bear."

Eleanor lifted Ringo in her arms and grabbed his paw.

"Thanks. This is Ringo. Say hi, Ringo." She waved the paw and affected her terrible British accent. " 'Ello, Ringo.' "

"Like from the Beatles?"

"Hey, yeah. You know 'em?"

"Had to. My mom and dad..." His expression dropped. To acknowledge them would be to acknowledge their loss. He sniffed, gave a slight shake of his head, and leaned back in his chair. "I listened to them since forever. They made great music. Rubber Soul's my favorite."

"Abbey Road."

"Both favorite. But everything they made was great."

"Yeah, they were the best," Eleanor said. "My mom used to listen to them all the time."

"My dad and Uncle Abe told me a little about your mom. She sounded really cool."

"They did?"

Jason nodded.

"They told me a lot. I know about magic and, you know, other things. Uncle Abe can be...scary? That's what they tell me. I haven't seen it. Is it really true that your mom was, uh, like him?"

"She was a demon," Ian said, pulling their attention. "Like me."

Ian's gaze never faltered. He did not blink. In Jason he beheld the impossible, and the impossible enticed him.

Jason stared back.

"That must make you great at hide and seek," he replied.

Ian said nothing.

Jason frowned. Under the older boy's stare he felt different, a stranger, someone cast upon the world without invitation. Before him was a demon, a boy not much older than himself, with dark eyes and a countenance that revealed strange calm. Everything he had known was ending, and while Eleanor radiated warmth, Ian was an avatar of discord, mistrust unveiled.

"Ian!" Eleanor said. She silently mouthed an angry stream of curses at her brother, gesturing for him to stop being hostile. He ignored her, never looking away from Jason.

Jason stared back, a smile creeping over his face, his eyes going manic. Madness could be a shield. Years of being an outsider had imparted that lesson to him.

Ian did not seem perturbed by the show of crazy on Jason's face. He stuffed his hands into his coat pockets and walked over to the overturned chair.

"Don't sit on that!" Jason said, seized by fear.

Eleanor jumped.

Ian stopped and glanced over.

"That—that chair doesn't want you sit on it," Jason said.

Ian blinked.

"It told you that?"

"Yep. I talk to chairs all the time. They're not as nice as couches."

Ian smirked. He lifted the chair and set it on the floor. Then he looked up at the gash in the wall, tracing the cracks that splayed over the plaster. He looked over at Jason. The stranger cringed, but fought not to show it.

"Angry?" Ian said. Jason didn't respond. "Makes sense. I'd be mad, too, if I were you. What would we think is weird?"

"Huh?" Jason replied.

"You were talking to yourself before. You said 'they'll think it's weird.' Did you mean something about this chair?"

Jason was silent.

"I get why you threw it," Ian said. "If my father was dying, I'd lose control. You must be losing it. Control. Your father doesn't have long, right?"

GIOVANNI DIAZ

An eerie stillness took hold of Jason, making his gray eyes shine like blades in the dark.

Ian watched, waiting.

Three of the chairs whipped around. They faced Ian, moving on their own, screeching against the linoleum. Ian looked over at them, unmoved. Then he smiled at Jason.

"I knew it," he said.

Eleanor went wide eyed. Understanding came in a rush of empathy. Her whole life had been the Gardens—magicians and werewolves, outsiders with strange abilities, people who took the extraordinary as a matter of course. But Jason had only his father (and perhaps Abebe Ngombe) to share in the wonders of their hidden kind. Around them was New York City, cathedral to the modern world, where the unique was only celebrated as an eccentricity. The truth was, even in a great metropolis, the extraordinary was gawked at, viewed with veiled disdain. There was no room for magic along the sleek avenues of Manhattan, the fading working class neighborhoods of Brooklyn and Queens, or the struggling tenements of the Bronx. The city streets were morphing into technological rivers carrying its people beyond the realm of wonder and into a future that scoffed at the slightest hint of anything beyond the material.

Jason had lived in that world for his entire life. He had been alone. Of that, Eleanor was certain.

"Hey, it's cool," she said to him. "You probably don't know how to control magic yet."

He didn't seem to hear. He was no longer staring at Ian, but at the chairs that had moved. His eyes trembled, and for a moment he seemed terrified. He blinked in quick succession and looked at Eleanor.

"The what?"

"You're a magician," Eleanor said, an excited smile on her face. "That's what you meant, right? You made the chair crash against the wall, and you were afraid to talk about it. Dude, it's totally fine. You know all about us, right, about magic, you just said so. So you don't have to be embarrassed. I wouldn't be able to control it either, if I didn't have places to practice. I bet your pops taught you some stuff, but still, it has to be hard outside of the Gardens. Here, look. Hey, fuck-face—" She waved at her brother. "Guard the door."

Ian did so, satisfied but still watching Jason as if he were a secret to be unraveled.

Eleanor looked past her brother and through the door's window. She saw no one, then opened her palm and closed her eyes. She whispered.

"Everything is nothing, nothing is everything..."

Jason's eyes lit up as a diamond of light coalesced and swelled over her palm. The diamond lengthened and curved with liquid ease into the graceful shape of a guitar player. She danced up and down, this minstrel of light, swaying with her instrument, and within her was a myriad of rippling colors, as if the fires of creation were revealed through her being.

Eleanor opened her eyes and smiled at her work.

"Pretty sweet, huh?" she said.

Jason gawked, lost in a warm cloud.

Eleanor nodded with appreciation. She let magic dissipate, releasing the thrumming warmth that filled her body. The guitar player dissolved into misty light that floated above them and faded.

"See," she said. "It's totally cool. We're used to crazy stuff. Bet weird things happen around you all the time, huh?"

"Uh," Jason replied. "Something like that."

"Yeah. That's how it's like when you don't have magic under control. I was like that in the beginning. Once, my pops asked me to get some eggs from the fridge so he could make breakfast. As soon as I opened the door, they flew out of the thingy and crashed into the ceiling. They were dripping everywhere." She threw open her arms above her head. "Everywhere! That shit was crazy. But you practice, and you learn. Besides, it's, you know, a hard time for you."

Jason ignored the last thing she said, veiling his dying father with an image of eggs dripping from a ceiling.

"Next time you should throw some butter on the ceiling first," he said.

Eleanor frowned, and then giggled. Jason was about to say that he wasn't sure what to call the things that happened around him, when footfalls clapped beyond the door. A sudden tightness seized his chest. His breath quickened, and sweat broke across his brow. He seized Eleanor's hand, unconscious of the action, aware only of those footsteps and what they meant. Eleanor had made him forget. For a brief moment he was just a boy making a friend. But the footsteps came closer, and they carried with them an ending he was unprepared to face.

Ian backed away as the door opened. Abebe was there, his eyes soft and sorrowful.

"It's time, Jason," he said.

The boy stood and felt as if he were drifting, the world falling away, leaving him alone within a dim tunnel leading to the end of the world.

Eleanor watched him leave the room. She stood, clutched Ringo, and wished she could say something to stay the pain he was feeling. But she knew there was nothing to be said.

Ian looked away, his thoughts on his mother and whatever feelings she conjured, veiled under the mystery of his heart.

Jason stepped into the hallway. The adults were there, watching him, their expressions mingled grief and awe. Abebe rested a hand on his back, but he slipped away, walking with growing agitation, his fingers trembling, his breath coming in hurried gasps. Yet no tears streaked his face. He went by Alexander, Rosie, and Percy, not seeing them, and followed the purple line to the nurses' station. Every beep and hiss reached his ears in the cadence of mockery. The lights above flickered and dimmed. He rounded the corner and saw the hospice doors a few yards away. His father's room was beyond.

He walked past the nurses' station, aware of nothing save the looming double doors. He reached them and laid numb hands on their smooth surface, pushed them open, and walked by the other rooms with their dying people.

He stopped outside of his father's room.

There he stood. Wind sighed somewhere. He licked his lips,

conscious of the sudden stillness of his thoughts. He reached for the door handle after an age, turned it, and walked inside.

He closed the door behind him, leaned against it, and glanced about. A red water pitcher sat the bedside table, beads cascading down its surface. A faucet gleamed under closed cabinets. Boxes of medical supplies rested a gray counter.

Jason looked everywhere but where he knew he needed to look.

Darius rasped.

Jason looked at his father.

He seemed to meld with the white sheets, not a man but a papier-mâché sculpture of a man, skin yellow, bones long, chest sunken. He wheezed. Wind cut against the window, as if mirroring the dying man's breath.

The first step was like walking through water. The boy moved in a daze, caught between the present and the past, remembering when his steps led him to the bed where his mother had lain withered, wide eyed, and dying. His father had been beside him then. Now he was alone.

He reached the bed and looked into his father's face. His cheekbones threatened to tear through skin. Veins throbbed blue and ugly in his arms.

Darius opened his eyes. The brilliant green rings dwindled, as if draining from life into death. They quivered in a flood of emotion. He reached out his hand and stroked Jason's cheek. His fingers were dry and frail and spoke of endings. Jason looked into his father's eyes. The boy's breath caught in his chest.

"Dad," he said.

"It's okay."

Jason shook his head.

"No it's not. You can't go."

Darius' lips quivered. He lifted shaking hands and held Jason's face, doing everything to feel his son, to take him in, to love him.

"Please," Jason said.

"I'm sorry, Papi."

"You're too young, it ain't fair."

Darius smiled sadly, knowing enough about the world to under-stand that the scales of right and wrong were weighed by a judge who transcended human notions of fairness.

"It's okay, Jase."

"No it isn't!"

"Listen: You're gonna be okay—"

"It ain't about me!"

"This time it is. My friends are gonna take care of you. They're gonna help you."

"I don't know what I'm doing. I can't control it."

"You can."

"No."

"Yes. You have to. For—for all of us."

Jason shook his head. Darius swallowed, grimaced, and beckoned him closer. Jason climbed onto the bed and slid beside his father. Darius turned to face him, a monumental task. Jason protested, but Darius pushed on and threw his arm over his son. They rested that way in the passing dark. Darius's heart thumped-paused-thumped-paused, beating against Jason's face. Jason willed it to fight, imploring whatever power that was within him to bring his father back to health.

"Uncle Abe can save you," he said. "He can make you like him."

Darius gave a curt shake of his head.

"He already tried. It won't work, Papi. Jason, please—"

"No." Jason's voice broke.

Darius smiled.

"This is one thing you can't control."

Jason sniffed.

"I'm afraid. Dad, they think I can do magic."

"You can."

"No. It's not magic. It's not."

Darius hesitated, something he could not say screaming in his mind. He swallowed, grimaced, and forced a smile.

"It is magic," he said. "It don't seem like it, but it is. When it gets scary, you just have to tell yourself that it's not real, just like always."

The room chilled. Jason gripped his father close. Darius held him and looked up at the ceiling. Black spots bloomed there, growing like abscesses, virulent darkness refuting the lie he had just told his son.

"I don't know," Jason said. "It feels wrong."

"It's okay. You're strong. You'll get to control it. And when—ah, fuck—" He grimaced. "When...when you're ready, you'll be able to use it to save everyone. You'll see. The vampires are the bad guys, and you're the good guy, and you're gonna be with other good guys now. One day you're gonna save everyone from the monsters. You'll make things right. You just have to remember—it's magic. That's all."

Jason shook his head. He buried his face deeper into his father's chest.

"Let's just go home."

"Jason..."

"I'm scared."

"That's okay."

"No. No, you don't understand—"

Darius almost laughed.

"I do," he replied. "I really do."

"You're not supposed to die. You're supposed to be happy, with me."

"I am happy with you. You remember that. You made me and your mother so happy. You are the best thing to us. And you're gonna be okay. I promise."

"Maybe Uncle Abe can—can take my power and give it to you. So you can live, so you can be happy, I don't care. I can die instead, please—"

Darius embraced him, holding tight.

"It's okay, Papi."

"No."

"I'm sorry. I'm so sorry this had to happen to you."

"I love you," Jason said. Those words flew from the boy's lips like a commandment dispelling any guilt his father carried.

Darius gripped his son with his remaining strength.

"I love you, Jason."

"I love you." Jason held with everything he had. "I love you."

They lay that way in the failing dark, the boy pleading with his father to stay, stay, ever to stay. Soon his voice trailed. The sky softened with the first infusion of gray morning light. Darius hummed "Hey, Jude" to his son, his voice cracked and off key. His eyes danced about and he looked through the window. Fog beat against the glass, and something hovered beyond for just a moment, a distorted shape lilting between dead trees. Darius blinked, and it was gone.

Jason struggled to keep his eyes open. He clutched his father, listening to his voice, and that way he fell asleep.

Darius stopped humming. He listened to Jason's breathing, the sweetest sound. He smiled and pressed his nose and lips into the boy's hair. The 7 Train clattered in the distance. Car headlights stretched over the window, refracting distorted shadows through the last of the morning fog. The coming dawn was silence beneath, a hush promising more snow.

Darius looked up from his son's hair and gazed at the black spots spreading across the ceiling. They gaped, deep maws revealing eldritch darkness.

He started into that darkness and knew what awaited him.

He breathed.

His heart slowed.

He breathed.

A black tunnel enclosed his vision.

Staccato breaths limped over his chapped lips.

The room darkened. Whispers spoke in reverence, wordless, voiceless, rising. Cold seeped under Darius' skin. The bed gave the slightest tremor.

Darius breathed in shorter bursts. The ceiling opened into a black portal, an undulating mass of shadows calling to him.

He held on, pain a distant shout, clutching his son to feel what was most important. Doing so, he stared out the window to see all that remained to him of the world.

The first fat flakes of snow spiraled beyond the glass. Darius smiled and watched the snow fall. His breath rattled as he exhaled.

He inhaled and the air tasted of cool water. Vision narrowed until all that remained was snow shimmering in the deep. The last of his being felt his son against him and watched the shimmering flakes dance through the black.

These things faded with all that was Darius Bardales, and he disappeared again and for the final time into death.

The room was still. Darkness was gone from the ceiling, leaving the crenelated tiles awash in pale light. But a single drop of black liquid fell on Jason's forehead, spilling out of the naked air. The pores of the boy's skin opened and drank this darkness, and he stirred and shivered. Something sighed that was not the wind. The sheet under him jerked once, twice, freed itself, and covered him as he slept beside his dead father.

And the snow fell.

ACT II

THE BOY OUTSIDE

1

They stood outside of the waiting room, each processing all that had transpired within the last few hours. Goodbyes had been spoken to Darius, hollow and hurried, the words feeble ambassadors for the emotions they felt. Their astonishment was great, their hurt, greater. But it was Jason who held them rapt, the boy focusing grief and bewilderment into muted awe.

Alexander stretched, then cracked open the door of the waiting room to look in on his children. Eleanor was curled in the chair, Ringo cradled in her sleeping arms. Ian sat rigid, eyes drooping, head jerking. Alexander's love for them spread in waves, deep warmth distilling confusion into clarity. They were safe. Nothing else mattered. But when he looked away, exhaustion swarmed, assaulting him with a volley of disjointed memories. Most vivid and cruel among them were the screams of the child who had gouged out his own eyes. Pablo. That was his name.

Alexander grimaced and rubbed his eyes.

Across from him, Percy leaned against the wall, glaring at Abebe. Doubt tainted his every thought, forcing him to search for something they had missed, some evidence of doom.

Abebe stared back, unflinching, patience obscuring all other emotion.

"That's it then?" Percy said.

Abebe spread his hands.

"You know everything that I know."

"Hate to state the obvious," Rosie said, desperate for information that would make sense of all that had occurred. A dizzying array of possibilities flooded her, each stemming from the boy. She crossed her arms and nodded at Abebe. "But that don't make a lick of sense. You being you, and all."

Abebe adjusted the cuffs of his shirt and smoothed out nonexistent wrinkles, taking a moment to consider their position and how best to make them understand his own.

"When Darius found me, I thought it some trick," he said. "I nearly killed him where he stood. But then he allowed me to possess him." He went silent, remembering. "That shattered any doubts I had. I experienced memories through him that only the real Darius could know. Believe me, Ms. St. John. I was as shocked as you are now."

All mischief and vagaries left him, unveiling a man who was tired, who had seen more than he had ever cared to see. And yet there was still an air of childish curiosity about him, as if he were aware that a great change was coming. He licked his lips, his eyes distant.

"I have lived for a very long time. I've known evil and goodness. I have witnessed–and been the cause of–many horrors. And every now and again, I have seen a miracle. The world is a strange place, both mundane and extraordinary. Yet never had I seen anyone return from the dead.

"I couldn't understand it. I still don't. What's more...when I take absolute possession of someone, there is nothing they can keep from me. A fully possessed person reveals all of their dimensions. They are open. But there was something in Darius that I could not see, some new part of him that pushed me away. It was stronger than anything I've encountered in anyone else. It should come as no surprise to you that Jason carries the same...obscurity. You can imagine my frustration.

"To make matters worse, Darius was already dying when he came to me. So, of course, I wanted to make him like us." He indicated himself and Percy. "I could not, and he did not want me to. My frustration turned to anger. Why had he waited so long to find me? Why had he not reached out to any of you? He claimed he was keeping us safe. I suppose there's some sense to that reasoning. If my brother or his brood discovered he was alive again, and that we were sheltering him, well, I believe there would be much disagreement on the issue. And of course, there's Jason."

The name carried the full weight of the mystery. They conjured the boy in their thoughts, along with all he was promised to do, and it was as if they were caught upon some strange current carrying them to an unexplored continent.

Abebe went on.

"Darius told me what Jason is–or will be—capable of doing. Despite my astonishment—or perhaps because of it—I believed him. How do you contradict a dead man? The truth is I want to believe him. If Jason can kill my brother and his children, then everything else is an afterthought."

"Why are you so anxious to see Manny dead?" Alexander said.

Abebe smiled. Blood vessels flared over his eyes, livid branches of crimson.

"My brother," he replied. "If he dies, then there will be no one who can oppose me. That is my motivation, yes, Magician? That I wish to use the boy for my own ends. Well, you're correct. But not for the reasons you think.

"Manny and I—we come from a cruel age. Barbarous. After we were reborn," he chuckled, his voice cold, "I realized that I had the power to shape the world however I saw fit. You may find this hard to believe, but I wanted peace. I had seen enough of what savages are capable of. Tell me, have any of you ever heard the screams of people being buried alive? I have. Thousands of years on and I can still hear them."

He squinted, looking inward through time.

"I wanted to do away with savagery. I thought I could wield my power to create a great global civilization, one that banished petty tyrants and their need to be worshipped. I wanted to see humanity rise beyond tribalism. But Manny put a stop to all of that. He doesn't wish for the world to change for the better. He wants humanity to tear itself apart. That way, he and his children can kill without question—an imperfect world for perfect monsters.

"You see now, yes? I could not stop him, and I still cannot. For all my power, I am nothing compared to him. He wanted a family that would rule from the shadows, and I had no choice but to help him build it. Yield or suffer. Werewolves, demons, they are my creations, my gifts to him. I have exacted cruelties upon his so-called enemies. I have counseled him, listened to him, absolved him...I have done all the things that any good brother should do. But I have always hated him."

He went quiet for a moment, his dark eyes working.

"I was only able to kill Darius because he allowed me to. But I cannot force possession against a vampire. I am shackled against them. That is my brother's will, and because of that they are unstoppable. I am not ignoring my share of the blame in all of this. Manny and I left our home and wrought cancer upon the world. That is why I must see him undone. Otherwise...no one is free so long as vampires exists."

They looked away from him. Terror spoke in their shared silence, the weight of years living in constant fear stamped on their faces. Each day free from vampires was borrowed time, a debt that would one day demand repayment. They all knew this.

"Now we have reason to hope," Abebe said. "Darius transcended death itself, and he claims Jason can kill Manny. What would you wager that he was telling the truth? I am willing to wager much. Everything."

Rosie tapped her elbow in thought, her mind working, puzzling together the morning's events and all that Abebe had said. Memories came to call, a lifetime of fighting an enemy that could not be beaten, of helping people who had no one else to turn to, of horrors, magic, and friends they had lost. She thought of Jason, and a thousand avenues opened, each brimming with possibilities both wonderful and nightmarish. He was the unknown, what could not yet be reconciled.

Yet two thoughts repeated, making her certain that Abebe Ngombe, the man they had reviled for so long, could be trusted.

If Jason could kill Manny Ngombe, what would stop him from killing Abebe?

And didn't that make Jason dangerous to him?

But here he was, asking them to care for the boy.

"I believe you," she said. "I'm even willing to say that I trust you. You could've killed us all tonight. That's why you came to us the way you did, right? To show us that you could've destroyed the Gardens whenever the hell you wanted. You've known all along where we were, but you did nothing about it. Shoot, it seems like you've been watching our backs. Well. What I'm trying to say is you're right. If what Darius told us holds water, then that boy is the key to all this. We have to give him a home, protect him. Ain't no other way. But hell if there ain't a lot of questions, and no answers I can see. I don't like that."

Alexander threw up his hands.

"Exactly," he said. "Darius came back from the dead. Okay, so, how? What did he mean about everything needing to be fixed? What are we dealing with in regards to his son? Is he a magician? Is he— what? Can we just bring the boy to Manny and let him have at it?"

Abebe adjusted his watch and wiped the lens with his thumb. The silver hands ticked over black.

"I do not know," he replied. "I doubt he is ready. Jason needs time to understand himself and gain control of whatever power he possesses. He needs guidance. That's what we can give him. That's what Darius wanted." He focused on Rosie and Percy. "I can think of no better foster parents than the two of you."

Percy scoffed.

"That simple, yeah?"

"Baby, we ain't got a choice," Rosie replied.

Abebe nodded.

"She's right. You don't."

"And what are we going to tell everyone?" Percy said. "I could smell Darius on the boy. They don't look exactly alike, but the resemblance is clear. Do you think no one else in the Gardens will notice?"

"You remember Darius' father, yes?" Abebe replied. "He was popular with women. It is not inconceivable to think that Darius had half-brothers or sisters, and that they too had children. Jason can be a relation. Your people may be astounded. They may expect certain things from the nephew of Darius Bardales. But they won't have to grapple with the truth. No one will question him living with the two of you. It will be expected. I would have recommended you to raise him, Magician, but your hands are already full."

Alexander shrugged, his children visible through the window behind him.

They fell silent. Abebe sensed grief rising through the deluge of their confused thoughts, as if a damp curtain weighed their shoulders. He smiled a sad smile.

"You are all forgetting the most important thing," he said. "What is at the heart of the matter." He caught each of their eyes in turn, picked lint from his sleeves, and shrugged. "It would appear that death is not the end."

Percy snatched off his cap and looked away. Alexander withdrew, his eyes moving over the floor, trying to unsee the dead boy in a basement. Rosie rubbed her chin and ticked a finger against her elbow.

"What is it then?" she replied.

Abebe opened his mouth, hesitated, and fell silent.

They stood outside of the waiting room, together with the unknown.

2

The red pitcher was overturned, its white cap spilled onto the floor. Clouded water streamed from the faucet. Medical supply boxes lay open over the countertop, gauze, bandages, and syringes strewn about.

Jason saw none of these things. He sat on the edge of the bed, and the corpse lay behind him. He had awoken nuzzled to a thing that was no longer his father, an avatar of absence in human form. He had not screamed or cried out. To do so would acknowledge the loss of both of his parents, and that admission would summon a tempest of pain, leaving him shattered.

Better to be numb.

He dangled his legs and gazed at nothing. His forehead tingled. He rubbed it and glanced at the ceiling. The last embers of dreams brought images of black rain falling through a forest of dead trees. The ceiling was white, stainless.

Dawn spilled gray through the window. Wind moaned.

Jason slid off the bed. The culmination of every child's nightmare lay behind him, and ahead of him the hallway shone in a haze. His feet moved without feeling and carried him out of the room.

He felt as if he floated down the hall, through the double doors, and towards the nurse's station. They both watched him, the blonde frowning, the Filipina rising with concern.

He spoke to them from a daze, not stopping, not looking at them.

"There's a dead guy in the room."

The Filipina nurse came around the station and stared after him, breathless, her hands clutched to her chest, as if that was enough to ameliorate her broken heart. She turned around and hurried through the double doors. The blonde nurse bowed and rubbed her temples.

Jason walked on, following the hallway around the corner, moving without thought. The fluorescent lights flickered as he passed, draping him in trembling shadows. He paid them no heed. Scratching hissed behind a closed door on the left. He did not hear. A door on his right slowly opened, revealing darkness and no daylight, and sobbing emanated from within. He did not look. Low music droned somewhere, a dirge fueled by melancholy harmonies crackling as if through cheap speakers, but for all he knew the strange music could have been the workings of his own mind.

He heard and felt nothing. The hallway went by as if it were of another world.

The others sat in the waiting room. Ian slept sitting up. Eleanor started from her dream, smacked her lips together, and frowned at the daylight. She forced her eyes open, stood, and walked around, shaking her head and slapping her cheeks.

Alexander watched her with a bemused smile. She continued to pace in circles, landing one foot before the other, walking an imaginary tightrope.

"You can keep sleeping, baby," Alexander said.

"Uh-uh. Shouldn't have fallen asleep. Just in case."

"In case of what?"

She shrugged.

"Monsters and stuff. Somebody's gotta protect us."

Alexander made to respond, then froze. He looked over her shoulder. Eleanor followed his gaze.

Jason stood there, the door closing behind him. He hadn't made a sound.

Ian's eyes snapped open, locking onto Jason.

Eleanor took a tentative step towards the boy. Jason looked at her, then at the floor.

"Aw shit," Eleanor said, knowing what the look on his face meant.

Jason took a shuddering breath, as Abebe went to him. Alexander looked away, the weight of the boy's sorrow dredging his own sense of loss. Rosie and Percy came together, each laying their hands on one another as if to ward away the specter of death. They had lost their friend once before, but this second loss was amplified on Jason's face, and for each of them it was somehow worse this time around.

Abebe knelt before Jason.

"I cannot imagine how you feel right now—" he said.

"I wanna go," Jason replied.

"Of course. I just need to speak to the doctor. Just for a moment. Okay?"

Jason didn't reply. Abebe stroked his cheek, rose, and left the room.

The others remained, each casting furtive glances, unsure of what was to come. Jason walked by them and sat the chair beside his luggage.

Rosie took a deep breath, then sat next to him. A momentary chill dappled her skin. She crossed her arms and legs and joined him in staring at nothing. They sat that way for a time. Then she looked over at him and saw the darkness under his eyes, days of little sleep etching lines into his young face.

"Reckon you're tired," she said.

Jason nodded.

"If you like, we got room at our place. You can stay there. Long as you like."

Percy watched them, a faraway look in his eyes.

"I'm sure you're used to better," Rosie said. "But it's got a bed, warm blankets—"

"Bed," Jason replied, a hint of a smile on his face. He looked around the waiting room and felt as if there were no world beyond its walls. A bed he could fall into was part of normal life, a thing taken for granted, evidence of a world beyond the hospital. Right now a bed was all he wanted. "Thanks, Ms. St. John."

"Rosie. Call me Rosie."

"Okay."

Eleanor took a furtive step, puffed her cheeks, and approached Jason.

"Uh," she said, "there's a lot of real cool stuff to see back home. I guess your home now? I mean…it's really cool, and I can show you, if you want."

Jason looked up at her. He wiped his nose with the back of his hand.

"Magic stuff?"

"Oh, a shitload."

"Cool."

He looked away and gazed at his boots. Eleanor sat the other side of him and laid an uncertain hand on his shoulder. He did not protest. A memory of sunshine and the sigh of ocean waves crept from memory, of his mother's laughter and his father's—

He launched out of the chair, knelt, and opened his backpack, not looking for anything, occupying his hands, his mind, burying his parents beneath the act of searching.

Alexander and Percy stood by the door like sentinels unsure of who or what they were guarding. Ian stared at Jason, singularly focused, unblinking. Rosie watched Jason's hands and knew all too well the cause of their desperate fretting. Eleanor fidgeted with her own hands.

See them: This cortege of outsiders, harbingers of magic and darkness, bound by the mystery of the boy, his retinue unanswered questions, his task monstrous and profound.

No one spoke for a long time.

JASON DID NOT HEAR when Abebe spoke of his father's burial being cared for. He made no acknowledgement for better or ill when Abebe promised to rest his father in the same plot as his mother in Calvary

Cemetery. A dull drone beat in the boy's ears, obscuring Abebe's promises that he would not have to be at the burial, would not have to see the grave until he was ready.

Abebe searched the boy's eyes, then sighed and looked away.

"The arrangements will be handled," he said to the others. "I'll see to them. Now is the time to say your...well, whatever you wish. Visiting his grave would not be wise for any of you."

No one moved. Their shared grief for Darius was an empty well, and to see his corpse would cause it to refill and overflow.

"Eh, if there's nothing else," Alexander said, "we should bring Jason home."

Jason walked with them through the hallway, unsure of where he was or how he got there. The wheels of his suitcase rattled and rolled, and his bag was a dull weight around his shoulders. He glanced to his right and saw Eleanor beside her father. Her hands were empty. He stopped. The others walked on a few paces, and then also stopped.

"Your bear," Jason said to Eleanor.

She glanced down at her hands. Realization came. She made to run back to the waiting room.

"I'll get it," Jason said. He turned and ran off without another word. The others watched. Eleanor went to follow, but Alexander grabbed her gently by the arm.

Jason entered the waiting room and stood alone in the hum of fluorescent lights. All was stillness, a place without strangers. He breathed deep and found a moment's respite in the solitude, release from curious glances, sorrowful silence, and unspoken questions.

But a greater mystery resounded through him.

"What am I?" he said, the words unbidden. He frowned as if someone else had asked the question. The faces of his father's friends amplified what he had always wondered about himself: how had he come to be? He had known something was different before his father had spoken of his past. The otherness, the strangeness, the sensation that he was a misplaced cog in the great machine of the world...

The lights flickered, snapping him from reverie. The comfort of isolation faded into cold air and bright light. He looked left, spied

Ringo, snatched the bear up, and enjoyed a surge of comfort from the softness of the stuffed animal.

He turned to go.

The hallway was black beyond the slender window in the door. He froze, seized by familiar dread, Ringo clutched to his chest. He closed his eyes and shook his head.

A series of groans scraped the floor behind him. He turned around, not wanting to. Every chair in the room was grouped together like rows of soldiers facing him at attention.

Jason backed away

The door whined open behind him. He turned and found obsidian darkness where the hallway should have been. Something shimmered there, a pale shape without definition, swaying this way and that. Jason looked away, holding Ringo.

The chairs screeched against the linoleum, a sudden barrage of banshee screams, and when he looked he found them encircling him.

"Not real," he said, closing his eyes, shaking his head violently. "Nope, nope, not real, not real, nope, not—"

Vertigo sent him careening, spinning the darkness behind his closed eyes as if he were falling towards a great chasm. He reached out, desperate to grab hold of anything, denying his senses and clinging to the knowledge that these strange happenings were the illusions of his heartbroken mind.

Laughter ripped him back to the world, and he opened his eyes to find himself face down on the floor. Two nurses walked past the room, both giggling over their smartphones. He looked around. The chairs were by the walls once more. He hurried out, and when he was a few steps into the hallway a great crashing resounded behind him. The nurses stopped and turned around. He kept going, rounding the corner, hurrying to the others.

He rejoined them, handed Ringo to Eleanor, grabbed his suitcase, and walked off without a word.

"Thanks," Eleanor said, but he did not stop or turn around. She stared after him, confused. Alexander squinted beside her, exchanging glances with the others, sending a questioning look towards Abebe. The demon watched Jason, his thoughts his own.

Percy frowned. The crash from the room had reached his ears.

"Did you hear that?" he said to Rosie.

"Yeah," she replied.

"I think he just threw some chairs against the floor."

"Can you blame him?"

"Suppose not."

They followed after the boy.

They stepped beyond the automatic glass doors and into the cold. Dawn painted the world gray-blue. Wind howled over the streets, whipping diagonal sheets of snow across the sidewalks.

Abebe led them towards a three-story parking garage adjacent to the hospital. The 74th Street Train Station loomed a few blocks ahead, the terminal green metal with large glass windows shivering under the clatter of a passing train.

Jason was silent. Eleanor walked beside him, searching for something to say. She looked down at Ringo, bit her lip, and offered him the teddy bear. Jason blinked at her, unsure of what was happening.

"Want him for awhile?" she said.

"I got him back for you."

"He told me he wants to hang out with you today."

Jason frowned at the bear.

"I didn't hear him say that."

Eleanor frowned back, noting the sarcasm. She threw Ringo up in the air. Jason caught the bear and stared at Eleanor as though she were crazy.

"Hey lookie," she said, "you saved his life. Now you have to protect him for at least a day." She pointed at him. "But you better give him back after."

Jason smiled.

"You're the boss."

"Hey, alright. I'm totally the boss." She pointed at Ringo. "Carful, though. He'll eat you if you're not nice to him."

"I thought bears only ate honey?"

"Oh, they eat people too, especially if they're dipped in honey. That's their favorite."

Jason looked at the bear in his arms.

"Please don't eat me, Mr. Ringo."

Eleanor leaned close to Ringo, nodded conspiratorially, and looked at Jason with deep seriousness.

"Doesn't look good," she said.

Ian watched them both, walking behind them, the corners of his mouth turned up into strange little smile.

Abebe walked up three concrete steps leading to a black gate. He opened it and entered the parking garage. The others followed at some distance.

Orange lamplight glowed over the diagonal line of cars rising with the sloping ramp, molding them into blurred shapes beneath the diffuse light of the garage. The shadows of pillars spilled over the ground and ceiling. The parking attendant's booth was far to the right, standing before the exit at 41st Avenue. Snow veiled the red and white boom gate.

Abebe led them up the ramp to a white van parked on the second level. Across from them were two cars—a jeep on the left, dark green, large tires streaked with dried mud, and a beige sedan on the right, a stick figure family—mom, dad, daughter, and cat—smiling from its bumper.

Jason stopped and stared at the stick figure family, transfixed, something in their simple lines calling to him.

Abebe opened the driver's side door of the van. He brought the sun visor down and caught the keys waiting there. They jingled as he threw them to Alexander. The magician caught them, flourished his fingers, and they were gone. He almost blushed. The sleight of hand was a near-habit.

"This vehicle is safe," Abebe said. "Do with it as you wish."

They kept their distance, as if expecting the van to morph into some hungry monster. Mistrust still lingered, an instinctive hesitation to all things connected with Abebe Ngombe. Percy grimaced, a part of him knowing they were being overly cautious, another part of him thinking they were not being cautious enough. He went to the van and peered inside the windows, looking over the leather seats and the spaces behind them. The van was empty. He sniffed. The layered scents of fresh plastics and rich leather coursed into his nostrils.

"Would you like to peer under the hood?" Abebe said, a sardonic smile on his face. "I've been known to hide imps within engine blocks."

Annoyance dripped from Percy's gaze. He turned to the others.

"It's safe," he said.

The sedan's horn screamed behind them, echoing in rabid tones throughout the garage.

Alexander threw his arms over Eleanor and Ian, igniting spirals of metal shards over his palms. Percy stepped towards the car, growling from deep, fists clenched. Rosie slid a pearl-gripped 9mm pistol from a holster concealed in her coat. Tendrils of blue light seeped between her fingers, a spell emanating from deep within her, soothing her nerves and steadying her hand so there would be no hesitation or misfires.

Jason stood entranced. The world about him blurred, leaving the sedan in stark relief, as if it were a sacred relic stumbled upon in a dream. Ripples of cold broke over his skin, and deep silence engulfed him, giving way to droning that bled from some unknown place. Darkness inside the car swelled with the droning, and out of that darkness the boy beheld something emerging, some formless thing coming together to reveal a truth he could not stand to face. Sweat soaked through his undershirt, his mouth dried, and he shook his head.

"Not real," he said.

The car horn blared, as if in defiance.

A deep well of dread erupted within the boy, drowning his thoughts. He clutched Ringo and stepped backwards, wanting nothing more than to leave, go to bed, and forget everything. The droning shattered into hundreds of voices whispering with broken tongues. He shook his head against them, aware that the others did not hear them, aware that his father had told him time and again that these and other oddities were the internal manifestations of a power he did not yet understand. They would vanish. They had done so before.

The car horn screamed again. In its cacophonous bleat, the boy felt something alien but familiar, an otherness that ever scratched at him, rising out of unconsciousness, cold, certain, and terrible. It was part of him. And yet it was as if this great emptiness seeped into him from nowhere, crying out for his attention through fits of chaos. He groaned through clenched teeth and pursed lips, pushing against that awareness as he always had, as his father had taught him, hoping to hold out until the day when he could take control, when the otherness would be felt no more.

"Not real," he said, shaking his head for emphasis. The discordant voices seethed, and then faded.

The others did not notice him. The adults strode toward the car, seeing only stillness beyond the windshield. Abebe motioned them back. He focused on the sedan. The stick figure family smiled.

"Eleanor, Jason, would you please close your eyes and cover your ears," he said. Eleanor looked to Jason and nearly cried out when she saw the wide eyed terror on his face. Abebe did not turn back to them, but when he spoke again his voice hissed from dozens of places, as if a swarm of locusts buzzed upon the air. "Do as I say."

They both did so, Jason hurrying, Eleanor uncertain as she stepped away from her father.

Alexander realized what was about to happen a moment too late. The roiling metal over his palms withered to smoke, and he made to cover Ian's eyes. But his son batted his hand away and stepped towards the elder demon, drawn to a silent storm building around him.

Alexander grabbed Ian's arm, pulled him back, and that was when the air began to drip blood.

Thick droplets spilled across the ramp, splattering on concrete and misting the air scarlet. Wails pierced the stillness. A harem of shadows peeled themselves from the pillars, stepped out of the dark corners, and merged with that bloody haze. They writhed as they moved, wretched things contorted into monstrous shapes, a pack of abominations with burning red eyes (many with more than two), demented faces, and anatomies that were blasphemous to creation.

They vanished into thin air and reappeared over the sedan like flies swarming carrion.

Ian watched with rapt attention, his mouth hanging open, his own shadow by his knees sighing as if astonished.

The adults looked on with grim resolve, loathing what they saw, but readying themselves for whatever the shadows revealed.

Dozens of rats sprinted from beneath cars, their shrill screams adding to the din as they raced out of the garage. Some of them collapsed into twitching masses of flesh and fur, foam spilling through their clenched teeth.

Jason opened his eyes. He gave a start, horrorstruck at the writhing mass of darkness. His hands fell from his ears, and their screams unveiled savage imaginings in his mind, scenes of depravity and violence he had never thought of. He looked at Abebe and saw not Uncle Abe, but a creature with caustic red eyes shrouded by a retinue of shadows that reached with clawed hands and screamed with cruel mouths. Jason trembled, the dread of his own struggle falling away as shock took hold. He had heard the stories. But to see such power was something else entirely. He looked right, saw Eleanor near, and stepped in front of her so she would not see if she looked. But for him it was too late. He could no longer look away.

Eleanor did not open her eyes. She hummed loudly to herself, snatching this melody or that, remembering her training with her brother enough to know that she did not want to see nor hear what was happening. Cold raced through her, and bits of the demon's deluge filtered in, causing nausea to tiptoe at the edges of feeling. The music in her mind swelled as she focused on it, shining enough for her to almost forget the surrounding dark.

The shadows bled in and out of the interior of the sedan, the trunk, and under the hood. They touched, scratched, and tasted, their senses filtering into Abebe's mind, exposing the myriad traces of day to day life that went on in the vehicle. The sultry aroma of coffee merged with the metallic sweetness of blood–a nurse's car. The oils from tiny faded handprints ingrained into the rear windows, ink staining the passenger seat, and cat hairs scattered within the recesses of the back seat. A portrait of a family, fed to the great demon by his imps.

The shadows shrieked, and then they swarmed the nearby jeep, some moving like insects, others like marauding chimps. Abebe sifted through their perceptions, searching for spells, for another demon's shadow, for any sign of an unwanted watcher. He found nothing. The shadows moved from the jeep to the van in a violent surge that nearly made the others flee. They held their ground, but each of them grunted or cried out as the eldritch tide passed. The shadows inspected the van, satisfied their master, vanished, and then reappeared at both ends of the ramp, rampaging.

They blanketed the garage, hiding in dark places on every level, hanging from the ceiling, crawling over pillars, watching, listening.

They beheld the parking attendant, an Egyptian man with a luxurious beard watching comedy videos about two trash talking robots on his phone. Pictures of a new car engine lay on his desk, and handmade robotic actions figures stood guard around the windowsill. Posted on the exterior of the window was a memorial card to a maintenance worker who had died a month before, an older man with a crooked grin and white hair.

The attendant shivered, racked by a sudden jolt of fear. He frowned at the darkness beyond the window and raised the volume on his phone to blot shrill tittering just on the edge of hearing. Pipes, he told himself, or the wind. The trash talking robots let loose a string of profanity, and the attendant laughed. But his eyes kept darting towards the dimness, and he was grateful that full daylight was nearly here.

The shadows spied a family wheeling their grandmother to a car, she in mid-tirade over her perceived mistreatment by them, her children and grandchildren rolling their eyes or frowning. All of them were seized by dread that they did not want to acknowledge, and even the old woman fell silent. The youngest granddaughter stopped, looked at a pillar, and would swear for the rest of her days that she had seen some strange creature dip behind it. She snapped a photo with her phone, looked, and frowned. There was nothing remarkable in the image, and yet the darkness on the screen seemed swollen, about to burst. She hurried back to her family. Her grandmother snapped back into nagging, but the girl did not mind anymore. Her grandmother's whining voice was a comfort against whatever had passed.

The orderlies, who had been smoking cigarettes before the main entrance earlier on, were now walking hand in hand to their car on 41st Avenue, their shift over. Snow roiled about them, casting their faces into silhouettes. They both stopped, one with a shaved head and green bubble jacket, the other with a well kept flat top and blue pea coat, and looked about the streets. All was quiet. The one in the green bubble jacket shivered, and his boyfriend pulled him close, suddenly all too aware of how alone they were, of how deep the surrounding snow. Without a word they both hurried to their car, their gazes clinging to the pale light spreading morning over the streets.

The shadows went beyond.

For blocks around, people slept, awoke, drank coffee, readied themselves for work, argued, had sex, or stared out of windows in bleary hazes. They walked the streets, got into their cars, and clamored onto trains. A group of friends ate bagels over cards, their poker game still going. A mother threw cold water onto her daughter's face to wake her up. An older brother beat his younger brother over a television show they streamed. A family shared a happy breakfast at a Colombian bakery.

These things and more, so much more, surged into Abebe Ngombe's senses, his horde of imps sampling emotions, feeding him sights and sounds.

There were no threats, no others like him.

A silent command whispered across the ranks of shadows. They dissolved into darkness wherever they were, brief streaks carried on the wind like ash. Blood faded from the air, leaving the muted orange lamp-glow of the garage diffuse in the pale morning light.

Abebe frowned at the sedan.

Eleanor opened one eye, tiptoed to look from between Jason and her father, and saw everything was clear. She pulled her hands away from her ears.

Abebe said nothing, watching.

"Jason," he said. "Please come here."

Jason did so, all too aware of the others watching him. He stood beside Abebe, his eyes darting from the car to the demon and back again. Abebe once more looked himself, his face pensive and kindly. But the thing he had become was burned into Jason's mind. He forced himself to step closer, clinging to the memory of man who had been so kind to him, the only one left who knew his father the way he had.

Jason made to speak when, one by one, the sedan's doors flew open and closed again, clattering open and shut, creating a rhythmic pattern that echoed in the garage. He took a step back, but Abebe stopped him with a gentle hand. Jason shook his head, staring at the sedan, fear bubbling to anger.

"Stop!" he said.

The last of the doors slammed shut. All fell still.

Jason panted, his eyes darting left to right, his hands trembling.

"I didn't—" he said. "I—I didn't know I was doing that, I didn't mean to—"

"It's fine," Abebe replied. "I guessed it was you, but I wanted to be certain. Of course you did not do that on purpose. " He turned to the others. "This is nothing you all haven't seen before, yes?"

They were silent, each one considering what the sudden outburst of Jason's unchecked power meant. Rosie holstered her gun, but only after a moment's consideration. Alexander nodded, but his eyes were distant, unsure. Percy remained standing before them, as if to shield a waiting blow.

Eleanor frowned at all of them.

"Yeah," she said, thinking nothing of the strange behavior of the car. "I told him shit like that happens all the time. It's not a big deal for magic—for people like us."

Abebe smiled at her.

"You see, Jason," he said.

The boy nodded, but he stared at the ground, cheeks convulsing, eyes blinking in rapid succession, Ringo squeezed between his hands. A blank space filled his memory from just moments before, and he knew in that time he had nearly reached some truth about himself. He shivered. He did not want to remember.

Alexander cleared his throat, nodding his head from side to side.

"It, eh, seems we have a lot to teach you, Jason," he said. "Like Eleanor said, it's no problem."

"It's magic, hon," Rosie said. "It can run wild if you don't have any control over it. Don't feel bad. You ain't been trained."

Jason scratched his head. Another voice took hold of his thoughts, one that he welcomed, that transformed fear into a skewed and silly approximation of the world.

"Do I need magic diapers or something?" he said.

Rosie furrowed her brow, unsure of how to respond. Eleanor snorted and giggled.

Ian watched, his dark eyes revealing nothing, that strange smile still on his face. His shadow growled at his side, and the growl was almost like a purr.

Alexander frowned at him, wishing he knew what was going on in his son's mind.

Percy rocked on his heels, as if arguing with himself. He grunted and went to the sedan, once more inspecting. The stench of heated metal assaulted his senses, mingled with everyday smells and the bitter and acrid aura left behind by his father's imps. But beyond these things, he found nothing out of the ordinary.

A look of mild hurt crossed Abebe's face, his son's distrust of him grating. He said nothing and led Jason to the others, not waiting for Percy to finish his inspection. He gently nudged Jason ahead, and the boy stood beside Rosie. He stared up at Abebe, a ripple of fear still fresh in his eyes

Abebe read that fear as shock at witnessing his power.

"I know," he said. "Terrible."

Jason shrugged, clinging to the memory of Abebe's shadows to blot out the deeper and unknown thing bubbling beneath the surface. He remembered the scurrying rats and spied some of the dead ones.

"You could be a really good exterminator," he said.

Abebe smiled. Percy rejoined them, and Abebe looked at him. Between them were their long years together, cementing a deep love that was tarnished by distance and doubt. Percy looked away, unsure of what he felt. Abebe sighed within, locking away the many things he wanted to say to his son, knowing they had to wait. He moved his gaze over each of the others, as if measuring them. His eyes fell on Ian last. Neither spoke, but both nodded, understanding clear between them: There would be time enough, time for Abebe to reveal many secrets, time for Ian to learn.

Alexander grimaced and held his son.

"I believe," Abebe said, returning his attention to Jason, "that you are now in good hands. Better than mine. So—"

"Please don't go," Jason replied, whispering, staring at Abebe with urgency.

Abebe shook his head.

"I must."

Jason looked away. But he nodded. A twitch rippled over his cheek.

"I'll see you again though, right?" he said.

"Do not worry," Abebe replied. He looked at Percy. "I'll always be near."

"We, eh," Alexander said. "We owe you a debt, and our—our apologies."

"I assure you, Magician, that's not necessary. You would've been foolish not to fear me."

He looked them over one last time. Then he smiled.

"Well…"

He turned and strolled down the ramp, hands clasped behind his back, his fingers moving in tune to music only he could hear. The shadows unpeeled from the pillars and dark corners, trailing him like a regiment or marching savages. They fell over him in a wave that darkened the ramp in total. Then pale morning light broke through the stygian blackness, swelling until the shadows faded into their natural places.

Abebe Ngombe was gone.

Jason stared into the empty space and understood that the life he thought he knew was darker and broader than he had ever imagined. He looked at his own hands, wondering what secrets were stitched into them that would make him one with a world where a man he called "uncle" could diminish into coils of shadow.

Alexander laid his hand on the boy's shoulder. Jason looked up at him in a daze.

"It's going to be okay," Alexander said.

Jason blinked. His gray eyes seemed to reflect no light. He let Alexander lead him to the van, where Ian waited by the door. He winked at Jason.

"Ian," Alexander said.

Ian gave an apologetic smile and stepped out of the way. Jason entered the van and slid into the window seat. He laid Ringo on his lap, buckled his seat belt, his hands automatons, and sat drained, weighed down by loss and questions.

Rosie went around the van, patting Ian's head as she did so, and got into the passenger's seat. Alexander entered the driver's seat and popped open the rear door. Percy placed Jason's bags inside, closed the door, and entered the van. He sat behind Jason. Their eyes met in the rearview, each a mystery to the other.

Eleanor paused before Ian.

"You okay?" she said.

Ian stared at her the way a crow stares, eyes dark and unreadable.

"Never better," he replied.

Eleanor frowned. A seed of dismay swelled, coupling her conversation with Rosie from earlier with Ian's strange demeanor.

"His dad just died," she said, keeping her voice to a whisper.

Ian's expression did not change.

"Again," he replied. "He died again."

She sighed, blew a strand of curls from her face, and got inside the van. Alexander watched through the side view mirror, frowning with concern. Ian followed after his sister. He slid the door closed and looked at Jason.

Jason looked back. Blood swirled over Ian's eyes, and then receded into the whites. Then Ian smiled. Shock coiled through Jason. He was still surprised even after what he had witnessed with Abebe. To see a display of demonic power from someone as young as Ian seemed wrong. But a part of him was thrilled, awestruck that the world held such creatures.

Alexander started the van, backed out, drove down the ramp, and stopped before the ticket booth. The parking attendant slid the window open and blew into his hands. The voices of the trash talking robots buzzed within the booth.

"Hey, hey," he said, an amiable smile on his face. "It's mad cold. Good to see some daylight."

"You have no idea," Alexander replied. He searched the dashboard for a garage ticket. Rosie opened the glove compartment and found both the ticket and a fifty dollar bill. They settled with the clerk, told him to keep the change, and drove on through the empty street.

Jason watched the sidewalks rush by. Trees reached bare branches over cars, parking meters, garbage cans. Their withered features were too much like the dead face that had belonged to the thing that had once been his father. He looked away and once more found Ian staring at him. He looked from Ian and caught Alexander's eyes in the rearview, and Rosie's in the side view. Eleanor shifted beside him, her eyes glancing his way every so often, and a cold weight pressed into the back of his head where Percy stared.

He clutched Ringo, closed his eyes, and knew that in a van with magicians, a demon, and an immortal werewolf, he was the curiosity.

3

They left the van. Percy ripped off the license plates, punched through the windshield to remove registration tags, and then peeled the VIN plates from the doors and the engine block. Jason cringed at the harsh whine of torn metal, and for a moment he remembered something out of a nightmare, a fusillade of shrieks that pierced his bones. The memory passed, and he focused on Percy's hands as he tore both license and VIN plates into pieces, ripping them easily and then chucking them into multiple garbage cans along their route.

They walked through snow, silhouettes in swirling frost, each longing for release from the wailing cold. The Gardens rose ahead, promising warmth and respite. Alexander remembered the horrible drawings Abebe had threatened him with only hours before, so to see the buildings still standing relieved some of his doubt. But he knew he would not be fully comforted until he saw their people were safe.

The white buildings and bare trees seemed to hover in the snow. Jason marveled as they climbed the red brick steps and passed beyond pillars, seeing his father's home unfold out of stories and into reality. He sometimes imagined the Gardens as some Gothic manor or great castle of old, where apparitions and sorcerers traded secrets within crypts. But the complex was like many others throughout

Queens, weathered bricks standing tall, a collection of lives veiled behind windows glittering in daylight. That such a place could hide such wonders. He wondered if it was real. He looked at Eleanor walking beside him, remembering the diamond of light she had molded into the facsimile of a musician, and knew that it was.

"No such thing as ordinary," he said, whispering to himself.

"Huh?" Eleanor replied.

"What? Uh, nothing. Nothing. How are you?"

She furrowed her brow at him, confused.

They walked through the entrance tunnel and emerged onto the path. Buildings slept around them. The group wound around gated trees and ornate lampposts, squinting against icy wind. Figures were visible in the distance, huddled and moving in the morning chill. Alexander and Rosie looked to Percy.

"Can you make them out?" Alexander said.

"Looks alright," Percy replied. "Far as I can tell."

"You sure?" Rosie said.

Percy nodded, relief clear on his face.

"It's Charlie Ruiz and Martin Gleason. They're alright. Heading home, I reckon."

Rosie grabbed his hand and exhaled.

They walked on.

They reached the fountain, and Jason stopped. He approached, standing beneath swaying branches lathered white, looking deep into black waters frothing against sheets of ice, remembering how his father had often spoke of how much he had loved the fountain, how it had been one of his favorite places in the Gardens.

His father...

He caught a knot in his throat, pushed it back, and turned to the others, seeking to forget.

"Sorry," he said.

"That's alright," Rosie replied, shielding her eyes. She was about to say something else, when a security jeep rolled up. They froze, all unsure of what to expect. A stuffed pink elephant dangled from the rearview, and a fresh cigarette was clutched in the guard's gloved hand. He drove by without acknowledging them, a relaxed smile on his face, as if he were lost in some pleasant dream. The jeep rolled on, vanishing into the snowfall.

Rosie and the other adults exchanged a look. She nodded them away from the children.

Eleanor blew a raspberry through her lips, opened her palms, and caught falling flakes. Ian leaned against a lamppost, and its light flickered off. Jason spied Ian's shadow stretched over snow in perfect mimicry of its master. He shuddered, feeling somehow that it was mocking him.

Eleanor went to Jason with a few snowflakes cupped in her palm.

"Wanna see something cool?" she said.

"Okay."

She looked over at the adults, over at Ian, and closed her eyes. The snowflakes rose from her palm like auroras and swirled until they coalesced into a crystalline polar bear loping in place. Jason smiled with genuine awe.

"That's even better than the other thing you showed me," he said.

"Ya think?"

"But is Ngombe controlling them..?" Alexander said from the adults' huddle, his voice rising.

Eleanor looked over at her father, shrugged, and blew into her hand. The bear faded into a snowdrift. Then she smiled at Jason.

"Your father probably showed you stuff that was way cooler—" She seized up, mortified.

A visible gloom swept over Jason.

"I'm sorry," she said.

Jason shrugged. He turned away, looking at the buildings, at the playground standing farther down the path beyond a low fence, at a copse of trees behind a gate across from the fountain.

"You grew up here?" he said.

"Uh-huh."

"It's nice."

"Where did you grow up?" Eleanor said.

Jason shrugged.

"Doesn't matter."

Eleanor was about to protest, when the adults returned.

"Ian, baby," Rosie said. "Are you getting any vibes, anything off?"

"Actually, I was just thinking how nice this all is," he replied, a bright smile on his face. "There's nothing wrong that I can see. Mr. Ngombe just had that guard...distracted. He's not possessed. I think we're fine."

"Do us a favor, yeah," Percy said. "Keep aware. If you notice a single thing off—"

"No problem, Uncle Percy."

"So," Alexander said, going to Jason and clapping his hands together. "I understand Rosie and Percy offered you a room at their home. It's not as nice as my place, but I think you'll like it."

Jason said nothing. He looked around, uncertain.

"It won't be any trouble, honey," Rosie said. "I told you, we got an extra room. It's yours if you want it."

Jason thought for a moment.

"Do you want money?" he said.

Rosie reared back as if he had just spat in her face. Jason saw his mistake and rushed to explain himself.

"Just...I have some money from Uncle...from...do you call a demon mister? It's not on me, but he said it's in the bank. Anyway, if you want some for food or...whatever..?"

Percy cringed and turned away, knowing the boy was in trouble.

"What makes you think that we're the kind of people who would charge a boy rent?" Rosie said.

Jason shrugged.

"I don't know what kinda people you are."

"Your daddy give you the impression we take advantage of kids?"

"No, I was just—"

"I'm betting he didn't. I'm also betting he told you that he was family to us."

Jason stared at the ground. Rosie sighed.

"That means you are too," she said. "If you're worried about earning your keep, we can see to it that you do. But that'll come in time. Right now, you need a place to call home. I know it won't feel like it, but considering the alternatives, I think you'd best accept this for what it is. Alright?"

Jason looked down the way they had come. The shadows of branches were black and trembling. He could see buildings in the spaces between currents of drifting frost, and for a moment a sense of peace took hold. It faded soon after, leaving him stranded in a wasteland of uncertainty. But for a sliver of time, he did feel some connection, some warmth linking him to the Gardens.

"Sweetheart?" Rosie said.

Snow kissed Jason's cheek, the cold bringing him back.

"Okay," he replied. "Yeah. Thank you."

"Alright, then. Well." She looked from Percy to Alexander. "It's been an evening."

"We'll see you later today," Alexander replied. He bent before Jason. "We're glad you're here. It's hard, I know, but, eh, think of this place as your birthright. You're home. Okay?"

Jason nodded, but his eyes were far away, lost in a maze of confusion, afraid to focus on any one emotion.

Rosie laid a gentle hand on his shoulder, gesturing that it was time to go. The boy waved at the Demidovs, turned to follow Percy and Rosie, and then stopped. He lifted Ringo in his hands and looked into the bear's black button eyes. Then he turned around and offered it back to Eleanor.

She glared at him.

"I told you, he wants to stay with you," she said.

He placed Ringo in her hands. His eyes were wide and wild, filled with sudden crazed light.

"Trust me," he said, "he doesn't."

He walked off, the wheels of his suitcase groaning in the stillness.

The Demidovs watched. Wind lifted snow from the ground and swirled into temporary phantoms. Eleanor looked up at her father.

"What were y'all talking about?"

"When it would be best to bring him below," Alexander replied. "And other things. We'll talk about that later. Just remember, what your uncle told Ian goes for all of us: watch if anyone is behaving in strange ways. We must be cautious."

Jason was fading into the white curtain, passing as if from out of time and into another world. Melancholy took hold over Alexander. The boy was too young to have lost so much. But something like hope whispered in his heart. Alexander could not name the feeling, but he held to it, allowing for the notion that perhaps things would turn out well.

Wind bit. Tree branches hissed. Alexander shivered, the long night seeping into his bones. He motioned for home. Ian walked beside him, but Eleanor hesitated, seeing Rosie, Percy, and Jason as specters in the haze. Snowflakes meshed with her hair, shimmering like starlight sewn into dense fabric. She wondered at a feeling rising from deep within, as if she stood near a precipice that beckoned her to plunge into a deep and unknowable ocean.

Ringo dangled from her hand, swaying. She turned, saw Alexander and Ian waiting, and ran to join them.

Their footprints were geometrical patterns on the ground. Surrounding them were others, a frenzy of misshapen prints that should not have been, slowly being filled by falling snow.

4

Rosie opened the door to their apartment.

Percy carried Jason's suitcase through the vestibule, and Jason followed after them, hefting his backpack. He looked around the living room. The walls were adorned with photos of horses standing silhouetted against desert vistas, or running along the edges of corrals. A book of mathematical puzzles sat a table beside a rocking chair. Across from the rocking chair was a table carrying a computer tower, its innards glowing neon green through clear panels. Video games were piled in neat stacks beside the computer's monitor. Boxes of circuits, motherboards, smart phones, GPSs, computer tablets, and a whole array of gadgets were stacked across from the games. A work station branched off from the computer desk at a 90-degree angle. Screwdrivers and a soldering kit lay open over a green mat in neat rows. A computer tablet lay disassembled, revealing gold bands connecting wires to circuits embedded in green plastic. A round black clock hung above the work desk, its long hands glowing red over binary ones and zeroes. In the center of the living room, two Winchester Rifles hung crisscrossed above a flat screen television that was linked to video game consoles. Tall speakers stood at either side of the television. A sofa of deep blue sat before the entertainment center, and a wireless record player lay upon a bureau besides it, flanked by hip hop records on one side and jazz crooners on the other —Nas and Nina Simone at their heads, respectively. A bay window draped with golden curtains let in pale light at the end of the living room. Snow danced beyond.

Jason took it all in.

"You guys like video games?" he said.

Rosie gestured at her husband. Percy shrugged.

"Technology's a marvel," he said. "Hungry?"

Jason shook his head.

"Alright. Shoes, then."

Jason took of his boots. The warmth of the carpeted floor pulsed through his socks and seeped into his skin.

Percy noted the look on the boy's face and smiled, kicking off his own sneakers.

"Perks of being married to a magician," he said.

"One of many," Rosie replied. "Want to see your room, Jason?"

Jason nodded and followed them past the kitchen. He looked inside for a moment, taking comfort from what was usually his favorite space in any home. A round dining table stood near the left wall, and pots and pans hung over a small island at the kitchen's center. Jason smiled with approval, for a moment imagining himself cooking there. But the soreness of his feet, metallic pressure beating at his eyes, and hollowness in his heart reminded him of why he was here. He went on down the hallway, and his smile dissolved.

More pictures lined the walls, faces beaming down at them from the past. He saw Rosie and Percy just married, embracing against a background of trees and rolling hills. He saw them seated with the Demidovs in a red booth at a café, Eleanor throwing her hands up and yelling in celebration, Ian smiling his strange smile. Their familiar faces shone from a third photo, along with others standing on a cobblestone street before Rosie's restaurant. He recognized Cedric McGill from his father's description of him, a burly man in a black leather jacket, someone whom Darius had spoken of with deep affection.

He saw a photo that made him stop.

His father stood on a rooftop, Percy and Alexander at either side of him. The Manhattan skyline glimmered in the background. Darius' face was younger, his hair golden brown, but Jason recognized the sadness lingering in his vivid green eyes, despite his smile. His arm was draped over a younger Alexander. Percy was the same as he was now, cold and timeless, blue eyes bright. Calm radiated from the photo, as if it were not a picture at all but a portal into a moment in time that would never end.

Percy stood behind Jason and looked at the photo, remembering. Rosie leaned against the wall across from them, a deep ache of sorrow for the boy pushing aside her exhaustion.

"That was our first year here," Percy said. "We were having a bit of get together. Already been through a lot by then, so we tried to enjoy ourselves from time to time."

Jason said nothing.

Percy took a deep breath, made to speak, but realized there was nothing more to say. He urged Jason on.

Rosie opened the guest room door. Long shadows painted the white walls within like hooded figures holding vigil. A bed covered in a white comforter lay beside double windows that looked out over the playground seven stories below. Dark blue curtains framed the windows, held open by golden ropes. A closet stood closed across from the bed. Beside it was a tall dresser. A bookshelf lined with all manner of well used books stood on the wall beside the entrance, and a wooden desk and chair stood to the right of the bed and window. The floor was carpeted, radiating that same warmth.

"Do you like the color?" Rosie said, indicating the walls.

Jason hesitated, then nodded.

Rosie smiled.

"I won't get offended."

Jason shrugged.

"Blue's more my thing."

Rosie rubbed her eyes, willing wakefulness, and placed her hands against the wall. Percy laid the suitcase on the floor near the bed.

Rosie closed her eyes and whispered. The walls began to ripple as if she were dropping stones into still water. The white paint shifted into yellow, faded into green, and brightened into a soft baby blue. Percy examined his flat cap, picking vagrant strands of lint from the checkered print.

Jason looked from one to the other and understood that for them this was normal.

Rosie backed away from the wall.

"How's that?" she said.

"How do you do that?" Jason replied, feeling stupid as he spoke, unable to check his awe at what they regarded as mundane.

"We'll show you," Rosie said. She frowned. "You ain't never learned any kind of magic?"

Jason shifted from one foot to the other, twitched, and scratched his head.

"He told me he couldn't do it anymore. He said being alive was his greatest magic trick."

There was no need to specify who "He" was.

Rosie exchanged a glance with Percy. Percy's expression urged her to let it be for now. He nodded for the door. They went.

"The loo's right over there," Percy said, pointing to a door across the hall.

"The what?" Jason replied.

"The bathroom, sugar," Rosie said.

"If you need anything, we're right across."

"So, I just...stay here, then?" Jason said.

Percy looked at him for a moment, remembering a time ages past when he too was alone amongst strangers.

"That seems to be the way of it," he said. "Believe it or not, I know exactly how you feel—suddenly being in the care of strangers, not knowing where you stand. So let me promise you this: you're with friends. Your father was no fool, was he?"

Jason shook his head.

"And he trusted us, yeah?"

Jason nodded.

"Right, then." Percy spread his hands as if to say "that's that." He waited to see if Jason would say anything else. The boy just looked around the room.

Percy sighed.

"Like I said..." He pointed in the direction of their bedroom.

"Get some sleep, sweetheart," Rosie said. She indicated the door. "Open or closed?"

Jason stumbled over his words and smiled a defeated smiled. He knew it did not matter.

"Open."

They left the door open and turned to leave.

"I—" Jason said. He sought the right words through an amalgam of emotions. Exhaustion, the strangeness of so suddenly living with people who were until this moment just stories, and the loss he refused to acknowledge all conspired against him. Frustration relented to an air of quiet defeat. "I guess this is weird for you, too. I mean, you don't know me, but you've all been really nice. So. Thanks."

"Sure," Percy replied.

They walked out, stopped before their bedroom, and faced each other. Percy covered his face with his hands. Rosie reached up, pulled his hands apart, and kissed him.

"It'll be alright," she said.

"How do we know that?"

She did not reply. Instead she led him away. He looked back at the open door, as if through it waited a riddle that, once solved, would birth answers no one was meant to know.

"Maybe I should stay up with him?" he said.

"We both need rest."

Rosie led them to their bedroom and stopped by the threshold. She was assaulted by the fact that they now lived with a boy fated to carry out a monumental and gruesome task. She reminded herself that he was a child above all else, scared and confused and lonely. She hoped that was something she would not forget.

The springs of their bed creaked as Percy sat. Rosie slid the gun from its holster and laid it on their mattress. The bed sheet folded over the weapon like ocean waves, and the gun sunk into the mattress where it would rise into her hand if needed. She threw off her coat and slipped under the covers. All things drifted away, and she was soon fast asleep.

Percy lay beside her, twisting his cap round and round in his hands. Sleep would come. But for now he replayed the entire evening in his mind, from the warehouse to the hospital, seeking some pattern or detail that would reveal—

Reveal what?

He saw his father, and Darius, one after the other in his mind's eye. A chamber of emotion was pierced inside of him, blotting all doubt and mistrust in a torrent of love for the father that he wished he could deny, and grief for the friend who was lost to them once more. He clenched his jaw. Something made him certain that he would not be allowed many moments like this. The boy promised dangers ahead, and he would have to be strong. But for now he took his wife's hand and let himself weep in silence.

Jason stood alone. Grief crept across his heart, causing him to look around for anything that would serve as a distraction. He peered out the window at the falling snow. The flakes drifted like pieces of forever, and he felt as if he were of them, a thing shaped from mystery to shine for a brief moment and then return to the unknown. Peace came again, comforting him with the idea that perhaps he and everyone else were part of some greater whole, a cosmic tapestry composed out of infinite experiences. On and on they flowed, recorded somewhere in time and perhaps beyond, every moment of life catalogued into some divine ledger, a collection of questions leading to the ultimate answer.

These things he could not put into words. But he felt them as he watched the snow fall.

Cold rattled the window. Air howled within the closet behind him, shattering reverie. Jason blinked and took a deep breath. An otherness took hold in the room, a presence that seeped out of a separate reality. This presence was no stranger to the boy. It always came when he was exhausted or distracted, casting ripples of dread, an unwelcome force that he had come to expect in the quiet.

He set his backpack down, went to the closet, inched the door open, and peeked inside. Dull morning light illuminated wire hangers. He opened the door all the way and looked around, leaning in to peer upwards while gripping the outer doorknob. Something brushed his hair. He jumped backwards and laughed with relief when he saw a dangling chain. He pulled it. Light bloomed from the fixture and coated the bare shelves.

He left the closet door open, went to his suitcase, and unzipped it. A dozen small candles encased in glass were scattered over his clothing. A pack of neon-colored lighters lay among them, four remaining out of five. He pulled out a green lighter and went to work laying the candles about the room. He set three before the closet, two by the entrance, and another three on the window sill. He laid the remaining candles at each corner of the room and lit them one by one. The flames scattered undulating light across the walls, the carpet, and the furniture, swaying this way and that over pale wax. Much of their light was lost to gray morning.

Jason examined the candles from the center of the room, stuffed the lighter into his pocket, and ran a shivering hand through his hair. His breath shaking, he opened his backpack and rummaged around. His hands worked past an E-book Reader, a worn cookbook, and a notebook with "My Recipes" written on the cover in chaotic print. He pushed aside a small blue photo album and seized an MP3 player with the headphones wrapped around it. He pulled it out and crawled onto the bed, taking the pillow and leaning with it against the wall so he could face the window at a diagonal. He left the curtains open.

Snow and silence were one. A deep hush embraced everything, and he wished it would remain unbroken, shielding him from what was coming. But he knew it would not be so. He intertwined his fingers over the MP3 player, as if in prayer, and waited for the stillness to be shattered.

The closet light dimmed, flared, and then flickered in a diminishing pulse. Each beat of light was weaker than the last, as if the light itself were a failing heart.

Shadows fell over the entrance threshold, darkening the hall beyond. A low sigh whispered from someplace, and the bedroom door began to inch close.

The closet light blared in a brief moment of protest, dimmed, beat once, twice, a final time, and then died. Darkness took hold, complete and cavernous.

The bedroom door came to a sudden stop, swung backwards, stopped again, and then eased shut with a click. The dim line of daylight beneath the door dissolved into black.

A blur distorted the darkness in the closet, as the chain began to spin from out of the gloom and into the swelling glow of candlelight, whistling as it went round.

Jason placed the headphones over his ears with trembling hands.

The closet door slammed shut. The spinning chain rattled within.

Jason gave the closet a thumbs up, as if in mockery, masking his growing disquiet with sarcasm. Then he turned the MP3 player on and pressed play. The first mournful licks of "While my Guitar Gently Weeps" poured into hearing. He focused on the coalescence of sound, the melody crying over the splash of cymbals, the march of the rhythm guitar, and the steady backbeat of the bass.

The closet doorknob twisted left and right, as if in tune to the music.

Daylight swelled through the window. Snow fell, the shadows of flakes drifting over Jason.

But then the darkness came, as it sometimes did before he slept, bleeding over the window in viscous folds, blotting daylight, enshrouding the room. Candle glow bloomed in answer, bathing the walls and ceiling in strange shadows.

The spinning chain continued to whip within the closet.

No matter the time, no matter the place, these strange happenings occurred if Jason was exhausted and alone, rising out of whatever caged power was within him. He had been told not to fear these things. He had been promised that they were no more than untamed magic, something he would one day control. He had learned long ago that if he let the restless shadows be, they would allow him the same courtesy, and that it was best to leave doors open and objects unattended and to never mind the dark. Otherwise, locked doors would shudder with violent outbursts, objects would be ripped from their hiding places, and fearful hallucinations would hover just on the edge of seeing.

But regardless of the assurances, self or otherwise, these outbursts filled him with terror. His heart raced, his jaw clenched, and his senses were ablaze with the notion that reality was collapsing and allowing some outer awfulness entrance to a world where it did not belong. The only comfort came from hiding—within music, within the pages of a book, or within daydreams. These were his guides to sleep, gentle companions leading him away from the uncanny and into the realm of slumber. There, all could be forgotten.

He took a deep breath and hugged his knees.

"Not real," he said, letting music take hold. He wrapped himself in the blanket. Cold emanated from the darkened window, caressing his face, but it was oddly soothing. He looked into the darkness beyond the panes of glass, and for a moment felt as if something beyond was beckoning him. A sudden urge to fling the window open and jump took hold. He grunted and looked away, folding himself deeper into the blanket. Warmth threaded through his body, inviting him to lose himself to sleep. He began to drift away.

The wooden chair thumped on the floor and tumbled end over end until it stopped before the bed, facing him. Jason's eyes flew open. He stared at the chair, and it seemed to stare back.

"Not real," he said.

The closet doorknob fell still, and the chain within went silent. Jason nodded along to the Beatles, but he felt some presence pulling his attention towards the chair. He looked at it again. Unease crept under his skin. He closed his eyes and struggled to focus on the song, seizing each note as if they were buoys leading him to shore. A sliver of comfort lit in his stomach. The worst had always been a sudden whisper, a violent movement, a touch of something cold against his skin. It would come, and it would go, and the darkness would sometimes vanish, would sometimes remain, but always leave him in peace. The chair was no different. Sleep would soon find him, and the next day would seem almost normal.

He hummed along with George Harrison, letting the beauty of his voice and guitar carry him to the peaceful space great music can lead you to.

The closet door flew open. A rancid groan seeped into hearing, cracked and wet, severing Jason's emotional connection to the music. He gave a sudden start and stared with alarm. The groan ended with a hoarse cry, as if a great beast were taken by surprise.

The chair rose a foot off the floor, hovering, and the groan came again, low and undulating, growling first and then rising into a piercing shriek.

The closet door trembled. It drifted a few inches, stopped, and then slammed shut. The chair fell to the floor at the same time, and the shrieking went silent.

Jason trembled all over.

"Not—not—"

Pounding boomed against the window. He looked and saw flickers of movement, frail things pressing against the glass and vanishing into the blackness.

The closet door crashed open, went to swing shut, and froze in mid-motion, as if two opposing storms pushed against either side.

The window rattled.

Jason looked from one to the other, shook his head, and pressed the headphones to his ears. He rocked back and forth with the music, grimacing as the candles nearest the closet began to waver.

A nasal moan emanated from beyond the window.

A guttural bark boomed in answer from the closet.

Jason pulled out his lighter and pressed against the wall. The closet door swung back and forth. The nearby candles blew out one by one, making each movement of the closet staccato like animated characters in a flip book.

Something moved within the closet, a bloated silhouette stuttering in the dark.

Jason turned away and wrapped the blanket over his head. The closet door slammed shut. Thumps crashed, and long scratches hissed from within.

The bedroom door opened. Jason peeked from within the blanket, hoping against hope for daylight. Darkness peered in at him, so deep and complete that he became certain that the hallway, Rosie, Percy, and all things connected to the world were now gone. As if he was hovering in a space between worlds. The remaining candles did nothing to illuminate the darkness beyond the door, a vast midnight without end.

The candles by the entrance flickered. The pounding at the windows intensified, and low and strained voices seemed to be crying out from afar.

Jason clutched the lighter, his thumb pale against the spark wheel.

"Not real, not real, not real..."

Doubt was a tormenting storm, plaguing him with questions. The groans, the dying candles, the pounding at the window, and the voices beyond were something new. His insides were ice water.

The closet door opened once more, and an outline of something blacker than the surrounding darkness was there.

Across the hallway, Percy stirred. Rosie's breath was the sweet cadence of sleep, broken from time to time by snores. He slid from the bed, not wanting to disturb her, threw on a T-Shirt, covering the four horrendous scars running diagonally across his torso, and stepped out of the bedroom.

The shadows of daylight stretched through the hallway. He walked across, went to Jason's room, and found the door closed. He frowned, wondering why the boy had changed his mind, and then listened. Deep silence answered from within. Cold slid around him, and he shuddered. He gripped the doorknob and turned it for a peek.

The door was locked.

Percy went to let go, then hesitated. A spark of panic flared in the back of his mind, urging him to break down the door. He argued with himself, listening, waiting, allowing logic to deflate trepidation. He imagined scaring the boy out of sleep. He saw the confusion, the accusation, and the remembrance of Darius' death in the boy's eyes.

He shook his head, grumbled, and let go of the doorknob. Then he went to his room and slipped into bed, pressing close to Rosie.

"Not real, not real, not real..." Jason said, rocking back and forth.

He hugged his knees. The candles by the entrance died as one. With them went the candles at the corners of the room. A barren country of darkness lay beyond the glow emanating from the window sill, marooning Jason in an island of shivering light. The windows boomed until he was certain the glass would shatter, and the far away voices grew into a tumult of hoarse cries on the verge of panic.

The darkness beyond the bed was still.

The song ended. An electric hum and clicking like the scraping of a record player's needle came through the headphones. Jason snatched them off his ears, clutched the MP3 player in a shivering hand, and clicked the screen to life.

A jumble of letters and numbers filled the screen.

"Nah," he said. "Nah, come on, man."

Wet footsteps smacked in the darkness beyond the remaining candle glow.

Jason gasped and sparked the lighter to life, feeling trapped between the violent shaking of the window and the coming footsteps. He moved the flame around, looking this way and that. There was nothing.

The footsteps walked on.

"Nah," he said. "This isn't happening. It ain't real. It's me. I'm doing this, it's me. I can stop it. Stop it, dumbass. Stop now. Stop it!"

The footsteps went silent. The window fell still.

The candles on the windowsill dimmed.

Jason's breath raced. He swallowed, reached for the candles, and added the lighter's flame to their dwindling fire, his eyes darting from the window to beyond the bed and back again. The wicks took and shone brighter. He nodded and turned back to the darkness.

The footsteps sprinted. The window boomed once more. Jason screamed and crashed against the wall. His back roared with pain, the lighter's flame died, and the candles on the windowsill trembled.

The running footsteps reached the edge of the bed, and then vanished.

Movement caught Jason's left eye.

A dead candle floated into view, hovering over the overturned chair. It rose once, twice, and then was hurled upwards without a sound.

Strangled laughter erupted from the darkness. Frenzied shrieks pounded against the windows. Jason screamed and covered his ears.

A growl exploded from somewhere beyond the bed, thick with crazed malice, spraying droplets of darkness across the bed sheets. The screams and shaking of the window ceased.

Silence took hold.

Jason panted, no longer a person but a collection of fears. The MP3 player's screen blared to life. He did not want to look. He looked.

Be my friend...

Be my friend...

Be my friend...

The same three words scrolled upwards over the screen. He tossed the MP3 player, the headphones clattering.

A putrid glow bled from the shadows by the entrance, illuminating the bookshelf. Books hovered before the shelves, open and dangling as if they were lolling tongues, and single letters were scrawled over each book by a crazed hand.

B E M Y F R I E N D

Jason fought for a solid breath, for calm, not understanding what was happening.

The books fell, but made no sound. The glow diminished, returning the bright obsidian beyond the bed. Deep quiet fell over the room. No footfalls, no groans or grunts, no crashing of doors.

Jason waited.

Something shimmered on his right. He turned around slowly, not wanting to see, unable to stop himself. There, hanging in the pitch, was a white face leering at him. As quick as he saw it, it disappeared.

Jason threw himself under the blanket, screaming for Percy, for Rosie, for his father, shouting at the top of his lungs, his throat becoming a ragged thing. But he knew they would not hear him. He knew that he was alone.

Footsteps smacked towards the bed, and then stopped. Jason clenched his jaw. He tried to still himself, struggling to stay quiet.

Voices erupted beyond the blanket, a barrage of mangled plea—screaming, crying, begging, accusations, maniacal laughter, and endless gibberish, some ungodly chorus tearing through reality to get the boy's attention.

A scream like that of an undead bear silenced them all.

Jason shivered under the blanket.

"No," he said, his words wet and thick. He clenched his eyes shut and gritted his teeth. "Go away."

There was no movement, no sound, and yet arms wrapped themselves around him, were under the covers with him, holding him close. Before he could scream, a frigid hand slid over his mouth. A large mass pressed against him. It had materialized under the blanket as if it had always been there, waiting in the hollow spaces and cramped creases, spawned out of nonexistence to revel in the boy's terror and savor his warmth.

"Wanna be my friend?" it said, its voice warped, each word dripping decay.

Jason's muffled screams answered.

"Shh," it said. "All I want is a friend. Say yes."

Stench oozed into Jason's nostrils, the reek of battlefields and butchery, the mingled sweetness of decay, filth, and withered skin.

"Be my friend," it said, the last word reverberating like a bestial oath, blind desire without care or reason.

Jason groaned through the fingers over his mouth, tears streaming. He clenched his eyes shut and nodded.

The thing holding him hissed with satisfaction.

"Yeah," it said. "Good boy. We've been dying to say hello. Now we're gonna have some fun."

The candlelight beyond the blanket went dark, the last candles extinguished as if their light were physically ripped from them. The thing clutched Jason tighter and made a wet noise. A sudden sucking sensation pulled at Jason, and he felt as if a piece of himself were being torn from his mind and connected to something old and hungry and cruel. Thoughts became a jumbled mash, confusion took hold, and his limbs were saturated by an invading presence like liquid rot.

His eyes faltered, consciousness broke apart, and all went black.

5

Snow fell, and ocean waves crashed with reverential silence. A gentle breeze brushed black blades of grass against Eleanor's legs, and upon touching her skin the foliage transformed into iridescent shades of green.

She closed her eyes and smiled.

She stood atop a hill rolling among many, and everywhere the grass bent beneath the breath of the sea. Catching a snowflake falling from the star strewn sky, she beheld within its fractal shape an entire universe pulsating like divine clay. Matter churned in great clouds across expanses, painting the far reaches of space with cosmic flame.

The snowflake drifted from her palm, joining those that fell about her. Within them she witnessed other universes and the same dance of particles: protons, electrons, neutrons, quarks, forces known and unknown composing existence into being.

This snow landed on grass, melted, and trickled in pale streams towards the silent waters. Somewhere in the waves the snow rose again towards the innumerable stars and fell across the world once more.

Silence was all, a blind alchemist aware of itself through infinite creations.

And Eleanor knew: here was the truth of all things.

Everything and nothing.

Never and always.

"The silence that once was."

The words came unbidden from her lips, and snow enveloped her and spoke with no voice. She listened and agreed to what was offered. Then she dissolved, becoming one with all that ever was and would be, the cycle of being fading in and out, never into forever and back again, always.

A scream devoured the silence.

Eleanor opened her eyes and saw snowflakes hanging petrified in midair. The scream enslaved the sky from one unseen horizon to the next until the snow ruptured into caustic dust that ignited white flames over the hills.

Horrors rose from these flames, and blood seeped from the earth, drenching Eleanor's feet.

A figure wreathed in a black hood appeared before her, and her heart sank. Surrounding the hooded figure were nine prostrate creatures feeding on endless rivers of blood. The hooded figure offered Eleanor its skeletal hand. Eleanor looked on its face and saw a beak and empty black eyes. She backed away. It screamed, white fire consumed the hills and the sky, and abominations danced.

The hooded figure threw open its robe. Eleanor beheld emptiness beneath. Things long not of the world reached from that emptiness and made to embrace her.

In her hands awoke the faintest shimmer of star-fire...

Eleanor awoke.

The dream collapsed into the confines of sleep, and she groaned and knuckled her eyes against daylight. The hiss of cooking whispered into the room, bringing with it breakfast perfumes: the welcoming sweetness of blinis mingled with the sultry scent of bacon and eggs. She looked around, piecing together images from the dream— darkness, snow, an otherworldly peace broken by some final thing that lit fading strands of terror through her. But the dream faded, leaving an imprint of something profound that she could not understand.

"Sleep okay?" Ian said.

Eleanor jumped, clutching her chest and glaring at her brother seated at the foot of the bed. He was dressed in a black vest lined with baby blue, a cream shirt, and a black tie with blue stripes.

"What in the actual fuck?" she said.

"Dad said to wake you up, but you were mumbling something in your sleep." Ian cocked his head to the side. "You should never wake someone up from dream."

"Thanks, Grand Master."

Eleanor knuckled her eye, yawned, and smacked her lips together. She gave Ian a searching look, concern making her alert.

"You okay?" she said.

Ian smoothed his tie.

"Sure. It was a strange morning. Left me curious."

"Just curious?" Eleanor said, incredulous. Ian shrugged. Eleanor threw up her hand. "Dad's best friend comes back to life, somehow has a son, and you're 'just curious?' "

"What else should I be?"

She stared at him.

"I love you and everything, but you're fucking weird, man."

He smiled.

"I just think that things will work out for the best."

"Yeah, yeah. I was mumbling? What was I saying?"

Ian just looked at her. Eleanor rolled her eyes.

"What?" she said.

"Just want your honest opinion first: what do you think about our new friend?"

She frowned.

"Jason? He seemed cool. I mean we just met him, what do you want me to say? His dad just died. Probably not a good time to, like, judge him."

Ian kept looking at her, knowing there was more. Eleanor relented.

"I feel like he's different," she said. "In a good way. I don't know how else to say it."

Ian leaned closer, interested.

"Different how?"

Eleanor made a confused sound in her throat and swirled both hands through the air.

"Just different. I don't know. His dad's a fucking legend, of course he's gonna be different."

"Do you trust him?"

"Just met him. How are you not getting this?"

"You didn't answer the question."

She thought for a moment, clutching Ringo to her side without realizing.

"I think he's like us," she said. "You know, after mom died...that changes you. So he's just like everyone else here. He knows what it's like to lose someone. That makes you see things differently. I trust that. What's Pop always say? Perspective, whatever. Makes you know what's important and stuff. Do I trust him? I don't know, but he seemed nice, even though he was really sad. I like him." She yawned. "It's too early."

"First impressions are important."

"No, I mean it's too goddamn early, numb-nuts."

"It's almost three."

"So? We ain't got nowhere to be."

She flopped back down on the bed. Ian stood and flipped the covers from her. She groaned and covered her head with the pillow.

"Aw come on," she said.

"We do, actually. We're going to Aunt Rosie's. Remember?"

Eleanor peeked from beneath the pillow.

"Oh. Yeah."

She sat up, blew curls from her face, and cringed at the mustard gas emanating from her mouth. Ian smiled and ruffled her hair. He went to leave.

"Hey," Eleanor said. "What did I say in my sleep?"

"You repeated 'everything' a few times, like when you're meditating. Then you sort of groaned, like you were scared. Maybe you're practicing too hard?"

"Your face is practicing too hard."

But she frowned in thought, mumbling "everything," tasting the word on her tongue. It brought her the memory of grass and falling snow. It brought her black waves shimmering under endless stars. She looked out the window. Snow fell outside over a battalion of jubilant children conquering hills on sleds.

She turned to ask Ian if she had said more. He was gone.

He walked down the hallway with his hands stuffed into his pockets, whistling John Coltrane's "A Love Supreme," affecting the air of a well-to-do man strolling at leisure. He went through the living room, turned right past the piano and into a hallway, and peeked into the kitchen.

Alexander swirled a pan of eggs while guiding three plates that floated on an invisible current past Ian and into the dining room across from the kitchen. The plates landed with precision on the table before their respective chairs, surrounding a large bowl filled with fruit stuffed blinis, a plate of bacon, a carafe of tea, a French Press filled with coffee, three porcelain cups, and three glistening glasses of water.

"Pop," Ian said.

"Eh?" Alexander flipped the scrambled eggs, turned the burner off, and faced his son while still swirling the pan. His shoulders and arms were ropes of muscle, and his stomach was a mound underneath his tank top. A coating of flour infested the left side of his thick mustache.

"Eleanor's coming." Ian pointed at his own face to indicate his father's. "You have flour on your mustache."

"Here?" Alexander pointed at his forehead, staining it. "Here?" He stained his cheek.

Ian laughed, stuffing his finger up his own nose.

"Ah," Alexander said. "Of course."

"What did we tell you about all those drugs?"

Alexander gaped.

"Eh? What kind of way is that to speak to your father? I don't have to feed you, you know."

"Yeah you do."

"Go away."

Ian made to go, looked at his father again, and stopped. The veins of his eyes beat with blood, and something came through to him from his shadow, standing out among the constant flow of sensory information fed to him by his dark half.

"Pop?"

"Mm?"

"Why is there blood on your forearm?"

Alexander blinked with surprise, and then caught Ian's shadow crouched beside him. Its red eyes flared. Alexander looked at his forearm, noticed the faintest speckle of crimson there, and frowned at his son.

"What have I told you about using your other around here?" he said. The shadow remained near him. He pointed at it. "Get that thing away from me."

The shadow dissolved into the floor, but Ian continued to stare.

"I didn't mean to, Pop," he said. "Sometimes it can't help it. And you didn't answer my question."

The gunshot roared in Alexander's memory. The boy's blood had gushed from his ravaged head and steamed upon the cold floor. He remembered its heat on his hand.

"I—" he said.

"Don't lie," Ian replied. "You were about to lie."

Alexander looked at Ian for a long time. Love swelled in him for the boy. But his son's curious gaze saw too much, and Alexander nearly shuddered for a reason he could not name. Or perhaps he did not want to.

"I had to do something very unpleasant last night," he said. "That's all I'm going to say about the matter. If I keep something from you, it's for a reason, and I expect you to respect that. Okay?"

Ian nodded, but still he remained, his head cocked, that too-wise expression in his eyes.

"Pop," he said. "You're feeling bad. Let it go. I know whatever you did, you did to protect us."

Alexander blinked, stunned.

"You have to protect the people you love," Ian said. "No matter what. Sometimes that means doing bad things. But I know you. Whatever happened, you did it for a good reason. So don't feel bad."

"You should always feel bad for..." Alexander couldn't finish. He exhaled and shook his head. "You should never do anything bad, if you can help it. You understand that, right?"

Ian smiled.

"Sure."

Then he walked away, whistling.

Alexander pulled the flour from his mustache, forehead, and cheek with an absent wave of magic. The white powder spilled into the sink. His throat constricted. He could still hear the boy's frenzied screams and smell the copper of his blood. He washed his hands, wrists, and forearms, unsure of how he had missed the stain before. But of course there wasn't much blood left.

Eleanor wouldn't have noticed it.

But Ian...

He watched the flour dissolve into the running water along with the faintest streaks of pink. Twisting the hot water knob to its conclusion, he grimaced as steam rose from his forearms, but forced them under the scalding water, as if that were enough to wash away the killing of a child. The water hissed, steamed billowed, and he cried out as he yanked free. Pain subsided in waves of release, and Alexander wondered at all the things that had transpired in just a few hours. The warehouse seemed like something out of another life, something he wished would remain forgotten. He knew he would never forget.

Eleanor's laughter sang through the hallway, and Ian's voice murmured underneath. A door closed, and Eleanor's mocking voice followed.

A great burst of fresh air rose in Alexander's chest. He shook his hands out and twisted the faucet's knobs so cool water would come, then washed his face and turned the water off. The horror was his to carry, but life transcended it in layers of love and laughter and learning. There was also mystery, the events at the hospital plaguing him with curiosity, wonder, and fear. He dried his hands and smiled despite dread or perhaps against it. His children were still here. They loved him, and they were his. He replayed his son's words and, loath as he was to admit it, Abebe's words as well, and understood that both had said true things on the nature of guilt and necessity. Of the burdens one must carry through their lives to protect their loved ones. Of the cost of righteousness and mercy, sometimes purchased by blood.

The boy had torn his own eyes out. His mind had been shattered by something incomprehensible. There had been no hope of revival, of reprieve. Ever would he be trapped in that warehouse, no matter where they would have taken him or what medicine or magic they would've used to heal him. He had to be spared from the horrors he had witnessed. The bullet had been quick and clean, eviscerating the memory of the vampire's frenzy. If the cost for a child's peace was his own guilt, then Alexander was willing to pay.

But sadness burrowed through him, planting a dull weight he knew he would always carry. Beyond that was his responsibility to his children, and a promise to help care for his best friend's son. Life called, and Alexander Demidov had to answer.

He nodded to himself, took the eggs and made for the dining room.

The sink gurgled behind him.

He turned with a furrowed brow and walked over to it. Pink water frothed from the drain. Alexander frowned with distaste, again remembering the heat of the boy's blood splattering his hand. The water rose a few centimeters, and then drained in a swirl of bubbles.

Alexander stood there for a moment, wondering. Eleanor's voice pulled him back. He carried the eggs to the dining room table, trying to push the horror of the morning out of his mind.

He did not see the drain spit a bubble of blood.

. . .

ELEANOR GIGGLED with a mouth full of blini and chased the mashed sweetness with tea. Alexander chuckled at her joke, shoulders quietly rising and falling.

"The best part is you can make the whale sound for a long, long time," she said. "As long as you want."

"And watch the reaction on the victim's face."

"Exactly." She slapped the table in approval. "Fuck yeah. You get it, Pop."

"Hey. Language."

"Shi—I mean fu—"

She growled. Alexander shook his head.

"Just like your mother," he said.

"Sorry. Anyway. Two whales in a bar." She laughed again, snorting. Alexander pointed at her tea. She drank, still giggling.

Ian came in and took his place opposite her. Alexander pushed the bowl of blinis his way. Ian ladled three onto his plate, glanced at his father's arms, and went for the sliced apple in the fruit bowl.

"Took ya long enough," Eleanor said.

"You annoyed me into meditating."

"Awesome."

"Are you anxious?" Alexander said to his son.

Ian shrugged. "

Kinda."

"So you are human," Eleanor said. "Thank god. Seriously though, it was a long night. I'm so hungry."

They ate.

Alexander looked from daughter to son, the events of the early morning writ upon their faces in a menagerie of emotions. Excitement thrummed through Ian's calm like a sustained musical note. The boy had always been curious, and after taking in Jason, Alexander was not, nor could not, be surprised at the need for Ian to find out more about the stranger.

Eleanor's jokes and laughter was a veil over a train of confusion. The mention of the unexpected events etched uncertainty on her features. The day before, Darius had been long dead, and Abebe

Ngombe was an enemy. But Jason waited a few buildings away, living evidence to the change the early morning hours had brought.

"Listen, both of you," Alexander said, wiping his mouth and laying his napkin beside his plate. Eleanor laid her fork down. Ian stabbed his into an apple slice. "This morning—well this morning changes everything for us. That is not an exaggeration. I wish it were. We thought many things, but sometimes what you think and what is true are completely different. I don't know what all of this means, but I do know that having Jason here will be complicated. You may be confused. That's okay. Things change. They are strange at first, and then they become normal. But no matter what, no matter how this boy affects things, this family, the three of us here, will be whole. If we love each other always, then we will be okay."

Eleanor and Ian exchanged a look.

"Pop, it's cool," Eleanor said. "The whole thing is freaky with, y'know, Satan being our friend and everything—"

"He's not really Satan, Ellie," Ian said.

"Whatever, you know what I mean. And then there's Mr. Bardales coming...back...to life. But Jason's still just a magician's kid, just like others around here. Or, okay, maybe a little more than that. I mean— okay, shit, now that I think about it, it's weird. It's weird. But I can move and make stuff with my mind. I'm used to weird."

"Yeah you are," Ian replied.

"Shut up."

Alexander stared at his son and saw an emotion he could not name hiding behind his jab at Eleanor.

"And you?" he said.

Ian shrugged.

"Like Ellie said. I have questions. I have a lot of questions. Can I say something?"

"Uh oh," Eleanor said.

Alexander gestured for his son to go on.

"I get why you let Jason come here. But, if you look at it, it's hard not to be a little worried. His father dies, comes back to life, and has a son. When has that ever happened? We all know better: dead is dead."

Their mother, Alexander's wife, drifted through the space of silence that followed. Ian gripped the knife and moved it like a metronome over the table.

"I think," he said, "that you should let me watch him."

"Ian!" Eleanor replied.

"No," Alexander said.

"Pop—" Ian said.

"I said no. Forget it. Ian, do you understand what would happen if you were caught?"

"I'm only talking about watching Jason. Uncle Percy and Aunt Rosie would understand. We're the only ones who know who he—"

"They would be furious, and so would I," Alexander said. "Percy wouldn't trust you anymore. He barely...we would be forced out of here. We would have to make a life outside, and believe me, we don't want that. We wouldn't last long without the protection of the Gardens."

"Mr. Bardales did," Ian replied.

"Everyone thought he was dead. There are people looking for me, Ian."

Dejection crept into Ian's face. Alexander sighed, took his son's cup, and poured coffee into it. Ian perked up and took the cup in both hands as if it were an offering not to a boy, but a man.

Eleanor frowned, looked away, and wrestled with a bit of jealousy.

"It's not the worst idea," Alexander said. "But—and I know I talk about this a lot—Darius was my best friend. I cannot disrespect his memory by having you spy on his son. We have to trust him. We have to treat him like he's one of us."

Ian sipped his black coffee, smiled to himself, and placed the cup down.

"He can still cause trouble without meaning to."

Alexander shrugged.

"And one of our werewolves can decide to let themselves turn without going down to the Den. But that has not yet happened. We have to live with risk, Ian. There's no other way to live."

"Okay. Then I have to ask: are you sure Mr. Bardales didn't fake his death the first time?"

A hard look crossed Alexander's face. He remembered Darius charring in black and crimson flames. He remembered screaming, blood, and stench.

"Yeah," Ian said. "There it is, right there. I saw that same look on Uncle Percy's face this morning. He really did die. So this is scary. Makes me worried. I just want to keep our people safe. Just like you. But, okay, you're right. Mr. Bardales is the reason we all have our home in the first place. So, we should trust his son. Fine. I can do that. To be honest, this is kind of exciting. Right, Pop?"

The hidden question was clear to Alexander: What is Jason? What is he really?

He will kill the vampires. Those words clanged in Alexander's mind. Hope and foreboding grappled, toppling one another. Though they had all agreed to keep Jason's task secret from his children, he saw in both of them wonder over the boy. They knew there was something different about Jason Escoto. What should he tell them? How much should he keep from them?

"He's different," he said, giving a little to spare a lot. "I think it's safe to assume so. But for now it's extremely important that you don't have any expectations."

"You just said everything's gonna change," Eleanor replied.

"Yes. I believe that. That does not mean that it will change according to how you think it will."

"Well, Jason's definitely a magician," Ian said. "Right, Ellie?"

Eleanor danced her head from side to side.

"Well, maybe. We both think he moved a chair by accident last night. This morning. Whatever, I'm tired. Ya know, like how I was moving stuff by accident when it was time for me to start learning magic?"

Alexander leaned forward.

"That so?"

Eleanor noted the interest on his face.

"What did Mr. Bardales tell you when we were in the waiting room?"

Alexander rapped his knuckles against the table.

"I cannot tell you about that yet."

"That ain't fair!"

"Come on, Pop."

Alexander raised his hand for silence.

"There is something...special about Jason," he said. "When the time is right, you'll know. I promise. But right now, I need you to trust me. There are some things that are still too big for you."

"Balls," Eleanor replied, tossing her napkin. Ian tapped his finger against the rim of his mug, frustrated. But they both let it go.

"In time, Jason will begin to learn how to control magic," Alexander said. "I'd like for both of you to help him. But I don't want you pushing him too hard, or expecting too much."

"So you want us around him?" Ian said.

Alexander stroked his mustache.

"Yes. I have my apprehensions, but...I want you two to get to know him. I think that's one of the reasons why Abebe wanted you both there. He wanted Jason to make friends. He's going through a hard time, something you two definitely understand. So make him feel welcome. However, if you see anything strange or...just be alert. If anything happens, you come to me, or your aunt and uncle, straight away."

Ian nodded.

Eleanor crossed her arms with sudden doubt. A ripple of cold air tumbled against the back of her neck, and flashes of her dream intruded on her thoughts. She grimaced, remembering how Rosie had asked her to keep an eye on her own brother. That made two she had to spy on now. She suppressed a groan of frustration, shook herself off, and caught the question in her father's eyes. She took a deep breath and made the okay sign with her thumb and index finger.

But then a thought hit her.

"Wait," she said, frowning as she replayed what her father had just said. "You said 'one of the reasons.' Why else did Mr. Ngombe want us to come? We could've made friends with Jason over here."

Alexander rubbed his mustache.

"Well..."

A look of distaste tainted his eyes.

"Go ahead, Pop," Ian said.

"We're in it, right?" Eleanor said.

Alexander looked from one to the other.

"By bringing you two along, Abebe was making sure that you were involved. If something goes wrong, then you both could be held responsible with the rest of us. He's saying he knows that I love you two more than anything, and that we'd better be careful. Or else."

The siblings exchanged another look, she fearful, he curious, almost amused. Eleanor stood without a word and collected plates from the table. Alexander struggled to say something comforting, but his tongue would not work. The disgust on Eleanor's face reflected that she knew violence and terror were mere mistakes away. She stacked the plates and walked towards the kitchen.

"Ellie," Alexander said.

"I gotta wash these."

Alexander sighed and looked at his son. Ian watched as if in appraisal.

"Too harsh?" Alexander said.

"Had to be said," Ian replied.

"Help your sister with the dishes, eh?"

Ian got up, kissed his father on the cheek, and went into the kitchen.

Ian's shadow lingered for a moment, all slouched and bent in the wrong places. It stared at Alexander, cocked its head, and then followed after Ian. Alexander wished it were not a part of his son. He wished many things for his family that he knew could not be.

A bowl swirled in suds and hot water, floating under Eleanor's weaving hands. Ian dried the dishes as they came to him, his sleeves rolled up.

"We got a dishwasher, you know," he said.

Eleanor didn't respond, focusing on the dishes so as not to think about the unspoken threat against their family.

"He had to tell us," Ian said. "So we know to keep quiet."

"I'm not mad. Just...how many people do we know who've been killed?"

"You mean murdered?"

Eleanor fell silent. A sponge floated onto the plate and wiped hard at reddish berry juice.

"Whatever you wanna call it," she said. "I don't understand why it happens so much. I just don't."

Ian did not reply. He placed the bowl in the dish rack and caught the next plate as it floated into his hands. Snow fell beyond the window, and children screamed in play.

6

Rosie walked out of the bedroom in sweatpants and a T-shirt and found Percy seated on the sofa. She sat and leaned against him.

"Get any sleep?" she said.

"Not much."

"I figured."

"Been trying to sort it all out."

"I reckon you ain't having much luck with that."

"Not even close, love." He nodded towards the kitchen. "I made breakfast."

"How much of it did you already eat?"

He gave her a bashful look.

"I made more."

She kissed him.

"Why thank you, kind sir. Jason?"

"Still in the room."

His voice drifted, and his eyes were distant, as if he were contemplating some impossible vision on the horizon. He looked at her, and the fear on his face nearly made her pull away.

"What is he, Rose?" he said.

Rosie grappled with the question, hearing in it the same fears and

GIOVANNI DIAZ

doubts that were plaguing her. What was the child of a dead man capable of? What terrible power granted him the ability to kill vampires? She pieced together all she knew of the world, a lifetime of memory filled with magic and bloodshed, searching for some answer. But there was only mystery. She pressed her nose into Percy's hair and hugged him close.

"For right now," she said, "he's a kid. We have to start there."

Percy looked down the hallway and shivered against a sudden chill. He gripped her forearms, enjoying the softness of her skin under his hands. They stayed that way, each grateful for the other.

FREDDIE MERCURY CROONED THROUGH HEADPHONES, imploring the world not to stop him. Jason's eyes fluttered open. He lay sprawled on his stomach, the blanket surrounding him like frozen waves. Daylight filled the room. A little girl's shriek from outside pierced the last vestiges of sleep and shot him awake. Frigid air enveloped him. He shivered, rubbed his hands over his arms, and grimaced at the music thumping in his ears. He yanked off the headphones and tossed them aside, certain that he had taken them off when—

He blinked. Memory of the morning slammed into him, and he spun around the bed. He stopped, reaching out to balance himself, and examined the room. The candles were where he had left them, their wicks dead and burned low. Books were stacked on the shelves. The closet door was open, benign. The chair sat before the desk, and the curtains were open.

He remembered the chaotic spectacle that had led to the terror under the covers and attacked the blanket, kicking it off the bed, his mind creating evil shapes within the folds. But there was nothing underneath. He breathed hard, his eyes darting this way and that.

"It was a nightmare," he said. He knew it wasn't, but he struggled to wipe that certainty away. "It wasn't real."

The room tilted from side to side for a moment, and he groaned and fell back on the bed. Vertigo passed, but it left him feeling hollow, as if he had not eaten in days. He took a deep breath and rubbed his hands through his hair.

"I'm going crazy."

Those three words emerged with cold finality. He fell still, caught between madness and some other possibility he did not want to entertain. The laughter of playing children seemed to mock him, and he buried his face in his hands, wanting nothing more than silence and peace.

Two gentle knocks came at the door. He nearly screamed.

"Sweetheart," Rosie said, her voice muffled. "You up?"

Relief flooded him for a moment, but then he remembered the candles scattered across the room.

"Ju—just a second," he replied.

He jumped off of the bed and collected the candles from the floor. He crammed seven into his arms, when the door unlocked on its own and swung open. Rosie smiled at him from the hallway, thinking he had come to open the door, and then blinked with confusion at the sight of him at the center of the room, still in his jeans, all messy haired and holding an armload of used candles.

She looked around the room and spied a few of the remaining candles at the corners and on the windowsill.

"Okay then," she said.

A candle slid from the top of the pile and tumbled onto the floor. Jason flinched. Rosie came inside, making sure to keep a safe distance so as not to impose upon him.

"You always sleep with this many candles?"

Jason licked his dry lips and looked around the room for an answer. He laid the candles in a pile on the bed, turned back to Rosie, and scratched the back of his neck.

"I was testing them to make sure they all work the same," he said. He nodded as if the candles were a team of workers awaiting his approval. "Good job, guys. And girls. They can be both. I mean, it's hard to tell. But...they all did great."

Rosie watched, trying to read him. His tone was gentle, almost jovial, but his eyes were wide and wild with fear.

"It's alright," she said, opting not to push. "I need to sleep with a blanket, no matter how warm it is. I once knew someone who slept with her eyes open. Imagine waking up to that. Damndest thing. Some people just aren't comfortable in the dark. There's nothing wrong with that. Actually it makes sense seeing how our ancestors had a lot of reasons to be afraid. Predators and such. Ah, I'm rambling. It's just—well, it was already light when we got here."

"I just like them."

"Alright. I hope one day you'll tell me why. And that you're careful. Candles over a carpet ain't the safest idea, darling."

Jason was silent. Dark circles rimmed his eyes.

Rosie bounced on her heels and looked about. She turned to look at the bedroom door and had a sudden jolt of realization.

"Did you open the door from there?" she said, pointing from the door to where Jason stood.

He smiled and shrugged.

"Doors like to open."

"I see. Bet that happens a lot, doors opening and closing on you, things moving around when you're near?"

His eyes darted towards the chair.

"You can say that."

"Listen," she said, "I can't imagine how strange this is for you. And I want you to know that you can take your time getting adjusted. No one's rushing you to do anything. But I think it'll do us all a world of good if you can open up about a few things. That way, we can all better understand how to help you out. Like that door, for a start. It's natural for a young magician to show signs when they're nearly ready to start practicing magic."

"I know."

"You do? Good. That's alright. If this is something that's happening to you on the regular, we can help you out. There are people here who dedicate their time to training new magicians. That way, doors don't open without your say so. Bet that would be nice."

Jason looked at Rosie and struggled against the memory of how the darkness had deepened every time one of the candles had gone out. He forced a smile and nodded.

"That would make parties a lot less weird," he replied.

Rosie laughed.

"I bet it would. So you see? I want you to know that you're in a safe place. Ain't no one gonna kick you out over any strangeness."

"I mean, what's strange anyway, right?" He gave a nervous laugh. Rosie waited, doing her best to hide her confusion, hoping he would say more. Jason looked down at his feet. His eyelid twitched. She saw through the shallow armor of his sarcasm and beheld fragility, a tormented mind straining to hold it all together. She decided that was enough for the moment.

"Well," she said, standing. "Need some help cleaning up?"

"Thanks, no. I got it."

"Alright. We got some grub in the kitchen. Best hurry. Percy can eat."

She lingered a bit to see if he needed anything else. He only smiled. She nodded and left the room.

Jason stared after her, expecting the door to slam. It remained open. Long afternoon shadows played in the hall.

He bowed over, hands on his knees, his eyes working back and forth.

"What the hell, what the hell, what the hell," he said. With those words came the hope that the morning had been a creation of his damaged psyche, a nightmare imprinted on the waking world by grief and exhaustion. The notion of madness was almost a comfort. Coupled with an innate ability he did not yet understand, it would explain much. His body ached. Grief, lying buried alive in his mind, hidden and not dealt with, seeded horrible thoughts that bled into reality.

He breathed deep.

"It's not real."

His father spoke from the past, reminding him that stress could trigger his fears and desires to manifest like puppets fueled by anxiety. The darkness and the closing and opening of doors had begun years before, but he had connected them to his mother's death, and then to his father's failing health. He had endured, and Darius had indulged him as many candles as he needed.

But the morning's hallucination had been different. It had spoken. It had touched him. It had wanted a friend.

He gave a dry laugh. That made sense. He stood alone in an alien bedroom, in a place filled with strangers, in a world without his parents, a twelve year old boy aged beyond his years, forced to grapple with loss. Of course his imaginary tormenter had wanted a friend.

He pushed these thoughts aside, burying them with grief, allowing the morning to dissolve into afternoon light. Satisfied (lying to himself), he launched a barrage of slaps against his cheeks, jumped up and down, and shook himself out. His father's friends had taken him in, and it would be rude not to acknowledge their kindness.

He scanned the room a last time. The remaining candles lay where he had placed them. He went to them. Some were melted to uselessness. Others retained a half an inch or so of pale wax. Nothing seemed out of the ordinary, and yet everything did. Memories from the hospital came unbidden, the candle wax reminding him of his father's deathly pallor. He ran a hand through his hair and turned away from his father's dead body. He looked out the window at the snow still falling and tree branches swaying, and for a moment he went away from himself, forgetting everything and feeling as if he were the wind through the trees, liberated from all knowledge of grief and pain.

A scream pulled him back, the shriek and laughter of a younger child tumbling from their sled. Jason focused on the day ahead and tossed the candles into a trashcan by the bed.

He leaned out of the bedroom, toothbrush in hand, and scanned the hallway. Voices murmured from the kitchen. He crossed to the bathroom.

He spat water and toothpaste into the sink, rinsed his mouth again, and stared into the mirror. His eyes were haggard, deep gray waters against black shores, and in them he saw possibilities he did not want to entertain. The horrors of the morning weakened against the certainty that he had done it to himself. The horror that remained was that he could do such a thing, could fool himself with such darkness. Who was the frightened person looking back? He brought both hands to his cheeks and dragged them down so they stretched his lower eyelids and revealed the white orbs beneath.

The answer lay within those eyes. He was certain of that. He looked into them as if he they were great depths hiding all he needed to understand. The borders of his vision darkened, and his mind's eye fluttered with the swaying of many dead branches. He could hear them in the wind, whispering, calling, urging him to be among them.

He pulled himself away, and the vision scattered. He splashed water over his face and gripped the edge of the sink. The bathroom solidified about him, all pale blue walls, clean porcelain, and a shower curtain of deep red, everything standing crisp and real and contrary to the delusions of his addled brain.

"It's not real," he said, speaking against another world that stemmed from his imagination. He wiped his forearm across his wet face, turned off the water, and left the bathroom.

He walked towards the kitchen, following the music of Mobb Deep warning of harsh realities through street poetics and cutting hip hop beats. He stopped near the kitchen entrance and looked back with uncertainty, as if he had left something unfinished. Shafts of sunlight created slanted borders of darkness and light in the hallway. Within the dimness he perceived something unseen, a terrible waiting, as if the walls of reality were about to part and expose a truth he could not comprehend.

For a moment he saw another staring back at him, poised in the shadows, one just like himself, only...

He clenched his eyes shut and violently shook his head, breathing deep, holding out his trembling hand until it settled. He opened his eyes again. The hallway was empty.

He leaned so he could peek into the kitchen.

Percy and Rosie sat the round table, Percy chewing, Rosie pouring coffee into her cup. Percy thumped his fingers against the table along with the music emanating from a cylindrical speaker on the island countertop. A nearly-finished Sudoku puzzle lay beside Rosie's plate, the numbers written in ink. A pen rested on the page.

Daylight was a gentle haze illuminating them in comforting tones. Familiarity lit in Jason's stomach, seeing in the couple his father's stories come to life, drawing the boy to them. Yet he hesitated, uncertain of where and how he was supposed to fit.

Percy didn't even look up.

"Come and have some food then," he said.

Jason was still reluctant. Rosie offered a smile of such warmth, that for a moment he forgot everything but a sudden lightness in his chest. He went and pulled a chair across from them. Pancakes, sausages, and scrambled eggs waited on the table. Percy shoveled the last of his eggs into his mouth. He reached for the pancake warmer and offered it to Jason.

"Thanks," Jason said. He took a fork, pierced a pancake, and ladled it onto his plate. The music caught his attention, and he frowned, puzzled. "You guys like Hip Hop?"

Rosie pointed to Percy who took the pancake warmer and scooped three more onto his plate. He returned the warmer to the table and poured syrup over his pancakes. Rosie pushed the bowl of eggs towards Jason.

The boy did not notice. He stared open mouthed as Percy devoured two pancakes in less than a minute.

Rosie took a sip of coffee and smiled.

"Told ya," she said.

The merciless beat ended, and piano chords came next like bells extolling a sunset in heaven. Nina Simone's voice followed, haunting, airy yet powerful, summoning raw emotion even in those who could not understand her words. Rosie smiled and closed her eyes, engaged in a moment of bliss.

Percy grabbed the plate of sausages, laid two onto Jason's plate, and then took a number of them for himself. He seemed to be focused on breakfast, but he was watching the boy, noting the tension in his neck and shoulders, the exhaustion in his eyes, and the subtle trembling of his hands. Percy looked to Rosie and saw that she noticed as well. She mouthed one word:

"Darius."

He nodded, and what she had said before came back to him. Jason was a child first, one who had just lost his father. For the time being, all else had to be put aside.

Jason did not notice them watching. He ate, forking a bit of pancake into his mouth as if he were examining it.

"This is pretty good," he said, glancing at both of them, giving an uncertain smile. "Made it yourselves, huh?"

"You can tell, can you?" Percy replied.

"It always tastes better from scratch. Except if you suck at cooking. I thought British people were bad at it?"

Percy chuckled in his quiet way.

"Some are. Like anything else, it depends. No one thing is entirely true in this world."

"Oh. Uh, yeah, guess that's true." Jason took another bite and rolled it around his tongue. "You should try blueberries in the batter next time. Not too many, or else the pancake gets all messy. I mess it up sometimes, but it can be really good."

"You like to cook?" Rosie said.

"Yeah."

"Really?"

"Love to."

"Got a favorite dish?"

Jason leaned back and twisted his mouth in thought. For a moment, the tension faded and revealed a curious and intelligent boy sorting through an inner rolodex of his favorite meals.

"Fried beans," he said, a wistful look on his face. "Real beans, not canned stuff. Black ones. Scrambled eggs, white butter—that's sour cream, whole milk, and some salt mixed together—with flour tortillas, fried sweet plantains, and any kind of pork. I like to mix the meat in with the eggs. My grandma used to make that for my..." He almost said dad. He swallowed. "She made it a lot, I guess. She was from El Salvador, so she ate stuff like that all the time. You guys already know that, though. Never met her, but I learned her recipe. The trick is to use peppers and onions when you cook the black beans, and a little bit of olive oil when you refry them. You don't need a lot. The white butter puts it all together. It goes with everything: bread, plantains, eggs. It's like the glue. Huh. Never thought of it like that."

"Reminds me of Huevos Rancheros," Rosie said.

"Oh yeah. That was my grandfather's favorite breakfast. I think. Never met him either. But I made it a few times."

"It was my daddy's favorite."

"Cool. Is he around here too, like a werewolf or a magician?"

Rosie tsked and shook her head.

"Afraid he died some time ago."

"Oh."

The boy pushed the pancake around with his fork, hanging his head, embarrassed. Rosie smiled a sad smile.

"It's alright, sweetheart," she said. "You ain't said nothing wrong."

"I'm an idiot. You said 'was.' "

"Take it easy, darling, its fine. It was a long time ago. Before I even came to New York. I'll tell you what: if you want, we'll pick up whatever ingredients you need, and you can make breakfast tomorrow. That sound good?"

"Yeah. Yeah, okay. Latino food is my favorite. Well, I love Italian food too. My mom and dad…uh, I'm half and half, so we mix a lot. My grandparents were from El Salvador. Wait, I said that already… anyway, better to mix great food. But classic American breakfasts are also good. There's, uh, there's a lot of things you can make."

He shrugged and continued to eat. Rosie sipped her coffee. Percy watched him. A long silence took hold. Jason struggled against a swarm of thoughts picking at his mind, trying to find something to say that didn't sound awkward or ungrateful.

"Strange, yeah?" Percy said, picking up Jason's apprehension.

"The what?" Jason replied, pulled from his thoughts, blinking in rapid succession.

"This whole situation. You staying with us."

Jason looked from one to the other.

"You two comparing notes or something?"

Percy said nothing, waiting, measuring the boy. Jason shifted in his seat, feeling heaviness emanate from Percy's gaze as if his eyes carried the weight of centuries, pouring an ocean of experience over all who fell under them. Bit by bit the reality of his situation took hold, enveloping him with a sense of life that was broader and stranger than he had ever imagined. His father's stories were one thing, but to be seated with a werewolf who had lived untold years, and a magician who could manipulate reality, made him wonder again how he could possibly fit among them.

Then he remembered the morning. He twitched and shook it away.

Percy noticed, tensing slightly. He saw much in the boy, a wealth of awareness that spoke of conscientiousness and deep emotion. The picture he was forming of his friend's son was one he was beginning to like. But underneath lay something else, a constant apprehension that was palpable.

"I guess people are strangers until they ain't," Jason said.

Percy watched.

"Who told you that?"

"No one."

"Not your dad?"

Jason pretended not to hear. Rosie kneed Percy under the table.

"That's a proper way of seeing things," Percy said, remaining casual. "Reminds you that everyone has potential to be something more, if given half the chance."

"I guess."

"Thing about strangers is they only stay strangers when there are secrets between them. The more you know someone, the closer they are to you."

"I should be the one taking notes."

Jason frowned at himself and took another bite of his pancake. Sarcastic comments flew out of his mouth, constructing a wall he could hide behind. Guilt gnawed underneath. He focused on his plate, worried he had offended his hosts.

A half smile was frozen on Percy's face, hiding a swell of cold anger.

"Of course," he said, "you have to be cautious as well. You can't rush. Getting to know people can sometimes be dangerous, if you're not careful. A lot of strange characters about. I think you may know something about that."

Jason tensed, his fork clutched in his hand, his knuckles going white. Mocking and judgmental voices floated from his past, granted entrance by Percy's remark, reminding him of all the people who had feared him, shunned him, made him feel like an outsider.

He looked Percy straight in the eyes, his own suddenly filled with crazed light.

"That's true," he said. "People pretend to be nice to get something from you, or so they can make fun of you. Sometimes they even wanna hurt you for no reason. It can make you go crazy. And crazy people do crazy things."

Jason's eyes went over-wide, and his smile was nearly predatory.

Percy held his gaze, seeing past the feigned threat to frustration he recognized. His own demons knocked: faces and voices from deep within his well of memory, reminding him of how he had once been unwanted. He softened, admonishing himself for the hurtful remark.

"I suppose trust is a hard thing to come by," he said.

Jason shrugged and returned to his breakfast. The madness was gone, replaced by melancholy bordering on numbness.

Rosie glared at her husband. He lifted his hands from the table, defensive. She shook her head and leaned close to Jason.

"You haven't touched your sausages, sweetheart," she said.

"I like to eat my first pancake by itself."

"Hey," Rosie raised her hands in commiseration. "So, I bet there's a few things you'd like to know about us."

"It's not common to have breakfast with a werewolf and magician, is it?" Percy said.

"For you guys it is."

"Alright, maybe so," Percy said. "But I have to imagine that you're curious. It's alright to ask questions."

"I'm not too dangerous?" The words came unbidden. He looked from Rosie to Percy and shook his head. "Sorry."

"It's alright," Percy said. "I deserve that."

"No. You two are...nice, and I...I know what you're doing for me. You're right, this is just...different."

"New for us too, mate."

"Most definitely unexpected."

Jason nodded. He twitched, blinking hard, and thought for a moment.

"I am curious," he said. "It's just..."

He stared at his plate, trying to filter the right words through a haze of emotions, many he did not yet understand. Rosie took his empty glass and poured water into it.

"It's a lot to take in," she said, setting his glass down.

He took it and drank.

"Yeah. Like, I don't know where to start. Even though I know some stuff about you all and this place, it's like it's all coming in at once and I can't...I don't know. Does that make sense?"

"It does," Percy replied.

Jason took another sip of water, thought for a moment, and perked up with a sudden bolt of inspiration.

"Okay, I know. I've always wondered about your whole, uh, werewolf thing. Is it like you're wearing a really small costume when you look like the way you do now, like you're big inside but have to fit into your skin? Or is that how you really look, and your body changes into the, uh, werewolf?"

Percy squinted at him, uncertain if he was being sarcastic or not.

"The latter," he said.

"Oh. You must destroy a lot of clothes."

"I take 'em off before I turn."

"That makes sense. Hold up, even if you're in a hurry?"

"It all depends—"

" 'Cause, I mean, how do you get back home or wherever if your butt-naked? I know this is New York, but, still, someone would see you."

"I don't turn outside."

Jason was taken aback.

"You change into a werewolf in here? Like, Ms. St. John—"

"Rosie," Rosie said.

"Like Ms. St. Rosie can come in and find you all...furry?"

Percy nearly glared.

"Are you taking the piss?"

"What the—Why would I pee in here?"

Rosie stood up and took the pitcher of water to the sink, her shoulders shaking with laughter. Percy stared at the boy for a moment. Then he snorted and laughed in his quiet way. Rosie returned with more water, still smiling, and she and Percy exchanged a bemused look. Jason looked from one to the other and laughed himself, a crazed and unguarded sound giving way to gentle release.

They sat that way and ate together, a measure of light easing the air, filling the strangeness between them with something human and alive.

7

The phone rang in the Demidovs' living room. Ian slid the final dish into place within the cupboard and left the kitchen. Alexander stepped out from his bedroom behind him, buttoning his shirt.

"I got it," Ian said.

He reached the phone and answered. The line crackled.

"Hey...can...hurry..." Janet Olson's voice, far away, as if spoken through a windstorm.

Ian checked to see that no one could hear him. Then:

"Baby? What's up?"

"Can you...by....need...see you."

"Is everything okay?"

"Please...hurry..."

There was a click, then the dial tone. Ian frowned and redialed. The alien and monotonous beat of a busy signal answered. He hung up, thinking. Something in Janet's voice had sounded off, tension or perhaps even fear.

Alexander came into the living room, adjusting the cuffs of his shirt.

"Hey, Pop?"

"Yes, baby."

"Are we going to Aunt Rosie's right now?"

"In a few minutes. Why?"

"Janet just called. Mind if I go see her first?"

"Someone's in love," Eleanor said, singing from the sofa as she colored.

Alexander frowned. He remembered his conversation with Deirdre Olson, and the wary look that she always leveled at his son.

"Well..." he said.

"Just for a little bit," Ian replied, concern knotting his features.

Relief lightened a weight within Alexander. He saw in Ian what he wanted everyone else in the Gardens to see, most of all Deirdre Olson. He saw a boy capable of warmth and human emotion.

From time to time, he realized, even he needed a reminder.

"Okay. Not too long."

"Thanks."

Ian cut through the living room, took his coat from the sofa, and walked by Eleanor without rubbing her hair. She blew mock kisses at him. He ignored her. The phone call triggered curiosity and apprehension, and his shadow waited in the dim vestibule like a perched cat. It hissed, mirroring something close to fear. Ian threw on his coat and replayed Janet's voice in his mind, the strange way her words had cut in and out, the need in them.

He left the apartment, locked the door behind him, and went down the hallway. His steps clapped upon the tiles. Wind moaned as if the building were weeping.

He passed the elevator and went for the stairs. A sign reading "Maintenance - Work in Progress" hung from the doorknob, caked in rust colored stains. Bangs and pounding erupted from the stairwell, and weak lamplight flickered through the milky window. Ian looked at the door a moment, unable to remember any mention of maintenance being performed. The lettering on the sign seemed sloppy.

Janet's voice urged him on.

He called the elevator and went to button his coat. The elevator door slid open. He looked up with a moment's surprise, not expecting the elevator so soon. He went inside and pressed the Lobby button.

The elevator door closed.

"3" glowed red on a black screen, then vanished as the elevator began its descent. Metallic whirs and the humming of cables vibrated through the walls. Ian ticked each finger against his thumb, replaying Janet's voice and hearing something off beyond static and a faulty line.

The elevator trembled and hummed.

He thought of Jason. There was an air of something other about the stranger, something unreadable. Questions whirled through Ian's mind, and he found he was almost annoyed with Janet, wanting to sit once more before the boy, to watch and listen. But there had been something in her voice, something he could not place. His shadow growled beside him, mirroring his apprehension.

The elevator jolted to a stop.

Ian fell backwards against the wall, then regained balance. Wind cried through the shaft as the elevator shifted in gentle gradations. Cables creaked. Metallic dings echoed. Ian went to the console and pushed the Emergency Call button. The speaker crackled and purred electric as it rang out.

Ian waited. The ringing went on. He looked up towards the camera tucked into the upper right corner of the elevator and waved. The ringing continued. He turned back to the console and pushed the alarm button.

The elevator's light died, and the ringing ceased like breath cut short. Ian stood in darkness. The voice of the howling wind went silent. No sound reverberated through the elevator shaft. Ian's shadow growled beside him, its eyes staining the darkness.

Lights flared, and the elevator hummed back to life. Ian breathed deep and nodded up at the camera in thanks. Most likely no one had answered because they had worked quickly to fix the problem. He pulled out leather gloves from his pockets and slid them on. The elevator continued to descend, vibrating through his shoes. He frowned and looked at the screen, wondering why the ride was taking so long.

He froze.

The digits on the screen flared one by one. They read:

"L

-1

-2

-3

-4...

8

Eleanor slid the colored pencil into the margins of her sketchbook, closed it, wiped her hands, and looked up. Her father stood by the archway, sliding his coat on, watching her with a strange light in his eyes.

She gave him a concerned look, catching him in mid-reverie and sensing melancholy or perhaps regret.

"You okay, Pop?"

He did not answer right away.

"Da, darling, da. Ready?"

"Uh, yeah. Ready-spaghetti. I think you need this, though."

She got up, walked over to him, and threw her arms about his waist. He tensed for a moment, then received her with a grateful embrace. For a moment, all else was forgotten.

"You know I love you, right?" she said.

"I love you too. Where did that come from?"

She shrugged, pressing against him.

"You're a good guy. Good guys deserve to hear that people love them."

A burst of emotion cascaded through Alexander. He swallowed against his tightening throat, against the swell of gratitude for his daughter. A question drained the moment of some of its power: would she say such a thing if she had seen him with blood on his hands, with the gun smoking in his grip, and the boy's corpse at his feet?

He closed his eyes against the memory and held her tight.

They parted, and she brushed the tip of his nose and yanked on the ends of his mustache. The sadness faded into smiling lines crinkling the corners of his eyes.

"Okay," he said, the word filled with true happiness. "Go get your coat, baby."

"Okie dokie."

She went and returned, slipping her purple bubble coat over her red hoodie, smiling up at him.

The doorbell rang. Alexander frowned.

"One moment," he said.

He went ahead of her into the hallway, looked through the peephole, and then leaned his forehead against the door, burdened by the discussion that waited on the other side. It was necessary. It was inevitable. But he had hoped to put it off for as long as possible. He opened the door. Richard Horowitz stood beyond, hands stuffed into his pockets, eyes heavy. Alexander exhaled.

"I supposed this can't wait?" he said.

"We should talk," Richard replied.

Alexander held the door open and motioned him inside. Eleanor peeked into the hallway, and Alexander went to her.

"Pop?"

"It's okay. I just have to talk to Dr. Horowitz for a moment. Why don't you go ahead. Let your aunt and uncle know I'll be there soon."

"Should I tell them he's here?" She gestured at Richard, who lingered in the hallway.

"Of course. Eh, Ellie..."

He wanted to say that she didn't have to be in the habit of keeping secrets. But he knew that was not true. A piece of his heart broke.

"Just, eh, let them know I'll be there soon."

He widened his eyes to remind her: "Not a word about Jason."

She understood. He bent down, tapping his cheek with his forefinger, and she kissed him. Then she zipped up her coat and walked on, saluting Richard on her way out. The doctor smiled down at her and gently karate chopped her shoulder. But she caught heaviness in his eyes. As she looked back into the living room from the entrance, she felt as if she were intruding on something cold and terrible.

She locked the door behind her, walked past other apartments, heard televisions, music, and voices murmuring from within them. She hummed "Here Comes the Sun", emphasizing her favorite notes with "Do-Dos", and "Yeah-Yeahs." She passed the elevator door to the stairwell. There was no maintenance sign. She opened the stairwell door and froze for a moment. The dimness was deep, broken only by the orange glow of lamps hanging over landings, and the steps rose and fell like altars smeared in dying light. She breathed deep, accepted the fear unspooling in her stomach, and ran down the stairs as fast as she could.

She sang louder and jumped whole sets of steps, finally reaching the lobby entrance. She opened it and raced out to greet the fading daylight spilling through the lobby door, ran outside, smiled at the snowfall, walked down the steps, and followed the path to Percy, Rosie, and Jason.

9

The scent of Eleanor lingered, sweetness mingled with the waxy aroma of crayons and colored pencils. Alexander breathed her, and he was reminded of all that was dear to him: his children, his home, his life. He thought back to what Ian had said and knew his son to be right. He had to do whatever it took to protect what mattered.

But when he turned to Richard, all he could see was the boy screaming in the dark, his eyes a mass of blood.

He wiped his face and gestured towards the sofa. Richard sat.

"Drinks?" Alexander said. Richard shook his head. Alexander remained standing and stuffed his hands in his pockets. "So?"

Richard made a steeple of his fingers, looking over them, searching for a way to begin. His eyes were bloodshot. Snow melted on his jacket, rivulets pooling into the creases and rips of the worn leather.

"Eitan told me everything," he said.

Alexander leaned against a chair nearest the sofa and folded his hands together to stop them from shaking. Again he heard the screaming. Again he heard the crash of the gun.

"I must be honest," he replied, "This is not a good time to talk about this."

"It'll never be." Richard looked at Alexander. "You know I didn't want this. I didn't...you had no choice, Alexander."

"Stop. Just stop right there—"

"We were doing the right thing."

"Richard."

Richard looked at him for a long time, weighing Alexander's pain against his own and seeing in his friend a burden he knew he could never carry.

"There's nothing you need to say," he said. "I came because...if you want me to leave...if you want me out of the Gardens—"

"Don't be an idiot. I could've said no. We had to take the chance. We couldn't have known..."

"You were trying to do a good thing. This isn't on you."

Alexander was silent for a moment.

"Maybe," he said. But there was no conviction in his eyes. He threw up his hands. "You always have a home here. What happened —what's done is done."

They were silent. Richard's hands worked in circular motion, as if he were attempting to shape reason out of chaos.

"I knew that Greg was planning on staying outside," he said. "I should've told you, but he wanted to tell you himself."

"Does he know about...?"

"Not from me, but he has to know by now. As soon as I talk to him, I'll...I'll get him to come home."

"If he's still alive."

Richard's jaw muscles tensed.

"He's alive. He calls every few hours, lets my number ring once and hangs up. That's his way of...doesn't matter." He clenched his eyes shut and gripped the bridge of his nose. "We shouldn't have done this. It was stupid. I'm sorry. Truly."

Alexander nodded, knowing that the doctor was speaking honestly.

"If you want to keep this quiet," Richard said. "I'm saying no one has to know. That's what I wanted to tell you. People will be pissed if they find out. And scared. We've never had a vampire attack this close to home."

Alexander shook his head.

"No. We have to tell the Council everything. They need to know."

"Why?"

"Richard—"

"How will it help? What difference will it make? Just let it go."

"That's not how we do things. That's not us. We start hiding things from each other, and everything falls apart."

For a moment, he was overwhelmed by his own hypocrisy. He told himself Jason was different. What the boy was promised to do...

He let it go and pressed on.

"We tell them. All of it. That is who we are."

"Then I'll take full responsibility."

"There's enough of that to go around."

"You'll get a ton of shit for this."

"And what? I deserve it. I'll deal with the council, with whatever they want to do to me."

"This wasn't your fault," Richard said, filling each word with as much earnestness as he could. "None of it."

Alexander clutched his hands together and did not respond. There was nothing left to say.

Richard left. Alexander took a moment. Solitude beckoned, urging him to clear his mind. He sat down on the sofa, pulled out his silver cigarette case, took out a joint, snapped a flame into existence, and smoked. Tension melted, silencing the storm of accusing voices. A warm haze drifted through him, but he was not removed from the morning's events. In a sense he was closer, replaying all that happened through an objective lens. There had been no hope for the child. He had been destroyed by the terror he had witnessed, his mind devolved into a thing of pure suffering. But guilt burned Alexander. He nodded with morbid approval. It was a fire he was proud to endure, an emotion that separated him and his kind from their enemies. He would draw strength from the pain. He would use it to remind himself of who he was.

He stroked his mustache and remembered the blood hot on his skin. He knew there would be more blood spilled before his life was over.

This was not the time for reflection. Another boy demanded his attention. This one he had every intention of saving. What was more, if his best friend had spoken true, this boy would one day save them all.

He snuffed the joint against the cigarette case, returned it half-smoked within, and went to the entrance. He reached for the door-knob, and then noticed a folded piece of paper peeking from under the gap. He frowned with curiosity, picked up the paper, and opened it.

A child's drawing in crayon: a brown figure lying on a gray floor. Blood poured from its empty eyes and a ravaged hole gaping at the side of its head. Yet the figure smiled, a great exaggerated grin lined with yellowed teeth.

Alexander stared, aghast. Anger surged, and he threw open the door and stormed into the hallway.

No one was there. Fluorescent lights buzzed. Murmurs emanated from other apartments.

Alexander remained for a moment, clutching the drawing, his lip trembling. He could not imagine Richard doing such a thing. Then he remembered Abebe Ngombe. He had felt no hint of the demon, could imagine no reason why he would do this. But there was no other explanation. He waited, half-expecting Ngombe to invade his mind, or to stroll out of thin air.

Nothing happened.

He cursed under his breath, resolving to tell the others, and crushed the drawing into a ball.

When he turned back towards his apartment, he found a child standing in the doorway with its back to him, naked from the waist up. Crimson-black blood stained his neck and shoulders. A red crayon was in his hand, and he was coloring the side of his head beneath a wound of tattered bone and flesh, up and down, brightening the bloodstain in livid tones.

Alexander gasped, breathless. Reason left him, replaced by blind terror, an animal fear that locked him in place. Some deeper part of him screamed to run, but he could not move. The thing before him was an affront, a mockery to all that was sane in an ordered world. Despite the wonders and horrors the magician had witnessed, there was no reckoning with what stood at his door.

The door slammed shut on its own. Alexander blinked once, twice, and brought his hands to his mouth. He did not scream. All that emerged was a choking sound, as if a beast had been caught in a trap. Panic seeped in, and he looked about, searching for something familiar to grasp on to, some evidence of normalcy to disprove what he had seen.

But he was no longer in the hallway of his apartment building, not as he knew it. The walls were cracked and chipped. Paint hung in fetid sheets like drunkards leaning into sleep. Dust caked the floor, and corrupted light spilled from lamps encased in filth. Closed doors surrounded him, decrepit, damaged. They marched through a hall that seemed to go on and on.

Somewhere ahead, echoing in the darkness, came footsteps.

10

-26
-27
-28...

11

The faucet sighed against the clink of dishes.

Jason stood in the hallway, once more looking at the photo of his father. Numbness took hold, muting the impact of the image, casting Darius in a light of profound curiosity. Jason wondered who his father had been: what experiences brought him to that moment, what thoughts, loves, joys, and fears composed him into the man standing within the picture. He searched young Darius' face, but found no answers.

Then he noticed something he had missed before. A part of the picture had been ripped out, leaving a crooked border on the left side.

Percy stepped into hallway from the kitchen, looking in on the boy. He lingered a moment, but when Jason didn't notice him, he cleared his throat.

Jason turned to him.

"Why is this picture ripped?" he said.

"Oh," Percy replied, disappointment clear in his voice. "You noticed that then."

"Not good?"

Percy joined him before the photo, considering how to go on.

"Well," he said, "it brings up bad memories."

"What do you mean?"

"There was someone who used to be a friend of ours—your dads', all of us. He was in this picture. Then he did a terrible thing. More than a few, actually. Now he's gone."

"Gone?"

"It's nothing you need concern yourself with."

Jason turned back to the photo.

"Why didn't you just print a new one? You know, take him out that way."

Percy was silent for a moment.

"It's a bit of a reminder," he replied. "Sort of like a scar. Helps us remember to be careful of whom to trust."

"Did my…" Father. Dad. Jason couldn't say either word. He sniffed and wiped his nose with his arm. "Were y'all really close friends with this guy?"

A faraway look came into Percy's eyes.

"We were." Regret heavy in his voice. His teeth clenched with an audible click.

Jason noticed and felt guilty for pushing on. But curiosity could not be helped.

"He—he must've done something really bad to you."

"He tried to hurt Rosie, for one thing."

"How?"

Percy shook his head.

"She should tell you that. I shouldn't even have brought it up."

"What was his name?"

"Why do you want to know?"

Jason shrugged.

"Maybe I heard of him."

"Doubt that."

Jason stared. Percy saw something close to desperation on his face, as if this small bit of history would somehow bring him closer to his father. He relented.

"Matt. Mathew Moore. He was Phoebe's brother—that's Eleanor's mum."

"I know about Phoebe. I heard about her all the time."

Percy smiled.

"That doesn't surprise me."

"What did Mr. Moore—uh, Matt, do?"

Percy shook his head.

"Another time, mate. Come on. Keep us company, yeah?"

They went back to the kitchen, and Percy rejoined Rosie with the dishes. Jason offered to help, but they kindly refused.

The boy sat at the kitchen table and watched failing daylight seep into the lines of his palms. He flexed his fingers, weighing sunlight. His father had once told him that all life on Earth was made of stars, animated as if to dream what they could not. A spring of grief surged through the boy. His throat burned, and tears pressed against his eyes. He snatched his hands back, wiped his eyes with his sleeve, and pushed his father into depths where he was invisible, where he was not living or dead, where such words held no meaning.

He looked up and caught Rosie staring as she placed dishes into the dishwasher. He saw himself reflected in her eyes—slouched over the table, exhausted, alone. She smiled, looked away, and closed the dishwasher door. But she could not hide the pity she felt. That pity was another reminder.

A chasm opened inside Jason. He closed his eyes, pressed them into his palms, and clung to the darkness there.

In that darkness, silence.

"They should be here soon," Percy said, as he wiped the counter beside the sink with a towel. "Jason, are you alright with having a bit of a chat? We should all go over some ground—"

Jason heard Percy's voice as if it were memory, something half-dreamed, trailing into nothingness. The world went distant, almost forgotten, and his senses, thoughts, and emotions merged until all was still. No endings or beginnings, no death or life, nothing save a sustained peace that stretched beyond the confines of a boundless universe. This was where he wanted to be, floating in silence, a spark of light dreaming new dreams until one would take hold and spread across the cosmos like ink over paper.

Screams tore the silence apart and ripped him into a howling void.

He hovered in absolute black: no kitchen, no Rosie, no daylight, no Percy. Shrieks ravaged the emptiness, unseen specters undulating and booming, spitting and roaring, endless brigades of abominations raging against infinity. Jason slammed his hands against his ears and gasped.

"No," he said, his voice a pin drop in an ice storm. "No, no, no."

Something materialized out of the gloom, a pale figure veiled by visceral folds of matter that stretched and contorted around it. Fragments of a ballerina's dress shimmered, a purple tutu trailing and tattered. Black hair flowed. She did not move, yet came closer, as if the dark imagined her from one space to the next.

Jason shook his head, his hands a vice over his ears.

The figure offered a hand torn by decay and corruption. Long strands of darkness dripped from her fingers.

"No, no, no," Jason said, shaking his head violently, shutting his eyes. "You're not real, you're not real, this isn't real, not real, go away, not real."

The void shrieked in answer. The cold of her washed over him, the breath of catacombs. She came closer.

"Leave me alone," he said.

Screams penetrated.

"Leave me alone. You're—"

"Alright?"

"Not real!"

Jason snapped awake, leaned too far back in his chair, and crashed against the floor. Pain rippled up his arms and back. He almost welcomed it.

Percy and Rosie rushed to help him up. Jason staggered, tripped between the chair's stiles, and almost fell again. Percy caught him.

"You okay?" Rosie said.

Jason nodded, blinking in quick succession.

"A little wound up, are we?" Percy said, looking his head over for any gashes.

Jason gave a frenzied laugh as relief took hold.

"Yeah," he said. "I'm just peachy."

Rosie and Percy exchanged a doubtful look.

"What's not real?" Rosie said.

"What? Oh. Nothing, nah—I just had a bad dream."

"You fell asleep?"

"It's nothing."

Jason doubted the words as they came. He looked towards the living room, expecting someone or something to be standing there, watching him. There was nothing. He turned back to them, smiled an empty smile, and then looked at the floor in a daze.

"I was tired," he said. "I'm okay now."

"Do you want go to your room?" Rosie replied, "Get a little shut eye before Alexander gets—"

The kitchen cabinets exploded and vomited pots, pans, and glassware over the floor in a great crash. Rosie cursed as shards of glass tore through her sweats and bit into her right calf. Percy threw himself around her. A blue ceramic bowl slammed into his upper back with such force that it dissolved into fragments.

Jason pressed against the wall and covered his eyes. Quiet fell. He peeked through his fingers and stared at the aftermath. A mess of plates and cookware, glasses and bowls, piled on the floor. Shards of glass gleamed. The cupboard doors hung from damaged hinges, or lay broken on countertops.

A mug with a painted cartoon robot rested at Jason's feet. The robot looked up at him, its bright yellow eyes wide.

"Are you alright?" Percy said to Rosie, looking her over, running a hand down her back.

She nodded, flinched, and looked at her leg. Thin streams of blood dripped over her ankle, reddening the cuff of her sock. Percy saw this and glared at Jason. Rosie laid her hand on Percy's cheek, the single gesture reminding him of all that had happened in the last few hours. Percy collected himself. He nodded to the boy.

"Alright?"

Jason's mouth worked, but he struggled to speak.

"I'm sorry," he finally said.

Rosie braced herself on Percy's shoulder. She took a deep breath.

"You should've been here a lot sooner, sweetheart. We could've gotten this under control."

"I'm sorry," Jason said again.

"It's alright. It—aw hell." She grimaced. "It ain't your fault, you can't control it yet. Shoot, let me take care of this. Then we'll see to cleaning this mess up."

"I can leave," Jason said.

Rosie blinked as if she had been slapped.

"What?"

"I'll go. You don't have to—"

Rosie hopped forward, bringing Percy with her, glaring at the boy. Her eyes said everything she had to say about the matter. Jason looked down at his feet and let the subject lie. Rosie seemed like she wanted to say more, but she let it go and motioned Percy towards the hallway. He lingered for a moment, watching Jason as if he were an animal he had never seen. Then he helped Rosie from the kitchen.

Jason caught his breath, clutching a hand to his chest. Movement flickered to his right. He looked into the living room, and in the shadows before the window he spied a boy facing him. His features were veiled, yet something familiar emanated from the boy, recognition Jason did not want. He closed his eyes and shook his head.

"No, no, no, no," he said.

He opened his eyes. The boy was gone. He exhaled, bowed his head, and wrung his hands together.

Percy helped Rosie to the bathroom. She opened the door.

"Go back to him," she said. "I got it from here."

"Sure?"

"Get."

Blood dripped over her heel, soaking her sock. The sight of it gripped Percy with metallic fists.

"I'm fine," Rosie said. "It don't hurt none. I bet it's just surface deep. If it's worse, we'll call Doc Horowtiz. Scout's honor."

"You ever see unchecked magic that strong before?"

"Yeah, with Eleanor." Percy frowned. Rosie sighed. "Alright, this was stronger."

"What have we gotten ourselves into?" he said.

"Don't do that."

"What?"

"Don't start doubting. Keep all this in perspective."

"I am. I'm not sure you are."

"Meaning?" she said.

"You're bleeding, love, go have a look."

"Meaning?"

Percy hesitated.

"You're being a little too trusting. This whole thing—bloody hell, I don't know what you'd call it. The boy should've never been born in the first place. He's capable of goodness knows what. He's a stranger, but we're treating him like family."

"He is family. If Darius had come here like he should've, that wouldn't have even been a question. What's the matter with you? What, you think he's gonna wipe us all out? Blow the whole Gardens to hell? He's a kid, he's afraid, and he's got no notion of the power he's wielding. Most important of all, he's got no one else. Unless you wanna give him back to Abebe? I didn't think so. He made a mess. That's all."

"It's much more complicated than that."

"Maybe to you."

"Are you forgetting what Darius said he's meant to do?" he said.

"I ain't forget nothing. I just ain't afraid of babies."

Percy paused for a moment, the muscles in his jaw flexing.

"Is this because I can't give you a child?"

Rosie stiffened, her lips going rigid, hurt in her eyes. She yanked her hand away, hopped into the bathroom, and flipped on the light, all the while keeping her back to him.

"If you believe that," she said, "then you think very little of me."

She swung the door closed.

Percy stood for a moment, rubbing his neck, burdened by dread. The blood dripping over Rosie's leg twisted his fear into something tangible. The stranger in his home opened doors to unknowns he did not want to entertain. All of his long years, and he could not see every angle. Life had taught him you could only know as much as the world allowed. Change and chaos were marauders upending all things, leaving those left alive to scrabble among the wreckage and piece together an existence out of uncertainties. Immortality did not bring omniscience. Wisdom was the gift of time, and wisdom was recognizing that you could never know everything. That there were always surprises, and always things to fear.

He loved Rosie and wanted to keep her safe. He wanted to keep his people safe. Those were the things he knew for certain.

The rest...

He went to knock on the door, to tell her, but then dropped his hand. Perhaps he was being short sighted. Perhaps he needed to trust more. The way was unclear. He sighed and looked down. Droplets of her blood trailed over the carpet.

He went back to the kitchen and found Jason tiptoeing among shards of broken glass, pieces of a plate in his hand. He laid the pieces on the table.

"Leave it," Percy said.

"I messed it up, let me help."

"You wanna cut yourself? Think that'll make things better?"

Jason stared. Percy noticed more droplets of blood on the kitchen floor. He glared at the boy.

"Are you daft?" he said. "You're not helping. You're just in the bloody way."

He regretted it as soon as he said it.

Jason's face fell. He walked out of the kitchen and leaned against the wall outside. A voice spoke in his mind, offering a familiar option.

He could leave. He could run away and be alone. That would be nothing new. How many long lunches spent in a bathroom during his brief stint at school, the cafeteria a melodious babble he could not harmonize with? How many long days drifting alone, walking through an empty park, watching the world go by? How long had he spent with a book, sitting at a window, the spell of reading momentarily broken to remind him that he was not like the others he saw walking the streets? He looked towards the entrance door and felt its promise of escape, a life away from watchful eyes, the bitter peace afforded by isolation.

Wind cut against the living room window. He shivered, seized by cold. The question came like a taunt: where would he go? The answer was immediate and cruel, leaving him planted against the wall.

The clink of broken glass escaped the kitchen.

Jason looked down the hallway, towards the room he had slept in, and saw long shadows painted over its door. He turned away, remembering the events of the morning, remembering what he had seen moments before behind closed eyes, remembering the vision of the boy watching him. He told himself again that they were hallucinations, bad dreams, but he did not believe that. And though he felt Percy's anger like steam rising off of ice, he could not stand to be alone with whatever was waiting for him in the darkness.

He went into the living room and sat the edge of the sofa.

The doorbell rang.

Percy emerged from the kitchen and stuffed his hands into his pockets.

"I could actually use your help," he said.

Jason swallowed and stared at his knees.

"I don't wanna be in the way."

"You're not. I was angry. I said a stupid thing."

They stared at each other.

"You change your mind fast," Jason said.

"Perks of old age."

The bell rang again, then erupted into a melodious flurry in tune with rhythmic knocking at the door. Percy went to the door and opened it.

"Putting on a concert?" he said. "Bit early for you to be awake."

"Ha ha," Eleanor replied.

Jason perked up at her voice.

Percy saw she was alone and nodded towards the hall.

"They'll be here soon," Eleanor said, catching his meaning. "Ian went to see his girlfriend, and Pop had to, uh, talk to Dr. Horowitz, so—"

"Right," Percy replied, wanting her to speak no more of the matter for fear that she would inquire.

She followed him and made to greet Jason. Then she spied the kitchen.

"Holy shit, what happened here?" She looked from Percy to Jason. "Oh. I know what happened. Damn."

"I guess I just can't help myself," Jason said.

Eleanor cocked her head at the desolation in his eyes.

"You know it's normal for us, right?" she said. "It's part of the whole magician-thing."

He shrugged. Percy watched them.

"You said you needed my help?" Jason said to him.

"In a moment." He lingered, almost afraid to leave Eleanor alone with the boy. Paranoia caught him off guard, threatening to take control of his every decision. Shame followed, for as he looked at Jason he realized Rosie was right: he was only a boy. He made to speak, found nothing to say, and returned to the kitchen.

Jason smiled at Eleanor, but his eyes spoke of guilt and disappointment.

"Don't sweat it, dude," Eleanor said. "I told you about the eggs, right? It happens. You'll learn." Glass scraped against the kitchen tiles. She called out to Percy. "I can help too."

"Give us a second, Ellie."

Eleanor joined Jason at the sofa and inflated one cheek and then the other to a rhythm only she heard. Jason shifted, squeezing his hands into fists. He whirled and looked back at the hallway. Daylight faded inch by inch. The first glow of streetlight painted the walls. He turned back and drummed his fingers against his legs. Eleanor twisted in the sofa to face him.

"How you holding up?" she said.

"Great."

They were quiet.

"Sorry," Eleanor said. "That's a dumb question. I guess...I only remember a little of when my ma died, so it didn't really hit me the way it must be hitting you."

"Lucky you."

"Ouch."

Jason grimaced.

"Sorry. I just meant that..."

He didn't finish. Eleanor understood.

"I know," she said. "It sucks. But I still wish I remembered my mom, even though she died."

"Why?"

She shrugged.

"'Cause then I'd know her."

"You don't remember her at all?"

"No, I remember a few things. But it's like they aren't real or something. Like I made it up. Even though it would hurt a lot worse to remember her dying, at least she'd be in here, ya know?" She pointed to her head, hesitated, rolled her eyes, and pointed at her heart, sighing. "Yeah, sometimes I'm corny."

"You can be corny," Jason replied. His smile carried warmth. "That's cool."

"No it's not. That's why it's corny."

Jason shrugged.

"At least corny's honest. It sucks that you don't remember her."

"Yeah. But I'm still lucky. I got a lot of good people in my life."

Jason did not reply. Eleanor watched him for a moment, and then unzipped her bubble coat, letting it fall behind her. Plastic bags crinkled in the kitchen. Eleanor nudged Jason.

"How's he been?" she said, whispering.

Jason leaned towards her and responded at full volume:
"What?"

Eleanor urged him to keep his voice down. She pointed at the kitchen.

"I don't think he likes me very much," he said.

Eleanor shushed him with a finger to her lips. Percy emerged from the kitchen with swollen garbage bags in each hand. He looked at both of them, and then went to the door.

"Just be a moment," he said. "Have to go downstairs, can't throw these down the chute."

He left. The door clicked shut after him.

Jason rubbed his arms, trying to warm cold bubbling under his skin. Eleanor smacked his arm. He flinched and looked at her with surprise.

"Don't you know what this means?" she said, miming a shushing motion. "If he wants, he can hear you farting from like a thousand miles away."

Jason rubbed his arm.

"Wow, that's cool. Know what else is cool? Not hitting people."

Eleanor waved him away.

"Don't you ever worry he'd spy on you?" he said.

"Hey. He's my uncle. Watch it."

"Uncles can spy."

"Mr. Suspicious over here. I trust him. We all do. He can turn his powers on and off."

"What is he exactly?"

"Uh, I don't really know how to explain it. He's a werewolf who's lived a few hundred years. So...awesome?"

"How has he lived that long?"

"It has something to do with Abebe Ngombe. Oh, uh, your Uncle Abe. Don't think I'll ever get used to calling him that. He's like Uncle Percy's dad somehow. Even though they, you know, look nothing alike. Like an adopted thing. He gave Uncle Percy, well, immortality."

Jason stared at his hands again, going quiet. The mention of

Abebe dragged him closer to the morning, to what was lost and the strangeness of his new life.

Eleanor blew air through her lips in a syncopated rhythm.

"Bet you're pretty confused, huh?" she said.

"And there goes another one."

She frowned.

"Your aunt and uncle have been saying the same thing," he said.

"Well, you can't blame 'em, can you?"

He twisted to look at the hallway again. Eleanor spoke, but he did not hear. Streetlight glistened against the walls. Daylight creased the carpet, fading. Horrors linger beneath sun and moon. They abide no rules of time. But the coming dark tightened Jason's insides. Something in the abominable screams he had heard in that black space, that world he hoped was the workings of his agonized brain. Something nameless and without mercy, growing surer with every centimeter of darkness, sapping him of energy and will.

He wanted to tell Eleanor, to let it all out. But he imagined the look on her face, the realization that he was damaged. He shook his head, muttered to himself, and fell silent.

"Jason?"

He came to attention. Daylight was a trickle on the carpet.

"The what?" he said.

"I asked if I was being too weird, but it looks like you got me beat."

"Jesus, you ask a lot of questions."

"Sorry. I can be pushy. But, I mean, how else can you get to know someone?"

"I feel like you already know everything, the way you talk."

"You calling me a loud mouth?"

"Yeah."

She pouted. He rubbed his knuckles into his eyes.

"No," he said. "You're not a loud mouth, and you're the good kinda weird. Sorry, I'm not used to...friendliness. Are you a mind reader or something? It's like you know everything without me saying it. It's kinda nice, actually. Anyway..." He blinked hard and looked at the floor. Then he forced himself to look at her, and when he did an honest smile formed. "Wanna know something? I didn't think this place was real. I didn't think any of it was real. I thought it was all made up. Even when stuff started happening to me, I just thought I was crazy. I still kinda do."

"You're not," Eleanor replied, gesturing around the apartment, indicating her home, her world. "Either that or we all are. I mean I am, but I don't think everyone else is."

"If you're crazy, then I wanna be crazy too."

She blinked with surprise, and then smiled.

"It just feels weird," he said. "It's like hearing a story you really like, and then one day you wake up and see people from that story come up to you and be all like 'Hey, what's up? Want some breakfast?' It was almost better when I didn't see it in real life. Then I could pretend to be normal. This is normal for you. For me it's…"

He trailed off. Eleanor waited. She saw him puzzling thoughts together, trying to make sense of the whole of his young life.

"I just don't think I want it to be real," he said.

"That would make all of us not real."

"I guess."

"That would make me not real."

"Well, I didn't mean—"

"That wouldn't bother you?"

"I–it would now, but—"

"That's a little mean."

He gaped at her.

"I said it would now. Jesus, c'mon."

"How could you say that about my family? All the good people here? My precious home? I love them all so much."

She glared at him for as long as she could, then crumpled into laughter at the shock on his face. She fell on her side and rolled around, snorting.

Jason sagged into the sofa.

"You suck," he said.

"You should see your face."

He grimaced, looked sideways at her, and then chuckled. His

chuckle blossomed into a full laugh that harmonized with hers. Ease lived between them, and for a moment the shadows were not so deep.

"Everything you said makes sense," she said, sitting up. "I'd feel the same way. But I promise, you'll think differently once you see what this place is really like. There are a lot of good people here. They've all had bad things happen to them, and because of that they try extra hard to make this a real home. You're never really alone here."

"That might not be good for me."

"Being around people?"

"I don't do too good with them."

"You're doing okay with me."

"I am?"

"Yeah," she said. "You're kind of a bummer, but that won't last too long."

He turned to face her.

"Why do you think it'll get better?"

She shrugged.

"'Cause they do. They have to. Then you can be your real self. No one is themselves when they're sad. When you're sad, it's like you're half-a-person. But if you can get through it, you can be who you really are again. You just gotta be careful and not believe the things you think when you're sad. Even when they're true."

"I don't know if I believe that."

"Okay. Well, look at it this way: even the worst most horrible fucked up thing in the world ends. No matter how bad it is. Whatever happens after has to be better."

"Huh," he said. "You are crazy. But so am I, so..."

She nodded, okay with that.

"Most people..." he said, his eyes going distant. He let the thought hang. "I didn't have any friends in school."

"You went to school?"

"You didn't?"

"Here, not in the city," she said. "Not like all official and stuff."

"You didn't miss much."

"That's what they tell me. Still curious, though."

"Boring, long, bad food, and classes that don't really teach you anything. There you go."

"Sounds great."

"No one liked me. And I'm so bright and happy." He grinned an exaggerated grin and shot a thumbs up. She chuckled. He went on. "They called me 'Jinx.' That—" He nodded towards the kitchen. "Imagine that in front of other kids. Not all the time, but still. Things fell, flew off of tables, or went crazy. I couldn't stay. Too many people asking questions. I spent the last few years being homeschooled."

"Why didn't your–why didn't you come here sooner?"

"He said it would've been too dangerous." "He" resounded like an oath. "He couldn't be seen, or whatever. He said he wanted me to have a normal life for as long as I could. That's bullshit. He just didn't want to let me go. But that was okay. I didn't want him to, so I never complained. Also, I kinda didn't believe him anyway, like I said. Well, except when he talked about..." He looked at her with a sudden fierceness, a rabid curiosity bordering on obsession. "Do you know anything about vampires?"

Eleanor waved both hands no.

"We can't talk about that."

He sucked at his teeth and leaned his elbows on his knees.

"You too?" he said, shaking his head with disappointed. "He told me the same thing. I mean, he told me some stuff, but not a lot. It doesn't make sense. We were supposed to be hiding from them, from these horrible monsters, but he would barely talk about them. Why the hell did he even tell me about them in the first place? Don't you think someone should know how to protect themselves?"

"There's no protecting yourself against vampires. I'm curious about them too, but every time I ask someone, they get this look on their face like I just spat on their baby or something. There are some badasses here. I mean Uncle Percy: do you know who he is, and what he can do? Like really? They call him the King of Beasts. That's supposed to be a bad thing, but really it means he's the strongest werewolf alive. Werewolves are scary enough, even when they're not turned. And they call Percy 'king.' And even he won't talk about vampires.

"I tried last night with Aunt Rosie, and the way she looked at me really scared me. She told me the same thing I've heard before, but this time I understood. I thought, okay, I should just shut up about it. So then I tried again with my pop..." She saw the look on Jason's face. "Shut up. Anyway, I tried again, and it really, really clicked. I could see that he was afraid. My pop can do crazy shit. He's a real magician. And he was scared. Your dad didn't tell you anything because he didn't wanna give you nightmares. Vampires are real, and you can't fuck with them."

Jason was silent. A sudden desire flared in his stomach. His fingertips tingled. Excess saliva filled his mouth. The one thing his father had told him about vampires was the one thing he could not talk about with Eleanor. He wondered what she would say if she knew. His father had sworn him to secrecy, and it was a secret he guarded close. He assumed Rosie and the others now knew, but he would wait for them to say because he remembered how afraid his father had been the few times he had spoken about vampires, and how adamant his father had been that he would be in danger if others knew that he was meant to kill them. He saw that fear reflected in Eleanor. Yet instead of being afraid himself, he was frustrated.

"The answers will come in time," Darius had said. For now, it was supposed to be enough that he knew his purpose, a purpose his father had claimed would rid the world of an incredible evil. But if that was so, why had he told him so little? Why had his father been so certain that he would figure it out on his own?

He shook it off and chuckled like a condemned man remembering a joke on his way to the gallows. He would never get the answers from him now.

"I've seen that same look on my...on his face," he said, "whenever he talked about vampires even for just a second. I've never seen anyone so afraid. That's why I believed him about all this being real. That and the weird stuff always happening."

He looked to her for understanding. The same fear creased her face, as if she almost expected a vampire to melt through the walls. He hated to see it.

"Anyway," he said. "Sorry I asked."

"It's cool. I mean...I thought your dad would've told you a lot about everything else."

Jason shrugged.

"He always told me that I would learn a lot over here. Guess he was right. Like I said, I didn't mind pretending to be...whatever, it doesn't matter. Uh, let me see if there's some other stuff...oh yeah: is there really a whole other town or village under here?"

Eleanor compressed her lips as if concealing a great secret.

"I'm not gonna ruin that for you. You'll see it for yourself."

"Uh, okay. Think you can you show me around?"

"Oh yeah. I told you earlier, remember—" She froze, remembering the context of that telling. She brushed hair from her face. "I mean, yeah. It'll be a lot of fun."

"That'll be cool. Thanks. I like hanging with you."

He spoke in a matter of fact way, not trying to compliment or sway her, simply stating the obvious. Eleanor smiled to herself. Neither spoke. Jason scratched at his knuckles. He twitched and cracked the left side of his neck.

"Sorry about being a bummer," he said. "I swear I'm not always like this."

"Forget it. There'll be time for fun. Now you gotta—look, I'm just gonna say it. You gotta be sad. Your dad died, and you have to deal with it. Not like, 'Deal it, crybaby.' I mean, like...let yourself be sad. Otherwise...I don't know...you have to deal with it."

He was silent for a moment. Then he spoke as if releasing a long held secret.

"Know what they don't tell you about someone dying?"

"They say lots of things. I think that's 'cause they don't know what to say."

Jason nodded.

"That's because they don't wanna tell you the truth: the person who dies isn't here anymore. They're gone, and it's like they never existed. All I heard at my ma's funeral was how she would always be with me. But she ain't. She's gone."

Eleanor frowned. No rebuttal left her lips. The weight of her own loss pressed on her. She blew a strand of curls away and leaned forward in thought, burdened by the fact that she understood what he meant all too well.

Jason looked at her and knew that she did. He wished it were some other way for both of them.

12

Rosie leaned against the tub, her pant leg rolled up, revealing three cuts. One streaked the inside of her calf, the second was a shallow gash running horizontal almost behind the knee, and the last slanted close to her Achilles tendon. None were deep. Bloodstained shards of glass rested the edge of the sink, and tweezers lay beside them. Water streamed from the faucet, gurgling, and she dampened two folded paper towels to wipe blood from her leg.

When the bleeding slowed, she cleaned the wounds with disinfectant pads, tossing them red and then pink into the trash.

She took a deep breath. Warmth radiated under her skin, magic swelling, an extra sense akin to breathing, automatic and sometimes forgotten. She directed a surge towards her leg and through the wounds. Thick blue liquid flowed from within the cuts and knitted together into scabs. The surrounding muscles tensed and pulled, causing a momentary ache, but still she marveled at the way the cuts healed, reminded of the extraordinary nature of magic.

The scabs hardened. She stood and bounced up and down on the balls of her feet. Sharp pain bit, but the muscles worked as they should, and the scabs held.

She went to the toilet, closed the lid, and sat. Her hands dangled between her knees, and she took a number of deliberate breaths, collecting herself. Unease rippled through her, as if invisible insects crawled unchecked under her clothing. Percy's words echoed. There had been sense to them. Who was the boy? Should she be so trusting? What made him capable of killing vampires?

Her rebuttals were swift. He was a child, an orphan, afraid. The remaining questions were like half-written equations. There could be no answers, save what time revealed. For now they could only address what lay before them.

And what lay before them was a boy in need of a home.

They would help him. She would see to that. They would show him he did not have to be afraid. Then the answers would come, when he felt safe and ready to understand himself. And if, in the end, helping a damaged boy carried them to doom, then perhaps it was a doom Rosie St. John was willing to accept. Perhaps death was preferable to existing in a world where even a child was to be feared. Perhaps the right thing was all that mattered, regardless of the consequences.

Percy's last comment rang in her mind. He had not meant it. She knew him well enough to understand when fear and frustration made him say foolish things. The fact that they could not conceive together had never been a point of contention. She married him knowing he could not give her a child. And yet he acted at times as if she had made a great sacrifice for his sake.

She shook her head and muttered under her breath.

"Idiot."

She would make light of it and move on. There were more important things to attend to.

Nodding to herself, she clapped her hands together in affirmation, stood before the mirror, made a face at her reflection (the same face her father used to make at her, so many years ago, when the whole world was him and her and their small house among verdant desert plains and mesas that rolled all the way to Mexico), and splashed water onto her face from the still running faucet.

When she looked back up, she saw the back of her own head

reflected in the mirror. Her golden hair lay in unkempt waves over her shoulders, and her big ears protruded outwards. She reared back in surprise, and the back of her head and shoulders grew larger in the glass.

Disbelief seized her. The very air seemed to falter, as if reality were failing, allowing something other and awful into the world. Her senses slowed, dissolving her thoughts into a stupefied sludge of apprehension.

Something moaned behind her, the sound pregnant with longing and desire. Before she could summon the defenses built into the walls of her home, before she could scream or utter a sound, hands heavy with cold and saturated by the stench of rot seized her and turned her around.

Her reflection turned with her, revealing her face as seen by the intruder. For the mirror was no longer a mirror, but a projection of his vision. Had she been able to look, Rosie would've seen deformed hands moving away from her mouth and gripping her cheeks, pale and animated, as if shaped from moldy clay. She would've seen her features collapse into a mask of terror. She would've seen herself scream.

PERCY RETURNED. He came into the living room, looked at the children, peeked into the kitchen, and frowned.

"Rosie's still in the bathroom?" he said.

"Aunt Rosie's here?" Eleanor replied

Jason's stomach dropped. The room seemed to lurch. He looked at the hallway, and the shadows there were thick. Cold lapped his skin, dread coursed through his veins, and he knew that something was wrong.

Rosie's scream tore through the apartment.

Percy ran, a pale blur launching past the children. A whip-crack resounded in his wake. He appeared before the bathroom door, pounding his fist.

"Rose? Rosie!"

There was no answer. He tried the knob and flinched at deep cold biting into his palm. He shouldered the door open, cracking it down the center and scattering bits of wood helter-skelter. The door crashed to the floor, and he looked about the bathroom. Bits of glass shone in the sink. The faucet ran. Rosie's blood glistened on the lip of the bathtub. The narrow window above was closed and encased in snow that distorted the coming night into prisms of black and orange. He found no sign of her, seeing only his own reflection rabid and wild in the mirror.

He stormed out of the bathroom and went through the other rooms. The windows were all closed. The closets were full of clothing, discarded gadgets, packing boxes, jewelry, and plastic bins stuffed with undergarments and mementos. He checked underneath beds, behind dressers...the rooms were empty. He could not smell her. A cold stench supplanted all other scents. Panic flooded, and he spun around and around, helpless.

"Uncle Percy?" Eleanor said, calling from the living room, her voice hushed with worry.

He ran to her.

"You didn't see her walk out of here?" he said.

"I didn't even know she was here."

"You're sure?"

She nodded, wringing her hands together.

Percy's gaze found Jason. The boy sat beaded with sweat and clutching at the sofa. Percy lunged at him, deaf to Eleanor's screams. He ripped Jason from the sofa and slammed him against the wall bordering the vestibule, digging into the boy's collar and bearing his teeth like some feral beast. Eleanor ran to them, arms thrown out.

"Whoa!" she said. "Whoa, hold on!"

Percy pushed his face towards Jason's, his eyes blue fire, a growl tearing past his lips.

"Where is she?" he said.

Jason trembled as he stared at the hallway. They did not see, but he saw. Darkness bled out of empty space, lathering the walls and twisting the air into an otherworldly vortex. The ballerina emerged as if drifting from one world into the next, tattered and pale, the ends of her hair caught in the spiraling darkness, her purple tutu surrounding withered legs.

She beckoned to Jason.

"No," he said, shaking his head.

Percy slammed him against the wall.

"Answer me!"

The impact rattled the boy, and when he looked again the hallway was empty.

"You know where she is," Percy said.

"I don't know anything."

"You're lying."

"No, I swear."

"Where is she!?"

"Get off of me!"

Percy was ripped backwards, as if metallic hands snatched his hair, neck, and arms. He stumbled and crashed onto the floor, gaping, fury giving way to shock.

Eleanor covered her mouth, staring at Jason.

The boy floated in midair, wide eyed, mouth working without sound. Whispers sighed all about him, a harem of otherworldly voices fading into silence. He drifted down, landing gently on the floor.

Percy rose to his knees, eyeing the boy with something close to awe, unable to process what he had just witnessed. Eleanor backed away from Jason and searched blindly for Percy's hand. She found it, and he brought her close.

Darkness emanated from Jason, tendrils of shadows tainting everything they touched: the floor at his feet rotted into decrepit folds, and the walls nearest him dried and peeled. Long rivulets of black liquid dripped from the shadow's borders, splattering the floor and evaporating into withering plumes of mist that for a brief moment revealed spectral forms surrounding the boy. Then the undulating darkness receded into him, his skin breathing in shadows.

The phantoms dissolved, and the floor and the walls returned to their living states, save for a faint yellowing of their surfaces.

Eleanor and Percy stared, horrorstruck.

Jason remained for a moment, bowed, mouth open, eyes twitching. He laughed once, a joyless sound carrying with it the realization that he was not crazy, that all the fears of his lunatic mind were in fact true, a revelation of sanity unwanted. Then he turned and ran, throwing the entrance door open and escaping into the hallway.

Percy blinked, dazed. Eleanor looked about, unsure if what they had seen was real.

The bedroom door whined open like the sing-song of a bullying child. It crashed closed and then opened again, and again, screeching, booming, unceasing. Percy shot up, lifted Eleanor into his arms, and went to run out of the apartment. The entrance door slammed shut before them and then trembled with violent seizures. Voices moaned beyond, a cacophony of monotone wails.

Something spilled at Percy's feet. He and Eleanor looked up to see lamplight melting. The glow streaming through the window slowed into aqueous waves, and those waves collapsed into wilting particles of the deepest shade of red. It was as if night was bleeding, and empty spaces were torn open where the light failed. Deep blackness spewed from these wounds in reality, erupting in a bleak mist that obscured everything. The apartment aged in a span of seconds, peeling and breaking and bending everywhere. Dust hung in the air, holes opened in the floor and the walls, and furniture collapsed. The darkness reached the window, withering the remaining lamplight and blotting the outside world.

All was black and still beyond that window. Then pale things emerged and pressed against the glass like voyeurs, leering faces veiled by darkness.

Percy tried to snarl, to seem menacing, but all he could do was blink and hug Eleanor close. She buried her face in his neck, crying out with choked gasps, forgetting her own power beneath waves of incomprehensible fear.

The entrance door slowly whined open before them.

And then they came.

13

Jason ran out of the apartment, the floor under his feet a tether to a world that seemed to be slipping away.

He had floated. He had hovered in midair as if he were a prisoner to some otherworldly puppeteer. Darkness had spilled and was then absorbed by his skin. He had felt it fuse with his blood, the sensation natural, as if the darkness had satisfied a longing he could not name. Eleanor and Percy had borne witness, and through their eyes the nightmare was made real.

The hallway lights flickered as he ran. He turned towards the stairwell, pushed open the door, and bolted up the gray steps, running without thought, the world morphing into blurs and streaks.

He reached the rooftop door, bitter wind shrieking against it. His breath raced as he collapsed onto the steps.

Alone in the stairwell, away from questions that he had no answers to. Alone with the cold and the night and the silent battalion of voices that threatened to shatter an invisible barrier and reveal a truth he did not wish to know. Here sat the boy, Jason Escoto, son of the man once known as Darius Bardales, the first magician. Here he sat clinging to the fading hope that he was crazy, for that was the lesser horror. The greater screamed its presence from Rosie's sudden disappearance, from the look on Percy's face as he was ripped backwards by invisible hands, from the way Eleanor had backed away from him, and from terrible visions that had come in the morning and after breakfast.

The greater horror had always been with him. It followed, a constant presence that had oppressed his life like a great beast lurking under tumultuous waters, waiting for the right moment to open its jaws and devour.

The greater horror was truth.

And the truth was this: he was not crazy.

"Ma," he said. "Dad."

The words escaped unbidden, spoken to the darkness, swallowed by cutting wind. They released a tide of memories: his mother's hands as they worked knitting needles together, shaping a dark blue scarf into being as if working some ancient and truer magic. The stillness of the ocean somehow greater than the roar of crashing waves, as his father gazed from a beach frosted with snow. His parents' warmth radiating as Jason sat between them on the sofa, watching a movie, a family bathed in blue light. That same light over his mother's face as she worked from her laptop, looking over it from time to time to make funny faces at him, and the quiet and satisfied look on his father's face as they listened to music together.

Jason closed his eyes and traded the present for a gentler time.

But memory is a vast geography. Sweet meadows are surrounded by haunted lands that ever threaten to invade. Specters from the past crawled out of these infernal wastes and overpowered him, until Jason was once more alone with the underside of truth.

He remembered footsteps against his bedroom ceiling, walking towards him as he neared the edge of sleep, leaving distorted imprints on the cracked white paint. He would hide under his covers until the heat became unbearable, and then only risk sticking his mouth and nose out for breath. He remembered blurred faces peering through the cracks of doors, or malformed shapes vanishing into walls whenever he entered a room. He remembered whispers cutting through the sigh of running water, making him slip in the shower as unseen hands slapped the curtain. He remembered nights when darkness spilled over his windows and devoured all light, leaving him waiting for some strangeness to reach out and torment him.

In the past he had gone to his father, and his father had given him comfort. He had promised him that he was a magician in the making, and that all these things were illusions. But now the boy viewed these happenings through eyes weathered by loss, through a life no longer docked in safe harbors. He again saw Eleanor's face as she backed away from him, and he knew he was no magician.

"You lied to me," he said to the father who wasn't there, opening his eyes, nearly spitting into the gloom. He pounded on the step, his fist punctuating each word. "You lied to me!"

He shuddered and hung over his knees, his hair falling in thick waves, his shadow long and distorted over the stairs. He did not weep. Tears knocked, but he would not answer. To do so would be a final admission, and he would be rendered inconsolable, crying out to absence, surrounded by darkness hungry to adopt him.

Shame weighed him with the knowledge that he had brought something terrible to people who had tried to give him a home. Rosie's face appeared. That he had somehow caused her to vanish gnawed at his conscience. The rage on Percy's face sowed seeds of bitter guilt. And then there was Eleanor. He had scared her, and that broke his heart.

He sat that way for a long time, trembling. A word screamed through his mind. He would not say it. The word carried all the answers he never wanted, but he let it lie like unwanted pain, like an ignored disease, like a date with a firing squad.

He shook his head and stood, gripping the banister, looking down at the dimly lit steps. He knew where they led, and he knew he should've followed them out the first chance he had. He would rectify his mistake. He would leave and face the winter. He had no thought of his possessions, of being underdressed. Or perhaps he did not care. Perhaps deep down, he was hoping for a more final exit.

That thought gave him pause. With him gone, all that he had

wrought would disappear from this place and leave these good people be. Maybe Rosie would be returned, and she, Eleanor, and the others would have no more to fear from the son of a dead man.

A warbled screech filled the air, crying out from some unseen dimension. Jason clenched his eyes shut and knew it was not the wind. The air rippled before him, filling with darkness, and a pale shape began to resolve like a reflection over waves.

He shook his head.

"Go away," he said. The warped voice cried out. He stomped. "Leave!"

Wind whipped behind him. He opened his eyes. Dusky light filled the stairwell and nothing more.

He turned towards the rooftop door. Beyond waited cold, snow, and a great height to fall from. He did not want that. He knew nothing would be fixed or solved by leaving this world. He understood enough about loss to know that there was no glory or glamour in disappearing before your time. There would only be pain and regret forever embedded as shrapnel within those left behind, a melancholic chain tethering broken hearts. Yet he pushed the long silver crash bar, desperate to look into the curtain of snow from above, so he may clear his head and gain the courage to do what was necessary.

A voice spoke in his mind, urging him to go back. He could no longer run. He had to face whatever was happening and help the others find Rosie. Most of all, he had to face himself.

But he pushed and kicked at the door. It would not open. He looked for a lock, some mechanism to undue, but there was nothing. He pushed again, cursing, crying out. The door remained closed, and wind howled beyond.

He hung his head for a moment, and then began to walk down the steps. Frustration gave way to something close to relief. He would simply leave. Walk into the snow and become no more than a bad memory for these good people. With him gone, whatever horrid power he carried would leave the Gardens. That way, Rosie would be returned, his father's friends would be spared the burden of caring for him, and all would be well. New York City waited with its myriad possibilities, and he would find himself within its streets. A voice screamed protest in the back of his mind, but it was muffled by delusion, corrupted memories, and self-hatred, those wells of deceit, those devils leading broken hearts to bitter and unjust ends.

He reached the next landing and saw light spilling from the 12th floor through the door's transom window. He paused, feeling something calming in the pale gold streaming through the glass, as if a healing spirit were about to reveal itself and guide him to the right path.

The light flickered, and in the space left behind he caught his own reflection, blurred in the orange haze of the stairwell, contorted by shadows, seemingly inhuman. He looked away and continued his descent, passing the next landing, hopeless, for there was no escaping himself.

A door whined open a few floors below.

Footsteps echoed. The door clicked shut. The footsteps climbed down, dwindling with each flight. Jason stopped and waited, listening. Lights buzzed. A dim haze beat against shadows. Jason peered over the railing and down the spiral of banisters. He could see no one. The winding stairwell seemed to hold its breath under the footfalls.

Jason waited.

The lobby door whined open, sighed, and reverberated.

Jason released a long exhale and gripped the banister. Waves of relief cascaded up and down his spine. He did not know why. The decision was made. What did it matter who saw him now? He told himself he was worried about seeing Percy, or Eleanor, but he knew that was a lie. The truth was he did not want to be seen by anyone.

He pushed himself off of the railing and continued to climb down.

Whispers broke the stillness below, conspiratorial voices just on the edge of hearing.

Jason tensed and again peeked over the railing. He saw nothing but winding banisters.

The whispers ceased. Quiet held.

Something groaned.

Jason's skin rippled into gooseflesh. He backed up the steps with careful footfalls, making for the 11th floor. Cold slithered through the stairwell. The groaning stopped. Then rumbling resounded through the steps, beating at the walls, the banisters. Jason backed away slowly, every footfall working against dread.

The rumbling grew into an avalanche, as if many bodies tumbled down the stairs below. Then all fell to silence. The boy trembled. Lightheadedness made the steps tilt, and he leaned to the side and gripped the wall. The world righted itself in his vision. He peered again over the railing, unsure of what he expected to find, hoping to see nothing.

Footsteps exploded above him and rampaged down the stairs like a many legged creature. Jason did not hesitate, did not turn to look and see. He ran down, jumping steps, nearly tripping over himself. He reached the 10th floor and went to grab the doorknob, but there was no knob there. The window melted before him, revealing a black rift in reality where pale shapes moved through failing light. Jason's mouth worked in a silent scream. The rampaging footfalls above him neared. He broke and ran.

He reached the 9th floor. The door was gone, replaced by an opening unto pure darkness that roiled like the waters of a lake in a storm. Once more a pale hand reached out of the black and offered itself. Strips of flesh were ripped from its wrist and palm, revealing yellowed bone underneath. Strands of darkness hung from decayed fingers and dripped onto the floor near Jason's feet. For a moment the thunder of the thing booming above him faded. The white shape in the darkness spoke in its warbled voice, but Jason understood, heard the soft words of a little girl underneath.

"Come home," she said.

She offered her hand, and he saw her floating, all dark hair and pale skin, a white gown blossoming into a purple tutu. She beckoned, and a spark of something familiar and necessary shone through the chaos of his panicked mind. He reached out and brushed her fingers.

The memory of waking next to his dead father flashed through him as soon as he touched her. He staggered, unable to accept what was shown. He heard the thing above once more and ripped himself away.

He ran down. She screamed after him, but her voice was drowned under the thundering steps.

The stairs streaked by in a frenzied blur. The thing above bellowed. Its shadow blotted light and blotched the next landing. Jason jumped four steps, stumbled, caught his balance on the landing, turned for the next set of stairs, and ran into dozens of white mannequins.

They were waiting for him, their arms thrown open, their eyes and mouths painted with crayon, as if materialized from some cruel children's book, all garish hues and crazed strokes. Their bodies were bare and smooth, lifeless, and yet they swarmed as he crashed into them. A pair of arms wrapped themselves around him, and hands twisted into his clothing and hair and lifted him off of the steps.

The world became a havoc of distorted shapes. Hands touched his face and dripped frigid strands of darkness down his cheeks and neck. He tried to scream, but a hand clamped over his mouth. He screamed anyway, but no sound pierced the awfulness that muzzled him. He was carried down, riding a dead wave, catching glimpses of smiling mannequin faces.

The word Jason would not speak unveiled itself. The word transcended the meanings assigned to it through the ages, erupting from a cocoon of myth, superstition, psychology, and narrative, manifesting into the apotheosis of all horrors. The word was no longer a word. It was life without breath. It was existence trapped within the mausoleum of all creation. It was time, memory, love, and hope corrupted by the unceasing nightmare of endless being in a world meant for endings.

The word was a broken reality. The word was ghosts.

He was jerked and pushed until he was held over a great chasm that opened where the remaining stairs should have been. He fought, screaming his silent scream, trying to thrash against things that were no longer of the living world, things forgotten unto themselves, awful mimics of what they once were. They did not yield.

Folds of failing light dripped into the impossible darkness below, as something drifted towards Jason from above. Dead hands gripped the back of his neck and aimed his vision at the abyss, and he saw the bleeding light unravel into bits of corrupted matter before vanishing.

A great weight hovered on the edge of sensation, as if a behemoth spider dangled on its web. His hair reached upwards towards the unseen presence, drawn to it. The black hole loomed before him, yet he felt that if the dead let him go he would fall upwards.

The surrounding mannequins cried out, and from the corner of his eyes he could see their eyes and mouths swell into wide Os. Some held up hands as if averting their gazes from a great and terrible presence.

A guttural cry barked in his ear. And then the thing that had chased him down the stairs spoke in the voice he remembered from the morning, the voice that had demanded he be its friend.

"Just forget all about this," it said. Each word droned, broken things that were warped and cracked. Jason cringed, winter current charging through his veins where blood should have been.

"Do us both a favor, huh?" the dead one said. "Forget this and be a happy little boy. Let Uncle Matt take care of everything."

And then Jason was thrown.

He fell, and before the darkness took him he spied a swollen face grinning, triumphant.

He tumbled, careening until he pierced an invisible veil and broke into the depths of empty space. All light and orientation vanished. He rushed through the void, the absence between stars, where words like falling or rising lost all meaning. He was no longer a boy, but a blaze of consciousness that ripped through unending emptiness, reaching in desperation for anything that would remind him that he was human.

Figures materialized and faded. Agonized screams and howls rose and fell. Smeared visages whipped by. These things surrounded him, ever on the edge of seeing, as if he were the eye of some dread storm.

Then they suddenly cried out as one and went silent.

Low droning filled the emptiness. A pinprick glinted somewhere in the far darkness, a malevolent point of pure white that seemed to probe him. The sight of it gripped Jason's heart with talons of a secret and terrible knowledge. For in that fragment of white he recognized a terror he could not name, something locked deep in the basement of all dreams.

He clutched to the darkness as a comfort, shutting his awareness away from the white, knowing only that he had to get away. Some inner power surged, shielding him from the void, and for a moment he felt whole again, closer to a truth he needed to accept. Folds of shadow opened before him, and he saw the ballerina in the distance, white and purple, surrounded by skeletal shapes, calling out to him, frantic. He reached out to her, but was suddenly hurled, pushed by the will that had thrown him into the void.

Jason was lost, falling in no direction, an endless expanse at all sides, the world of the living already fading into something like fantasy.

All was darkness, rushing darkness...

He jolted awake from his bed as if he had crashed into it from a great height. He squinted and looked about. Much too bright sunlight infused the room. He shaded his eyes, sat up, and groaned from the leaden movement of his limbs. A bookshelf seemed to shape itself out of daylight, and on it he recognized cookbooks, comics, and novels whose titles stirred comfort. A water gun lay on the floor, sparking a memory of his old bedroom, his old life.

Disorientation held sway, and he doubled over, fighting for breath.

A knock rapped at the door.

His father leaned in, a bright smile on his face.

"Wakey-wakey, kid," Darius said. "Sleep okay?"

ACT III

FOR THE BENEFIT OF MR. MOORE

1

"-86

-87

-88"

The elevator drifted to a stop.

Ian watched the screen. The digits shone crimson against the walls, tinting the silver console like blood staining the edge of a knife. They signified something impossible, some otherness beyond his understanding. This was no possession, nor the weaving of magic. He knew those things well, had lived and breathed them. Here a presence worked unseen, some invisible awareness gloating at him. He felt it in his bones, a deep cold penetrating, as if many eyes watched with malicious glee. But still he could not believe. His mind fumbled for an explanation, but found only a heightened sense of danger, every fiber of his being calling for action or escape. Anger seethed at the lack of answers. His lip curled, and his fists clenched until the knuckles were bone white.

The digits vanished from the screen. All was silent, an oppressive absence of sound.

His shadow slunk around the floor and crawled over the walls, restless.

Ian rocked from side to side, rubbing his thumb against his fingers, seeking clear thought. The elevator swayed. The hoist ropes above and below creaked, and to Ian they sounded like the cries of dying men.

He pulled out his cell phone and thumbed the screen. It remained black. He pressed again, but there was no change. He held the power button, shook the phone, opened up the back cover to remove and replace the battery, and tried the power button again. The phone was dead. He stuffed it back into his pocket.

The elevator swayed. The hoist ropes creaked.

He looked up and registered a round grate in the ceiling. Beyond was the darkness of the elevator shaft. He brushed his tie, inhaled, and fell backwards into himself, his awareness merging into the space his shadow-self resided. Chaos howled there, a screaming network of neurons and veins pulsing, beating with an animal need to be free, to find who had done this to him and make them pay.

His shadow knelt beside him, slowly being filled with its master's full cognition. Ian's eyes frothed with blood, pools of bubbling crimson surrounding coal-black pupils. The shadow's eyes flickered and burned.

All sense of Ian's body faded into distant awareness. He looked through his shadow's eyes, and everything was deepened, etched out of some finer quality. But corruption also stood out in greater detail. Rust webbed the elevator's corners, dust and other particles pirouetted through the air, and the floor shone with the grit and stains of hundreds or perhaps thousands of different footprints and all they had carried.

The air was a cacophony: the hoist ropes rattled like thousands of crystals shattering against one another, the swaying of the elevator wheezed and creaked and whined, and Ian's breath filled the space with great rushes of wind.

The shadow moved, crawling up the walls and rising through the vent.

It knelt atop the elevator car, its eyes wounding the darkness of the elevator shaft. The hoist ropes gleamed red and silver around their sheaves and up into the black. The walls of the elevator shaft were drowned by a deep starless night. No other light radiated. No doors could be seen.

The shadow threw itself over the side, scurried down the car, and looked towards the bottom. Hoist cables disappeared into layers of darkness. Nothing more.

Ian searched for some hint or sign of illusion, but could find nothing. The shadow growled, a deep and hateful sound bearing its master's frustration at the cold truth: the elevator hung suspended between two impossible depths. He had been taken from his home and into some strange dimension.

A tingle of something that might have been fear ran through him. The surreal nature of what was happening was not lost upon him. But within the folds of his own private darkness he remembered who he was, who his family and loved ones were, and he was comforted. He would find a way out. And then he would find who had done this.

The shadow crawled upwards and over the car's roof. It slithered up the hoist ropes. Absence assaulted its vision, filling Ian with confusion: he knew of no darkness his shadow-self could not see through, but here he was engulfed. He carried on. The shadow ascended, following the metallic ropes up.

It climbed.

The elevator was swallowed, lost in the abyss beneath. The shadow was alone on the ropes. Ian's vision grew faint, dimming as the shadow attained distance from its master, the connection faltering. But it continued to climb, rising, rising.

Ian sweated within the elevator, his lip quivering. Tears of blood dripped over his cheeks, sizzled, and evaporated into drifts of corrupted smoke. He strained, pushing his other beyond its limits. There was satisfaction in the act, the demon child feeling his power grow stronger through resistance.

His shadow rose through silence and blackness. Long it climbed, beyond the counting of time, order, or any semblance of a rational world. Finally a shape materialized out of the gloom above. The shadow hurried. It reached the bottom of another elevator, scurried over the side, reached the roof, and poured through the vent.

And found Ian.

The shadow froze, its red eyes flaring, Ian's awareness like a taught rope about to snap.

A guttural shriek burst through his hearing, erupting from the darkness beyond the vent, and Ian's hold broke as the shadow fell screeching into the elevator.

His vision twisted and tumbled, and again he felt himself falling through his own mind. He slammed back into himself and reeled against the wall, disoriented, his stomach somersaulting. His shadow hissed before him, mirroring his shock and indignation. They had gone up. They had crawled together, following the hoist ropes. And yet moving upwards had returned them to where they had started. Nausea made Ian brace against his knees. He spat and took ragged breaths. The blood drained from his eyes, receding into the network of vessels, and he felt as if a long needle slid through his temples. His shadow flattened into the floor, and he felt his darker half recede into the back of his mind, unafraid but dumbstruck.

There had been noise, a scream. Ian had heard it. Nothing else had followed, but that sense of being watched deepened, as if others shared the space with him.

The elevator swayed in gentle gradations. Ian went to the console and pushed all the buttons, running his hand up and down.

The elevator swayed. The hoist ropes creaked.

Ian paced, punching the walls, glaring at the screen, the camera, shaking his head, unable to make sense of what was happening.

A sudden thought seized him. It was one word, a name.

Jason.

He hissed with realization. The stranger had done something to him. He had to have. Ian smiled a grim smile, anticipating how he would pay the outsider back. His father would want him to be sure, but there were no other explanations. This was some trick, some display of Jason's power. Ian would pay it back. He would—

Three knocks pounded at the elevator door, slow, deliberate, and sure.

Ian froze. Silence stretched.

Then came three more knocks. The elevator door began to slide open.

2

The bedroom door slammed, pieces of its frame scattering over the floor, and when it swung open again it flew from its hinges and crashed onto the wall across.

Quiet bled from the hallway and engulfed Eleanor and Percy. They waited, uncertain, their hearts pounding, their breaths a shared storm of panic.

The entrance door slowly opened, revealing a cold and flickering glow playing within a shroud of mist.

Slowly, as if peering in on old friends, mannequins leaned into view on either side of the doorway, their crayoned faces smiling, their hair withered strands of dead matter, their eyes exaggerated ovals with cracked pupils at their centers. They wore form fitting ball gowns of black fabric plagued with rips and holes, and necklaces of rusted chains adorned with cracked rubies rested against their bare necklines.

They spoke as one, their voices neither feminine nor masculine but some bastardization of the two, as if they were singing from a warped record.

"Per-cy."

They covered their faces with lifeless hands, and when they

removed them they revealed photo realistic masks of Rosie's screaming face.

"Wanna dance, Per-cy?"

Percy snarled. A low and deadly growl beat in his chest and reverberated through the floor. He placed Eleanor down, pushed her behind him, and opened his arms in challenge. His pupils flooded the entirety of his eyes, shaping them into murderous black orbs. His lips peeled back, revealing swelling gums and sharpening teeth. Snaps and cracks filled the air as his muscles and bones tore, broke, shifted, and reformed.

He began to turn into a werewolf.

He bent forward, howling, rage commanding the slow agony of transformation. Rips tore his shirt and cuts opened across his skin. His facial features erupted into a savage mask, as if crafted out of pandemonium. Yet never did his eyes leave the intruders gazing at him from the doorway.

Eleanor backed away, panic drowning all else. A primal awareness all sentient creatures share was awakened, crying out for her to run, to flee the coming beast.

But she could not look away from the ghosts in the doorway. They astounded her with the terror they evoked, summoning a level of fear so profound that it was akin to religious awakening.

Before Percy could fully transform, the ghosts floated in two by two, six in all. They surrounded him, the trains of their gowns dragging over the floor as they circled. He struck with a hand contorting by inches into a claw, but, moving as one, the ghosts were on him, their masks ripping down their centers to reveal mannequin faces with hollows for eyes and craters for mouths. Four bit into his limbs, another wrapped its putrid arms around the back of his neck, and the last straddled him with its legs.

It went to kiss him.

He roared, but the explosion drained into a man's scream. He had halfway turned, nearly transforming into an uncontrollable force, yet the werewolf now dwindled, bones once more breaking and reforming. His features deflated into a human face, and the blacks of his eyes dwindled into pupils once more.

He felt his monstrous power withering, leaving him drained, the ghosts taking from him his last hope of protecting Eleanor. He couldn't see her, but smelled her near, a clean scent like rain corrupted by the stench of corpses.

"Eleanor!" he said, panting, reeling. "Run! Ru—!"

Then the lips of straddling ghost puckered and kissed him. The world blackened, and he fell.

The dead threw themselves on Percy. The trains of their dresses coiled over his entire body, great black waves bleeding from their gowns in endless currents.

Eleanor was frozen. Her bladder released, and urine trickled down the inside of her legs. She did not feel it. She stared dumbstruck as the ghosts frenzied over her uncle, embracing him, kissing him, and gnawing at his limbs. He cried out to her, and she heard, but could not understand. He fell to the floor, and the trains of their dresses coiled him like constricting snakes.

Watching him vanish into the folds of black fabric sparked anger in her. Someone she loved was in trouble, and she remembered that she had the means to fight.

She took a deep breath (which was shallow and quick, but to her it seemed like the world), reached within, and called to magic.

A web of electric pain ripped her insides.

She screamed and fell to her knees. Tears welled, and her hands shook. She looked up and saw Percy almost completely enshrouded. The ghosts stroked his face and writhed against him, their dresses somehow unchanged despite their trains unspooling and devouring his body. Eleanor cried out in anger and focused all of herself on magic. Pain answered, beating against her bones, and she fell gasping.

She rolled around the floor, turned on her side, and vomited.

When she looked up she saw Percy's shrouded form hovering between the two rows of ghosts. They floated out of the doorway,

Percy carried upon some invisible tether, and vanished into the darkness and the mist beyond.

Eleanor got to her knees and stood. A barren ache pulsed against her insides, the hollows where magic had once lived. Darkness writhed about her. Tears streaked her face, and she stared in disbelief at the place where Percy should have been.

Something shuffled behind her, feet whispering on carpet. She turned around. A figure stood by the shattered bedroom door, obscured by shadows save for the obscene shimmer of its long blonde hair.

"Hi, darling," it said in a mangled voice, the scream of rusted hinges.

Eleanor knew. She knew right away. Her mind screamed, and every part of her revolted. She took a step back, shaking her head through tears.

The ghost watched her without a sound, its face hidden in the dark. Strands of hair rose one by one until they all floated, swaying like seaweed.

"I always wanted a daughter," it said. Its voice bled in and out of hearing, malformed and broken. "Please, Mr. Moore, can I have this one? I'll be so good to her. I always wanted a daughter. I always wanted a daughter!"

It reached with dead hands and charged Eleanor, crying with heartbreak and insanity welling from perfect desolation.

Eleanor ran out of the apartment. She ran without thought, seeing nothing save the need to escape. She ran through the dark and the cold of a corridor she did not recognize, and behind her the dead thing wailed.

3

The elevator door crawled open.

Ian watched in disbelief. There was no time to search for explanation, no defense he could muster. The lights in the elevator died, exposing him to the impenetrable emptiness of strange depths. The door came to rest with a sigh, and all that remained was the creaking of hoist ropes and the cold and silent air.

Then a haze spread over the walls.

Street lamps painted night, illuminating drifts of snow in amber. Ian blinked, took a step back, and crunched ice beneath his feet. He looked about. The elevator was gone, vanished. He turned around and found himself standing within a frosted playground under the watchful gaze of the Gardens, the windows in the white buildings shimmering. A black fence crystallized in snow surrounded monkey bars, slides, and swings sets. A concrete path wound beyond.

He stared, his fingers ticking against his thighs, anger overriding confusion and a sense of respect for the power that had taken him to this place.

"Like playing games?" he said. His voice whipped about the empty playground. Wind answered. His shadow stretched in three different directions over the ice. It growled, and he shared its tension, feeling mocking eyes watching, laughing. "I can play too."

He walked towards the gate, nostrils flaring, thoughts bent upon finding whoever had done this to him. It had to be the work of Jason, the stranger using his power for some unknown end. What that power was he could not say, but he was not afraid. He would find the boy. He would make him answer.

Laughter floated from behind him. He turned around. The shadows of trees swayed over monkey bars. Swings danced in the wind. There was no one.

'Keep playing," Ian said, his words dripping venom.

He walked on. Giggles came again. He ignored them, his face calm and composed, his eyes seething.

Icicles clung to the lips of slides. Ian bent, grabbed two, and snapped them off, gripping them like knives.

He threw open the gate and scanned the path. His other screeched, pulling his attention towards the ground. There he saw the shadow of the playground's fence like serrated teeth.

Seated on it were the silhouettes of children.

He whirled. The fence stood empty. He looked down on the ground again. The shadow children encircled him, each pointing a mocking finger. His own shadow shrunk before them, becoming a lifeless blob over the ice.

Ian spun around, trying to catch a glimpse of his tormentors. He saw no one.

Laughter erupted from the empty air.

He swung wildly, stabbing nothing. The icicles were snatched from him by invisible hands and tossed back and forth over his head, and laughter escalated in the mocking tones of children playing keep away.

Ian broke into a run, sprinting between fields. He scanned the surrounding apartments for movement, for a face in a window, for someone emerging from an entrance. The windows glared down at him like hollow eyes, their lights extinguishing one by one. He stopped, frowning in confusion. Dried paint stained the buildings' crumbling bricks. Tattered curtains flailed from broken panes. The entrances were boarded up, some doors torn and slumped.

Desolation was wrought upon the Gardens.

"Ian is a bad boy," a voice said, whispering in his ear. He started, backed up along the path, eyes wild, searching, seeing nothing. He ran again, seeking control in escape, in the act of moving.

He passed fallen branches with icicles rising from their bark. The fields shimmered as he curved about a bend and passed another scattering of branches, ran a straightway, curved again, and stopped. Once more he saw tree branches strewn over the ground, twisted lengths of ice rising from their withered skins.

He had run in circles.

He recognized nothing, and realization sapped his legs of their strength. This was not the Gardens. This was not the home he knew. He looked over the ground. His footprints were there, pressed into the snow, leading to where he stood.

Others followed, forming out of nothing, cracking the frost in a steady procession towards him. They stopped a few feet away. Ian turned to flee, but found a ring of footprints behind him. Blood dripped through a cone of streetlight and into one of the footprints. More splattered against his forehead, his cheek, until blood rained, staining the frost.

He looked up.

They floated there, children wearing school uniforms. Their faces were the porcelain masks of dolls, some pale, some tan or dark, grinning with exaggerated malice. Wigs shone brown, black, blonde or red in the glow of the lamp. Blood poured from their withered feet, misshapen things gray-brown with rot. Their eyes were cartoon-like, great ovals colored by bright crayon, but their pupils were black wounds seething with the memory of a vast emptiness, a waste without borders, profound and terrible and endless.

Ian went to run for the fields, but stopped before he took a few steps. There, standing in ordered lines as if placed by some demented hand, were other porcelain children frozen in poses of greeting, hands extended in waves.

Every one of them was waving at him.

"Ian's been a bad boy," they sang.

Then those who were floating fell, crashing into the blood streaked snow, their faces contorted masks of raving hatred. Their fingers wiggled as they swarmed Ian, enclosing him in a suffocating ring. All Ian could do was fall to the ground, balling up and covering his head and neck. Hands pulled and pinched, shooting cold through him. The dead children laughed.

Then a hush fell. The hands pulled away. Footsteps scattered.

Ian lay uncertain of everything. He removed his arms from over the back of his neck and looked around.

He was no longer outside.

Desks and chairs surrounded him, and moonlight fell through large windows, illuminating layers of dust and the mosaics of entropy that splattered the walls.

He got up, shoulders heaving, words lost to anger. A blackboard loomed ahead, and the letters of the alphabet ran above it, print and cursive over green paper.

He stood in an empty classroom. Worn coats and sweaters hung from hooks behind him. A closet was open on his right, submerged in an avalanche of rotted books. Ash clung to the tops of chairs in intricate patterns.

A hand gripped his wrist. He growled and looked left. A porcelain child sat beside him, its crayon colored eyes brown and wide, a rigid finger pressed over lips frozen mid-pout.

"Shh," the porcelain child said, its lips unmoving. "It's story time."

Unseen hands gripped Ian's shoulders and pushed him into the opposite chair. He looked around and saw all of the other desks now occupied by porcelain children frozen in poses of rapt excitement. Some held clasped hands pressed against their cheeks. Others leant forward over their desk like spectators at an execution.

Ian followed their gazes to the front of the class.

A large mannequin sat a chair before the blackboard. Its face was submerged in shadow. It wore a rotted football jersey with the number 88 melted into the polyester. Darkness dripped from hands that held a crumbling storybook.

Ian saw the title of the book done in a crude hand over the cover:

The Very Bad Boy

"We got a special guest today, kids," the storyteller said, his voice throbbing and shrieking all at once. "Whaddaya say, little man? Long time no see. Wanna hear a sad story?"

Ian's heart seized. He recognized the voice under the layers of corruption. Only one person in his life had ever called him "little man." But it could not be him.

The cover of the storybook flipped open on its own.

"Once there was a little boy who was made of shadow," the storyteller said. "He was a lonely little boy, because all the people in the town were afraid of him—even though his mother was also made of shadow and was really nice. The town worried the little boy wouldn't be like his mother. They thought he would be like all the other shadows in the woods outside of town. Those shadows liked to hurt people for fun."

Ian quaked with fury, and the grip over his neck and shoulders tightened. He bucked, rocking the desk back and forth, but could not get free. His eyes darted around the room, searching for anything he could use to escape. Moonlight spilled through the window in a toxic glow. There was no sign of life beyond. Around him, the porcelain children watched the storyteller.

"So the little boy had no friends," the storyteller said. "He spent time with his mommy and..." The storyteller growled, spitting the next word. "Daddy. The little boy had a sister, too, but she was too young to be any fun. So the little boy was mostly alone. No one played with him. The people of the town all thought that something must be wrong with him.

"But then his uncle came. And his uncle was also made of shadow. And his uncle knew many things about life, and many cool tricks. He loved the little boy very much. So they became friends and did everything together. Wasn't the boy lucky?"

"Ah," the porcelain children said, their voices dissonant.

"He was," the storyteller said. "He really fucking was. It should've ended there. They should've lived happily ever after. But the little boy wasn't good with that. The little boy was playing a mean little trick. Isn't that bad?"

Desks groaned, and chairs twisted. The porcelain children stared at Ian. He looked from left to right and saw their large eyes glaring.

"The little boy made the uncle believe they were friends, all so the little boy could learn his tricks."

"Liar," Ian said through gritted teeth.

A dead hand slapped over Ian's mouth, sending waves of decay through him.

Pages flipped in the storybook. Ian saw holes and burn marks interwoven through paper scrawled with deranged markings. The pages stopped on a sheet drenched in blood, and the blood spilled over the binding and hung like spit.

"The little boy liked to pretend that he was good," the storyteller said, his voice trembling, on the verge of breaking. "And his uncle believed him. So one day his uncle brought the little boy to a special place where he could teach him all of his tricks. And the little boy learned. And the little boy took those tricks and hurt his uncle with them. He broke into his uncle's mind and stole his most precious thoughts. He made his uncle scream and beg for the pain to stop. And then, when his uncle was so hurt that he couldn't even put two thoughts together, the little boy made everyone believe that his uncle had hurt him."

The porcelain children stood around Ian. They had made no movement nor sound. They were simply there, surrounding him. Crayon dripped from their eyes and over their faces, bleeding into holes in their skin.

Ian glared at his uncle. There was no more doubt about who he was. Matt watched him from the darkness. The book melted through his mannequin fingers, pouring blood over his green and white jersey.

"The town believed the little boy," he said. "It didn't matter that his uncle had been good and nice. We all fuck up sometimes, but he was nice! It didn't matter that his sister loved him, because of course she believed her son. It didn't matter that Matt couldn't speak up for himself because of what the little boy did to him. The little boy's father convinced everyone that Matt had done a very bad thing. So the little boy's father took Matt and...and..."

The ghost's voice drained into whimpers. Then he groaned and growled and whined, and the voices of the dead children seethed in disharmony—screams under rusted gears. The false moonlight flared crimson, spilling over the desks, the blackboard, the dead.

"The little boy's father made my sister do something very bad to me," Matt said, his voice dropping into the grinding of mausoleum doors. "So bad that Matt won't remember it. So bad that it always hurts. And everyone hated the little boy's uncle after that. They all felt sorry for the little boy, and even though they still didn't trust him, they let him be one of them. Shadows and all."

The storybook was a dripping mass of congealed rot in Matt's mannequin hands. The dead children's whining voices reached a shrill peak. Ian twisted and fought, but could not free himself. In his mind he felt Matt as a looming force keeping him from striking out, from possessing, as if his power was a match flame against a great conflagration. His shadow howled with helpless rage.

Matt's mannequin hand crumbled, splattering decay onto the floor and revealing darkness in the failed shape of fingers, as if composed by someone or something who had long forgotten what a hand was supposed to look like. Cracks spread over the dead children's doll faces. Their limbs dissolved into ash piling onto the floor, and in their wake the air twisted and folded in on itself.

"You see, kids," Matt said. "Even though Uncle Matt tried to do something good, little Ian hurt him. All so he could be accepted by the people of the village. All so they would feel sorry for him. But we don't feel sorry for him, do we? We know who he really is."

The blackboard warped like melting paint. Ian felt Matt, felt the wrongness of him, knowing that he was not supposed to be, that all dead things were meant to pass beyond the world. The dead childrens' voices sang their wasps' song, and their darkness spilled nearer.

"Ian is a bad boy," they sang. "Ian is a bad boy..."

"That's right," Matt said, looming closer, unseen.

"...Ian is a bad boy..."

"You hear that, little man?"

"...Ian is a bad boy..."

"Ain't no one gonna believe your bullshit over here."

"...Ian is a bad boy..."

"And what do we do with bad boys?"

Silence fell. Their doll faces were all that remained, hovering among writhing blankets of decayed space. Ian twisted, hissed, and spat, a demon child under the thumb of a greater darkness. A mass loomed before him, a malformed silhouette, and its presence was everything that was and ever will be the definition of ruin.

"What do we do with bad boys?" Matt said. "You gotta forgive 'em. Fuck yeah, you do. Yeah, you forgive 'em."

Ian froze, watching, waiting.

"See, Uncle Matt loves his nephew so much that he can forgive him. It's all good, little man. Life goes on. Life is what it's all about. We've all got nothing but nothing but time. To live...to learn...all that fruity shit."

Ian's shadow screeched, urging escape, urging suicide, anything but what it knew was coming. For in the silence following Matt's words, there lingered the promise of cruelty, the anticipation of retribution longed for in the depths of the netherworld.

Ian sagged against the pressure of the dead hands holding him. For the first time in his life, he knew fear.

"But a man's gotta pay for what he's done, right?" Matt said. The words dripped honey and smoke. "When you fuck up, you gotta be punished. But it's all good. You'll see. We're all gonna be one big happy family. You just have to learn your lesson."

The classroom disappeared within roiling walls of darkness. The smiling porcelain faces floated, inching through the air until they all nuzzled against Ian. Their mouths opened, and then...

Ian's screams spoke of what happened next. Of the vengeance wrought upon him by the workings of revenants. Some things are too horrible to tell. Some things are best left to the recesses of your mind, those wastelands that whisper to you from nightmares and fill your slumber with tossing and turning that you will, at best, forget in the daylight. But these denizens of the abyss flit through memory like grinning marionettes. You peek, but will not look. You hear, but will not listen. That is wisdom. For terrors should not be seen nor heard. They can never be prepared for. Should you be so unlucky to fall into their teeth, then all you can do is endure, hold to whatever is sacred and true in your life and hope that that is enough.

Ian's screams would have ceased the workings of ailing men's hearts. Ian's screams reached backwards through time and planted disquiet in his mother's insides and painted a frown over his father's face.

And underneath his screams, Matt's voice sucked and grunted like a feasting pig.

4

Footsteps echoed, one after the other.

Alexander stood mesmerized, unable to reconcile the sudden onslaught of the uncanny with what, a moment before, had been a late afternoon at home. He was trapped somewhere between disbelief and terror, the regions of his mind warring over the reality of the situation.

Then the apartment door swung open on his left.

Pablo lay slumped on his side, maggots writhing in and out of his eyes and the bullet hole in his head. Alexander stumbled backwards, wordless, remembering the child shrieking, remembering pulling the trigger and firing the gun.

The child was dead. He had to be.

Pablo's corpse raised its head and looked at him, a long thread of blood clinging from the wound to the floor.

"He's...making...me," it said, the words mournful.

The door slammed shut.

Alexander stared without seeing, his senses teetering, the world threatening to disappear.

The footsteps stopped.

Someone laughed.

Alexander looked down the corridor. A man stood veiled in the semi-darkness, hands in the pockets of soiled jeans. A football jersey was just visible, the polyester once green and white now blackened.

A spark of recognition lit in Alexander, coating the back of his throat with bile.

"Who are you?" he said, summoning anger to shield him from dread. The man watched, silent. "Who are you!?"

The man did not make a sound.

Alexander reached out to magic, ready to fight, to show this intruder the mistake he had made. But webs of electric ice tore through him as he conjured. He cried out and fell to knee. Sparks sputtered over his body, and smoke spiraled from his head. He reached out again, and the pain seared his nerves, making him scream. Hollowness beat through his veins, as if the very blood had been stolen from him.

Magic was gone.

The stranger stuck out a closed fist and opened it. Ash poured onto the floor, making a mound at his feet. The stranger then turned and strolled back into the darkness, and as he disappeared, a concussive explosion echoed through the hallway.

Alexander ducked, thinking he had been shot at. Silence answered, naked of the shrill ringing that followed gunfire. He stood, uncertain of what to do or what to think. He looked at his own hands, these extensions of his will, his magic, and saw the failing sparks. A fierce ache coursed through his muscles, and his mind reeled. What was happening? He spied something glossy in the ash pile and hurried over to it, desperate for answers.

He reached down and picked up a photo that was not supposed to exist. He had last seen it writhing in flames, remembered lighting it in his own hand, guided by fury. But the photo was now as clear as if it had just been taken, and the images within carried his heart to the borders of longing, rage, and terror.

Within the photo he saw himself seated beside Phoebe, laughing together over poker and beer. Next to his wife was a man grinning askance at both of them, a man he had once called brother, a man who had sometimes infuriated him and had eventually done the unthinkable.

Alexander remembered Ian's screams and finding Matt standing over his bed, eyes crazed and filled with blood. He had nearly beaten Matt to death, had seen to it that he was punished for his crime, had watched him draw his last breath.

Later, he had destroyed every image of him after finding Ian staring at one of his pictures in a photo album.

But this picture had been resurrected out of ash by a hand that had traversed a country no one was ever meant to return from. Terror cradled Alexander like a mother whispering obscenities in a baby's ear, for he now knew this was no possession or act of magic. He did not hear an alien voice creeping among his thoughts, or feel the pull of infernal fingers plucking at his doubts and desires. There was no heightened sense of reality, and no sudden awareness of the world's every detail. This was awareness without life, a malignancy livid in the walls, the floor, and the very air. He knew what had poured the ash, and all of him wanted to recoil from the incomprehensible truth that now commanded his fears.

He blinked, and suddenly Matt was looking up at him from within the photo. His eyes were green, his hair was brushed forward over a balding pate, and he carried a large bulk hidden by a black leather jacket and dark blue shirt. A cynical expression creased his rounded cheeks. He held a framed photo of his own within the picture: a black and white portrait of Eleanor and Ian seated side by side, both dressed up, both smiling.

Both dead.

Alexander covered his mouth.

"No," he said, shaking his head. "Damn you, no."

His gaze darted from the portrait and found Matt's face again.

Matt's features were now withered. His eyes were vacant holes that looked as though they were portals to a vastness beyond comprehension. His broken and yellowed teeth poked through rotted cheeks. Yet he smiled. The ghost smiled at Alexander.

Alexander stared aghast, his mind echoing revelations he did not want to entertain. Anger beckoned: that anyone living or dead could threaten his children, or threaten him. He clung to fury for it was a shelter against the truth, a bulwark of control against the unknown. He tore the photo in half, tore those halves into smaller pieces, and scattered them. He stared into the darkness, where the intruder—where Matt—had gone. Fury erupted into a roar, and he bolted after him. Reason urged caution, but it was a lone voice against sirens of rage, fear, and an animal need to see his children.

The hallway rushed by in one long blur illuminated by a strange glow. It stretched on, seemingly endless, the walls corroded, the doors sagging and warped. Once more a lone voice screamed in Alexander's mind, urging him to notice the abnormal length, the ruin, the impossible changes to his home. But all he could see was Matt's hateful face, both dead and alive, and the image of his children in the framed photo. He had to find Matt, whatever he now was. He had to make him—

Two children drifted into view out of the gloom ahead. They danced, twirling together, her dress and his tailcoat blurring as they spun across the floor. The girl had curls, and the boy had well groomed straight hair. There was wrongness in them, as if they were animated out of antimatter, shaped from substances too wretched to be allowed entrance into existence. They moved like marionettes, heads lulling this way and that, drifting without inner purpose.

Alexander slid to a stop, nearly falling.

They spun apart from each other, bowed, and then slowly looked up at the magician.

He screamed.

The dead faces of his children stared at him, their skin sunken, their eyes wastelands of darkness, and their mouths parted to pour blood over withered lips and collapsed chins. They shambled to him, arms out for an embrace, croaking with voices that had long forgotten words.

Their very presence was pure abhorrence, tormenting every atom of Alexander's being.

They went to him, unending streams of blood spilling from their mouths and coating the floor at their feet.

Alexander turned to run, but he found his dead children behind him, arms reaching. He turned back and found them once more. They were everywhere, before and behind, as if his gaze carried them wherever he looked. He stood dumbfounded. The cold of dead lands wafted from them. Their hands found him, and they pulled him to the floor with a force that sapped his will and drained him of all hope. There, they embraced him, running dead fingers over his face, through his hair, and against his chest. Their voices warbled from ragged throats, chattering mad lullabies, overloading his senses and distorting reality until his world transformed into a realm where his children were dead, where he had identified their corpses and had watched their coffins lowered into the earth.

The lifeless forms of his children then collapsed into his arms, and Alexander was powerless to do anything but cradle them.

He shook, babbled, and then screamed. The dead ones were limp against him, and his mind broke.

Beyond them, Pablo watched from the shadows, sadness etched upon his face, his hand pressing the red crayon up and down underneath his fatal wound.

Watching over all, Matt rocked back and forth, leering, his mannequin's smile the only thing visible in the darkness.

5

The dead are not known to the living. Not truly. They flit in and out of existence, shades that drift across our paths only to vanish before they can be understood. Rationalizations explain them away: the workings of exhausted or addled brains, the rampaging of electrical currents playing on nerves, the reactions to empty spaces that we fill with specters. Better that way. Better to believe ghosts are not real, things that can never be, the illusions of children or foolish and desperate minds.

But for those who come face to face with the waking dead, there is no confusion. They cannot be mistaken with beasts or cruel men, for the teeth of hungry ghosts threaten more than flesh. The shrillest wind cannot mimic their cries, for they speak from depths beyond the known universe, in voices composed from broken dimensions and failing memories. Their very existence is an insidious maze where they haunt their own lives in endless repetition, and the unlucky few who are taken into their grasps witness the living world become corrupted into exhibitions of rot.

So it was for Percy Bowles.

He awoke on his feet, wrapped in a straightjacket of shadows. He gasped and tried to move, but his limbs were pinned, and his strength useless. He looked around, wild eyed.

Cheval mirrors surrounded him. Between the mirrors were mannequins in their long black gowns, obscure in the dimness, their hands tucked under their chins as if in appraisal. The floor was wooden and warped and filthy. Insipid light beat from above, barely illuminating the space.

The mannequins whispered among themselves, their voices grating, just on the edge of hearing.

Percy caught his many reflections in the cracked mirrors. The black straightjacket writhed about him, leaving only his head exposed. In the center mirror he saw someone standing behind him, a broad figure in a football jersey.

"Whaddaya say, girls?" Matt said.

The mannequins fell silent.

Percy went rigid, his awareness warring with the memory of a man he had seen die upon his knees, executed by his own sister for an act unforgivable and irrevocable. Matt had been put down for what he had done to Ian. But the voice could belong to no other. Percy shook his head, unwilling to accept, but his senses were alive with the presence of wraiths, the cold stench of death, and something nameless assaulting him, filling him with wrongness, the certainty that the barrier between life and death had been penetrated. He gasped. The long years of his life, the wonders and terrors, had not prepared him for the reality of a vengeful spirit. Somehow Matthew Moore had traversed the beyond and now held him hostage. He thought of Rosie, bared his teeth, and writhed against darkness. But he could not move.

"This asshole's getting impatient," Matt said. "C'mon, hurry up. It's almost time for the party. Get him dressed. I want this limey fuck looking good."

The straightjacket molded over Percy until the darkness was like skin, taking control and stretching open his arms and legs. Pain screamed in his joints as the blackness twisted, pulled, and raised him into the air. Inch by inch the straightjacket transformed into a butler's uniform: black morning coat with long tails, a high collared white shirt that was stained and faded, a black tie frayed at its edges, white gloves missing fingertips, dirty gray pants, and weathered black shoes.

The uniform moved of its own volition, manipulating Percy, modeling him for the mannequins. "Oohs" and "Ahs" sang through the air. The uniform spun him. One revolution, and suddenly the mannequins were standing nearer, their faces adorned in crazed streaks of makeup.

They spoke.

"Perfect."

"Yes, a good and proper servant."

"He knows his place."

"Lovely, just lovely."

"He'll make us proud."

"Ooh, think of the guests! They'll be so grateful."

Percy was dropped to the floor, but was pulled erect before he could crumple.

Matt appeared directly to his left: a mannequin's face with swollen pink cheeks, a grizzly and cartoonish smile, and crayon colored green eyes. Their pupils were ragged holes, and deep within them shone malignant light, rancid and discolored, beating with malicious glee.

"Look at you," Matt said. "It's good to see you, homie. How the fuck you've been?"

The mannequins tittered.

Percy shivered, wrestling with incomprehension, fighting to conquer himself and take control of his body. The suddenness of the assault left him reeling, grasping for explanations. But reason abandoned him within Matt's dead gaze. He knew there was nothing he could say to stay the insane will of the ghost.

Matt appeared before Percy and pressed their foreheads together. Cold screamed into him, radiating from Matt's plaster skin.

"I've always fucking hated you," Matt said. "All your judging, your bullshit. You always thought you were better than me. Every chance you had, you made me feel like shit. For what? So you could be the big man. So you could look at me and say 'I'm better'. 'That's what it takes with pricks like you. You don't feel like a man until you're stepping on someone else. Wasn't enough that you already had everything handed to you. Wasn't enough that you tricked the woman I love into being with you."

Matt's voice twisted into a creaking roar. The surrounding mannequins hissed. Matt pulled back, and the roar diminished. His obscene smile conflicted with the ugly light in his pupils.

"You think it made you strong, making me look stupid?" he said. "Well, homie, it's my turn now."

Percy swallowed, seeing nothing but the barren truth in the crazed face before him.

"I watched you die," he said.

Matt's mannequin face contorted into a mask of rage. The smile twisted into a scream, the eyes went black, and the light behind them blazed into tendrils of darkness that hinted at the true form beneath the plaster.

"I'm not dead!"

The other mannequins screamed in kind, their voices rising into the shrieks of falling bombs.

Madness is a bastion against awful truths, a shelter from the things we cannot accept. Matt and the dead ones staked their claim within insanity's walls and rampaged against any who threatened to shatter their denial.

Percy cringed, himself teetering on the edge of reason. Such was the awfulness of ghosts, their presence enough to send a sane mind reeling within itself. He shut his eyes, thought of Rosie and the others, and clung to strength. Whatever was happening, he would wait, watch, and endure. He had to.

The ghosts fell silent.

Matt growled, and then laughed, a broken sound.

"You fucked up," he said, his face once more a garish smile. "See, I know Rosie loves me. But you tricked her. You made her think I'm something that I'm not. That's the only reason she married you. She doesn't really love you, homie. She wants to be with me, and I'm gonna show her. Then I'll have my family. You, and the Russian, and anyone else who tries to get in the way is gonna catch it. Watch.

"In a little bit, we're gonna have a party. And you're gonna help. You're almost ready. Just need one more thing."

A gaggle of rotted hands appeared out of the surrounding gloom and forced a mask over Percy's head. The mask went taut over his face and neck and twisted his head around so he looked into a mirror. His blue eyes stared out of a sad clown mask, the mouth contorted into a frown, the cheeks ruddy and pink, the nose a bulbous red.

The butler's suit went rigid, and suddenly Percy was bowing uncontrollably. He screamed through his teeth, summoning all of his strength to stop, but the suit began to throw him around, ending his bow and making him jig and flail as if he were a tap dancer having a seizure. He cried out. Matt laughed.

"You look like an asshole," he said. "Ladies, what do you think? He ready?"

The mannequins applauded, ash misting from their clapping hands.

6

Rosie's vision spiraled into focus. Slivers of light shone through the mire of shadows and haze, ordering themselves into rows of picture frames hanging on the wall before her. She blinked, tasted something foul on her lips, and shot up with a gasp. A blanket fell from her, and her fingers explored the lumps of a mattress covered by a stained and weathered bed sheet.

Memory rekindled: the bathroom, the strangeness in the mirror, the ghost.

She put out her hands and watched them shake. Then she counted her fingers from one to ten and back again, and closed and opened her eyes repeatedly to induce some evidence that this was a dream or the nightmare of possession. It had to be. Otherwise madness would usurp reality, supplanting rationality with psychosis. But no matter what she did, the room did not shift or dissolve from one blink to the next, and she still felt the dryness of the blanket over her legs, the failing softness of the mattress beneath her, and her own sluggish body.

She was awake, alone in a strange room, stolen from her home by a dead thing.

Cold saturated her. Sweat erupted through the pores of her skin. Her vision narrowed as a curtain of emptiness threatened to make her faint, and dread made an echo chamber of her heart.

Rosie forced herself to focus on a shivering finger and swayed it like a metronome from side to side. She breathed with purpose, easing her stuttering breath into a steady cadence, accepting the tide of panic seizing her heartbeat.

"Go ahead," she said, whispering to herself, remembering a mantra that had saved her from the avalanche of anxiety many times before. "You can't kill me, so go right on ahead."

Panic dimmed. She regained control and checked herself for injuries, for bleeding, for restraints, but found no sign of harm or capture. She then stood up, moving as if awakened from a long illness, and looked about the room.

Vases with wilted roses stood upon three dressers that were slumped against the walls. The dead flowers beat with strange luminescence in the gloaming. A deformed sculpture of a horse reared on a table at the room's center, its face melted towards the warped marble surface. Pictures lined the walls, and a single door was opened to a pale glow beyond the room.

Rosie focused on the door, sensing an unseen awareness there. The picture frames across from the entrance reflected a face drifting backwards and disappearing into the murk, scattering its ghostly visage across multiple panes. She did not see this.

She glanced at the many hanging pictures, threw her hand behind her, felt for a frame, and snatched it without pulling her attention from the door. She stole a glance at the photo, still tasting rancid sweetness on her lips, and then went rigid. Her muscles seized in her throat, her shoulders hitched, and a tempest took control of her heart.

She saw herself within the picture, standing in profile behind the bar of her restaurant, counting money but smiling at someone out of frame. Everything else within the photo was obscured by a dark haze, but she stood out in beatific glow. She strained to remember when this picture was taken and by whom, couldn't, threw it aside, and reached for another.

She was once more the subject, looking directly out as if staring into a camera. But she was not smiling or posing. Her expression was one of listening, the concentration of conversation. Behind her were other people, but they were blurs, and she again shone with the light reserved for saints and martyrs.

She shook her head with disbelief, stepped onto the floor still holding the frame, and then looked at the other photos. She was the subject of every one—endless images of her laughing, concentrating over books, oiling and cleaning her gun, spell casting from a meditative position, or looking across a table or bar or even over her shoulder as if speaking to someone mid-stride.

All of these intimate moments collected and collated by some unseen hand.

And it came to her. These were not pictures. These were memories.

She went to the table at the center of the room. One image lay there beside the malformed horse, and in it she was staring directly at the observer. Her face was dimmed, masking an expression of pity, but the observer's hands were visible and clasped within hers. Together they shone bright and golden, as if the observer had beheld in them all he had ever hoped for.

Rosie remembered that moment: Matt striding into the restaurant, reaching over the bar for a bottle of aged scotch, taking a long drink, and then calling himself useless. He had made a costly mistake during a raid to free captives from a possession parlor, one that had nearly cost Alexander, Greg, and Cedric their lives. He had come to Rosie's to obliterate himself with alcohol, and there she had provided some comfort. But his eyes had blazed when she had taken his hands, a conflagration of desire and feverish longing.

She had pulled away and told him in no uncertain terms that she regarded him as a friend and nothing more.

But those memories were missing. There was only this moment

from that night, a monument to her shaped from Matt's fantasies. In these images her skin was too smooth, her big ears small and dainty, and her lips fuller than they had ever been. This was not Rosie St. John, but the estimation of her in the mind of one who had never been able to let her go, one whom she had seen die, one who was now among them once more.

Terror engulfed her, vicious spasms of fear screaming through her skin. This could not be. She hugged herself, her sweatpants and t-shirt feeble against the cold radiating from within. Again she tasted the rancid sweetness on her lips, and she cringed and passed her hand over them. Her fingers came away covered in streaks of ash and some viscous dark substance. She wiped them on her sweatpants, backed away from the table, and then felt dead hands seize her ankles and dead lips kiss her feet, radiating waves of corruption through the core of her.

She screamed and ripped herself away. The hands released her. She looked down and saw no one, but her feet were smeared with the same ash and blackness that adorned her lips. Disgust overwhelmed her, and she fled the room.

Reality caught up a few steps into the corridor. She was in an unfamiliar place, perhaps not even of this world. The air pulsed with awareness. She froze and looked about, uncertain, her breath racing. Wilted flower petals were scattered over the floor, beating with rancid glow, illuminating a long and tattered carpet running the length of the corridor. A chandelier hung from the ceiling, but what were once shining columns and elegant arms was now a frenzy of wires, granulated crystal, and melted brass. The walls were ashen and had long forgotten their true color. Console tables leaned against them like drunkards.

A painting hung on the right, its gilded frame sagging, its colors stripped out of some hyper-reality where everything shone with manic glee. Within it was portraits of Rosie, Ian, and Matt posed upon a chaise lounge, as if they were some royal family from the eighteenth century. Rosie's and Ian's visages bore frantic smiles, and their eyes were over-wide and colorful, shining with reverence. Matt's face was unmistakable, his cheeks full and flushed, his green eyes bright, alive. He held a guitar by the neck and wore a black jacket with golden epaulettes. The painted Rosie leaned against him in a golden sleeveless gown that revealed her shoulders, and Ian sat her lap in a little sailor's outfit, dark blue trimmed with white.

Rosie stared, taking in the unmistakable madness of the work, seeing within Matt's painted features desire and arrogance, the countenance of a man who had traversed death to lay claim upon what he regarded as his. The impossibility of it all crumbled before the memories hanging in the other room. Matt had shown her what he had longed for in the impossible reaches of existence. That she had never conceived that a ghost could exist, even in her world of magic and darkness, mattered not in the face of what had befallen her. Mathew Moore was here now, holding her captive in a prison constructed out of his obsessions.

Terror gave way to fury. That anyone or anything would dare to take her as if she were some trophy to be claimed. That he would threaten Ian, or any of her loved ones. She bared her teeth, screamed, and ripped into the canvas. Shreds of the painting flew helter-skelter through the air until all that remained of the portrait was tatters. She huffed, her shoulders rising and falling, her fingers working with fury unabated.

A lone voice spoke in her mind, that keeper of logic urging clear thought. She scanned the corridor for other doors. That way she could hide and familiarize herself with her surroundings. Then she would wait and see if she was alone, and probe for a means of escape.

Matt gripped her shoulders from behind, false fingers pressing into her skin, casting ripples of nauseating cold through her flesh. She roared and struggled, but he only pulled her closer into an embrace. From the corner of her eye she could see his mannequin features and something more, an indefinable haze warping the air. Breath became thin through her nostrils and throat, and a dull flood took hold of her senses. Vision dimmed, sounds dampened, and awareness sank into the deepest part of her brain. She strained and fought, but her muscles gave only feeble twitches. She reached out to magic, sorting through the myriad of spells lying dormant within her for those agonizing concoctions that would assault an attacker's nerves and fears. But a metallic web answered, pouring gravel under her skin, as if magic was now an emptied river and she desperately trying to drink from its withered bed.

She slumped, and the ghost reached under her chin and raised it. The painting was before them, renewed. Matt groaned with satisfaction.

"I knew you'd like it," he said. His voice was that of a damaged record, prancing between octaves, warbled, mad. "That's just the first surprise. I built all this for you. You always said you've never wanted much, but fuck that. You deserve to live in a mansion." He elongated the word, stretching it, torturing it. Then he pressed his dead cheek to hers. "It's good to see you. For awhile I thought I wasn't gonna be able to come back, but I worked hard, got my shit together, and here I am. It was only a matter of time. And hey..."

He whipped Rosie around so she stared up into his crayon stained eyes, his cracked plaster face, and that stretched smile.

"I ain't mad," he said. "I know we had our problems, but all that's done. It was Percy, anyway. He got in your head. He made you doubt yourself. I know, I know, it's not good to start a new relationship when you're already in one–especially if you're married–but love is love. What we got–I felt it right away. I felt it as soon as I saw you. Ayo, I got something else for you."

He pulled away from her, floating backwards, his limbs unmoving. Suddenly, Rosie was thrust into a chair. They were no longer in the hallway, but in a spacious room with Megadeth and Metallica posters crisscrossed on the walls, broken bottles of scotch lining the shelves, a rotted New York Jets' helmet seated on a collapsed stereo system, and a four-poster bed adorned with burgundy canopy curtains that were streaked by burn marks.

The picture from the other room, where their clasped hands shone, hung the wall across from the bed.

Rosie moaned and tried to rise, but Matt appeared before her, seated in a chair not a foot away, and once more her mind was clouded in a dullard's haze. His will was a physical presence invading her senses, and silent voices urged her that this was right, that this was home and he her partner. She struggled, clinging to who she was, to her loved ones, to the Gardens.

A guitar hovered before Matt, its strings popped from the fretboard, its tuning pegs missing. Emaciated creatures that had perhaps been maggots wiggled through its body.

"I wrote this for you," he said. "You're gonna love it."

What followed were mangled notes strummed on a dead guitar. Matt's hands never moved, and his smiling crayon gaze never left hers. The song bore some melody, hints of romance and passion mired by insanity sown in his long dead mind. Matt hummed along, his voice rising with dissonant strings into a feverish crescendo, then falling to contemplative silence. His ghostly fingers picked and plucked the last notes, and the song faded.

Matt said nothing for a time, watching her. Then:

"Yeah? Alright, I knew you'd love it. Aw, you crying?" She wasn't. "That's cool. I wanted this to mean something. I wanted you to feel it."

The guitar floated out of his lap, landing gently in a crooked guitar stand. He leaned towards her, and his false hand stroked her cheek. She groaned, revulsion seizing all of her.

"I love you," he said. He kissed her, pressing an open mouth on her lips, and a torrent of screaming darkness engulfed her mind. She shrieked in her throat, both in rage and horror, but it came as nothing more than a whimper. He pulled away, pressing her face between his hands. "This is the start of our lives together. C'mon, ya gotta see the rest of the place."

The room was ripped away. Rosie was carried by some invisible force, her toes dragging over the carpet. Matt wrapped his false arm around her waist, and they floated through hallways and rooms, each one adorned with luxuries shaped by delusion. Everywhere were portraits of Matt and Rosie and Ian, everywhere evidence of Matt's obsession. Rosie's name was scrawled on walls and ceilings, as if by children, and crude drawings of her face accompanied the scribbles.

But Matt's face outnumbered hers: in paintings and pictures where he stood in regal poses, sometimes at the center of great smiling crowds, other times with Rosie or Ian or both, but most of all alone before rows of liquor bottles, or upon football fields, or some ornate ballroom. He was never the mannequin in the portraits, but an enhanced version of the man he had been in life, always with the appearance of strength. Yet decay tainted the walls around the paintings, insidious spider webs of rust and rot.

Matt carried her through double doors and out to a courtyard of dead grass, black and gray and lifeless in the still air. Porcelain children stood here and there, silhouetted in mist, some frozen in poses of chase, others seated together in circles for games of Duck-Duck-Goose. Two were in mid-throw, and though they did not move, a football passing between them, one to the other and back again. The porcelain children cried out with deranged joy as Matt and Rosie passed, their voices glass scraping chalkboards. Matt laughed.

"Look at this!" he said to Rosie, and all she could do was slump and be carried along, while all of her writhed inside. "Look at these little fuckers. They had nothing until I came along. I help them. Why not? Who's having a great time!?" The porcelain children cheered again. Matt went on. "Think the Gardens was something? I've built you a goddamn mansion."

Above them were turrets and towers hanging disjointed in the roiling mist, connected to nothing. Floating walls hovered on all sides, and within them were windows where specters stood, watching. Screams bled through the glass, muted like bombs falling in a parallel dimension, howling the truth that pounded against the façade of Matt's delusion.

He and the children ignored them.

Matt led Rosie through the courtyard and into the ballroom.

Chatter morphed into cheers as they entered. Mannequins adorned for a formal event stood on a black and white diamond patterned floor encrusted in dust. Round tables were covered with once white linens, and cracked plates and glasses were laid out upon them. The tables surrounded a large dance floor, and at its center was an altar before which a shriveled figure in a priest's habit stood.

A single table was apart from the others at the head of the dance floor, and there Ian sat dressed in a worn tuxedo, beside two empty high backed chairs. He was slouched over, his eyes drooping, the corners of his lips quivering. Rosie tried to call out to him, but all she could do was moan.

Here, surrounded by ghosts delirious with the delusion that they were still alive, horrid in their mannequin forms and putrid dress clothes, Rosie pushed through the muddied workings of her mind and pieced together what was to come. She shivered uncontrollably, true fear born from her helplessness and the slow dissolving of rational thought. Bit by bit, she felt herself fading, merging with the fantasy Matt had constructed

"You know what this is," Matt said. He dropped down to one knee, a stuttering and mechanical movement. Rosie nearly tumbled backwards, but unseen hands held her up. A large diamond ring appeared before Matt's green eyes, black splotches like carcinomas infecting the stone.

"You and I belong together," Matt said. "So?"

Rosie strained, trying to scream her refusal, but her vocal cords only cracked. She scanned the crowd of crazed plaster faces and found a lone figure standing aside from them. He wore butler's attire and a clown mask, and deep in the recesses of his eyes she caught sparks of blue quivering with sorrow. Recognition lighted, but Matt's will surged against her cognition, eroding it. For a terrible moment, everything felt normal. She screamed again in her mind, fury serving as an anchor to herself.

But Matt heard and saw none of this. There was only denial.

"She said yes!" he said, rising from the floor to take her into his arms. Applause and cheers erupted. Matt kissed her, and then Rosie was ripped back by a gaggle of mannequins in ball gowns, their crayon eyes and monstrous smiles encompassing her whole vision. Their unmoving hands somehow ripped at her clothes, and strips of a corroded wedding dress spilled from their plaster fingers and

GIOVANNI DIAZ

engulfed her. The folds of fabric seemed to sink through her skin, and her awareness sank into a pinprick of hazy light. All of her was contained within this feeble shimmer, scratching and clawing against an all encompassing cage. But she could not break through. She was a prisoner within herself, Matt's will pulling her body this way and that until she was nothing more than a doll satisfying his desire.

The harem of mannequins parted, and Rosie emerged from among them in a wedding gown, swaying on her feet. Her eyes drooped, but a painful grin stretched across her face as she went to receive Matt's embrace.

AND THEY WERE MARRIED.

The celebration began. The dead danced to broken music. Servants dipped in and out of the throngs, chief among them Percy in his clown mask, spinning and pirouetting as Matt saw fit. Ian sat at the Sweetheart Table, a smile breaking over his features, as if invisible fingers reached into his mouth and pulled wide. Rosie stood beside Matt by the table, arm through his, leaning her head against his shoulder, posing for a photographer wielding a camera with a shattered lens.

Somewhere Matt could hear Alexander weeping.

Matt took it all in, the happy (mannequin) faces, the joyful (hollow) look in Rosie's eyes, and the excitement (agony) in Ian's. Satisfaction filled him as he felt the warmth of his bride. He ignored the singular voice deep in the recesses of his damaged soul, screaming that this was all a lie. Never mind the falling sensation of doom that seeped from the memory of a vast emptiness. He felt only the power that had allowed him to make everything right, to paint the world as he saw fit.

He walked (stuttered) to the center of the dance floor and took a champagne glass from a passing waiter (a mannequin whose face was cracked in half) and raised it. The dancers stopped, and suddenly they all had champagne glasses.

That such joy could be his. That life could bear such fruits. His guests waited with anticipation. They were not ghosts inhabiting mannequins, denying the truth of their existence. They were friends. They were people. They were celebrating his rise into success and love.

His glass was cracked and filled with ash, but to him it bubbled gold and silver. He raised it to the heavens.

"To the living!"

ACT IV

THE BLACK FOREST

1

Eleanor ran.

Her breath and footfalls echoed through the gloaming. What had once been clean checkered floors and a warmly lit hallway was now a ruin of ash heaps, craters, and sagging detritus. Shadows enveloped the air, emitting a fetid glow. Ruptured doors, broken or hanging, rushed by. The ceiling swelled and dripped. Crude drawings and scribbles were etched upon ashen walls. Entrances to other corridors, spaces that had not existed before, branched off from the hallway, and in her rising panic Eleanor realized that there seemed to be no end to this place. Her home had been transformed into something withered and infinite, a self-replicating maze inhabited by absence.

A wail undulated after her, spurring her into full sprint.

"Darling," the ghost said, howling. "It's time to eat! I'm going to make you eggs. You need breakfast before school! Just come to mommy, come to mommy, mommy will take care of you, come to mommy!"

Cramps seized Eleanor's legs and midsection. She slid to a stop. The ghost shrieked, closer now, every word an audible kaleidoscope of decay. Eleanor covered her ears and looked about. She stood between three doors, two on her left, and one on her right. The doors on her left were broken, one barely hanging off its top hinge. The door on her right was stained and cracked but whole, and a pale glow bled through the bottom gap. She hesitated, sensing something barren waiting beyond that door, emptiness pregnant with terrible awareness, causing her to back away.

But the broken doors revealed nothing, layers of blackness that seized her senses with poison-tipped teeth.

"After school we can play hide and seek," the ghost said, its voice near, emanating from before and behind Eleanor. "But you have to do your homework first."

Eleanor chose the door to the right and threw herself inside.

She found the ghost within: a mannequin with brittle blonde hair, wearing a brown business jacket and pants. She stood before a rusted stovetop, her back to Eleanor, a broken spatula in her raised hand. The hissing of frying eggs filled the air, contrasted by the acrid stench of burning metal.

Eleanor gasped and turned for the door, but a wall greeted her. Shock took hold, freezing her for a moment. She suppressed a cry and searched for another way out. Clutter filled the room. Towers of boxes bulged with crumpled black papers, and everywhere were stacks of magazines with photo negatives of mothers and babies on their covers. Eleanor could just make out the title "Working Mom" on some of them, the once white block letters stained and blurred.

A square dining table stood a few feet behind the ghost, utensils and a plastic cup laid out.

Eleanor swallowed and watched the ghost. It stood there, silent, brooding. The air about it darkened, contracting and expanding on itself. It said nothing.

Beads of sweat dripped centimeter by centimeter over Eleanor's skin. She again reached out to magic, but immediately cringed against pain biting her insides.

The ghost stood there, the spatula in its hand, frying pan hissing.

Eleanor pressed against the wall, spotted a gap between the boxes to her right, and took a tentative step towards it.

A rattling sound emanated from the ghost.

"You know," it said, "I never have time to eat breakfast because you refuse to get up when I call you. I'm going to be late again. Do you want me to lose my job? Then neither of us will be able to eat. Is that what you want?"

Eleanor said nothing. She took another sidestep towards the boxes.

"Sit down!"

Eleanor started and cradled her hands against her chest. The ghost turned its head, creaking and cracking with every agonizing inch. Eleanor thought that to see its face would break her, rendering her a blubbering mess of tears and inconsolable shrieks. She nearly shouted for her father, her brother, her loved ones. But years of training as a magician gave her a foundation of calm in the face of horror. It was wisdom beyond her age, paid for by the loss of innocence. Though she had never known of anything like the deranged specter before her, one shade of darkness was akin to the next, and she understood that to succumb to terror would be the end.

So she hurried to the table, took a seat, and bowed her head. She listened to the clicking as the ghost turned back towards the stove. It sighed, a mournful sound accompanied by screeching like the sharpening of knives, and Eleanor's heart pounded. Her calm balanced on a wire. She took a shuddering breath and gripped the edge of the table, focusing on the cold pouring through her fingers, allowing the unpleasant sensation to blot out the offensiveness of the being standing near. Never had she felt something so wrong, a blight perpetrated upon the living world, threatening to unravel sanity. So she bit her tongue and focused on the pain, stomped on one foot and then the other under the table, and tensed her muscles until they throbbed.

This way she kept control.

A plate was dropped before her, clanging, spinning, coming to a stop. Eleanor trembled from the weight of the ghost inches away, its hand pressed against the table. She focused on the plate. Rusted metal shavings curled over the filthy surface, swelling from something moving underneath. The ghost waited. Without a word,

Eleanor reached for the fork, a curled thing like an arthritic finger, shuddered as she touched it, and dipped it into the shavings. She scooped whatever she could, darted a glance at the dead one, bowed her head so her curls obscured her face, and moved the fork towards her mouth. She poured the shavings onto her lap at the last second, then straightened and pretended to chew.

"Mm," she said.

The ghost stood there, silent. Eleanor waited for a moment, and then scooped another forkful. She made to pour the shavings again, when she tensed from something frigid writhing over her legs. She looked down and spied blackened maggots rolling off of her jeans and onto the floor. She swallowed, bowed her head, shut her eyes, spread her legs, and spilled more metal shavings. They drifted past her thighs and onto the floor.

The ghost ran a dead hand over her cheek. Eleanor cried out, dropping the fork. Then she clamped her teeth shut with an audible click.

"You see?" the ghost said. "Aren't they delicious? Mommy only wants what's best for you. I know you're getting older, but you're still young. I'm just trying to prepare you for what's..."

It trailed off, its hand beginning to shake on Eleanor's cheek.

"No, no-no-no-no-no," it said, its voice lowered to a hoarse whisper. "Not again, please, god, not again, don't take another one of my babies, please, don't let me miscarry again, please—"

Suddenly it screamed, and Eleanor was assaulted by a sensation of doom born out of misery. She clapped her hands over her ears and shut her eyes–

The screaming stopped.

She opened her eyes and found the ghost seated across from her. She spied pink lipstick traced over impossibly wide lips stretched into a smile, and mustard green eyes colored in with crayon. She looked away immediately, fighting spiraling waves of nausea.

"So, how was school?" the ghost said.

Confusion gripped Eleanor. She darted her eyes left to right, seeking some measure of sense in the madness. She noticed a few remaining metal flakes on her legs and remembered how easily the specter had been fooled. She swallowed, struggled for command of her body, and took a deep breath.

"School was..." she said. Her voice croaked. She cleared her throat and began again. "School was great. I, uh, I got a perfect, um, score...grade on a test...quiz."

The ghost stared. Eleanor focused on the plate.

"That's...wonderful," the ghost said, dragging the word. "Give it to me. We'll hang it up on the refrigerator."

Shit, Eleanor thought.

She swallowed.

"Oh, uh, well, the teacher didn't give them out yet. She's gonna hand them...hand them out tomorrow."

The ghost leaned forward. Eleanor saw the lower half of its mannequin features, the smeared pink lipstick and too-wide mouth. She shut her eyes.

"You better not be lying to me," it said.

"No. I—I swear. You'll see it tomorrow. Remember, uh, remember how you helped me study? We worked on it for, like, three days, and I got a perfect score. You...you were right, studying works."

The ghost hovered there for a moment, and then slid back, humming with satisfaction.

"That's my girl," it said.

"Yeah. That's...that's me. So remember how, like, you said I could go to...go to, uh, my friend Lily's place to work on...on our project for next week? You remember, you said right after school I could go. Lily..." Eleanor cringed, hating herself for mentioning her real friend's name, praying it would not somehow allow the specter to track her down. But she had to go on. "She's right down the block. It would only be for a few hours. Then we can...play...hide and seek..."

The ghost stared at her. A subtle tremor reverberated through the room, shivering through the surrounding boxes.

"I'm so proud of my baby," the ghost said.

"Yeah," Eleanor replied, frowning. "Yeah, thanks, mo—" She

couldn't say it. "Thanks. You're...you're the best. So, like I was saying, Lil— my friend's waiting for me, so— "

"Darling, it's almost time for bed, soon, isn't it? We should get your jam-jams on, and then I can read you a story."

"Uh. No. It's still...still early. So, I should—"

"Oh, did I tell you what my boss said about your essay on penguins? She said that you're as smart and creative as I am. Isn't that nice?"

Tears threatened to shatter Eleanor's façade. She dug her nails into her legs and pressed on.

"I get it from you," she said. She struggled, searching for some way to use the specter's delusion to escape. "You're—you're always telling me to work hard, so, that's why my friend and I have to do our project—"

"My boss doesn't have any children. She says a woman can't have a career and a family. She says that you can't be free if you have to raise children. But we prove them wrong, don't we?"

"Mom," Eleanor said, hating the word as it came out of her mouth. Tears streamed. That she had to waste that sacred title on a lunatic spirit. That such an impossible thing was happening. Rosie had vanished, Percy had been incapacitated and taken, and she could only imagine what else may have befallen her father and brother and the rest of the Gardens. She was aware that this was beyond reason, that she should be running and screaming, that she should be questioning her own sanity. But the truth stared at her with horrid crayon eyes, and to deny it would be to fall deeper into its grasp. She had run, and that had led her here. So she had to play along. She had to accept, so she could find a way to escape and help her loved ones if she could.

But to address the ghost as her mother, hurt beyond words.

"Mom, you're not listening. I have to go do my project."

The ghost stared, an aura of incomprehension darkening its features.

"You said I could," Eleanor said. "If I don't, I'll fail. It won't take long. Please, mom. Let me go."

"What did you just call me?"

"Mom," Eleanor gritted her teeth, nearly spitting through them. "You're my mom. Okay? Happy? Mom, can you let me go to my friend's house, please? Like you said."

The ghost stared.

"You're not my daughter."

Eleanor blinked.

"Who are you? Where's my daughter? What have you done with her?"

"M-Mom, what are you talking about?"

"Where's my daughter!?"

The table flipped upwards and fell onto the stove. Eleanor threw herself from the chair and ran for the gap in the boxes. The ghost darted, a blur. Eleanor reached the stacks and pressed into the gap, but the ghost seized her by the hair, unseen hands ripping her out. Her feet kicked inches above the floor, and she stared directly up into the mannequins snarling face. A torrent of accusations, whines, threats, and babble shrieked from the ghost, shaping the air into a wall of dead noise. Eleanor screamed, trying to shake herself free, but the ghost lifted her closer.

"Where's my daughter, where's my daughter, where's my daughter!?" the ghost said through the cacophony of its shrieks.

Eleanor thrashed and cried, reeling from the awfulness saturating her. A thread of anger sparked, and she seized it, inflamed by the ghost for it had dared to play her mother, had reminded her of what she had lost, had made her act as though she were her daughter when she was anything but. She gritted her teeth against tears and let rage take control.

"Up your fucking ass, you fucking asshole!" she said.

The ghost shrieked.

"You ain't got a fucking daughter, 'cause you're fucking dead, fuck-face!"

The ghost went rigid, its torrent of cries silenced.

"You hear me!? You can't have any kids 'cause you're dead. You're dead-dead- dead!"

The mannequin groaned, its snarl widening into a pained O.

"Dead-dead-dead!"

Eleanor fell to the floor. The ghost shivered above her, mewling, shaking, and then wailing with such despair that sorrow welled through Eleanor and erupted into a sob. The stacks of boxes tottered and then collapsed onto the floor, hurling hundreds of faded ultrasounds through the air. Smeared black and white images of fetuses sailed here and there, and the ghost gripped one with a jerk of its arms, brought it close, and wept.

"No, my baby, no, please, no," it said, rocking back and forth, pressing the ultrasound against its face.

Eleanor watched it, saturated by sorrow. The stove and table sank in on themselves, and the walls peeled like burnt flesh. Eleanor nearly reached out to the ghost, hearing in its sobs loss she never wanted to understand. But, despite her pity for the dead thing, awfulness still clung to it, repulsing her. She stood up, turned around, and found the walls behind her dissolving into sagging folds. Beyond was the hallway, bleeding mist into the room.

Eleanor ran out, crying as she heard the ghost screaming for the child she would never have.

2

Eleanor collapsed, spit clinging to her lips. She wiped her mouth and looked up. The ceiling swelled in places, strips of paint dangling. The floors were pocked and splintered and slanted and covered in inches of ash. Doors continued to line the hallway, cracked and bent, marching ahead into desolation. Shafts of drear light shot through their eyeholes, casting a feeble glow.

Her home, the world she knew, reduced to a grim spectacle of what it was, as if she had stepped through time and emerged upon the ruin of all things. She whimpered, her muscles seizing, her heart thundering, all of her thoughts clustered around the succession of events that had sent her running. The hallway stretched before and behind her. Shadows saturated spaces between shafts of goblin light. A nameless silence blanketed everything, amplifying the terror in her heart.

The dead had risen. She was certain. The child accepted what the others had so desperately fought. She knew magic. She had heard the ravaged screams of werewolves and had suffered a demon to claw at her soul. But this was none of those things. She could have been blind to the horrors that had stolen Percy and deaf to the cries of the phantom who had so wanted to adopt her, but still she would have known that ghosts now infested her home. She shivered. "Ghosts" was just a word. The reality of them permeated skin, smothered with the atmosphere of an alien world, reached down into the depths of a person and twisted.

The hallway beat with distortion, a diorama of haunts, existence contorted into something that should never have been. She looked left and right, searching for some means of escape, for hope. But the life she knew had been devoured by a phantom dimension, a jealous realm of specters where the people she loved were taken, where the dark spaces were chasms carved out of time.

"What the fuck," she said, was all she could say. She hunched over and wept, wracked by sobs, crushed by silence, a child alone in architecture wrought by dead hands.

She wept until a hollow wind billowed through the walls, sighing and shrieking through cracks like wraiths harmonizing over a wasteland. She wiped her face and shook out her hands to steady herself, then looked around and tried to take in as much of the hallway as she could. Expectation crept over her skin, as if the shadows teemed with unseen specters, horrors waiting for the right moment to strike. She watched. She waited.

Nothing.

She trembled. Wind whipped, and dust spat. The hallway was a broken kaleidoscope, slivers of light jagged against the encompassing dark. Eleanor felt as if she were staring down a mineshaft. Vertigo seized her. She braced against the floor, closed her eyes, and breathed. The world steadied. She hugged her knees against the cold and looked about the doors and darkness and ruin and knew not what to do.

She thought on Jason.

It had begun with him. He had brought ghosts to the Gardens. What she had been certain was the unchecked magic of a budding magician had actually been the workings of revenants. How? Why? He had seemed so afraid. His eyes had been tired, sad, and always moving. Had he known? Had he hurt them on purpose?

Even here, she could not think on it for long. To do so, to believe that the boy whom she had felt an instant connection with could do such a thing, would send her into a pit where there was no escape. To believe that Darius, the man who her father had loved as his own brother, the man who had discovered magic, would allow such horrors to pass, would shatter her faith that anyone could be trusted.

Had it all been a trick of Abebe Ngombe's? The great demon. That seemed obvious, save for the fact that it made no sense. He could have destroyed them at his leisure. He had shown them that. Did the manner of destruction make the difference? Did he want Jason to be the instrument of their end?

These ideas were beyond her. She rested against her forearms and wanted to stay this way. To dissolve.

A glimmer of hope sparked her to action. Magic had failed before, but that had been in the face of a ghost. Here was a moment of stillness. She folded her legs together, rested one hand into the other, closed her eyes, and let her thoughts rise to the surface. They assaulted, variations of orchestrated panic screaming at her to run, to hide, to fall, to weep. Her heart raced. Cold bloomed in her belly and surged through her insides. A glaring whiteness bubbled over her vision, and for a moment the world blurred until she thought she would faint.

She breathed.

She breathed.

Her heart slowed to a drum beat. She let each thought scream and rant, accepting them the way a parent tolerates a child throwing a tantrum. Panic dissolved into heightened awareness, and fear dulled to a sporadic flame. Her hands stilled. Clarity blossomed into control.

She was Eleanor Demidova. Her own name rang out, tethering her to life, to memory, to all she had ever been. She was a magician, and no ordinary child. She needed to find her family, to tell them about everything that had passed, and to warn them that Jason was somehow connected.

The shadows loomed with promises spoken in silence by wraiths.

But in her hands and heart were magic and all the light that life carried.

"Everything is nothing..." she said, reaching out, opening every pore, every cell, to power.

Metallic emptiness answered, seething through her veins. She pushed against the barrier, her thoughts digging through cold and pain to the magic that had to be waiting underneath. Sweat beaded over her skin, exhaustion commanded for release, and her head ached. But she strained, seeking, searching, every inch of her taut as she grasped for what she knew was already hers to wield.

A great crack ruptured inside of her, unleashing a deluge of power. She screamed, shock underlining agony, as if she had been pushed into a furnace. But she did not let go. She fell to her knees, pounded the floor with her fist, and collapsed into the dust. But she would not let go. She writhed, rivers of sulfur boring through her, a thimble trying to contain the ocean. Yet despite the ropes of pain coiling around her, something wild and beautiful beat like star fire emblazoned upon clouds, a presence radiating enchanted light.

Her nerves shrieked. Pain roared across her sight, and the many-colored folds of magic succumbed to crimson-black waves. Eleanor could no longer endure. She shut the internal valve against the flood. Agony faded into aches, and twitching muscles danced through her body. She lay on her back and panted, tears staining her cheeks. Coughs racked her chest, and she rolled onto her side and vomited. Ribbons of bright blood shone in the steaming yellow sludge.

After, she lay on her side, shivering and pawing at the floor.

She frowned at the feel of cool earth sucking at her fingertips.

She pushed herself onto a shaky elbow. A bed of grass was beneath her, interlaced with flowers of every color that spread for a radius of a few yards. She rose to her knees, cringed, and dipped her hands into the growth. Cool soil spilled through her fingers, and she grabbed a handful and laughed. What miracle here: the alchemy of life risen from halls of death. Her pain ebbed under a tide of bliss, as if the grass under her knees and the soil coating her hands filled her with the ever present love of all things, a secret song waiting to be heard, a power veiled and obscured, but never diminished.

Rot gripped the outer rim of the oasis and swelled into a landslide of decay that devoured the grass and flowers. Eleanor gasped, wobbled to her feet, and watched as the earth blackened. She backed away, shaking her head, her physical pain forgotten, replaced by sorrow that drowned her heart.

Her own vomit weighed against the wilted blades of grass.

Despair pinned Eleanor down and clamped jaws around her throat. But soil and tatters of bright green grass still clung to the creases of her palms. She looked at her knees and saw the same there. Her mind worked, bouncing from the horrors she had endured to the brief surge of life she had summoned. Aftershocks of pain flared through her, evidence of magic resurrected. Questions crashed against one another. She searched through them for an answer. She found none.

She looked about the hallway and remembered all that had led her here. Her father smiled from memory, and a clear need to find him, to find her brother and the others, took hold. Purpose shone, muting the shadows. She would search for her family. She would find them.

And then...

She exhaled, looked again at the earth and grass still clinging to her hands, and steeled herself.

"Just walk," she said, cringing at the sound of her own voice. Shivers wracked her. She hugged herself and scanned the doors. "Just fucking walk."

She took a step. Then another. Ash hissed against her feet, casting ripples of fear upwards. But she walked on, taking the dark world in, stretching her senses to meet whatever lay ahead.

The sound of her footfalls became one with the crying wind. She passed endless doors and signs of ruin. Silence held sway, orator of a dead world. A dreamlike fog took hold, diffusing the flow of time until she felt as if she drifted through unstructured eternity. But she went on, clinging to the memory of light. She would not forget. She would shine within if no light beat without. She would fight her way through blackness and pain to stand with her loves. What happened then, they would face together. And if she were to remain alone, then she would summon fires that would make the dead halls scream. She would burn and sear her end into the flesh of oblivion itself. For magic was hers. And she...she...

Music choked by static blared through a door on the right, ripping Eleanor into awareness. She jumped and ran. The music cut off as quickly as it began. She bolted a few yards, but forced herself to a stop. The hallway stretched on before her, door after door into an uncompromising miasma of absence. The music had been the first sign of anything after she could not tell how long. She remembered the crazed ghost, how horrible it had been. But it was now known to her. She had escaped it. The emptiness stretching before her was all that was unknown, all that waited unseen, undreamt, terror in its purest form. Wind sighed. Ash tittered. Eleanor reasoned that the wind had to be coming from somewhere, and perhaps windows waited beyond the door, windows that could help her see where she was, or escape. She knew it could be a trap. But even that might lead her closer to her loved ones. The alternative was all about, silent, absent, unending. Confusion swirled, but she threw it all aside.

She went to the door, twisted the knob, and pushed.

Eleanor's nostrils filled with acrid sweetness. She covered her nose and squinted through swirling dust. Beyond a short vestibule sat stools before a bar littered with rubble. Broken bottles formed a pyramid of cracked teeth behind it, reflected in a mirror caked with rust. Round tables sat across from the bar, beer bottles and shot glasses standing upon their surfaces, their labels dried up, their rims warped. Four televisions, spaced a few feet apart, were mounted to the corners of the room. Their screens were dark and still. Framed pictures and decrepit sports banners hung the walls. Dead light shone from nowhere and painted everything the shade of irradiated clouds.

She made to take a step forward, stopped, and inspected the door. She unzipped her hoodie and rolled it into a ball. She hesitated, cradling the hoodie, unwilling to let it go. She thought again of her family, and then stuffed the hoodie into the inside corner of the door. She stepped inside and let the door sway to a close. It stopped against the hoodie, leaving a space of a few inches. Eleanor pulled. The door bounced back against it.

She entered the bar and scanned its shadows, but spied no mannequins, no hidden figures. She stopped between two tables and looked up at the photos hanging the walls between them. They were all of happy get-togethers, dully lit portraits of drinking and pool playing and partying. The faces in the photos were mangled blurs, skin colored shadows peering at her.

But in each photo one face was clear. Eleanor looked upon it and gasped.

"Uncle Asshole?" she said.

Mattew Moore toasted with confidence from the top photo, squinted over his pool cue at the cue ball from the center, and cheered with a host of sports fans in the last.

Eleanor shook her head, her mind racing, not wanting to understand. The blurred faces surrounding Matt seemed to stare into her, their distorted features somehow seeping through her skin. She shook them away and focused on Matt, on what she knew of him, but still could not piece together why she was seeing him here. She glanced at the bar and then looked back into the photos. Decay and rot had claimed the once dark walls and warm tones, but there was no mistaking that the bar in the photos and the bar she stood in were one and the same. She looked again at Matt's face. She knew his face from the photo Ian kept of him, a secret she kept from their father. There had been stories, whispers stolen from late night visits with Percy and Rosie—of Matt and his obsessions, his pride, his greed. These ugly things warring with his humor, passions, and warmth. Two portraits of the same man, each a morbid curiosity for Eleanor. Here was the monster that had hurt her brother. Here was the man who had been her uncle. His green eyes were bright, penetrating, and alive.

First Rosie, then Percy had been taken. Eleanor's stomach dropped with realization.

"No," she said. "No fucking way."

The dead had come. Her uncle was a dead man. If the rumors were true, then he had all the reason in the world to hate her family. The dead had come. And Mathew Moore had come for them.

Eleanor reeled. She looked around some answer, for anything. Stillness. She steadied herself, walked deeper into the bar, and spied a tiny hallway sloping down into a small room. A pool table glared under gray light emanating from an open door that led outside.

Eleanor gasped, almost ran, but caught herself. She kept calm and walked between the tables and high stools, her eyes darting from side to side. The broken bottles were warped puddles of color in the failing mirror, and the stools sagged against themselves. She spied other pictures, and in all of them Matt was surrounded by blurred faces—dancing on the bar, toasting shots, and sitting around a table laden with red cups and coins. Eleanor did not feel his eyes upon her, but the blurred faces were like wounds in reality itself, waiting for some silent signal to bleed out from the pictures.

She reached the hallway with the sloping floor. Rolling arcs of pale light danced against the walls. She entered the room, squinting against the glare emanating from the open door at the back. The pool table rested askew on the floor, one leg broken, the other three cracked under the uneven weight. Pool balls were embedded into the walls, as if someone had thrown them in a rage. Two tables sat opposite sides of the room, cigarette butts tinted black and green in ash trays. Stacks of boxes stood at the back of the room, flanking the back exit.

Eleanor quickened her pace, hurrying for the open door. Wind blew against her, engulfing her in the acrid stench of burnt metal. She reached the threshold, peered out, and gasped. White flames smoldered against blackness, a great conflagration hovering in emptiness. The fires burned cold, casting frigid ripples through Eleanor's shirt. She hugged herself and tried to peer beyond the flames, but found only dark and cold. The fire shifted and swayed. Figures faded into seeing within the flames, faces drifting like dreams before crumbling into nightmares and then nothing. They darted in and out, seemingly unaware, moving as if repeating patterns over and over.

A single face stood out to Eleanor, appearing for a brief moment besides smoldering silhouettes. She clutched at her chest and felt her heart cry out. Her mother's curls were just like her own, and her mother's face smiled at something she could not see. Eleanor went forward and reached out. Her mother's face collapsed in upon itself, withering, burning, gone. Eleanor froze, her voice a squeak in her throat, tears stinging her lashes. Another face appeared, her father's, and her mother's face leaning towards it, and they whispered together, their faces beaming. They turned outward, smiled, and held between them a baby in a red bundle, the only other color in the white fire. There was a flash, and then her parents and the baby crumbled into the flames.

Eleanor had seen the image before, many times. She had traced the lines of her mother's face in the photo of the day she had been born, had marveled at the happiness radiating from both of her parents. She realized that she was witnessing memories unfold in the flames. Whose memories? She had asked her father who had taken the picture. He had gone grim and silent, the way he always had when he remembered her uncle.

A solid and gruff face emerged glaring from the fire. Eleanor recognized her grandfather and understood that she was seeing her uncle's memories burn within this waking tomb.

A screech, static, and then the riff of distorted guitars blared to life behind her.

She whipped around.

Mannequins stood at the pool table, or sat upon stools and chairs, drinks in their hands, unlit cigarettes sagging in their upraised fingers, pool cues resting their sides. Silhouettes stood in the bar beyond, and music crashed like static and broken glass. Dread crept through Eleanor's insides and made her legs weak. She gripped the doorframe. She was no longer alone.

3

"Papi," Darius said. "You alright?"

Jason looked at his father. In an instant a great library of memory — sights, sounds, emotions composed of years—vanished into the realm of the unconscious. The Gardens and its people, ghosts, magic, the death of his parents, and every painful recollection of his young life dissolved. He prodded at the sudden emptiness, sensing a chasm where once so much had passed. Had it all been imagined? Apathy answered, pulling him away from fading visions and placing him here, in his bedroom, before his father.

His father.

Jason focused on Darius, and the emptiness was filled with a love so great that nothing else mattered. He let doubt go and allowed joy to take hold as he leapt from the bed and threw his arms around him.

"Whoa," Darius said, laughing. "Mornin' to you too, doofus."

Jason squeezed, unable to let go, gratitude singing through his blood.

"Bad dream?" Darius said.

A collage of sights and sounds whirled in Jason's mind, pulling him, begging him to remember. But he pressed against his father and let them fade. Golden morning light infused everything. Birds chirped, and the day was new.

"Doesn't matter," he replied.

"Sure?"

Jason nodded and smiled.

"Well alright," Darius said. "C'mon, let's go help your ma with breakfast."

"Mom," Jason said, the word electric, coursing through him like holy light. Again a silent cry came from deep within, clawing. He pushed it aside. The warmth of daylight was reflected in his father's eyes, and he basked in the certainty of the moment, the safety of morning, the knowledge that all he had ever wanted or needed was exactly where it was supposed to be.

They walked the hallway towards the kitchen and the sizzle and crackle of breakfast. Morning light glinted. The floor was soft under his feet, easing tension sown by what felt more and more like distant nightmares. These terrible visions were fading, sepia monsters diminishing into the horizon. But they cried out, silent voices shouting from an unknown space deep within. Jason searched himself, wondering, apprehensive, trying, but not wanting to under-stand. When he looked at his father, warmth spread across his chest, releasing him from all doubt.

Together they walked through the living room and into the kitchen.

She stood there, pale and black haired, golden eyed, her slender hands working over the stove. The lines of her face spoke of kindness and humor, patience and intelligence. She turned to them, smiled, and tasted a dab of butter from her finger.

"Hey, baby," she said. "Wanna help me scramble these eggs?"

"Y-yeah."

"It's alright?" she said, her eyes laughing as she launched into an old Looney Tunes routine that they both loved.

Jason beamed.

"It's alright."

"It's okay?"

"It's okay."

He went to his mother as if emerging from a tangle of dark trees and into a meadow. He hugged her and pressed against her side, breathing her in. She ran her fingers through his hair, playfully picking at the wild strands. Stillness lived between them, perfect understanding shaped from silence. Nothing more needed to be said.

Jason wrapped his hand around the handle as she stirred eggs in a bowl and poured them into the pan. He took a spatula, pressed around the edges of the eggs, and pushed them towards the center. His parents worked behind him and beside him, preparing tea and coffee, bacon and fruits. He listened to them talk and joke as he scooped the eggs into a bowl. He brought the bowl to the table and felt his father's hand muss his hair, his mother's fingers tickle the back of his neck, and all was softness and love and golden light.

They ate. They talked and laughed, and Jason forgot everything that was said. He sat in a sweet haze, speaking without thought, savoring warmth, food, the sound of his parents' voices, not noticing the disjointed way time skipped from moment to moment.

He brought dishes to the sink, ran the water, and looked out the window to the sidewalk. The sky was gray. Jason blinked, a flicker of question darting through his mind: from where this golden light? The sidewalk was empty of pedestrians and cars. Winter branches swayed over a yard of dead grass.

A lone figure stood across the street.

Jason walked towards the window.

"Papi," his father said, calling him from the dining room.

"Baby," his mother said.

Jason felt their voices luring him away, but inner need pulled him closer to the stranger. Warm light faded into gray as he neared the window. And he saw. The figure outside was a boy in a black hood and dark blue jeans. His back was turned. His head was bowed, and his curled fingers twitched. Nothing on him stirred from the wind.

"No," Jason said, unable to understand why. The figure's head jerked to the left. Jason looked away, gripping the window sill, his breath seizing in his chest. Something horrible waited. He was certain without understanding why.

He swallowed, backed away, and focused on the radiance of morning light that resolved throughout the kitchen, washing away his fear of the boy outside. Both of his parents smiled at him from the kitchen entrance. He went to them, and together they walked into the living room.

His father read, and his mother frowned over the day's crossword puzzle. Jason joined them on the sofa, opened a notebook nestled on the wine colored coffee table, and flipped through magazine pictures of gourmet meals pasted onto the ruled pages. Recipes were written in the wild print of his hand. He traced them with his finger, looping over the frantic pen strokes as he read along, committing them to memory. The paper was soft under his fingertips, and he frowned, wondering at how delicate the sheets were.

Wind cried, rattling the living room window. Black curtains flanked it, billowing despite the window being closed. Jason looked out to where a modest lawn had gone gray and yellow, and beyond stood the boy before a chain link fence. His back was turned, his hood was up, and his fingers were curled around the green wire, staining all they touched to ash.

Marion's fingers curled through Jason's hair, lulling him to close his eyes. He opened them a fraction and saw the curtains were now drawn over the window. He knew not how they had closed, but he did not care. He let himself sink deeper into his mother's caress, embracing the sweetness of slumber, a narcotic haze invading awareness until vision shattered into fragments.

A shriek, a swarm of hands, and then a skeletal face erupted at him from a dark space.

He shot up, clutching his chest, panting for breath. He sat on the sofa. Golden light infused the air, surrounding him, and he surrendered to it. The vision was already fading, fading, gone. His mother and father both looked at him, smiling, loving, unalarmed. Marion offered the crossword puzzle. Darius draped an arm over his shoulder. Between them, Jason felt only safety and love.

But disquiet thrummed with every heartbeat.

He got up, kissed them both, and felt their eyes on him as he left the living room. He made his way to his room. Books were scattered everywhere, bookmarks marking varying places in some of them. Pictures of Bugs Bunny adorned the walls, and heroic action figures stood atop shelves and video games cases. He closed the door, closed his eyes, and pressed against it. The very air seemed to soothe him, yet a warning voice crept under his skin. He sent a flurry of slaps at his own cheeks, hoping to beat apprehension out of himself, and opened his eyes.

Something sat on his bed.

Worry erupted, pounding, a frantic voice screaming through duct tape. He walked over to the bed as if approaching a wild animal.

Ringo the Teddy Bear sat on the pillow.

4

Static coated music poured through the speakers, freezing Eleanor in place. She stood transfixed, animal fear seizing her muscles and pulling them taut. She fought to move, working as if through mud, and ducked right, behind stacks of sagging boxes containing battalions of beer bottles. She struggled to quiet her breathing. Music screeched and coughed, rock and roll devolved into a harem of electric banshees.

Eleanor put her hands out and willed them to steady. Their shaking subsided. She collected scraps of remaining courage and dared a peek around limp edges of cardboard.

Mannequins were scattered about in poses of celebration and play throughout the bar, a forest of silhouettes blocking her view of the main entrance. Their voices erupted as if a door had been opened on a party in full swing: laughter, excited shrieks, and babble billowing against the musical cacophony.

She darted once more behind the boxes.

"Shit," she said, whispering under her breath. "Shit, shit."

She clenched her teeth and fists, seeking clarity through a torrent of panic. The frigid light of the white fire beat against her from beyond the back door. She peered over its long fingers of morphing flames and into the surrounding dark. A great cavern loomed, composed of shade that deepened the farther out it stretched. For a moment she considered that the vastness was nothing more than an illusion, the fire dancing within the confines of unseen walls. But wind moaned, tainted by the stench of burnt metal carried across some impossible distance.

Escape waited in that expanse, release from the bar and its denizens. A voice screamed for her to run, to risk it, for she was once more near the delusional dead and felt their madness like radiating ice. No longer did she believe that they would lead her to family. Better to dare the dark and the unknown than to be stolen into their desperate hands.

But she remained, unable to face the colossal dark alone. The blackness poured terror down her insides, and she could imagine no light strong enough to pierce its heart. How far did it go? Where did it lead? Awareness beyond comprehension lurked in that emptiness, beckoning, an ancient malice composed of eons. Her magic was weakened, perhaps broken. And what was magic against the void?

Everything, an inner voice whispered. But she was too scared to believe it.

She looked away, relieved even in this realm of phantoms to pull her gaze from the darkness, and once more peeked over the boxes.

The ghosts were there, seated on stools, standing by the dart board, and leaning near tables. Two stared at each other from either side of the hallway door. Rotten cigarettes dangled unlit in their hands, and cracked beer bottles were raised or tipped back to their always smiling mouths. They were dressed in ripped jeans and stained miniskirts, shirts and blouses, their clothing faded against the many shades of their skins. Beyond the poolroom were others clustered at the bar, black against the fetid light, and nearest Eleanor a mannequin was bent over the pool table, its back to her, cue stick slumped in its hands.

None of the mannequins moved, and all of their gazes were averted from the back door.

Eleanor ducked and looked once more beyond the flames and

into the darkness. A deeper terror bloomed, fueling her to face the lesser of her fears. She looked around for some distraction, some way to capture the attention of the dead so she could escape the bar. Bottles pressed against her back through the moist cardboard. She imagined hurling one of those bottles against the wall, drawing the dead away from her so she could flee.

They'd look at where it came from, dumbass, she thought.

They would find her. And then...

She saw no other way save for crawling or walking quietly, hoping she would not be noticed. But she remembered the ghost that had tried to be her mother, how quickly it had attacked her, how aware it had been.

Frustration took hold. She nearly screamed.

Then it came to her.

She remembered the grass and the flowers, the flutter of life beating for a brief moment in the hallway. She had not been able to choose what she conjured, had barely been able to retain control, yet there had been power in those blades of grass, something unspoken and pure. Tendrils of pain still burned under her skin, reminding her of what summoning magic could cost in this place. Perhaps it would be too much this time. Perhaps it wouldn't work.

But she saw no other choice, save the abyss beyond the fire. She arranged herself into a meditative position, closed her eyes, and reached out.

Pain answered, mauling her insides. She struggled to keep quiet, clamping her mouth shut. But waves of fire swelled under her skin, and she screamed.

Among the dead, heads turned towards the boxes.

Eleanor held on, straining for magic to work through her. Images of green and vibrant life swelled in her mind as magic ruptured the ghostly veil and bled into her veins. A spark, a crack, and then magic erupted, seizing all of her. She embraced the flood and went beyond pain, beyond her body, a vessel wielding the ineffable. A voice screamed that this was too much, and somewhere in the distance she felt cuts ripping her body. But she pushed on, channeling her will through the realm of the dead.

Foliage of the deepest green blossomed, a waterfall of plants and flowers overwhelming the bottles behind the bar, surging through the rust colored floor, and shattering pictures of Matt and his revelries.

The dead went silent as one, and they each drifted towards the greenery. They moved in stuttering motions, reaching to touch what was no longer theirs. They gasped and cried out, engulfed by a sense of oneness, forgetting their attempts at reclaiming life, remembering, for a brief moment, the beautiful mystery unifying all things.

Eleanor released and fell back into herself. Pain howled, and she fought for breath as blood oozed from the gashes on her forehead, cheeks, arms, torso, and legs. She stood, dazed, weak, and shambled past the dead entranced by the life she had summoned. Blood dripped with her every footfall, staining the grass shooting out of the broken floor.

She limped by the bar, surrounded on either side by awestruck ghosts, and reached the front door.

It was closed. Her hoodie was gone.

Blood seeped into her eyes. She wiped it away and pulled at the door. It would not open. Behind her she heard the screams of wraiths as the foliage decayed and withered to ash. She pounded against the door, her arms carried by adrenaline, but the door would not move. The ghosts shrieked in pain and anger, and then fell silent.

She turned, blood saturating her shirt and jeans, the world dimming, and found them all staring at her. One, a slender mannequin with Korean features, cradled the hoodie in its hands as if it were a holy relic.

Eleanor turned from them, pulled at the door, screamed.

Dead hands seized her, and the bar spiraled as she was snatched by one ghost and then another, each clamoring to touch her, to feel her blood, to taste life once more. She struggled, cried out, but could no longer feel pain. Sight and sound spun together in a mangled web.

She was dropped.

She hit the slopping floor by the poolroom and was jolted into awareness. Behind the bar, vines and leaves dissolved, spilling the remaining bottles against the floor in a landslide of ash that revealed the large mirror in its totality. Streaks of rust and filth crisscrossed the glass, but enough reflection remained to reveal the dead to themselves. They stared, their mannequin features (some stained by Eleanor's blood) smiling. Yet their pupils went wide, and cracks ruptured across their false skins. Through the cracks erupted tendrils of darkness that warped the air around them, shattering the delusion that living faces stared back from the mirror, unveiling their true nature.

They wailed, revealed to themselves, the antithesis of life. No longer could they be deluded. Here, beyond Matt's lie, the terror they had fled seized them with cruel teeth. Their arms shot up in stuttering motions, all supplicants to a god that could no longer hear them.

Eleanor dragged herself across the floor, pulling her limp body, trailing more blood as she reached the poolroom. The ghost with her hoodie jittered after her, screaming and holding her hoodie out as if in offering. Eleanor summoned the last of her strength, stood, and stumbled to the back door. The ghost shrieked behind her, throwing out its hands to ward off the great darkness beyond.

Eleanor froze by the threshold, gripping the door frame, wanting to give up, to bleed out and die rather than face the black.

But she took a step. Then another. She limped past the white fire and its morphing images of Matt's memories, and went on into the darkness. Emptiness engulfed her, muting all sound, all light. She stumbled, deaf and blind, and there, in the absence of all things, swallowed as if by a gargantuan mouth, she fell.

5

The teddy bear was innocence: black button eyes, cute nose, a creature of comfort.

But to Jason it was the herald of nightmares. Buried emotions clawed out of his subconscious, whispering things he did not want to hear. Recognition taunted, allowing him to glimpse the bear's origin, but not fully see it. Fragments of sights, sounds, and people drifted in and out of his mind's eye, only to fade, making him feel as if he were untangling endless threads at the center of memory.

Jason turned away. Golden light seized him, warmed him, assured him that things were exactly as they were supposed to be. He smiled. Relief took hold. This is what he wanted and not the other.

What other?

The bedroom invited him to explore. He searched through his books and toys, and was overwhelmed by gratitude. He found a coloring book, went to sit on the floor, and fell backwards onto living room sofa. His mother was beside him, smiling over knitting needles as she composed a blue scarf. Disorientation spun a veil over Jason's senses, and he was certain that he had been somewhere else. But when he looked at his mother, he was overcome by the relief of something precious being returned.

Markers were laid out in a perfect row on the coffee table, every color denoted by bright rectangles printed on the white cylinders. He reached out to them, but hesitated for a moment as his eyes darted this way and that, searching for a truth he was desperate to never find. Warmth embraced him. He laughed his crazed and melodious laugh, took a purple marker, and colored in shapes on a page that he could not make out.

A whirl of air brushed against him, and then a baseball slapped into the glove covering his outstretched hand. He blinked. Branches sighed above. He was...he had been...He felt the weight of the baseball in his glove and savored it. His father stood across from him, smiling. Jason palmed the ball and threw it back. Autumn leaves crunched underneath, golden light beat through branches, and the wind blew with crisp sweetness. But again that wrongness—this was not the outside world he had seen beyond the window. His father threw the ball, but he let it sail over his shoulder.

Where was he? Where..?

His mother's ponytail soared as she hefted weights over her head. He was once again in the living room, and he mimicked her, pretending to struggle against great weights of his own. She laughed and lovingly told him not to make fun of her, and he went on, going through the routine that always put a smile on her face, until he stopped and realized that he had just been...

He sat between them on the sofa, a plate of rice, beans, plantains, and chicken on his lap, the brilliant colors of a sci-fi movie exploding over them from the television, a blanket containing their warmth. Confusion tickled his mind, but then the warmth ran comforting hands over his skin. Things could stay this way, beating with love and gratitude, always.

The plate of food was suddenly gone. He looked down, wondering, questioning, and then felt his parents nuzzle closer at either side of him. He sighed with relief, but still the doubt echoed in his mind, as if shouted from a dream.

When he caught movement from the corner of his eye, when he

recognized the shape of the boy outside, he knew he could ignore it, never look at it, ever remain here where he belonged.

But he looked.

The boy stood with his back to the window. The world hurled past him, dropping him down a cavernous well of confusion and certainty, the two emotions taking hold of everything. He stood from the sofa and hurried to the bathroom.

Warm water ran through his fingers, but when he splashed his face the water went frigid. He gasped and looked at himself in the mirror. His eyes shone gray against the golden light, and in them voices whispered like the dead rising from opened tombs. He splashed his face again and looked left.

Ringo stared at him from the window sill.

6

Eleanor drifted through the abyss.

Stygian blackness encompassed everything, layers of darkness crafting a realm of endless absence. The sky was a pinprick, the whole of the earth a piddling of dirt when compared to the magnitude of the void. She fell or floated, uncertain of which, for there was no meaning in these words, no direction. The whole of creation seemed to be a sliver of hot coal flaring its last against empty space. And Eleanor was less than dust, a speck of consciousness ever tumbling through a dead universe.

But she was not alone.

Folds of oblivion coiled over her, through her, probing her being with invisible talons. Silent voices whispered, offering release from the dark and the cold, if only she would let go, forget herself, become one with the void. Their voices were not voices, their words not words, but some nameless communication born out of the eons, undeath incarnate seeking the newly dead to join its ranks. Eleanor's thoughts folded into a shield, clinging to themselves in cyclical patterns that danced across her mind like the passing of seasons. Her family, her home, her joys, her struggles...They anchored her, keeping her whole against the onslaught of spectral offerings.

A voice penetrated. She pushed back, clinging to memory, to herself. The voice released her, and for the briefest moment, an instance that may not have been, she glimpsed a white and beaked face receding into the depths.

The prying darkness retracted, but was ever near, saturating the abyss. As if Eleanor were trapped within the mind of some nether god, a lone thread of being among countless neurons. Incomprehensible emptiness overwhelmed her. She struggled to not become one with absence, counting every agonizing second so she had something to hold on to.

She tumbled.

Then she heard the screams.

Voices cried out, undulating across untold distances far and near. Some trembled with heartbreak, wails pleading for exoneration from the endlessness. Others shrieked with hatred that raged like the origin of all violence. Babbling and gibberish bled in and out of hearing, words that were once human now reduced to deformed soliloquies repeating endlessly to any who would listen. Low moans sagged, somehow making the dark deeper, a physical substance caging its inhabitants. Reigning over all was the silence that was not silent, the nameless language of the void itself.

All of these voices bore into Eleanor, stripping away her humanity, peeling back memories of life and light until she longed to vanish, to blink out of existence before she was consumed. The abyss pried at her, cajoling, inviting. She receded deeper into herself, remembering the cold kiss of snow, the warm weight of sunlight, the taste of water, the power of magic flowing through her.

Magic.

Shapes emerged around her, spectral figures dancing on the edges of sight, swaying, spinning, gone. Bone white structures bloated with corruption floated past, and monuments shaped into uncanny forms moved like the inhabitants of ocean depths. Emptiness, and then a writhing chain of skeletal figures clothed in rags was revealed, stretched endlessly across the expanse, some seeing Eleanor and reaching out, babbling in crazed tongues.

All came and went as if they had never been, fading, leaving Eleanor once more to drift.

How long? What was time without life? Each moment of awareness dragged Eleanor closer to insanity. She clung to memories, but they unraveled strand by strand, slowly stripping away who she was. The abyss slithered over her, and once more the voices were there, offering release if only she would become one with the silent congregation of the undead. Their longings rent her insides, making her wish she could claw herself out of existence. She pushed, struggled, clung to that which was dissolving.

Again she thought of magic—what was that word? What was its meaning? In the mad laps of thought that kept her whole, the memory of candle flame flickered to life, burning blue to yellow to gold, swaying. She remembered its warmth, its contours, and its gentle pulse that had kept the shadows of the Dungeon at bay—

Heat flared, and it was no memory.

Warmth pulsed somewhere deep inside. She raced to it, wading through the shield of memories until she melded with her own depths, where the fire of magic and all its makings still burned.

Against terror, against the absence of all hope, the magician closed her eyes and threw herself into that flame. A familiar mantra seeped through the cycle of her thoughts.

Everything is nothing...

The flame swelled, and searing fingers seized her. Agony blared across her being, but she clung to it, letting pain consume emptiness as she dissolved into an infinitely colored fire. The void screamed offense and assaulted, an avalanche hurling against the blaze. She again heard silent voices offering release: pleasure, power, all that would steal her away from pain. She held on, wavering but burning bright. Anguish cried, screamed, and then sang as she leapt beyond it and transformed into a great fire warring against the abyss. Her entire life cascaded about her as the wheeling of stars, each moment etched into a mosaic of quivering light.

So much love. So much loss. All of it spinning, a galaxy of being shining in rebellion against the void. All about her, remnants of life bloomed into existence, atoms joined together in defiant dance. Water and fire and air and earth, star flame and gravitons, forces weak and strong sewn together for a brief moment as if to say here we are, here is life, here in the face of nothing is everything.

For all that, the magician focused on her life, her loves, their smiling faces, filling her with true magic, that binding force that joins humanity where there should only be bloodshed and grief. The galaxy roared, her memories stars and planets hurling through emptiness. The darkness trembled: How impossible this light.

Eleanor transcended form and thought and beat brightly like a wound in death. Nothingness warped about her, melting, tearing under the magician's power.

She was every moment, every second, and every inch of life itself. She would not be held. The void was ruptured by her fire, and the galaxy that was she erupted through the wound and spewed like a geyser of holy light. She opened up and sang and her voice reverberated through death and into time—

Cold.

The floor sent chills through her skin.

She opened her eyes. Her vision swam. She lifted her hands and watched them sway, spin, and coalesce. Her skin was flushed pink under long globules of darkness that slowly evaporated. The cuts and the blood were gone.

There had been fire. She remembered that. There had been a bright light in a vast darkness.

The rest...

She groaned, gagged, and vomited clear liquid. She spat the last and wiped her mouth with her arm. Chills embraced. She shivered, ran her hands over her body, and felt bare skin. She hugged herself and squinted at her surroundings. She was kneeling on a filthy red carpet fringed with gold that flowed down a long room. A faded mosaic of dancing women was printed onto an arched ceiling. Lamplight spilled from lanterns mounted along the walls, glinting against rows of mirrors that paralleled each other. Mannequins stood before the mirrors, some with brushes in their hands, others clutching straw-like hair in unfinished braids. They were all dressed in formal wear, staring into crayon colored eyes reflected in the blemished glass. Light shimmered to Eleanor's right, and she looked and found her own mirror. She was naked and disheveled. Her hair clung to her cheeks and brow, and the last tendrils of darkness wafted from her forehead like threads of smoke.

A message was written upon the mirror, each letter made of filth:

Where's Eleanor?

She processed the words through her dazed mind, squinting, mouth hanging open, each letter a mathematical riddle. She hugged herself tighter, looked back at her own face in the mirror, and saw a gaggle of pale faces hovering behind her.

She fainted and saw no more.

7

Ringo stared.

Cold water dripped over Jason's face. He looked into the bear's black eyes, and the golden warmth faded, revealing a chill underneath.

Jason looked away and splashed himself again. The blissful warmth returned, but fear tainted its edges. He turned the faucet off, wiped his face, and looked into the mirror.

Eleanor stared back.

He almost screamed, stumbling backwards. Something in her face stilled his fear and spurred determination. He gripped the sink and looked closer. Eleanor was haggard, her hair clinging to her cheeks and forehead in drenched clumps. Behind her was a host of encroaching shadows, and though she did not seem to see Jason, her eyes bored into him, imploring.

He blinked and she was gone, leaving his reflection.

She was a phantom in his memory, something felt but not understood. Her name floated somewhere, a wave of the tongue and a movement of the lips forgotten. But he knew her face. He knew the warmth her visage evoked, truer warmth emanating from a soft place where fear and grief existed not as monsters but as broken hearts in need of consolation.

"What's happening?" he said, clutching his hair, the air somehow thinner, as if weakening to reveal another layer of reality seeking to pull him in. The golden warmth wiped away questions and discomfort. But Eleanor's face remained seared into his heart, and the overwhelming happiness brought by the golden light warred against the doubt she had sown.

He looked again at Ringo and stared into the bear's button eyes. A barrage of questions crashed. How had he gotten inside? When had he ever been given such a gift? Why did he think of the stuffed animal as "he"?

He closed his eyes and pounded the flats of his hands against the sink. Wind rattled the bathroom window, rising.

He opened his eyes. His parents stood at the open door. He had not heard them. They were there.

"You okay, baby?" his mother said.

Her voice softened doubt, each word sowing unfettered joy into his heart. Eleanor's face flashed, and he grimaced, but kept his gaze on his parents and let the warmth surge. Pieces of a nightmare, he told himself. Unwanted visions intruding like jealous harridans. Such is the nature of bad dreams, that they cannot abide happiness.

"Yeah," he said to his mother. But as he looked at his parents, another volley of questions crashed through the haze. Why had he not heard them? What had they done yesterday?

He wiped his eyes and ran wet hands across his hair.

"Uh, what day is it?"

They smiled down at him, blinked, and then his father wrapped his arm about his mother's shoulders. Something in the way his father's hand dangled sent a wave of déjà vu cascading through Jason. He saw his parents in his in his mind's eye, standing exactly as they stood now, but at a park, on black rubber mats. Jason was looking down at them from a jungle gym, exhilaration coursing through him from being so high.

The memory vanished.

"How about we go back and watch the movie, kid?" his father said.

"Okay..." Jason replied. He furrowed his brow. "What movie was that again?"

"Ooh, I'm gonna get some popcorn," his mother said. "And you can't stop me." She walked off, smiling. His father looked at Ringo, walked into the bathroom, and grabbed him.

"Come on, papi," he said to Jason. He turned and walked out, and Jason threw his hands over his mouth and gasped.

The hand clutching the teddy bear was rotted. Torn flesh revealed yellowed bones and graying cords of muscle.

His father walked away.

Jason stood alone. The golden warmth rushed him, but Eleanor's face and his father's dead hand were the first pebbles of a landslide. He longed to dive back into the warmth, to drown in endless happiness and comfort. But questions stormed. He looked into the mirror. He saw his own face where Eleanor's had been. He saw his own eyes all gray with slivers of white, and in them was grief and loss and all the things that seemed impossible in this place. Yet they were there, ghosts, wraiths who would not be silenced. A leviathan broke the waters of his subconscious, and with it came unbearable loss.

"But they're here," he said, unsure of what he was saying, certain of why it was said. A tombstone shone black in his memory. "No. They're here. They're right outside."

He closed his eyes and let the warmth take him, but Eleanor's gaze broke through the golden light and freed memories from their imprisonment: the fearful looks of his father's friends, the cold glint of hospital light, and the feel of a dead body resting against him—its dull and papery skin. These memories were not someone else's. They were his. He knew them from pain and grief. He knew them from the chaos of confusion and change. He knew them from Eleanor's face, something he could never conjure in his imaginings.

Dust sprinkled his brow. He touched the granulated particles, looked up, and beheld a cracked ceiling. Gray light filtered through the window, dimming the golden haze, revealing shadows and pock-marks on the walls.

He looked again at the mirror.

He saw the boy standing behind him in the reflection, his back turned.

Jason ran out of the bathroom.

He stood in the hallway, the carpet under his feet stiffening into coarse wires. The glow of a television painted the walls, and he knew his parents waited, and with them was safety and warmth and love that could not be measured. The closed door to his bedroom stood beside him, and behind it was the truth. He knew. He knew with every beat of his heart. The boy outside was now within, waiting behind that door, and with him came the ending of everything that Jason had ever wanted.

But Eleanor's face had been haggard and lost, and something was wrong, so very wrong, and he could stop it. He knew he could.

He walked down the hallway, stopped at the threshold, and stared in at his parents cuddled together on the sofa. Between them was a space waiting just for him, where the golden warmth would never fade, where he would always be beside them.

He swallowed back tears, still refusing them. But his voice was thick, and his features nearly crumpled.

"You're not real," he said, whispering.

Love was a chorus of pleas and invitations, and the space between his parents begged to be filled.

His father had lain beside him, paper-thin and empty. His mother's tombstone shone black over a green field, and the Manhattan skyline had towered in the distance like monoliths erected from his grief.

His parents sat before him and he knew them to be memories. The space between them called, and the golden warmth surged, whispering, comforting, and he too would be a memory, and together they would fade away.

Somewhere, people who had taken him in were suffering. Their names and faces were mirages. But Eleanor's face was clear, and in her suffering Jason saw what he was running from, what he had always run from. The rest was a jumble, but he knew somehow he was responsible for what was happening to the girl in the mirror.

So he looked at his parents for the last time, wanting to reach out and always be with them. They smiled happily at the screen. They did not see him. For that, he would always be grateful.

He turned and walked down the hallway.

He opened the door to his room.

The boy stood there, his back to him, staring at clouds and rain and dead branches through the window. Fear grounded Jason to the spot, but he reached out with a shivering hand and touched him. The boy turned.

He bore Jason's face, but his eyes were empty black sockets that stared into the heart of him and brought it all back.

The death of his parents...

The endless haunts...

The Gardens...

The stairwell...

Eleanor...

An entire life remembered in an instant.

Jason shuddered, but stood his ground. He would not run. Not anymore.

The boy raised a withered hand and pointed behind Jason.

A portal of darkness spiraled where the walls had been. The ballerina was there, half-veiled by shadows, reaching another dead hand to him. One final rush of love and warmth surged, begging Jason to stay, to run from these dead things and their foul truths.

He took the dead girl's hand and stepped into the darkness.

8

For a moment it had all been a dream.

Eleanor lay nestled in warmth. Folds of a blanket embraced her, stretching every second into an ocean of relief. It had to be morning, and she, waking from a strange and vivid nightmare, could now rest before the day was begun. She shifted onto her side, enshrouded by a sweet ache coursing through her body, in no hurry to wake up.

Cold fingers dragged over the top of her hand. Her eyes shot open, and with sight came memory. She recoiled, looked about, frantic.

Wine colored curtains surrounded her, hanging from a canopy swaying in dusty light. She got up on her elbows and frowned at the folds of a red gown draping her body.

"What the fuck?" she said, picking at the coarse ruffles accentuating her skirt. She slid down to the foot of the bed, got on her knees, leaned out of a gap in the curtains and found that she was in a bedroom. Fetid candlelight stretched shadows over burgundy walls ragged with holes. Cracks crisscrossed a wooden floor. Two tables sagged at opposite corners of the room, and pictures were stacked upon them.

Eleanor listened for a moment. Candle flame sputtered. She

looked around, clutching her hand, remembering the cold touch over her skin. She saw no one.

She slid off of the mattress, her bare feet protesting against the cold and tacky wood, and then tiptoed to each corner of the bed respectively so she could peek around the corners. Bureaus sat on either side, their drawers hanging like lolling tongues.

She looked around the rest of the room and spotted a large oil painting hung on the right wall.

In the paining, Rosie sat smiling on a plush green chair, Ian to one side of her, and Eleanor to the other. Eleanor's painted self wore the same red gown she wore now, while Rosie was in a golden gown and Ian in a tuxedo. Behind the chair stood Matt, his smile wide, his cheeks flushed, and his eyes green. He wore a dark suit that disappeared into the background, making him seem like a floating head just above Rosie.

Eleanor glared, disgusted. Everything about the painting seemed exaggerated. Their eyes were too wide, their smiles strained, forced. Only Matt seemed at peace, his grin forming soft jowls that were pink and alive.

Eleanor backed away from the portrait, looked about, and went to one of the tables to look at the photographs.

They made her curse under her breath.

She was in every one, unconscious and posed with ghosts: seated on laps or stood beside their formally dressed mannequin figures. The faces of the dead were warped, hinting at other faces hidden behind their facades, bug eyed and manic and sometimes monstrous. Eleanor's was the only image that was whole, her expression slack and her eyes closed.

Eleanor destroyed the photos, screaming and stomping her feet.

She did not see the ghost drift down from within the canopy bed, where it had been watching her sleep from its ceiling. It floated past the curtains and landed without sound.

"Now, the waltz is all about the three count," it said behind her. "You must keep the rhythm in your head at all times. 1-2-3, 1-2-3, 1..."

Eleanor slowly turned around.

The ghost was dressed in a burgundy suit, white shirt, and black pants. Its arms were raised as if it were holding an invisible partner in white gloved hands, and its hair was a tangle of blonde strands dangling over its crayon colored eyes.

It swayed from left to right.

Eleanor backed away.

"...2-3," it said. "There. Practice that. The others have already done so, and they're dancing now. You're late, young lady. You already missed the wedding, but Mr. Moore is very forgiving. He still wants you there, so you must be prepared to waltz. 1-2-3—"

The ghost suddenly sputtered. Eleanor backed into the wall, and then was jolted by a splash of panic as she realized there were no doors in the room.

The ghost stared at her, its silence corrupting the seconds into cruel eternities. Then it gasped, the desperate sound of a dying man trying to breathe.

"No, the performance was wonderful," it said, as if reassuring someone. "Everyone can be tighter on their count, don't be so hard on yourself...hard on your...1-2-3, 1-2...But I can't be...I can't. Please, doctor, there must be...I have so much more to...They need me to show them how to dance...My students need me to...3...3...3...3..."

It suddenly raised a bent leg in a stuttering motion and pirouetted, spinning, spinning. Eleanor tried to look away, but fear held her in place.

It stopped and focused on her.

"Ah," it said. "That's better. Everything's fine, plum. You're here for a lesson? Good. Here we all dance. Here we're all happy together."

It launched at Eleanor, spinning, arms outstretched.

"Time for your lesson: 1-2-3! 1-2-3! 1-2-3!"

"Fuck-fuck-fuck-fuck!" Eleanor said. She pounded against the walls, wanting nothing more than escape. The image of a door took hold of her thoughts. Heat exploded through her, her skin tingled, and a great churning of imagination, matter, and power erupted from her mind and escaped through her fingertips.

A doorknob swelled into her palm.

She did not think. She clutched it tight, twisted without looking, stumbled backwards, and fell on her ass. The ghost was nearly at the door.

"Close!" Eleanor said.

Invisible tethers launched from her, and the door slammed shut. It boomed as the ghost crashed against it. Then the door quavered, and Eleanor realized it was attached to nothing, standing in midair. It fell upon the floor and exploded into a swarm of buzzing lights that evaporated.

Eleanor looked down at her hands, breathing hard. Magic surged warm and alive under her skin, not a trickle but a rapid, as if she had stepped from a stream and into the depths of a wild river. There was no pain. Only the familiar ache from weaving the impossible into existence. A wall had crumbled, a barrier had been removed, and every breath sang with magic.

She looked around and waited for the ghost to waltz through the trembling dusk. All remained still. She stood with a grunt and collected herself.

Light blared, sickly and pale, illuminating a black and white diamond patterned floor under her feet. All about Eleanor were mannequins frozen in mid-waltz, specters adorned in suits and dress gowns, arm in arm, smiling. Beyond the dance floor was a curtain of darkness. One by one the dead turned their heads to look at her, many shades of faces with too-bright eyes that never blinked.

"Look at you," Matt said.

The ghosts released their partners and began to applaud as Matt appeared behind Eleanor at the center of the dance floor, a large mannequin in a tuxedo, hands in its pockets, deformed fingers poking through. His green eyes locked onto Eleanor's.

"All grown up and ready to party."

9

They walked hand in hand through a tunnel between worlds.

The darkness churned, spinning about them like an unending storm. Jason saw faces forming and dissolving within the tumultuous shadows, contorted by silent screams. The ballerina's hand tightened over his, and he looked at her floating ahead, a pale specter in a purple tutu, her hand cold and dead in his brown fingers. Revulsion seized his heart, but disgust was undercut by a tantalizing sense of familiarity. He recognized not her, but the core of her ghostly presence meeting something within, as if a dormant part of his being began to stir and whisper secret knowledge.

The ballerina stopped. Jason waited.

Mist bloomed all about them, engulfing the tunnel and revealing a shrouded land of barren trees reaching heavenward like mummified saints. Bare earth radiated cold through Jason's feet. He stood on a path in a forest whose branches met in neurons of brittle wood above. Roots writhed over uneven land, deformed earth sloping into the fog.

Emptiness sighed through Jason's hand. The ballerina was gone.

The path wound ahead, surrounded by clouds of mist that beat gray and spectral through the forest. The trees were black and twisted, ancient things contorted into spirals of grim geometry. Jason turned around. The path was blocked behind him, a wall of tangled branches rising into bloated hills. Beyond, patches in the frothing clouds revealed the peaks of mountains.

Jason searched the trees for his dead companion. There was mist and forest and nothing else. He looked ahead and steeled himself, remembering Eleanor's face in the mirror and the kindness she and her family had shown. The path beckoned. Perhaps doom waited. But it no longer mattered. He had to go on.

He took a breath.

There was no air to breathe.

He started, clutching at his chest, pulling through his nostrils and then his open mouth for what was not there. His eyes flew wide, panic seized, and he fought for oxygen. His lungs screamed in anticipation for the agony they were about to endure. But no agony came. Realization cascaded, even as he continued to fight for breath. He was not struggling. There was no pain. He let go of the natural impulse to breathe, waiting to drop dead, to fall to the ground gasping. Lightness and ease worked through him instead.

He did not have to breathe.

He looked around at the trees as if in accusation. They surrounded, silent, veiled. He flipped them off, yelped his strange laugh, and followed the path through the black forest.

The trail inclined, leading him over a small hill. He reached the top and saw the path curve past a wall of trees whose trunks were bent in poses of supplication. The mist roiled, dripping over every branch, caressing bark, root, and earth. Jason walked through the cold embrace of fog, alone in a silent land, emerging from the mist and continuing through a world that did not breathe.

Tree branches reached into the trail, their tips curled. Cold earth seeped through Jason's toes, coating the soles of his feet, triggering nostalgia he could not place. He looked through the mist and beyond the veil of trees and felt something pulling him. Not memories, but their ghosts speaking from beyond space and time, whispering with voices that spoke of a home he had always secretly longed for.

The path carried him into a valley, and the ground rose about him in slopes of tangled roots. He followed the trail as it descended, leading through a veil of perpetual shadow.

The path leveled and opened into a circular clearing. Jason stopped, peering through the bright darkness at slender trunks twisted into agonized contortions. Branches swayed above, rattling together. Jason tilted his neck to both sides, cracking it. His eyes were wide. His mane of hair frenzied. He walked into the clearing, stopped at its center, and looked about in anticipation of something he both feared and desired.

All lay still.

Then something floated between the trees. Jason stiffened. The old mantra tumbled through his mind.

Not real, not—

He buried fear under resolve and kept his gaze on the thing circling beyond the clearing. It was real. He saw it, its presence the breath of ice. He turned with it, moving as it moved, watching it inch closer through the mist. It floated out of the trees and across the trail, a specter formless yet with form, obscuring all it passed in a curtain of emptiness. It reentered the forest, vanished into the tangle of trees, made a half-circle, and stopped directly across from Jason. It hovered there, the silhouette of a man manifesting out of the skeletal branches and writhing mist.

It floated into the clearing.

A rubber skull mask hid its face, and a bowler hat sat tilted on its head at a rakish angle. The decayed remnants of a long tailed dinner jacket flowed over pinstriped pants, and its feet were bare and curled. It circled Jason, floating, watching the boy through eyeholes that offered no light.

It spoke. Its voice was absence and sand.

"Beyond the black...beyond the pitch...behold a stranger in your midst."

It hovered before Jason.

"Forgive the rhyme. It has been so long since we've entertained.

433

The years come and go, and they do drag-drag-drag. Ah, but manners-manners. Allow us mine."

It raised a gloved hand to its hat, spun it with a flourish, and bowed. The crown of its mask was stained by an inkblot of ash that formed a smiley face over wrinkled rubber.

"We are the Emissary," it said. "Ever at your service."

It rose, twirling the hat back onto its head.

"We have waited a long time to meet you, such a long-long time, yes."

It hissed the last word, stretching it into the skittering of dead leaves.

Jason stared at the Emissary, ordering his thoughts, terror and wonder warring until a clear center took hold.

"What are you?" he said, his voice barely a croak.

"You don't know?" They stared at one another. "Ah, but you do, yes. You know. You've always known."

"Don't play with me. I'm not—I'm not afraid of you."

Its laughter was the howl of sandstorms and spilled blood. It leaned into Jason's face, its empty gaze engulfing his.

"Yes you are: Hiding all your life, praying, wishing us away. You fear us because it is right to fear us. Has that kept you safe? We wonder-wonder, yes-yes-yes."

"Answer my question."

"You answer it."

Jason's eyes flared with anger.

"You're wasting time. Something's happening to my friend. I have to help her. I..."

He trailed off, overwhelmed by the knowledge that he was not sure what he was supposed to do, or if there was anyone in need of help at all. Perhaps Eleanor's face in the mirror had been part of a trick meant to lure him into this place and stand him before the wraith. Perhaps the Emissary was the one who had taken her, and this, the final torment before it ended them both. He fell silent, eyeing the Emissary with suspicion, waiting for the unknown. But recognition still brushed at his mind, making him certain that the thing before him was not the gluttonous creature that had taken him in the stairwell, but something else, something as familiar as his own skin.

The Emissary stared, its perpetually grinning mask seeming to darken.

"The longer you play the fool," it said, "the longer your friends will suffer. Yes-yes-yes—friends, not only the bright girl. They are all suffering, and it's because of you. Only incidentally, we assure you. But you cannot help them until you stop lying to yourself. There is much to tell, much you must learn, but you waste time on a question you know the answer to. So we will ask, and we will not ask again." It opened its arms. "What are we?"

Jason trembled against memories of so many frightened evenings spent cowering in his bed, whispering against encroaching nightmares. Of days waiting for some impossible horror to peek from behind the veil of death, a collection of haunts woven into the fearful tapestry of his life. He stared at the Emissary without anger, without fear, a boy beyond the point of exhaustion.

"You're a ghost," he said. "And you've ruined my life."

"All of it?"

Jason shook his head, numb.

"I never wanted this. But you...things like you...won't leave me alone." He spread his arms open, a near maniacal grin forming over his face, his eyes betraying something close to madness. "Well. Here I am. You gonna help me, or kill me? The boogeyman likes to kill kids, right? Then do it. I ain't running. I don't care anymore."

"Ah, poor-poor child," the ghost replied. "How you misunderstand. But you're hysterical. Perhaps you should take a breath."

Jason reared back as if insulted. The Emissary chuckled.

"Oh, that's right," it said. "No air to breathe. Funny that."

The ghost circled him, its hands clasped at its back. Jason stared through the black earth to the meaning of the Emissary's words.

"I'm dead?" he said.

"Yes. You've always been." It stopped, leering at the boy, its mask grinning. "At least...halfway."

"You're either dead or you're not."

"Wrong-wrong-wrong, so-so wrong. Is it intentional? Let's see, hm. You're no idiot. Far from it. In fact, if you had been anybody else, you'd be correct. But, ah, you've always known how different you are. The problem-problem is that you've spent your life being incomplete. And so you're confused. Well then, allow us some questions that will make things clear: how does a dead boy survive in the living world? How is he then able to exist in a dead land? Answer: he's dead and alive, the son of a living woman, and a dead man. That's you, walking between two realms, one half of each."

Jason's mind worked, his brow furrowed. He looked at his hand and wondered what secrets lay under the skin.

The Emissary watched and waited.

"I can't be..." Jason said. It was all he could manage.

"But you are," the Emissary replied. "Poor boy. What secrets your father kept from you. He should've prepared you. He owed you that much."

"What do you know about my father?"

"So-so much. He only gave you half-truths. He thought he was protecting you. How very stupid of him."

The Emissary floated towards Jason. Cold rushed over his skin, but he did not shiver or recoil. A secret part of him delighted to be so near the ghost.

"You think we torment you," The Emissary said. "No. You torment yourself. In all your denial, you've hidden yourself from the truth. You would not face what needs facing. We could not reach you. Your will is much stronger than you know, much stronger, yes. You would not allow us to prepare you for your task."

Jason stared at the ground. A barrage of thoughts flew in some final attempt to convince himself that he was crazy, that the Emissary was the heart of his madness manifested into this surreal and grim form. A dead and gloved hand reached under the boy's chin and raised it. Jason stared into the hollow eyes of the mask and beheld darkness that was still and profound.

"It's time you heard all of it," The Emissary said. "It's time you understood who and what you are. We ruined your life? No. We protected you from the emptiness, doing all we could to keep you safe from the countless dead who are drawn to you. They don't realize it–or perhaps they do–but they need you. We all need you. Everything depends on you."

The Emissary let go, floated over to the trees, and stared beyond. Jason stroked his chin where the ghost had held him, and once more that dormant part of him stirred.

The Emissary gazed into the forest. Trees rustled and sighed.

"Story time," it said. "A long and sad tale, yes-yes-yes. But you must listen well. Will you?"

Jason hesitated, then nodded, somehow knowing that the Emissary would know his response. He felt the ghost in the earth, in the lifeless air, and in the trees, a presence ever watchful.

The Emissary spoke.

"Once there were two brothers, grandchildren of a cruel king. This king took his throne by force and led the most dangerous and savage of his warriors through an ancient jungle. They attacked village after village, killing many, enslaving and cannibalizing their captive foes, and sacrificing the most innocent by burying them alive in the deepest parts of the jungle. The king thought himself a god, you see, and decreed that so long as his people sacrificed lives in his honor, he would be appeased. He would keep his tribe healthy and strong, and he would never die.

"They conquered the jungle, and the king reigned. But he had an unlikely enemy. His son, the prince, was different: a good man, a man who wondered at the stars, a man who saw value in life. He detested his father and all he had done. He rebelled. He failed.

"The king then went to his grandsons and laid a knife before them and offered them vengeance. But the brothers were wise, yes-yes-yes, the youngest especially. They knew the king told lies. They knew they were being tested and were not yet strong enough to defeat the king or save their father. So they swore fealty to him. They showed their allegiance by burying their father alive. The king was satisfied, and counted his grandsons as his most trusted of devotees.

But it was all a lie. The brothers were biding their time, waiting for the perfect moment to take their vengeance.

"Years passed. The oldest brother became the greatest warrior the tribe had ever known. The youngest was brilliant and far seeing, a sage and a wise man. They were feared and respected, and they honored the king's word. For the king had remained strong, even unto his old age.

"The eldest felt the time was right to strike the king down, but the youngest knew they were not yet strong enough. The king commanded the loyalty and fear of his people. They would not oppose him again. The younger brother counseled patience, waiting for some secret sign, a moment of weakness.

"That was when the jungle began to speak."

The Emissary went silent, and its silence was joined by whispers from the forest, strange and haunting voices seeping through the mist.

"The brothers heard them," the Emissary said. "Beckoning...Calling. Each wondered if they had gone mad. But they confided in each other and confirmed that what they heard was real. The voices spoke to them and them alone. The voices promised that they would help the brothers win their vengeance. The voices ushered them into the depths of the jungle where no living thing dwelled, straight to the heart of the sacrificial lands where their father and countless others had been buried alive. There they found a cave where no cave had been, a deep and dark place leading into the earth. It was from this cave that the voices came, whispering promises of power and vengeance. Their father's voice cried among them, and the eldest rushed inside. The youngest cried out to him, afraid to enter. But after some time, alone with the deep shadows of the jungle, alone with the presence of forces cruel and malicious, he too followed, screaming his brother's name.

"Deep within the earth, among a maze constructed from the faces of the buried dead, they discovered darkness with no equal. This darkness knew itself. It was aware. It knew the brothers and had called out to them. And the darkness made the brothers an offer: join with it so they may spread it across time, and it would reward them with life everlasting.

"The eldest saw vengeance and a chance at power. The youngest saw possibility, the ability to see the world unfold over centuries and to one day control it. The brothers accepted the darkness. They made their covenant. The eldest had been rash and fearless, and for that he received a savage gift, the most awful power that he could use to terrorize and consume. The youngest had been wise, cautious, and was transformed into a being that could know the hearts of humanity, that could bend the world to his will.

"They emerged from the cave, and the night wept at their presence— for they were no longer men.

"They fell upon the village. Vengeance was theirs in bloodshed and possession. The eldest drank the king's blood, and the youngest fed on his misery. They devoured the king's men, blood and soul, while the people bowed on their knees and prayed to be spared.

"None were.

"They struck out from village to village, the eldest drinking blood, half-crazed with the joy of killing. With each life he took, he grew stronger, for he did more than just kill. When he drained his victim's blood, he took their souls and made them into cursed things that forever serve him. So it was. So it still is.

"The youngest took his first victims from among his enemies in the king's tribe. He possessed them, breaking their wills, feeding on the ecstasy of their misery and torment. He kept them like cattle. But something unexpected happened: some of his victims began to change. They did not break and babble like most, or kill themselves like others. No. They fell into deep sleeps. What they saw in their slumber, we cannot say. Perhaps the same darkness the brothers had seen. But then they awoke. Days and sometimes weeks would pass, and they would change into horrible beasts of uncontrollable rage and destruction. Or they would see their shadows move and feel their wills scratch against the minds of others. They derived joy from torment and pain. They learned to break and possess souls.

"And they, too, were no longer human.

"The brothers took these creatures as their servants. They passed from the jungle that way, roaming into new lands, spreading across civilization, they and their children spoken of in terrible legends.

"The eldest longed for his own children. He regarded his brother's creations as lesser, for these creatures would die, while the brothers lived on. He wanted others like him, and the darkness wanted this of him as well, for through them its hold over creation would become stronger. And so, over millennia, he has selected few, those whom he has come to cherish. He offered them a gift only he could give, and they have carved their name into nightmares alongside their father.

"You know their name. We know you do."

Jason did. He stared, breathless.

"As for the darkness—the brothers were true to their word. They carried it with them across the Earth, and it has grown beyond measure. The moment the brothers accepted its offer, it seeped through the fabric of life and into death, making its kingdom where once there was silence and mystery. All who live must die, and once death was a release. But the darkness has transformed death into a prison. None escape it. Death has been corrupted, and we must hide from the terrors that make their home in the void. But they find us. They always find us."

The Emissary's voice strained, its words howling with silent grief.

"Do you understand?" it said. "Death has been broken. Countless dead linger on. Throughout millennia, all who have died since the brothers emerged have been unable to pass away. So long as vampires exist, we dead cannot pass. We are trapped. We howl and scream and lose every part of who we are until all that remains is madness...and something much worse than madness. Something no one was ever meant to become.

"Can you imagine? Everyone and everything that has ever lived trapped together in an unending abyss."

The Emissary went silent. The forest sighed. Jason shook his head, a colossal weight settling in his heart, causing every part of him to shake.

"No," he said. "This is too much. It can't be true. It just can't."

The Emissary made no movement. Blackness slashed across the sky, a great rent in heaven. The clouds vanished into a vast expanse of nothingness, and the nothing howled and screamed and laughed and babbled, eons of voices imploring and pleading and threatening, creatures and people who had once lived thundering upon the forest like the heart of madness bleeding over creation.

Jason fell to his knees, hands slapped over his ears, screaming.

The clouds rushed over the darkness as quickly as they had been removed. Silence resounded. Jason sat stunned, his hands limp.

"Would you like to know what ghosts are?" the Emissary said. "We are everyone. And we suffer. Oh, how we suffer."

They whispered from the forest, a host of the dead, their voices carrying through the mist. Branches clicked and clattered, and Jason looked up to see phantoms sitting among them, or appearing between the trees, apparitions muddled in the fog. Black eyes opened throughout the mist, and the trees themselves leaned closer to the clearing like dancers falling in slow motion. Figures resolved out of the empty spaces, not walking, not gliding, but emerging as if darting in and out of an invisible curtain, appearing in one world and then the next.

A music box chimed.

The ballerina appeared behind the Emissary, her back to Jason, her black hair sailing through the breathless air. She danced, a rusted music box embossed with the design of a cat chiming in her cupped hands. She leapt onto her pointed toes, curled her arms over her head, and danced en pointe.

"Another story," the Emissary said, "and this one is brief, we swear-swear-swear.

"Once there was a boy named Darius Bardales. He was the son of a demon and a werewolf. He was expected to become one or the other, like all of their kind. But he became neither. He refused the darkness. In doing so, he almost died. He should have died, yes. Instead he awoke from a long sickness and could do strange and wonderful things. He had found light, rebellious light, hiding somewhere in all that emptiness. The light clung to him, and he wielded it, and he taught others to wield it, and magic was born.

"Years later, after doing many strange and terrible and wonderful things, Darius helped to establish a home for all those who did not want to succumb to the darkness, a place where even monsters could be free. There they could hold to their humanity, be more than the tools of a hungry machine. But he could not enjoy this freedom. The eldest brother, the first vampire, Manny Ngombe, coveted Darius and wanted him to be his child. He would not rest until Darius was his. Darius knew to what lengths the vampire would go. He did not want to see his friends hurt, or his home ruined. But he also saw an opportunity to wield the darkness against itself. He hoped in his hands, the power of vampires could be used for good. He accepted. He became a vampire. He used his power to help shield and hide his people and their home. But he was a vampire still. He drank blood. He took lives, oh, so many lives, and from those lives he created slaves that would serve him as all who fall victim to vampires serve.

"But unlike the others of his kind, Darius examined the plight of his victims. Many of them had been terrible, had deserved to die. But none deserved what they suffered, and when Darius learned the truth of all things, he hurt, oh, he hurt so much. And something more: in peering into his own darkness, he had made a discovery. Something of the light, of magic, had remained in him. The dead ones, those whose lives he had taken, clamored around that light. The dead cannot peer into the living world save through the will of a vampire, and theirs is a horrible sight. But through Darius' magic they saw true life. They saw beauty and balance. They saw everything and nothing conjoined in an eternal dance.

"Much as the darkness had spoken to the brothers, the light spoke to Darius and the dead ones. If the dead ones so chose, they could have given themselves over to that light. They could have let go. Oh, what bliss, for in the light they would dissolve. They would be no more, returned to the silence that once was. But theirs would be a temporary victory, selfish-selfish, for the darkness has consumed countless souls who cannot escape it. So the light made Darius and the dead ones an offer: come together in the light without dissolving, without letting go, and Darius and the dead would be reborn as one man. That man would be a magic trick, an illusion, a wraith pretending at life. He would have little time, would struggle with ill health, for the light had to struggle to keep him alive. But in him would be the seed of salvation, and through the womb of a living woman a child would be born who would be of both worlds, who could wield the magic of true death, who could shepherd the dead into the living world and use darkness against itself to shatter the terrible prison and return death to what it once was.

"Do you understand, child? Do you see? Your father gave up his life, and we dead sacrificed our chance at peace, so you could be born, so you can make things right again. Death must be repaired, and for that to happen, the vampires must die. So long as they exist, none can pass away."

Jason rocked back and forth, shaking his head, blinking rapidly, swarmed by the Emissary's bitter truths. The phantom's words were true. He knew it from the very soil of the black forest, from the horror of the ghosts in the mist, their memories of the void bleeding into him as if they were his own thoughts. A single question pierced his near mania, and he seized it, hoping it was the string that could unravel the entire story and make it all untrue.

"Wait," he said. "But my father died. If—if he was a vampire, and he died before me, then how did he die?"

"Sunlight, dear child, yes: some legends are true. The light of the sun is where the dead may escape, disappear, and by doing so they leave their captors weak and mortal once more. Their true age catches up to them. But just try-try-try and get a vampire near sunlight. Ah, a fool's task. Even if a vampire should want to step into the light of the sun, their subconscious need to survive would stop them.

"Your father made the first demon possess him so he could die. He sacrificed his free will, his life, to have you. He made your dear Uncle Abe understand the monstrous thing he and his brother had brought upon the world. Against our wildest hopes, the first demon has renounced his creations. But, sadly, Abebe Ngombe cannot just simply possess his brother and the other vampires and walk them into the sun, no. Your father had to allow him in. No other vampire would do such a thing.

"But rejoice, child, for you are here, and no longer is the sun the only enemy of vampires."

"But if all you need is sunlight to escape—"

"What always happens before you see a ghost?"

Jason remembered all too well. Darkness would appear, shadows blooming from nowhere, obscuring daylight.

"The dead do not know the touch of the sun," the Emissary said. "How we long for it."

Jason stared, speechless, the truth a cage he saw no escape from.

"Of course, this is all simplified," the Emissary said. "Easy-peasy-lemon-squeezy. Whole lives condensed into story, so you may understand. The full tale will take time for you to learn, but learn it you must, learn it you will. For now-now-now, know what we speak is true: you are dead, and you are alive. You are both doorway and shepherd to we who wander the darkness. These haunts that have brought you so much pain, many are just accidents, collisions with vagrant ghosts. They find you, for you shine in the void, and they cannot help but infest the living world through you. Can you fault them? All they have known is darkness. They may not understand the terror they have caused you. They are mad, locked in the repetition of their lives. The minutia of life is a treasure to we of the abyss. To open a door, or to sit-sit in a chair, makes us feel as if we are alive again. There are those of us who deserve your pity.

"But the void is limitless. Many things linger there that have lost their humanity, or were never human at all. Your servants have shielded you from much, but your denial has made us weak, and now a usurper has come. He..."

The Emissary trailed off.

Jason shook all over, his facial muscles twitching in unison to the panic growing inside. He hugged his knees. He scanned the forest. Wraiths shifted near the tree line, their forms melding and melting into the inky mist. The ballerina danced, her hair a comet's tail composed out of the netherworld.

All of them once people, some or perhaps all those that his father had killed. His father, one half of his life, the man his mother loved, a kind man, a good man, had drank the blood of others and had ushered his own child into the heart of a war over death itself. The Emissary's truths shattered any illusion Jason had that he was mad. He could never conceive of anything so horrible, so cruel.

He looked again at the dead ones among the trees, at the Emissary. How long had they suffered? What was left of their lives? They were quiet and still, but through their silence radiated emotions spoken in a silent language only he could decipher. Fear and longing, need and hope, a desperate alchemy of collective thought consuming him, pushing him to see through his own pain and into the deeper wound that was ravaging existence. The boy listened, uncertain at first, then marveling at the fact that he understood them, as if he had stumbled on a language he had always known, but had never heard. He heard it now. He heard the pleas and desperation of the dead.

He stood, and without a word to the Emissary, walked to the trees. The Emissary watched. Jason stopped before the border of the forest and reached out. Gray, black, and yellowed hands reached back, some decayed and skeletal, others like smoke. They stroked Jason's fingers. He shivered, closed his eyes, and allowed sadness to give way to a sense of returning home. He stepped over the tree line and walked a few feet into the forest. There, wraiths surrounded him, a legion of ghosts welcoming the boy into their world. Jason felt beyond the cold, the fear, and into their hearts. Once, they had been human. No matter what they had been in life, in death they were all victims. And he could help them.

He closed his eyes and felt something awaken, stirring from a self-imposed exile. Suddenly he was aware of the dead as if they were extensions of himself, appendages to be utilized at his will. He opened his eyes and gasped, the feeling alien, frightening, filling him with certainty that a part of him was truly inhuman.

He backed away from the dead, walked back into the clearing, and stood before the Emissary.

The Emissary drew nearer.

"You feel it," it said, its hands clasped together as if in prayer. "You are awakening. Good-good-good. You are beginning to see, to open yourself, to embrace what you have run from for so long. Can you hear our silence? Yes. We now have hope. For the first time in countless years, we hope. We see in you what will be made right. You can save us. You can end this nightmare. You have that power. A terrible road awaits, but terrors will walk it with you, will guide you. If only you stand with us."

It offered its hand. Seams were ripped through the glove, and blackened strands of leather shot out like bristles. Decayed patches of skin peeked under the tears. Thick globs of darkness dripped from the wrist.

One final beat of terror seized Jason. He stared at the dead hand, knowing now what it meant, seeing in the rot the misery of a countless number of souls.

"It is...too much," the Emissary said. "No one deserves such a burden, no-no-no. Especially not a child. But pity alone is not enough to save us. If you do not end this, you are dooming everyone who still lives. Do you understand? Everyone dies. You are already a ghost."

Jason looked into the emptiness of the Emissary's eyes and read pain, grief, and suffering there. The dead cried out, their voices a mournful wind beseeching, pleading.

He took the Emissary's hand.

"I can hear them," he said, whispering as if sharing a treasured secret.

And then he laughed, gripped by sudden relief. The crazed sound fed upon itself, horror transforming into necessary madness. His eyes were wide with terrible wonder. Such awfulness had been laid at his feet, a dreadful reality unveiled. And yet he was unafraid. Or perhaps he was so afraid that the emotion transcended anything his mind could comprehend, and instead morphed into a savage joy. For the unknown melted before the fires of truth, and in that truth he had discovered who and what he was. He was not inhuman. He was more human than any who lived for he understood that everyone was tethered by invisible shackles in an infinite prison.

A prison he could destroy.

"I can—I can even feel them," he said. He stared wide eyed at the dead ones beyond the trees. "I can feel their pain. I can feel yours. And I know I can do something about it."

He laughed again. Here was purpose. He peered into himself and realized that he had always sensed the awful truth waiting. It was not ghosts he had feared, but what their existence meant. But instead of being overwhelmed, he now felt connected to something greater than himself. He had a purpose in the world. He would stand for the dead and free them. If terrors they were, then a terror he would be. And he would visit that terror upon monsters that deserved every bit of it.

His father had been right about something after all.

"I'm the good guy," he said, astonished.

The Emissary cocked its head, staring.

You're crazy, Jason thought. He laughed again. So he was.

The forest sighed, trees swayed, and the ballerina pirouetted around Jason and the Emissary, spinning with undead grace.

The Emissary hissed with satisfaction.

"A step, a first step, yes," it said. "The dead are here to serve."

"I have a lot of questions. But later. Right now, my friend is in trouble. I don't know what, but something took her. It was the same thing that took me in the stairs. I can...I can feel it. It was a ghost." He frowned. "Hold up, I don't understand. It...was a ghost, but it wanted to get rid of me. It took me and threw me into a hole, and then I woke up and I was with my parents. I was with them. I thought–but then weird things started happening, and I saw Eleanor's face in the mirror. That's how I knew it wasn't..." He laughed a dry and humorless laugh aimed at himself. "...real. You're telling me I have all this power, and that ghosts need my help, but that ghost in the stairs wasn't like you. It didn't need my help. It wanted me gone."

"And now we've come to the fool," the Emissary replied. Shrieks and cackling laughter broke through the forests. Anger and resentment and even a bit of pity spilled from the dead ones, as if they were a stadium crowd berating a failed athlete. "The usurper. Remember what we told you: You denied us, and through denying us, you denied your own power. That made it possible for those dead wandering through the void, to sometimes reach you and penetrate the living world. Your servants have been able to contain many of them, yes, but the fool is strong. His denial fuels him."

"What do you mean?"

"Many of the newly dead cannot accept what has happened to them. That is no surprise. Some become so lost in their denial, that they convince themselves they are still alive. They collapse into their own minds, reliving their memories over-over-over again. At first this is a comfort, even blissful. There are many joys and pleasures in the land of dreams. But in time their memories become distorted, for they are still drifting in the blackness, surrounded by terrors. The truth-truth slowly seeps in and distorts what they remember of life, corrupting their memories until their minds become ruins. They persist in their denial, on-on-and-on until they can see nothing beyond themselves. They go mad, locked in memories that are no better than haunted tombs. In time, the true terrors of the void find them...but no need to speak of such things now.

"One of these pitiful beings has usurped you. His name was once Matthew, and he was killed in the very home your father built. He has clung to its memory, and that memory has kept him close to the Gardens. His denial is so strong that other dead ones have taken refuge in it, merging their memories with his. Remember, wherever you go, you open a door for the dead to come through. Because you denied your own power, you have not yet learned how to shut that door. And when you arrived in your father's home, you drew the fool and his followers to you, for even in the abyss, he has remained close."

"I made this happen?" Jason said.

"No, child, no-no: you let this happen. We were not strong enough to stop the fool, not without you. All those years, your denial has shackled us. Worse-worse-worse, you shackled yourself. Perhaps we should've let other ghosts threaten you sooner. Perhaps then your father would've made you see. Instead, he comforted you and bent the truth and did you no favors. You convinced yourself it was magic, and so your power is like an unchecked fire. Tell us: do you like to float?"

Jason remembered hovering before Percy and Eleanor. He glared at the Emissary.

"That was you," he said.

"No. That was you. Just a sample of what you will do once you gain control."

"But—alright, so this Mathew guy's strong, he has all these ghosts with him. How is he doing what he's doing, how was he able to make me see my..." He stopped, his throat seizing, the memory of his parent's warmth still near. He steadied himself. "I saw my parents. They're dead, but I was with them."

"It is not his power, but yours that he wields. You have left it untouched. The fool was drawn to this, and you let him in. Remember an offer of friendship?"

He remembered: Matt assaulting him in Percy and Rosie's apartment. He remembered the blackened windows, the candles, the face, and the crazed voice whispering in his ears.

Jason sneered.

"That was him? He scared the shit outta me."

"Rightly so. Make no mistake: the fool and others like him are something to fear. Even in life, he could not be trusted. He was once kin to your father's closest friends, an arrogant man, a fool then and a fool now.

"When he came to you, we tried to push him back, but he and his acolytes are strong. He would have taken us into him, had we struggled. We had to flee, your lowly servants remaining only to watch and hope that you would somehow stand against him. But you were afraid. He made you accept his friendship. By doing so, you allowed him to take hold of you, to peer into your memories, to understand your power. You let him in and now he has control. He has constructed a world from his dreams and has given refuge to all those dead who follow him."

Jason twitched and shivered, his fists clenching.

"Oh, yes, be angry," the Emissary said. "The fool has stolen what is yours. He could not destroy you, but he could distract you. What you experienced, the love and light of your parents, was all a collection of memories. It is the same for those who refuse death, who wander in the void, lost in their own minds. They construct bittersweet fortresses, all to hide from the truth. Had you remained, your memories would've decayed, and you would have lost-lost yourself to them.

"Do you see now? You were able to escape because you finally accepted the truth. And so, here we are, and your friends are in danger."

"I only saw Eleanor—"

"The fool has taken all of them: Percy-Percy Bowles, Rosie, Alexander, Ian...they are known to us. He has sucked them into his own private world. If they remain, they will die, and then they will awaken in death as his slaves, and bit by bitty-bitty-bit, his fantasy will spread until it devours the Gardens and who knows what else? Other dead ones will flock to him, to dwell in his false mansion."

"Why didn't you tell me this from the beginning?"

"What would you have done?"

"I–ask him nicely to stop—what the hell do you think I would do, I'd stop him! It's my power!"

"Power you've shied away from. And now it answers to another. He will not give it back willingly. You must take it from him. But how will you do that? We wonder-wonder, yes-yes-yes. "

Jason looked at the forest, the ghosts, the Emissary. He felt them like a different kind of air in his lungs, like the unspoken knowledge of blood coursing through his veins, and once more there was the sensation of appendages beyond him, awaiting his command. The Emissary's question repeated in the shared silence of the dead. They were part of Jason, and he of them. The forest seemed vast, a place beyond reckoning, a universe of infinite mystery waiting to yield its secrets. Perhaps by understanding its mysteries, he would further understand himself.

"What is this place?" he said. He whispered, as if realizing he stood somewhere sacred, a holy land that could change the course of time. The Emissary leaned close. Jason could not understand how, but he knew the ghost was smiling.

"A parting gift from your father," the Emissary said.

"He made this place?"

"He is this place."

Jason blinked.

"What?"

"We entered life through your father," the Emissary said. "We were one with him until we became one with you. Much of the magic that remained to him was at work keeping himself alive. But there was still enough in him to grow the forest out of himself, a refuge for your servants, created out of your father's very soul. We expected this place would vanish when he died. But it remained, and he did not vanish into the void like so many other lost souls, no. He became one with the forest. He is the forest."

Roots slithered through the earth, wrapped around Jason's legs, and brushed his fingers. The trees swayed. The wind whispered, and love enveloped Jason.

"Of course, your father had selfish reasons to make this place," the Emissary said. "He wanted to make sure your mother had somewhere safe to be when she passed."

Gratitude nearly sent tears gushing down Jason's face. He fought for control, swallowed, and dared a question he had been too scared to ask.

"She's...she's here?"

The Emissary turned to the side and gestured towards the ballerina. She pirouetted and came to a perfect stop, her arms slender and curled above her head, her ankles crossed. Then she spun near to Jason. He shivered, gasping against all the things he had held back, all of his grief, all of his fear, and all of his love. She came to him, a dancing ghost, her face hidden by sheets of black hair.

She reached out and laid her hand on him as she danced. A train of memory took him through their brief life together—every moment, small and large, the frustrations, the joys, each and every second a triumph of existence in an impossible universe. His mother spoke no words, but no words were needed. All of her resounded through him in a cadence of unending love. She said: all of me will always be a part of you. She said: should the foundations of existence collapse, I will still be a part of you. Forever.

She released him and continued to dance. The music box chimed a bittersweet lullaby.

"Is she—is—" Jason said. It was all he could manage.

"She does not truly know you," the Emissary replied. "Or this place. To see her son suffer the way he has would be too much for her. She is as she was as a child. In a sense, this is her fortress against the void. We owe her that. But deep-deep within, she recognizes you. We let her be this way, a child without care. She is here for you, yes." The Emissary gestured to the roots brushing Jason's legs. "They both are."

The roots caressed Jason's hands, then slid down his legs and sunk back into the earth. Jason felt his father all around them, not as a man, but as a silent and overwhelming presence that filled him with determination.

"But this place cannot hold forever," the Emissary said. "There are terrors that will devour us all, unless you stand against them."

Jason looked at his mother, at her dancing as a child, and could think of no better reason to fight. His eyes were wide and bloodshot when he turned back to the Emissary.

"Where is he?" he said. "Where's Matt?"

"You already know that. All you have to do is find him, and we will follow."

Jason clenched his jaw, resolve steeling him. He closed his eyes. No more would he hide from the things that he feared. He opened himself to the bitter passages of his mind, where truths he had called illusions waited, where his veiled power had been caged by his refusal to accept them. There he felt the many appendages that were beyond him, but his to command. Cold washed over his skin, and a great inner darkness rushed from his depths and overwhelmed his senses. He embraced the onslaught of darkness, awash with the alien sensation of being himself and something more, something beyond, letting the last of his fears howl and fall silent.

For a moment he saw the boy outside, floating out of the black, his empty eyes staring at him. And then he was seeing through those same eyes, looking at the world through the gaze of death, at one with terrible knowledge that he had hidden from for too long.

He was the dead thing. That was the truth that he had run from. Now he let death course through his veins, and when he opened his eyes they were empty and lifeless, emanating tendrils of darkness.

"Ah," the Emissary said, smiling.

Jason marveled at the black forest, seeing through it to the secret netherworld beating over everything, a shimmering network of animated death connected to the all encompassing void. He gasped, looking at his hands and seeing them yellowed and corpselike. His own thoughts emanated in great vibrating strands of translucent darkness, and he felt all of the Black Forest and its denizens as if they were a part of him. On his command the trees rocked and swayed, the clouds blackened, and the dead poured into the clearing, a parade of corpses enshrouded in mist. All of this should have been overwhelming, but to him they were as natural as drops of rain, as shafts of sunlight, as the innumerable stars in the heavens.

But his hold over these things faltered, and he saw through the forest, space, and time to where waves of his power were being sucked by a malformed swollen thing like a tick feeding on existence. Matt was visible, yet far, not in the sense of a physical and measurable distance, but across an expanse of thought. For the dead world was commanded by the power of the immaterial, by the mystery of the mind.

All of Jason's thoughts locked onto Matt, and suddenly the world around him felt as malleable as clay in his hands. Fear had caged him, had kept him from being whole. But now he was fear. Now he was a dead king seeking vengeance on the wraith who had stolen his crown. His thoughts shaped a path that followed his siphoned power, and those unseen appendages pulled at the very fabric of the Black Forest and ripped open a tunnel of darkness behind the Emissary.

Jason no longer felt like a person, but like an idea, weightless, without form. His feet left the ground, and the dead cried out and touched him, shrieking with horrid joy. A weight vanished from within, as if he had lived life holding his breath and had finally allowed himself to exhale. He floated towards the tunnel. There was no more doubt.

"Follow-follow the leader, yes-yes-yes," the Emissary said. It floated behind Jason, its mask smiling wide, and they both vanished within the black folds of the tunnel. The ghosts of the forest followed, an undead host disappearing into the churning dark.

The tunnel closed behind them.

She remained, dancing on her toes, and the trees bent about her, swaying with her endless song.

10

Eleanor did not hesitate. She didn't wait for Matt to speak another word. She saw in his gaudy and exaggerated features madness and desperation, the greed of a tyrant feasting on a starving land. Anger fueled her, and magic burst through her skin in shimmering lines of heat. She threw up her hands and screamed as columns of flames spiraled into existence, writhing scales ignited out of the naked air. A part of her was amazed by the powerful display, unable to comprehend how she had done such a thing. But rage focused her on her enemy, cutting away all other distractions.

The fire charged Matt, reaching within a few feet of him. There it convulsed, thinned into sputtering streaks of lightning, and crumpled into clouds of ash collapsing over the dance floor.

Eleanor panted through gritted teeth, stunned. The ghost smiled at her. She screamed again, conjuring a roiling orb of flame that spawned long necked hydras. They struck, roaring.

They dissolved into ash and splattered on the floor.

Eleanor shivered, muscles aching, head throbbing. A dull current of pain beat at her nerves, as if she had just pressed the world over her shoulders. She seized calm and breathed life into the diamond patterned dance floor. A riot of green blossomed, transforming the space between her and Matt into a meadow rife with purple flowers and lithe saplings. Eleanor urged them on, feeding them from that secret well inside of her.

The foliage came within inches of Matt, froze, went rigid, and then withered into pools of decay.

Eleanor reeled. Hollowness echoed across her insides, her power dwindled. Tendrils of steam rose from her body, and she shook with frustration as the ash and rot was swallowed by the floor.

The ghosts made no sound. They surrounded her, their crayon eyes smiling with the desperate light of cultists, their heads twisted like a gaggle of vultures waiting on a dying animal.

Then they applauded as one, their hands coughing clouds of dust.

Matt gestured at Eleanor, and the dead ceased their clapping.

"Ain't she something," he said. "Late, but worth it. That was one hell of a show, even though we could all tell it was fake. It's cool, you're young. You missed the wedding, though. But, ayo, don't be pissed at her. It's been so long since I've seen Eleanor, that I forgot to invite her. She was, like, three or four or some shit, last time I saw her. Wow, can you believe that?" He stared at Eleanor, his false eyes unblinking. "You're getting big. Been hearing so much about you from my friends, about all those cute little magic tricks you've been pulling off. They send you to a camp or something? Anyway, you definitely caught my eye, and I'm glad you could make it. Come over here, give me a hug."

Eleanor glared, not moving an inch. The red gown gripped her, digging into skin and seizing control. She tensed and looked down at herself in horror, then fell backwards onto the floor, struggling. Something within her pushed back, refusal transforming into tendons of air that strained against the strangling threads of the gown until the red folds sagged and were inanimate.

Matt grunted with surprise. He hesitated a moment. Then he was above Eleanor, face to face, teleported from once space to the next. She tried to crawl backwards, but dead hands rose out of the floor and gripped her.

"Stubborn," Matt said. "Just like your mother. I knew we were related. Don't be sad. I'm impressed. Takes a lot to impress me, ya know? Not an easy thing to do." He stared down at her, his mannequin features rigid, twisted into an impossible smile. "You got your ma's heart. I see that. Her lip too, from what I hear." He chuckled. "We can use that around here. You'll liven up the place."

Eleanor shivered between breaths, rage muting exhaustion.

"Fuck you."

"Oh! There's that lip again. That was my favorite part about your mama. But, hey, I'm still your uncle. You can't talk to me like that. Why you acting so pissy? There's nothing wrong here. It's a celebration! By the way, did you pay attention to those dance lessons? They were expensive, you better've learned something."

"Where's my family?"

"Jesus. No hug, not even a hello. I'm your family. That ain't enough? I thought you'd at least be excited to meet me." He stared at her, assessing. "You're tough. That's good. You need to be tough, gets you through the bullshit. Gets you to where I am today. Look at these people. Think they hang out with just anybody? Nah. These are a special class of people. My people. You'll like 'em. They'll make you feel right at home."

"Dead things don't have a home."

Matt bellowed, and the dead screamed with voices blasphemous to all creation, rabid and deranged shrieks rising from the bowels of a broken universe. Darkness fell, a livid curtain of seething emptiness that left only Matt's mannequin face visible. Its smile was contorted into a hateful scream, and its eyes were craters shining with two points of unforgiving light.

"I'm alive, I'm alive, nothing can kill me!"

Eleanor screamed back.

"Where's my goddamn family!?"

The screams broke. Eerie light seeped out of the darkness, and the surrounding dead reappeared like reflections smeared across black water. Matt was silent, his features smiling once more. A nearly imperceptible groan droned from somewhere, reverberating with the true voice of emptiness.

"Your family," Matt said. "Your fucking family. You sound just like your father, you know that? That's all he ever talked about. It's great, unless you're not part of it. Then you're on the outside. Then you're always reminded of where you don't belong. But we're in my house now. I'm your uncle, stupid. I'm your family."

"You ain't family. You're an asshole."

Matt laughed, his mannequin features contorting into a grin once more.

"Family don't hurt each other," Eleanor said.

The surrounding ghosts echoed Matt's laughter.

"See, it's all good," he replied. "You're just a kid. You don't know what you're talking about—family don't hurt each other, fuck outta here."

"No, you don't get it." Eleanor grinned, her eyes glinting with malicious light. "I know family can make mistakes. But if they love each other, they're always sorry. They make it right. They don't try to hurt each other for no reason. Like when you tortured my brother."

The laughter vanished. Droning silence took hold, morphing into a growl that slathered Matt's anger over the darkness.

"You don't know what you're talking about," he said, his voice seething.

"Everyone knows what you did, you sick fuck. How old was my brother when you possessed him? Six? Seven? Did that feel good, torturing a little boy?"

Matt's growl swelled. He leaned closer, the mannequin face shaking.

"Your brother deserved everything I did to him."

"Then why you dead now?"

The ghosts screamed again. Matt's voice erupted into a gravelly bark that rendered them silent. He glared at Eleanor, but still smiled.

"You stupid little shit," he said. "You don't know anything about anything. You wanna see something? C'mon, I'll show you how little you know."

The surrounding dead vanished into a curtain of blackness.

The ravaged shriek of a crying child gripped Eleanor and sent spasms through her stomach. A dull amber glow infused the dark. She lay on a concrete floor, still pinned by dead hands. Matt was beside her, and both stared at the back of a boy with dark hair who screamed from the floor. Eleanor could make out nothing of his features, did not see the blood and gore splattered over his fingers, nor the pale corpses frozen in their final death throes surrounding him.

But she did see her father and Percy standing before him. She beheld the gun in her father's hand.

"Pop," she said, lunging and crying out. Dead hands held her down. Her father made no notice. She gaped, a dull croak escaping her throat. "Dad?"

"This already happened, stupid," Matt replied. "Just sit back and watch what a good man your daddy is."

Eleanor screamed and shut her eyes at the explosive clap of the gunshot. Cold fingers pried her eyelids open. She watched the boy collapse into a heap, watched his blood ooze over the floor, watched smoke rise from the back of his ravaged head.

She looked up at her father and saw the same smoke rising from the muzzle of his gun.

All went black. The fingers pulled away from Eleanor's eyes, the mannequin faces faded into view, and once more they surrounded her in the fetid twilight. She swallowed and shook her head.

"No," she said. "I don't believe it."

"You're dad's a liar," Matt replied. "It's why he's so dangerous. He'll say and do anything to get what he wants—like tell his kids lies about their uncle. I bet he never even told you that you were born a demon."

Eleanor froze. Shock and incredulity spread through her. She shook her head, the disgust of disbelief written on her face.

"No way. You're full of shit."

"Nah, it's true. You almost died and everything. Of course he didn't want to admit it to himself. But I knew. So did your ma. I'll let you ask him in a bit. If you're nice."

"Where is he!?"

"See, that wasn't very nice. If you apologize and stop yelling at me, I'll bring him to you. If not, we can wait. I got all the time in the world."

He turned away from her. Smiling faces watched. Hatred burrowed into Eleanor, making her strain against the dead hands coiled about her arms and legs. But she relented, seeing no other way, speaking as if forcing a rock through a straw.

"I'm sorry."

Matt waited, his back turned.

"I'm sorry, Uncle Matt. I'm—I'm being very mean, and—and you don't deserve that."

Matt whirled around, his smile somehow larger, the green crayon refreshed over his eyes.

"There's my little niece," he said.

The hands released Eleanor, vanishing without sound. Matt came to her and offered his own. The faintest beat of pity flickered in Eleanor as she stared at the horror he had become. In him, there lingered longing, a depth of panic that underlined every word. As if he was clinging to a drowning buoy in an unmerciful sea. But still she hated him and had to force herself to take his hand, to let him raise her up, to stand looking up at him in the façade of familial bonding. She did all these things and was made instantly older by it, a part of her youth destroyed by the understanding that monsters could be born from broken hearts and damaged minds—that monsters could be anyone.

The dead ones gushed over the false reconciliation, sighing with reverence and wiping away imagined tears with tattered handkerchiefs.

"Ain't that better?" Matt said. Eleanor swallowed and nodded. Matt leered at her, his false fingers pressing into the back of her hand. "Now we start the party."

Harsh light blared, revealing the rest of the ballroom. Ghosts were joined together for a waltz, their faces smeared with demented clumps of makeup, accentuating features already exaggerated by the wild curves of their smiles and the jagged ovals of their eyes.

Among the crazed faces, draped in a wedding dress and smiling like a child's doll, was Rosie. She was locked in a waltzing pose, awaiting her captor. Her eyes found Eleanor's, and through their droopy haze they screamed. Eleanor cried out and lunged towards her, but Matt pulled her back. Eleanor looked about and spied Ian a few couples away on Rosie's right. He was stooped and limp in the arms of a mannequin in a garish pink gown decimated by rips. His eyes rolled, the whites fluttering. Eleanor groaned, but saw there was no sense in calling out to him. She searched for her father among the waiting dancers, but did not find him. Her gaze landed on the butler in his sad clown mask, standing rigid beyond the dancers, a stained towel draped over his arm. Eleanor blinked in surprise, recognizing something familiar in his stance.

Percy wanted to scream, to hurl his strength at the ghosts and tear them apart. But his voice would not work, his body was no longer his to control, and Matt's voice ever chuckled in his ears.

"This is all I wanted," Matt said to Eleanor. She looked up at him, finding his crayon eyes staring into hers. "All of us together like this— family, friends—one big ass celebration. As long as I'm around, you never have to worry."

"Yeah, yeah, this is great," Eleanor replied, speaking through her teeth. Matt's lunacy crashed full force, sparking caution, coding her thoughts into sensitive algorithms programmed to incite no anger in the ghost. She looked at her brother, at Rosie, at their helpless forms, and knew she had to tread lightly around Matt's power. "Thanks— thanks for putting all this together, Unc—Uncle Matt. Would, uh, would you mind if I got to dance with my pop?"

The ghost stared.

"It doesn't have to be the first dance," she said. "But, it would be really nice of you if my dad and I got to dance, 'cause then I—I could tell him what a great night I've been having with you. I mean, we all have." She turned towards Rosie and her brother, unsure of what she was doing, but letting her words work. "Right, guys? Hasn't this been great?"

Rosie grinned, her muscles twitching, her cheeks swollen and pink. But her eyes glinted with understanding. Her head trembled in the slightest nod.

Ian sagged like a junkie in the midst of a high. His eyes fluttered, and drool drenched his chin.

Eleanor turned back to Matt with a bright smile.

"See?" she said. "We're having a great fucking time."

Matt's silence opened a wealth of terror in Eleanor's heart. In it she could hear her deepest fears cackling.

He sighed with paternal warmth.

"You're a sweet kid," he said. "You're dad's being punished right now." Eleanor tensed. Matt went on. "You saw what he did. He's a very bad man. When you do bad things, you have to be punished. Or else, what? There needs to be justice. But it won't be forever. You'll get to dance with him. Maybe at the next party."

Eleanor's jaw quivered, worry and anger coiling over her. The image of the dead boy returned, but she refused it. She would not believe it of her father. And if it was true, then she would be the one to confront him. She would not stand by as this deranged specter exacted his vengeance. The notion that Alexander was someplace worse than this transformed worry into a near debilitating terror. She did not fight it. She let fear work its awfulness, accepting its possibilities, and slowly reined in the stampede of her mind.

"Oh," she said. "Okay. I understand. He needs to learn his lesson. Butt—but if I see him, I can tell him how mad I am at him. Then he'll feel bad. That way, he'll really learn his lesson. See what I mean?"

Matt stared. Silence stretched.

"Everyone's waiting on us," he replied. "We can talk about this later. Now..."

Music warbled into hearing, as if spinning from a tangle of broken pipes. The dead waltzed like a menagerie of toys fueled by a sputtering engine, twirling across the ballroom floor. Their shoes and heels were unmoving yet somehow kept pace with the whimpering count of the waltz. The music churned, melodic strings clashing against dissonant bass tones.

The ghosts danced. As if to forget the horrors they had become. As if life could be shaped out of movement.

Eleanor suddenly spun, lifted from off the floor, invisible hands pressing her into another mannequins' embrace. The dancing dead were blurs in her vision, a kaleidoscope of phantoms. Between the waltzing ghosts she spied her brother, his head rolling over limp shoulders. Rosie was a streak of white in Matt's arms, her teeth bared in a screaming smile, her eyes heavy.

They spun away, revolving through the menagerie of the dancing dead, and Eleanor was cast from her partner and into Matt's arms. Rosie waltzed around them, partnered with a mannequin woman.

"I gotta say, I'm happy you're here," Matt said to Eleanor. "For a second I was worried you weren't coming. It's cool, I ain't mad. That was kinda my fault, actually. We really gotta work on, whaddaya call it, communication. You're starting to understand that I'm all about family. Ask everyone here, they're always going, 'Matt, you work so hard, you want the best for everyone. Your family should see that.' And I tell them, 'Don't worry, give it time'. And ya see. Here we are.

"Those were some cool magic tricks you did. Everyone says so. See, we all knew you were gonna be something, after coming outta that coma. We thought you were just like your brother, your shadow moving and shit. But you changed it up. Couldn't have been more than two, three years old, but you said 'Fuck that, I ain't gonna be no demon'. It was crazy. Of course your father denied it. Begged us to keep that shit quiet, so, you know...But I always knew what was really going on.

"I admit I forgot about you because there was so much going on. But my friends, they couldn't stop talking about you, and I was like, oh, that's right. She must be something special now. You've grown into something amazing, kid. I think, now that you're here, we can really liven the place up. It needs that extra something and you're the one to do it. Now that you're here, we can make this place even better. You can use that power of yours, and life will be great."

They danced. The ghost lifted her in the air, Eleanor drifting above the reach of his outstretched hands. They spun, and then she was dropped into his embrace once more.

"Don't get it twisted," Matt said. "I know how to move. Listen: I'm real happy you're here. Not just for the magic shit. That's great and whatever. But seriously, I always wanted a daughter. I don't know what it is, but little girls calm me down, make me remember what's good about life. You give me hope. A'ight, it's cheesy, but there ya go. You and me, in time, I think, are gonna be close. Oh snap, here comes the switch."

Eleanor was thrust from Matt and into the arms of a tall and thin mannequin whose narrow face curved like a vulture's beak under a monstrous grin. Its voice was a metallic buzzing in her ears.

"...steer carefully now, don't take the turnpike, oh, sure, great time, yes, great time, the audit revealed some troubling figures, and I didn't think dancing could feel like this, you've really made this a great time, I'm sorry, but I just don't feel that way about you anymore, can't we be adult about this, there's no reason to stretch this out, the blonde woman's wedding dress compliments her hair so well, just one scotch, that won't kill me, just one dance with her, I see why Matt loves her so much of it is unfair, you can't tell me what to do, one more drink, just one more drink, I won't have any problem getting home, there's always something we can do, I'm sorry, I need to leave, I'd rather not talk about it, but we're all here now, that's all over and done with, that new operating system is something, really something, really, really something, really something—"

Eleanor was pulled from his grip, spun, and thrust into a new partner whose dry plaster skin clashed with the moist fabric of its suit. A dead hand pressed into her back, and a new voice shot into hearing, rapid fire words careening at her from everywhere, the ramblings of another ghost mixing its old life with their dance.

She went that way, spinning into the arms of this ghost and that, beings who were once men and women and everything in between, now half-empty entities dancing to shield themselves from the pain of their own existence. Matt danced with Rosie at the center of the ballroom, keeping her to himself, raising them off of the floor, spinning. Eleanor was passed from ghost to ghost, the room a blur of twirling mannequins in dresses and suits, each one pouring clouds of crazed speech into her ears.

She struggled in the embrace of her next partner, a woman who spoke single words between long stretches of yowls. Eleanor pulled and twisted, fighting to get free. Matt cheered, and the dead cheered with him. But underneath their celebratory cries was a mournful chorus of wails. Eleanor looked toward Matt and realized he was singularly focused on Rosie.

An idea came.

Her show of force against him had failed because he was somehow able to dictate to the other ghosts what it was they could experience. He manipulated their senses, his delusion their delusion.

But now he was distracted.

The pull of another ghost dragged her to the next dancer, a bloated mannequin with a bald pate rimmed by gray hair. This wraith spoke in grunts and jittering noises, pouring nonsense at Eleanor. She closed her eyes and wove a pattern of magic, straining against the reinforced barrier created by the collective dead. Inch by inch a rose composed of light materialized between them, its petals folds of honey-gold tapering into a silver stem. The ghost stopped its rambling and fell still. A subtle hissed escaped it, and then it dropped Eleanor to the floor. It raised its hands to the luminescent rose, cupping it as if warming itself by a fire. Others nearby stopped their dancing and looked, some gasping.

Eleanor hurried, crawling past the dancers and towards the sweetheart table. She lunged beneath it, the tablecloth cold against her neck. There she stopped for a moment, catching her breath. She sat up on her elbows and watched the ring of ghosts staring at the bright flower.

The flower dissolved strand by strand, peeling into embers and becoming no more.

The halted ghosts swayed, dumbfounded, then came together like automatons and returned to their dance. But the balding ghost remained, staring at its own hands, torn between the false life erected out of Matt's illusion and the memories of its real life rising in ephemeral fragments. Senses and emotions had been summoned by the flower, its true light peeling back the folds of darkness in the ghost and revealing that which could not be replicated by dead hands. A life: an endless series of happenings born from thought and sensation and something more, something nameless, that silent witness at the heart of all things.

Matt's words came to Eleanor as she watched the bald mannequin, the way her uncle had spoken of things to come. A thought clicked through her working mind, and she looked on all the ghosts with heartbreak.

"They think they're alive," she said. The luminescent flower had shattered that delusion for the lone specter, had revealed the awfulness of its existence by comparison. The others had not been close enough, their delusion strengthened by each other. But Eleanor's partner had been alone. It still searched the air before it, mewling and whimpering.

It came to her then.

She forced herself into a seated position, planted her fists against the floor, and breathed deep. Pain returned as she struggled against a cold and unclean force surrounding her, Matt's will a rancid barrier that had doubled after her first attempt to depose him. The single flower had been a minor work, but now great magic was needed, and she pulled through the barrier, summoning great torrents of power, even as her muscles ached and her head swam. She would reveal to the dead what they could not see. She would unveil the truth piecemeal, and perhaps that would somehow release them and her family from her uncle's clutches.

Or they'll turn on you, she thought.

But still she breathed, focusing on the pain, accepting it even as it swelled. Need gave her the strength to endure.

You were born a demon.

It came as a slap. A deep pit opened in her stomach. Fragments of feeling bled through: dread, pain, and sickness morphing into elation, the release of some cold dark thing that had once been a part of her.

She could not know if these emotions were memories or imaginings, and yet they seemed true.

"Okay," she said, nodding, wiping her eyes, accepting that perhaps it was the truth. If she had been born a demon, then so be it. It did not change who she was.

Another thought came:

If you were born a demon, then you beat it.

You beat it.

A smile flickered across her face.

She watched the bitter spectacle of the dancing dead. Pain flared through her, but she didn't give a shit. She breathed, letting calm take hold, summoning magic until it filled every cell. Her muscles screamed. She gasped under the weight of pain, her voice strangled, but still she conjured, taking hold of the threads of creation. She shaped them into what she knew the dead could not deny.

First came light.

A luminescent flower blossomed before the loner who immediately seized upon it, sighing. Others bloomed between couples on the outer rim of the dance floor, pulsating, shimmering with multitudes of color. The ghosts stopped and stared, seeing in the light some sacred thing long forgotten and undreamt of.

More flowers blossomed among the next ring of dancers, and then the next, until only Matt and Rosie danced, surrounded by entranced wraiths.

Then came the heavens.

The darkness of the ceiling rippled into folds of fire: green, purple, and blue, auroras shaped out of nothingness. The cries of the dead scraped against the music, as they looked from the flowers to the shimmering magic above, witnessing the magnetic clashing of forces stemming from creation.

Matt danced on with Rosie, but his head began to spin, seeing his acolytes no longer waltzing, hearing their awed cries.

Faster, Eleanor thought, conjuring, channeling, beyond pain, beyond her own body.

Then the shaping of the earth.

A tsunami of soil and grass erupted through the floor and coalesced beneath the dead, the dark green blades pressing against their legs. This time, their delusion interrupted, the phantoms gazed at the meadow with open wonder, some reaching shivering hands to touch the greenery.

All about them life revealed itself. Grass swayed, the aurora pulsed, and the flowers beat with light.

Eleanor was beyond herself. She knew the silent language of all things, merging the mechanics of existence with the wonder in her heart, weaving them together into magic that transcended all she had ever known.

Matt froze with preternatural stillness, awed and horrified.

Rosie fell to the floor with a grunt. The bonds holding her vanished, and she clutched at her face as spasms took hold of her cheeks. She took a breath, frowned so as to still her contracting cheek muscles, looked about, and saw Eleanor glowing under the sweet-heart table. A swell of pride shattered the noose of horror that had gripped her. Then she blinked, searched through the mannequins, and found Ian writhing in the grass like a drunkard trying to rouse himself. She pulled herself over to him, crying out against the waves of pins and needles assaulting her body. None of the dead noticed. She reached Ian and grabbed him. He shook, his eyes rolling into the back of his head, lost in seizure.

"Ian," she said, managing to move her lips despite the mask of knives gripping her face. She brushed hair from his brow. "Ian, baby, come on, you gotta get up."

He lulled in her arms, his tongue sagging against his bottom lip, a desperate sound rising from his throat. Rosie thought for a moment, searching for clarity, for cause and effect, for pattern. Familiar warmth tingled about her. She blinked with realization, looking at the grass under them, feeling in it the same source of magic that she had known for so many years, hidden from her by Matt's yoke, now returned through Eleanor's will.

She laid Ian onto the ground and placed her hand on his forehead. She drew from the grass, pulling magic into her, and a familiar spell bubbled, taking shape out of the components of her mind. A bluish light radiated under her fingers, and the spell surged into Ian, soothing the onslaught he had endured with waves of calm that coursed through his brain, triggering the good memories of his life to come flooding out, to return him to who he was. Rosie felt as if she was trying to pry through a metal wall, but the spell breached and poured into the boy, planting seeds of relief, rousing him.

Percy limped into the grass, ripped off the clown mask, and shambled over to Rosie. He knelt beside her and laid his hands on her shoulders. Unrestrained relief glowed in both of their eyes, but Rosie continued to work. Ian fell still, his eyes closing, the seizure stopped. Percy looked about at the dead, and the magic holding them rapt. He reached out to the grass and felt life surge like some silent force reclaiming the world.

Eleanor transformed into everything that had ever been and ever will be.

The dead reached out to the singing heavens, cupped their hands over the pulsing flowers, touched the blades of grass.

The grass died under their fingers, sending ripples of agony through Eleanor. But creation beat through her, and for every shoot of grass that withered away, a new one rose in its place.

Whimpers and cries and groans emanated from the ghosts, for in the child's magic they beheld life and knew themselves to be death. The surrounding darkness began to fade under a grayish light emanating from somewhere not of Matt's making. The music slowed to a groan that screeched and fell silent. Silhouettes of furniture began to resolve out of the shadows: a blue sofa, a computer desk, portraits of horses, Rosie and Percy's living room reemerging from under Matt's delusion.

Alexander spilled out of the failing shade beyond the ballroom, his face tear-streaked and worn. He landed on his knees, the false corpses of his children still clutched in his arms. Pablo emerged beside him, the bullet hole a ghastly chasm in his head. He touched Alexander's shoulder and pointed. Alexander looked and beheld magic at work, and as he did so the false corpses crumbled to ashes.

Pablo went to the outer rim of the dance floor, dropping the red crayon he had been using to color the skin beneath his ravaged skull. He stared up at the aurora with empty eye sockets, and the hint of a smile twitched on his face.

Alexander blinked with wonderment, forgetting the false corpses he had held, feeling something familiar within the weaving, something he was too scared to hope for.

Slowly, the darkness failed. The aurora painted the dead with shimmering color, the grass rose and clung to their legs, wind pierced through their formal and decayed clothing and burrowed into the unknowable place where their true forms lingered. And somewhere in what remained in each of their hearts and each of their minds, a beautiful knowledge was awakened. They looked at themselves and knew the abominations they had become, and their moans harmonized with the crying wind. But within the light and life around them they remembered themselves to be once one and the same with life, beings that had walked the earth. The flowers of light swelled into incandescent bouquets, and from them came a silent song beckoning the dead to release themselves and be free. The ghosts answered, transfixed, each drifting towards the roses and dipping their fingers into the liquid light. There they began to dissolve.

And then Matt shattered it all.

His scream erupted as if it had been caged at the center of the earth, an explosion of hurt, greed, and desperation. The dead succumbed as one, ripped from the light like marionettes on strings. Matt was at their center, his mannequin face a mask of indignation, his anger transforming their revelation into hatred.

Once more the dead were slaves to delusion.

And they swarmed.

Some lunged at the ground and others rose up into the air, their mouths widened into contorted black holes that vomited acidic darkness over the grass and the flowers and the aurora's light.

A vicious jolt crashed into Eleanor, the fire of magic besieged by the dead man's will. She screamed and was slammed onto the floor, and all about her the grass decayed.

Ghosts fell onto their knees and began to inhale the regurgitated darkness, taking with it the earth, wailing as they did so. Others spun in the air, the aurora bleeding drip by drip into their mouths.

The flowers withered into clouds of ash.

Wind screamed with Matt's voice, a herald of its master announcing that this was his world. He charged out of the encroaching darkness, tore the table from above Eleanor's head, and loomed over her. He glared, his cartoon-colored eyes contrasted by the offended snarl of his mouth. Eleanor's magic wilted, and the decayed and ruined architecture of the ballroom bled into being.

"Just like your fucking father," Matt said. Eleanor groaned, dazed, trying to push herself up, to reclaim the threads of magic. Matt floated off of the ground and hovered horizontally over her, centimeters away, the awfulness of his existence emanating in drafts of putrid cold. "I try to help you, and you spit in my fucking face. You think your little tricks are gonna work? We know bullshit when we see it. You can't trick us. We have a good life here, and I'm not gonna let you ruin it. Looks like you need an education, just like your brother, huh? Fine."

The porcelain children parted the air behind Matt, silent, their faces contorted into angered masks.

"My kids here are gonna show you a few things," he said. "Then you'll respect me. Then you'll know who—"

The demon slammed into him, Ian's shadow a red eyed bullet streaking and screeching across the darkness and laying into the dead man like wrath itself. Ian emerged from the dark, his eyes furnaces of blood that were ready to consume any and all that came too close. Matt cried out in shock as the shadow coiled about him. Ian felt as if he were prying at an infinitely heavy door, but the terror and pain that radiated from underneath fueled him. He opened himself to desire, to the need to feed upon ultimate suffering, to the orgasmic release of inflicting torment.

Eleanor writhed on the flood, struggling to get up.

The porcelain children swarmed Ian, and he snarled as they pulled him down and clamped their mouths over his flesh. But his eyes were still ablaze, his shadow screeching, biting, piercing, promising pleasures, threatening pain, doing all it could to break Matt's will.

Eleanor strained against spasms, fighting to rise up, to protect her brother. She fell with a cry, her every muscle trembling, the ballroom spinning.

Warmth enfolded her. Her muscles eased and fell still. She looked and saw Rosie across the dark, shining like a blue priestess, one hand clutching Percy's shoulder, bracing against him as she cast her spell. Eleanor felt as if the embers of fire were being stoked within her. She breathed, got to one knee, and stood on shaky legs. Magic bubbled, trembling under her skin, calling for release.

The dead encircled Ian and the porcelain children, and as one they vomited the fabric of an abominable reality, the skeleton of a dimension of horrors that coalesced into negative space closing over the boy and his attackers. They wanted to take him from this place, to trap him in tortuous worlds that he could never escape. Ian sensed the space changing, strange shapes materializing in the spewed blackness. But he did not care. He saw Matt and only Matt, his thoughts a dagger stabbing over and again at the revenant.

The aurora was gone, and the floor was slick with rot and decayed blades of grass, but Eleanor was rejuvenated by Rosie's spell and once more felt an indefinable life force pulsing through everything. She summoned power and let it build until it became an unbearable pressure begging for release. She transcended her body, becoming one with magic, and the very air became an extension of her will.

She conjured.

The aurora rekindled above, tensed like a contracted muscle, and then burst with tongues of multicolored fire that crashed onto the ghosts encircling Ian. They were seized by whips of light and shook as if in the throes of religious awakening. The dread reality vomiting from their mouths erupted into a great conflagration, a column of flame roaring into the dark. The porcelain children gasped, released themselves from their prey, and looked on in wonder.

The fires of the aurora hurtled towards Matt as he struggled against the shadow, but broke apart as they neared him. His will was still strong, his delusion refusing Eleanor's magic.

Ian made no notice of the magic raining down, or the writhing dead, or the blood spilling from the wounds gouged into his face and arms from where the porcelain children had mauled him. The surrounding fire burned to nothingness, and he stood and limped towards Matt, his eyes vats of boiling blood, his face written with every curse ever spoken. Matt writhed, his false mouth an abyss of hate, and he glared back at the boy as the shadow rampaged over him like an insect.

The dead ones were engulfed by Eleanor's fire. Some remembered lives they had long forgotten in the madness of the void, entranced by memories returning in all consuming visions. These retreated into themselves, and their mannequin forms fell limp as they once more haunted the halls of their own memories, refusing reality.

Others, less than a few, saw in the sacred flames the truth of their condition, and it was these who allowed themselves to dissolve, to be no more, and for them there came peace.

But Matt's devout clung to the will of their master, their mannequin forms untarnished by the fires. They shrieked his delusion into being, a wretched darkness that consumed the magic holding them captive.

Eleanor fought back. She was revitalized by Rosie's spell, transmuting magic into rebellious life, hurling light from the aurora at the dead, guiding a bombardment of her own creation against the denizens of emptiness. Each time the dead ones devoured her fires, she felt as if a thousand swords slashed her. But she fought on.

Exhaustion curled parasitic limbs over Rosie, making her spell wane, and will weaken. Percy saw and bit into his arm and spilled a circle of blood around her. She reacted without thought, drawing on the ancient power in his blood, transforming it into light and magic that seeped through her pores in a red mist, merging that power with the spell fueling Eleanor to fight on.

Magic warred with death. Torment warred with madness.

Throughout all of this, Alexander was like a man coming out of a delirium. The corpses were gone, and he stared about, unfocused, blinking, his mind unable to process what he was seeing. There was a tugging on his fingers. He looked and saw Pablo with his empty eye sockets staring at him. Guilt seized Alexander once more, but the boy cupped his hand, shook his head, and then pointed at Eleanor.

Alexander blinked, uncertain if what he was seeing was real. A torrent of emotion writhed in his chest, grief battling hope. He looked into the hollows of Pablo's eyes. The gunshot roared in his memory, and he saw the blood, and the slumping of Pablo's body. Guilt screamed with the shrillness of a fanatic accusing one of heresy.

"I'm sorry," he said.

Pablo shook his head and gripped his hand.

"Help them," he replied, his lips unmoving. He pointed again to Alexander's children.

Memories broke Alexander's daze. It all came back: the nightmare that had taken him, that had posed his children as corpses, and that had held him captive in a world between life and death. He remembered the figure in the hallway, remembered Matt's photo. He blinked with sudden clarity, looked at his daughter, and knew such relief at seeing her alive. He swelled with pride, watching her wield power that no other child could wield. He looked at his son standing like something shaped out of perdition as he squared off against the demented ghost, and the need to stand with him, with both of them, overcame all else.

He let go of Pablo's hand and felt the familiar thrum of magic flow around and through him, awakening a power he had, for a brief and awful eternity, forgotten.

Eleanor blazed with light. She moved as if from out of a dream, her arms upraised and swaying, orchestrating forces that composed the world. The dead ones eroded her fires with the darkness of their delusions and stormed at her. Their mannequin faces crumbled, revealing chaotic shapes that had long forgotten how to be human. They screamed into existence the fabric of a nightmarish reality that surged against her in great waves, and within this darkness she beheld whole other dimensions, each one designed to steal her from this place, to trap her, to make her lost. She summoned a wall of burning light, and there, darkness and light clashed, surging against each other. The light eroded the dead dimensions from within, but wilted against the constant barrage screamed into being by the ghosts. Eleanor trembled against the cold weight of death engulfing her. Tears streamed down her face, the aurora began to fade, and the wall of light collapsed about her in sagging sheets.

It would not be long before she fell.

They came as an army of fire, blazing figures rampaging against the folds of corruption surrounding Eleanor. She froze for a moment, and then shouted with unencumbered joy as Alexander Demidov emerged out of the gloom like a sorcerer of old, skin alight, hair whipping, arms upraised. The army of fire consumed the dread realities attacking Eleanor, and then surged at the ghosts in a barrage of flame and fury. The burden on Eleanor lessened, and she pulled with all of her might upon magic and that other indefinable force that channeled life itself into her hands.

Grass swelled into long blades that seized the struggling ghosts, and the aurora thundered down in hammer strikes, freezing them where they were, surrounding them in the mystery of life itself. They struggled to pull away, torn between their master's will and the magic entrancing them. The army of fire merged into a surging wave, and together father and daughter waged war against the delusional dead.

The demon assaulted Matt with a host of temptations until they were all the ghost could see. Something weakened in the wraith, his already crazed mind giving in as if he were an alcoholic locked in a room full of glittering bottles. He went from railing against the invading force to welcoming all it promised.

Ian pounced, penetrating into the frenzy of Matt's mind, fusing his will with the dead man's. The shadow merged with the panicked mannequin, and Matt fell inward and vanished.

A torrent of the dead man's memories flooded into Ian: so many voices and events speaking from times past, each one like a scroll the boy could unfurl and understand at the speed of thought, all of them windows into the truth of the man the ghost had once been.

Ian saw himself in them. He saw the moment that had defined his young life, the night his uncle had possessed him witnessed through a different set of eyes. He experienced what his uncle had felt in him, and the seed of a terrible understanding was planted, giving the boy knowledge of himself he had either denied or had been unaware of. He staggered against the weight of what Matt revealed and struggled to bury it so he could return to his task. Control of the dead man was within his grasp, the multitude of emotions and desires in Matt the key to taking command of his faculties and ending his dominion.

But before he could take hold, before he could seize possession, a memory of screaming endlessness erupted from the deepest and darkest part of Matt, overwhelming Ian with all the terrors of the void. He gasped and fell to his knees, inundated by visions of absolute nothingness where beings beyond description made their home in a place without time, order, or mercy. Endless dark captured him, howling with the ravaged and pleading cries of the itinerant dead, piercing with the truth of death itself. Ian froze under the stranglehold of the terror awaiting all living things. He had never known a greater fear. He stared blankly from his knees, seeing nothing.

What Ian experienced, Matt experienced as well. He remembered what he had created a world to forget. And once more, Ian had been the pebble that set the avalanche loose.

A roar thundered, Matt's agony exploding over everything. The dead swelled. What remained of their garish faces and mannequin bodies melted, releasing their true forms veiled and incomprehensible beneath folds of ruin. Hints peeked from beneath the roiling absence: limbs contorted in impossible angles, faces with features misplaced, twisted, monstrous, beings pretending at being human but no longer remembering how. The gluttonous and manic aspects

of their personalities shaped them into bastardizations beyond definition, and something more, something awful, an amalgamation of
fears held together by the desperate need to exist. To see them fully
was to renounce reason.

They devoured Eleanor's aurora. They drowned the long shoots
of defiant grass. They opened mouths contorted into impossible
shapes and swallowed Alexander's flood of fire. The truth of who
they were came through them from their master, and with that truth
emerged the full brunt of awfulness that had been buried under their
shared delusion.

Both father and daughter cried out. The ocean of magic that had
flowed through them was now lost, as if blocked by sheets of mile-
thick ice. Mere trickles teased their senses, and without magic, both
fell to the floor in exhaustion and pain. Rosie collapsed as well,
emptiness overpowering her. Percy held her and watched as ghosts
materialized like a tribe of nightmares shaped out of a madman's
mind. He turned away, unable to make sense of what he was seeing.
Rosie raised herself up, leaned against him, and shut her eyes.

The dead fell upon them, taking them one by one.

They were caught by corrupted and overlong limbs, melted and
shambling forms pinning them, sitting on their chests, and coiling
around their necks. Faces like things retched up by a dying god
appeared and disappeared.

The living struggled: Eleanor cursing and biting, Alexander
screaming his children's names, Rosie tossing her head in a wild bid
to get free, and Percy prying himself away with beastly growls, only to
be taken once more by an orgy of death.

Only Ian was still, his eyes vacant and far seeing, a strange smile
on his face as the dead wrapped themselves over him.

All light failed. Eleanor saw blackness and blurs. She heard her
father screaming, and then heard his screams go muffled. The air
trembled under a guttural voice rising into a bellow. The dead
screamed in kind, their voices a shared lament for all the things they
could never be again.

"My so-called fucking family," Matt said, his voice an earthquake, encircling them, coming from everywhere at once. The dead continued to scream, some rambling, others tittering, their cries inhuman. "Why can't you let me be good to you?"

Things without a name tightened their grips over Eleanor, and a host of faces emerged from the darkness before her. They were like masks made out of ancient skin held taut in invisible hands. Their eyes and mouths were crude lines emoting nothing. Behind them, a massive shape resolved into seeing, a great mountain ghoulish and deformed. Eleanor could barely make it out. Doom drummed in silent percussion, filling the child with the promise of all that was unclean. And she knew there was nothing more she could do.

"I try to get us all together," Matt said. "I made the goddamn effort. But all I get are lies! No more. You didn't kill me back then, and you can't kill me now. I'm still here. I'm in control, and you're gonna respect that. You're all gonna fall in line."

The faces loomed before Eleanor and the others. Their dead mouths and eyes began to open.

"You hurt me, Rosie," Matt said. "You're gonna have to work hard for me to forgive you. But I'll show you. You love me, you'll see. This needs to happen so you'll understand that I'm right for you. You have to let me in. Then you'll be part of my world, and we'll make things good again. You hear me, Eleanor? That goes for you too, for all of you. I'll forgive you when I see you finally understand that I know best. Then we'll be a family. Then we'll have a life together."

The dead faces opened their eyes, revealing glass orbs with green irises and too-large pupils. The mouths stretched wide until the lips thinned into rings of rot, unveiling phantoms within that laughed and cried and howled and reached out with emaciated hands.

Eleanor tried to pull away, to shake free, but the dead themselves were the darkness, and they imprisoned her, offering her to a fate she could not fathom. She heard the tinny strings of a waltz creaking from somewhere, ushering her towards madness and the beyond.

Here was the end.

A shockwave boomed like muted thunder.

The dead tensed, their yowling voices disappearing into a curtain of silence. The faces and the abominations they vomited retreated into the dark as if burned.

Matt whimpered.

"No," he said. "No, god, no."

Fog unfurled, illuminated by spectral light. Whispers hissed from out of the vapor, calling Matt's name, laughing, taunting.

The Emissary's chuckle rose above them.

The fog expanded. Shapes moved within. And then Jason was there, coalescing within the vapor, hovering at its center, tentacles of darkness emanating from him and transforming into mist.

Eleanor gasped. She went to call out to him, but dead hands clamped over her mouth, and Matt's voice growled in her ear.

Jason opened his eyes to reveal empty sockets that searched the surrounding dark. He felt the dead as if they were extensions of himself: their thoughts, emotions, and memories flowed into him, a storm of sensation stretching awareness well beyond his body and giving him understanding. The ghosts were the neurons of an ethereal brain and he the stem capturing control of its functions.

But there was another, a parasite gorging on his influence over the dead. Jason reached out to them, surprised at how easily he was able to push aside the usurper, and their rage transformed into confusion and awe, for within the boy they sensed something terrible but true.

But he could not control them.

He would have to make them see.

"He's lying to you," Jason said to the dead, speaking with an ancient and silent voice that had waited eons for him to shape into speech. "You're all dead. Do you feel it? I know you do. If you keep listening to him, you'll never be free. But I can save you."

They heard and screeched and cried out, for still they clung to their denial and Matt's delusion. Images of who they thought they were flooded Jason, bastardizations of their lives warped by desperation. Jason shuddered, but absorbed these visions. He thought for a moment, and then sent a silent command to the ghosts of the black forest. They acquiesced, saturating him with memories of the void, of the true state of the dead. These he funneled out to those in the outer dark, and their responding screams spoke of heartbreak, of rabid grief for these memories mirrored their own.

"If you hide from it," Jason said to them, "it'll find you. But if you help me, I can end it. I can give you peace."

A sudden barrage of postcard images and saccharine emotions assaulted the ghosts, Matt once more attempting to blind them to his will with promises of a false life. These penetrated beyond his acolytes to those of the black forest and to Jason himself. Many of Matt's acolytes clung to these delusions, their doubt turning into anger against Jason. But others understood the lie. They saw in Jason's words the tragedy of what they had become. They let themselves be taken into him, and Jason felt his power surge.

The fog deepened.

Jason reached out to those in the dark who still clung to their denial, showing them the black forest, letting them see and feel its sanctuary, its truth.

"I can keep you safe," he said. "You can make it yours, be whatever you need to be until you're finally free."

Matt's voice resounded:

"Liar! Liar! Liar!"

But more of his acolytes gave in, feeling hope for the first time in endless years. Matt had given them illusion and pleasures, and the boy offered bitterness. But within that bitterness was absolution, a fight worth struggling for, and a world that they could shape into their own.

"You'll be free," Jason said to them. "Just stand with me, and we'll all be free."

Still, they doubted. Jason felt their desperation emanating in waves of panic. Matt beat at the center like a rabid tick, clinging to his delusion and the source of his power. He sputtered, casting random thoughts throughout the dead. But these thoughts were decrepit, broken, the truth eroding his delusions.

Jason pressed, his very presence drawing the dead closer to themselves.

Footsteps echoed. A silhouette stopped at the edge of the mist. It emerged.

Jason stared into his mother's face.

"Baby," she said. "What's wrong? I heard you screaming. Were you having a nightmare?"

Jason looked up at her from his bed. The fog was gone, replaced by the familiarity of his room. Concern was writ on her face, sweet and kind, inviting no judgment. Warmth embraced him, promising relief. She went to brush hair from his brow. He succumbed to her touch, joy rising in gentle waves that were pulling him in—

He remembered Eleanor's face. He remembered the Emissary and the Black Forest.

"No," he said, slapping her hand away.

She stared, eyes hurt.

"Jason," she said, her voice begging for her little boy to accept her love.

Darius appeared behind her, laid his hands on her shoulders, and smiled with concern. Jason fell into those eyes. The warmth deepened, sliding into him, and golden light illuminated the room.

"He had a nightmare, Dari," his mother said.

"Aw, man," Darius replied. "You okay, papi?"

Jason longed to say yes, to tell them that he was okay, that he was exactly where he needed to be—

"My parents are dead," he said. The words flew out of his mouth.

"Jason!" his mother replied.

"You're dead."

"That's not funny, kid," his father said.

"You had a nightmare," his mother said. She patted herself down. "See? I'm right here. Got all my parts."

"You're not my parents. My parents are dead. They'll always be dead."

Their faces were shrines to broken hearts. Longing cried out in the boy, making him want to embrace them, erase all pain from their lives. But behind them he saw through the golden light to the cracked walls and the damaged shadows. He looked at his parents and let heartbreak wash over him. Beyond heartbreak waited truth shaped from the depths of time, long years of bloodshed and terror that saturated the world with that which was worse than his own pain. Jason knew his grief was one with a tragic tapestry that needed undoing. He was meant to bring an end to the suffering of the dead, and the only way to attend to his task was to accept his own pain.

"My parents are dead," he said. He did not allow himself to shed even one tear. "You ain't them."

He watched the illusion of his parents go cold and pale, then bloat, and finally wither into skeletal figures that collapsed into ash that filled the room. Fog poured through the fallout, and darkness surrounded. He was once more among the dead.

He had always been.

"So what?" a voice said behind him.

He turned. His mother was there, but a decayed thing, skin gray and corrupted, hands shriveled, eyes empty, hair limp and brittle over exposed ribs.

Her hollow eyes stared straight into his.

"Is this what you want?" she said, croaking. "Is this better than what we've offered you?"

"You're not my mother."

"We might as well be. Where do you think she is? Or your pops?" Darkness swelled over the specter, receded, and revealed the dead avatar of his father. "Do you think the truth is better? Why? What's the point? You're too young, anyway. You're not supposed to know about anything so...so fucking horrible. You're supposed to be happy. Instead, you refuse my kindness.

"Is this what you want? Do you want to live your life knowing this is what your parents are?"

The dead moaned from the darkness, succumbing to Matt's words.

"I want my friends back," Jason said. He glared at the ghost. "I'm tired of your lies. I want what's mine."

"Your friends?" Matt replied, his voice acid through Darius' mouth. He laughed. "You don't even know them! You think because they liked your pops that they're just gonna forget about this? They're gonna get rid of you first chance they get, maybe even kill you. They're not nice people. Me, I'm a nice person. You're in pain, kid. You need a break. I can give you that. I can make you forget this whole thing. Imagine it: this isn't real. You're sick. Your parents are so worried about you. They're watching over you as we speak. You can go back to them right now. You'll wake up and forget all about this. All you have to do is let go. No more nightmares. No more scary things. Just happiness."

Jason was silent for a moment. Doubt broke the surface of his mind and made him wonder where he would stand after all of this was done. He called Eleanor and her family his friends, but they were his father's friends. Were they not still strangers to him?

The mist threaded about him. He coiled his fingers through it, feeling the cold of what waited there, the unbearable truths he had learned. He remembered the warmth of his kitchen, of his parents near, the surety of a love that would never end. All of it so close, a few words away.

Something green flickered beneath his feet. He looked down and saw a single blade of grass standing within the mist in open defiance of absence. He saw in it the dream of time and life that was kind and hateful, pleasurable and painful. He saw existence and all of its horrors and wonders. He remembered Eleanor's face in the mirror. In it he had seen fear, but also determination. And he knew: life was not what you wished it to be, only what you made of it. He looked at the wraith before him. He shook his head.

"All lies," he said.

The dead puppet of his father glared, and then was ripped backwards. The darkness beyond the mist groaned like the hold of a ship full of prisoners.

"You wanna talk about lies?" Matt said. The darkness was his voice, booming. Jason spun around, trying to see everywhere at once. "Wanna know about your friends?"

Alexander emerged out of the darkness, hanging in midair, his chin lulling into his chest. Invisible hands dug into his hair, yanking his head up so he stared wild eyed at Jason.

"Why don't we ask our friend here how many people he's killed," Matt said. "Go ahead. Ask him about the kid he shot in the face. Or about all the times he turned my sister against me. Ask him about the time he considered killing your father."

Alexander and Jason locked eyes. Guilt pulled Alexander's face into a sorrowful mask. Before either could say anything to the other, Alexander was ripped backwards. Percy emerged next, struggling, teeth bared.

"How about asking our buddy here about how he abandoned your pops, huh?" Matt said. "How he left him alone to face a vampire, because he was too chicken-shit to stand with him. Ask him if he's ever eaten anyone. Go ahead, see what he says. Or this one..."

Percy was hurled backwards. Ian flew out, dangling by one arm, eyes blank, a dull smile on his face. He caught Jason in his gaze and perked up, looking without fear, without anger, somewhere between curiosity and excitement.

"'Poor Ian,'" Matt said, his voice a mocking singsong. "'His disgusting uncle hurt him so badly. He's such a good boy, even after everything that happened to him.' No one asked me why I did it. No one ever wondered what I saw in this...thing. You think he cares about you, or any of your friends? You think he won't turn on you as soon as he sees something in it for himself."

Ian went to speak, but was snatched back with the others. Rosie flew forward, grunting and pulling at the invisible force gripping her by the hair. She looked at Jason and shook her head, her eyes pleading with him not to listen.

"Liar!" Matt said. "Liar-liar-liar-liar! All this one ever did to me was lie. The fucked up thing is I still love her, even after all her bull-shit. But she couldn't tell the truth to save her life. She tell you what she did before she was the great spell maker, huh? Ask her how much she used to charge to suck dick. Ask her about the people she's robbed and killed. Ask her how she broke my heart, without flinching."

Rosie was ripped backwards.

"You're throwing away everything for liars, murderers, and a whore. You don't know these people. Not like I do, not even close. You don't owe them anything. I offer you paradise, and you shit all over it for strangers. But it's not too late. You can walk away. You can leave me to my family, and I can leave you to yours. Whatever happened, I still love them. So don't worry. I'll take good care of them, teach them to be right.

"Just go with your parents. They're waiting for you in the real world. You deserve better. You can have better. Walk away. Just go, and the rest of your life will be golden, little man. Golden."

Jason considered. He looked into the dark.

"What about Eleanor?" he said. "What's she done?"

Matt was silent. All of his cajoling, his desperation, and his angry pleading sent realization flaring through Jason. The boy grinned, a cruel and dead smile shining with malicious glee beneath empty eyes.

"Know what you just did, dead man?" he said. "You just showed me that you're scared."

Matt screamed, his voice raging, commanding the dead to seize Jason.

They didn't.

Matt sputtered, screamed again, but the dead would not obey.

Jason finally understood. It had come to him at the end of Matt's desperate tirade, the absolute knowledge that the power the ghost wielded belonged to him, and no other. Doubt vanished and released a weight in his chest, and with that release, came control. The dead were not a part of him. They were him, and his will was their will. The shift of power rippled through the revenants, the denial that had been crippled by Eleanor's magic, now broken by the truth of Jason's certainty.

For Jason, Eleanor had been the final spark. He saw through Matt's memory to the wonderful things she had created, just as he had seen life shine in the lone blade of grass. Eleanor was existence as it should be, and the boy understood that in order to protect life he had to accept his role as the savior of death.

The fog swelled over the darkness, revealing Eleanor and her family. Dead hands gripped them, but these hands dissolved into ash. The dead themselves faded into the fog, their horrid forms veiled, now silhouettes, and this way they were closer to their lost humanity.

Matt continued to scream, but Jason silenced him and then ripped him into the open with a thought. Matt wailed, a pitiful sound, the crying of desperate child. His mannequin form exploded, rupturing dust over the ground. He was there, crumpled, a corpse surrounded by the broken shards of his mannequin body. He pressed the cracked pieces of his mannequin face to his true face, trying to piece it together.

"I'm not dead," he said, whimpering. "I'm not dead. I'm not—"

"Oh, Matty-Matty-Matty," the Emissary said, charging at Matt from out of the mist, ready to wreak vengeance. "So good to see you again, Matty. Time for you to pay, Matty."

"No," Jason said.

The Emissary stopped without a word.

Jason vanished into the fog and reappeared before Matt. He stared at him with his black hole eyes, bent low, and lifted Matt's chin.

Matt gasped as all of his memories flooded into the boy. The darkness of Jason's eyes transfixed him.

"Look," Jason said.

A rift opened, swallowing Matt, and he fell and fell and...

Matthew Moore started awake, shivering, a sheen of sweat coating his skin. He sat at the bar. The melodic crash of Metallica blared, a procession of guitars and bass following the march of beating drums. Matt clutched his chest, feeling the languid fabric of his football jersey. He saw himself in the mirror across, a brutish man with intelligent green eyes and cherubic jowls, his hair thinning and brown. He stared at himself, overcome by relief.

The bar was empty. Stools were arrayed to his left and right. Weak pink light shone from a neon sign blinking at the window announcing K.C Moore's to the world. The music stomped through the speakers, echoing. Dread hovered at the edge of Matt's relief. He stood on the stretchers of his stool, leaned over the bar, and found an open eighteen pack of bottled beer beside freshly washed glasses. He grabbed a bottle, placed the edge of the cap against the lip of the bar, and slapped it off with the palm of his hand. The cap ricocheted without a sound. He drank with greedy abandon, relishing the bitter sweet bubbles pouring past his lips, over his tongue, and down his throat. He paused, took a breath, and drank again, finishing. He stood the empty bottle on the bar and looked up at a television screen showing a running back pounding through flailing linemen, only to be hit from the side, fumbling the ball. Another screen followed a rushing hockey forward missing the puck as he slapped at it.

Matt stared at these things, the failures on the screens summoning some grim certainty he could not comprehend. He looked behind the bar and saw pictures hanging to the left of the mirror. He got up on unsteady legs, walked around the bar, and looked at the pictures. He saw himself in each and every one, surrounded by strange blotches and blurs shaped out of gritty darkness.

"The fuck?" he said. Each image pulled at his attention, as if they were portals luring him into the past. The edges of his vision softened. A carousel of memories spun all around him, saturating him in a bevy of emotions and experiences that carried faces and smells and sounds, pains and pleasures, places both loved and hated and uncared for, the whole of a human life.

"Nah, I'm not doing that," a voice said behind him.

He turned around and gave a violent start. The bar was gone. He stood in a basement he had not seen in years, a place whose filth he could still taste like metallic ash coating his tongue. The flickering glow of an electric lamp sent erratic shadows dancing over smooth concrete walls and the orchestrated chaos of painter's cloth on the floor. Concrete steps rose into darkness at the back of the basement.

Matt went still, remembering every detail of what happened in this place so many years before, not wanting to see it again. But he saw himself seated a few feet away, a lithe and muscular teenager with vivid green eyes. His hands dangled between his knees and a gun lay at his feet. Sweat soaked through a Megadeth t-shirt, folding the leering image of a skeleton into quarters.

Matt gaped in wonder and fear, watching his past unfold, unable to look away. His father, Patrick Moore, stood beside a dartboard, his arms crossed, his features muted by shadow.

A stuttering breath trembled from the right, and Matt looked and saw Phoebe seated beside three five-gallon buckets of plaster. Her face was buried in her arms and knees, obscured by curls. Her hands were raised as if in supplication, blood dripping in streaming rivulets from their slender forms and coating her arms. A hammer stood on its eye before her feet, lathered in blood, flesh, and yellowed bone.

Beyond the hammer lay the dying man.

He convulsed on the floor, naked, a frail creature with a bouquet of pink tulips tattooed on the lower right of his abdomen. Spit bubbled from his lips and over his dark features, and his eyes rolled white in their sockets. A dead man lay to his right. He was squat and brown and missing one side of his head. Blood and brain matter coated the floor around the corpse in abstract streaks.

Matt's younger self rocked back and forth, shaking his head, a stubborn light in his eyes.

"I ain't fucking do this," his younger self said.

"Put him out of his misery," Patrick replied.

"Nah. You made us do enough."

"You telling me Phoebe's got more balls than you? Huh? Man up. It's a hard world. Demons posses people. It's what we do. Now you can let him suffer, or you can finish him off. I don't really give a shit. All I know is I ain't doing it for you."

"Matty, don't," Phoebe said, raising a tear streaked face. "I'll do it. Just go."

His younger self waited for a moment, as if holding out was a great act of defiance. Then he picked up the gun and walked over to the man. Phoebe cringed, covered her ears, and looked away. He pulled the trigger. The gun roared, clashing against the walls, a bitter flash of powder and smoke. The convulsing man's head rocked against the floor, and then was still, a smoking crater of flesh and bone where his cheek had once been. His younger self grimaced against the report, clutching at one ear in pain.

"My fault," Patrick said. "Should've brought ear plugs."

"Fuck, dad," his younger self replied. Pain and something worse was etched across his face.

Matt remembered the ringing, the sensation of metal wire in his ears, the sting incessant. Those things had been nothing to the hollow pit of regret that screamed for the dead man at his feet to stand up, to be well, to walk away and live on. He watched his younger self fighting to suppress the sickness bursting through him.

"I can't watch this," he said.

Something moved on the stairs. He looked up and saw Jason there, gripping the twisted balusters. He whipped away, for the boy was a portent of doom, a harbinger of the unknown come to claim him. He saw his father approach his younger self and clap him on his shoulder like a coach congratulating an athlete. He turned his back to the scene.

Jason hovered before him like some horror out of a children's fairy tale.

"No," Matt said, overcome by invading snakes of dread, feeling some bitter truth about to open its lips and speak. He backed away and covered his eyes and prayed to wake well away from horrors and darkness and murder.

Warm daylight spilled over his skin.

He opened his eyes to the sight of green leaves dancing in and out of an open window. Shafts of smoky sunlight drifted into what had once been his living room. The carpeted floor, the low rolling table, a basketball by a closet overflowing with laundry, posters of Metal bands, a guitar stand beside a leather chair, all the chaotic geography of a place he had once called home

He once more saw his younger self, a few years older, with love handles beginning to bulge through his white tank top. His younger self took a swig of beer and stood the can on the table beside three crumpled empties. He tweaked the knobs of an electric guitar in his hands and squinted as he strummed and tuned, the electric twang clear and clean over the reverb from the amp.

"I think you're good," Phoebe said. She sat across from him, on the other side of the table, a sleek black guitar glinting in her hands.

"Mm," his younger self replied. "You ready?"

They bobbed their heads to a silent count and then strummed together, their speakers an explosion of fuzzy dissonance. Phoebe's fingers danced over the fretboard, and Matt watched his younger self strum chords he could never forget, an apocalyptic rhythm underscoring the frenetic assault of his sister's melody.

A brief moment of peace was his: standing there, engulfed by one of the few memories of his life that carried with it something beautiful and complete.

His younger self peeled off a final lick with squinted eyes and puffed out cheeks. Phoebe laughed and threw a crushed beer can at him. In the soft daylight, she was like an angel of mischief. How like her daughter she looked.

Daughter? he wondered.

"It's time to stop hiding, Matt," Jason said.

"No," Matt replied, the word bursting out of him. "Please, just let me stay here."

The daylight failed, dripping like melted wax. The living room vanished under bleeding darkness. Long ropes of cold overcame Matt and dragged him through the space between his memories, pulling him past the myriad experiences of his life just out of reach. He clawed at them, praying for purchase, knowing but unable to acknowledge where it was he was bound.

He felt hard concrete beneath his feet, and flickering light beat against the dark from two rows of gas lamps hanging parallel over gray walls. He whimpered, knowing what was to come. Phoebe was there, her face no longer bright. Her eyes were red rimmed, scalded by tears, and her expression was rage chiseled out of granite. Alexander stood beside her, a revolver glinting in his hand. Rosie was beside him, and Percy stood with his arms crossed against the opposite wall, turned away as if unable to look at what was about to happen.

Others were there, many of their faces glimmering outlines in the dark. Matt recognized Cedric McGill, his features stoic, his eyes betraying the pity one has for a rabid animal. Deirdre and Hank Olson were beside him, both expressionless, their hands clasped together. Close by were Radek Stempian, Eitan Verad, Richard Horowitz, others...all a mixture of anger and disbelief.

Panic seized Matt. He stared among the familiar faces and found grim resolve, people who would not be swayed from their task. Something he had not wanted to remember faced him, something he could not abide. He followed their gazes to the floor and saw himself shivering on his knees, mumbling, laughing through tears, and bleeding from a vicious cut over his inflamed left eye.

"No," he said, overwhelmed by the deepest sense of horror he had ever known, for now he knew what was to come. Cold hands gripped him out of oblivion unseen, forcing him to watch.

"Look," Jason said in his ear. The boy hovered beside him, an eyeless face in the dark.

Alexander stepped out from the group. His knuckles were red with Matt's blood. He stared at the babbling man on the floor with intense hatred, his lip curled, his eyes merciless. He pointed the gun at Matt's head, pressing it into his scalp. The babbling man looked up at him, tears streaming, eyes wide with terrified lucidity even as the words careened past his lips.

"...the boy is no good I did you a favor he will kill us all you have to believe it was good it felt really good I made him scream the little bastard deserved it asked for it I possessed him so I could stop him and he liked it cause he's a little shit..."

Alexander glared at Matt and saw sorrow and panic in his eyes, as if another were inside, begging for him to see that he could not stop speaking, that he was saying what was beyond his will to stop. Alexander looked away, a moment of doubt taking hold, making him drop the gun an inch away from Matt's head. Matt kept rambling, talking of the possession and Ian, of the joy it gave him, of all the horrible things the boy deserved.

Alexander raised the gun to finish his task and pressed his finger to the trigger, when Phoebe snatched the gun from him. He went to take it back from her, but she pressed the gun against Matt's brow in a fluid motion.

"No!" Matt said, screaming at a memory he knew would never hear him, desperate beyond anything to spare him from the inevitable. "Phoebe, please, no! Please, god, no!"

Phoebe pulled the trigger. The gun spoke. The memory was obliterated by waves of darkness erupting from everywhere, drowning everything in an endless ocean of undying that revealed once and for all the thing he had run from, the thing he had stolen Jason's power to conceal, the thing that he had lost his mind denying.

He was a dead thing, a ghost flailing blindly through a void teeming with ancient horrors that babbled and laughed and screamed and sang. The memory of his birth into oblivion engulfed him, and he saw nothing else.

There was no more hiding.

Here was the truth, and nothing more.

To Eleanor and the others all huddled together, it had been an instant. Jason had consumed Matt with a shroud of darkness spewed from his eyes, and then released him screaming like a tortured child. The ghost collapsed onto the ground, a bloated carcass of rot, the final pieces of his mannequin face collapsing to the ground and shattering into dust. He writhed, shaking the ruin of his head, babbling, mewling. Darkness smoked from a wound in his forehead. The space about him wavered into distortion, and he took on the form of an agonized blur.

Jason drifted down to the floor, assaulted by the barrage of loss emanating from Matt, a great mass of pain, regret, and sorrow. Jason trembled, aware of the void, of the great terror constantly felt by the dead. To Matt, it was a monster endlessly chasing him, and all of Jason's anger turned to pity. He could not hurt the ghost, would not banish him back into the unending emptiness.

Power beat through him with a simplicity that he could not believe. His thoughts were forces of death, and without his denial and without Matt or any other specter blocking him, he marveled at the connection he felt with the netherworld. He reached through the dread dimension of the void with that growing extrasensory awareness. A wound opened in the air, bled darkness, and revealed the Black Forest. He had beckoned, and it had come. The Emissary appeared at his side and sighed with satisfaction. The ghosts of the forest murmured and whispered, among them Pablo who walked to its edge and reached a hand to touch the low branches of a tree.

Alexander gasped as he saw the boy appear at the forest's edge, a myriad of emotions making him numb.

Ian stared with fascination at the trees and the mist, and then focused on Jason with the wonder of one who knows many incredible things are to come.

Rosie and Percy were in each other's arms, both terrified and in awe.

Eleanor smiled. Despite the horror, despite the darkness, there was something in the forest that she recognized. For a moment a brief wisp of light beat within the mist and the trees, and the magic inside of her responded by shimmering over her hands.

Jason looked at Matt for a long time. The ghosts of the forest–Matt's acolytes now no different, save for their shared wonder—awaited his word. Anger beat through them for their once master, and for themselves. But there was also grief and pity. The void was always there, a layer of filth underlining everything, driving them all to madness. Matt had simply succumbed.

Jason spoke his silent command. Mist enshrouded Matt, and there, whimpering, weeping, he was transported into the Black Forest. A measure of gratitude rippled through his once-acolytes, and Matt was now among their number. Jason felt him as he felt the others. Grief and anger still beguiled the wayward ghost, but relief was there as well, for he recognized respite in the trees. The branches beckoned. Paths parted through the mist, revealing a boundless land of hills and mystery. And within, Matthew Moore disappeared.

The other dead remained.

"Go," Jason said.

They remained. He felt them like chess pieces he could force into movement, but he waited, wanting them to move of their own will. They surrounded him, distorted shapes with terrible faces and absent eyes. The living watched, feeling the wrongness of beings that should not exist. Pablo looked back at Alexander, smiled a sad smile, and vanished into the fog. Alexander shivered, struggling not to weep. Eleanor watched with horrified fascination, wondering at the brief moment of magic she was certain she had witnessed in the dead land. Ian smiled. For what reason, none can say. Rosie shook her head, her rapid mind already understanding that this is what Darius had meant, that this was the power coming to wreak havoc upon the vampires. Percy swallowed and grimaced, seeing before him a force he knew could not be contained, save for the will of the boy.

Jason looked among the dead faces. The Emissary floated before him, silent.

It bowed.

One by one the dead followed.

Jason felt it then: what he had taken back from Matt, the piece of himself that had lain waiting all his young life. He did not see the boy outside among those dead faces, for the boy outside was now within.

The dead bowed, and their silent voices whispered fealty. Then they began to fade backwards into the forest, all ghosts of the forest now, his servants, dissolving into mist. The Emissary remained, floating before Jason. The mist itself roiled, thickened, dissipated, and the forest was gone.

And they were in Rosie and Percy's living room.

Alexander wiped his eyes, saw his children, and hurried over to them. Eleanor flew into his arms, and Ian joined their embrace. Rosie and Percy fell in with them, and they huddled together at the center of the living room. Outside it was night. Snow fell. The clock on the wall read 3 AM.

Jason bowed his head, and when he looked up again his eyes were gray and alive. The Emissary remained. He looked at the ghost, and the ghost looked back. The others broke from their embrace and stared. Save for Alexander, they were still adorned in the ragged clothing Matt had selected for them. Their eyes were wide and wild, their expressions uncertain, and Jason realized that they were not looking at him but at the Emissary. Jason made to speak, but instead rubbed his head and barked a maniac laugh. He shook his head and mumbled to himself, longing to express remorse, not knowing how to begin.

Eleanor stood. She stumbled, and then limped towards him. Alexander went to pull her back, but she raised her hand to stop him. Jason went to her, unable to look at first, and then forcing himself to meet her eyes. Between them was life and death, the ineffable powers that had saved them all from a madman. Eleanor frowned, trying to piece together all she had seen and heard. Of one thing she was certain: he had saved them. She had seen and heard all Matt had offered, and she understood that Jason had given up happiness to save them.

She smiled.

Jason smiled back. Then, without realizing what he was doing, he embraced her. She started, wide eyed, and almost pulled away. But then she brought both arms around him, and they held each other, both relieved that the other was alive.

Jason pulled away. He seemed almost embarrassed. Eleanor shrugged, as if to say "shit happens." She looked over his shoulder at the Emissary and took an involuntary step back. Alexander reached out and held her, and the others waited.

"Yes, bright child," the Emissary said to Eleanor. "You are right to fear us."

Eleanor and the others looked from the Emissary to Jason with expectation. Jason went to speak, but the Emissary laid a gloved hand on his shoulder.

"Allow us. We are the Emissary, at your service. We have much-much-much to tell…"

ACT V

MAY THE DARKNESS SAVE US

1

The Emissary told.

It told much of what it knew.

Jason watched the horror on their faces, the despair in their eyes, and the concern over loved ones and others who were lost to the void.

He saw distaste, hatred, and fear when the Emissary spoke of vampires.

Most of all, he saw the way they looked at him when it was over—when they knew all he knew, when they understood that it was up to him to set death right again.

Silence lingered after the tale was told. Cool light infused the air and softened the living room into hushed blues. Streaks of amber unfolded across the sky, and shadows stretched, fading into an ethereal haze that unveiled shattered doors and damaged walls.

But around the Emissary, all was darkness and absence, the light failing before reaching the wraith.

They had gotten out of the clothing Matt had picked for them and into familiar wear: Percy and Rosie in sweats and t-shirts, Eleanor in an oversized sweater and her father's coat. Ian had his wounds cleaned by his father and then healed by Rosie. Then he put on a baggy pair of jeans and one of Percy's shirts emblazoned with a Wu Tang Clan logo. Alexander was still dressed as he had been, but discolored splotches stained his shirt.

The ballroom outfits had been placed in garbage bags, and there they had dissolved into soot.

They each processed the Emissary's words.

Percy combed through his history for any moment that may have hinted at the terrible truth they had been told. He reeled to think that the centuries he had lived had been at the cost of all those trapped in a lifeless prison. Guilt took him, as he realized that he felt gratitude for his immortality. He would not hide from it. Though he wished it not to be so, and though he resolved to learn the full scope of the truth and help Jason on his quest, he was too old and too tired to deny his own feelings. He knew to rule over oneself was to know thyself, and he clutched tight to Rosie's hand and shivered both with gratitude that she was here and from the realization that, should Jason fail, she along with everyone else would find themselves in the vast emptiness of undeath.

Anger thrummed through his heart. That Darius would leave them so ill prepared.

He shook his head.

"Bloody fool."

"On that we agree, Percy-Percy Bowles," the Emissary replied, knowing who Percy was referring to.

"Why didn't he tell us, then?"

"There was, perhaps, some wisdom in the magician's reticence. He could not have known how you would react, or if you would have even believed him, no-no-no. Would you still have taken the boy in? Would you have tried to summon a loved one out of the depths? What if-what if-what if...too many possibilities. The magician should have told the boy all, should have helped him to understand his power, and together we could have shown you the truth. What's done is done. But he was not wrong in another respect: this is dangerous knowledge. You are all now burdened by a plan that has many enemies, both in life and death. To know the dead is to invite them in."

"This is madness," Percy said.

"The worst kind, Percy-Percy Bowles."

Percy fell silent.

Rosie attended terror as if it were a contaminated thing, something to be respected but locked away. Matt's voice slithered in her memory, and she understood his madness, could not fault him for it.

She refocused on Jason, on what he needed to do. Darius had said the boy would kill the vampires, and now she understood if not the how then the why of it. The vampires' awfulness retched inside of her, making her lip quiver and her eyes burn. They would pay. The words beat like a refrain through her mind. They would pay.

How many have I sent into the pit? Alexander wondered. He stared at his hands, at their strong ridges and broad knuckles, remembering all the times they had worked death on people who had threatened his life and the lives of those he had loved. Always that justification: to protect, to uphold righteousness—but at the cost of blood and, now he understood, people's very souls. Phoebe looked at him from beyond time, and he hung his head to think of her in an endless place of emptiness and horror.

He looked up at the Emissary.

"My..." he said. But then he looked to his children and became afraid of what the answer may be, of what they would have to face if their mother was in fact a lost and insane wraith.

The Emissary watched him, sighing gently.

"Never-never fear, Demidov. The one once known as Phoebe belongs to the forest."

Alexander gasped. Eleanor clutched her father. Tears spilled, and she could not help but laugh. The faintest smile crept over Ian's face. Rosie clutched her hands together as if in prayer, and Percy rocked back and forth on the sofa.

"Can we see her?" Eleanor said.

"No," the Emissary replied. "You would not want to see her, bright child, no. Not this way. Perhaps in time. For now, know she is as close to peace as the dead can be."

Alexander held both of his children close.

Ian smiled, his head resting on his father's shoulder, wondering over all he had seen within Matt. Such darkness. Such pain. The brutality he had suffered was forgotten, buried in the countless sensations he had stolen from the ghost. How they had expanded his knowledge of suffering. How that knowledge would strengthen his ability to do what was necessary in protecting his home.

He looked at Jason and understood the boy had come for them when he could have fled, and that loyalty was something that won the demon's respect. Beyond that was the knowledge that Jason was a portal to mystery, to the itinerant dead and all they would unveil. Excitement hummed within Ian. But there was something else in his look, a faint glint, the strangest light, as if a secret knowledge had been imparted upon him and him alone.

A storm of emotions beat within Eleanor.

Through exhaustion and pain, she had been granted relief. Her mother was, if not safe, at least in a place with those who were fighting against the dark, who remained something close to whole.

Then there was the magic that had offered succor in a place of death, that mysterious power that was life itself. It had been entrusted into her hands, and Eleanor had been able to wield it against the dead. Why her? She did not know. But she was grateful.

She thought of her uncle and wondered at his claim, that she had been born a demon. A near-overwhelming sensation took hold, a tide of confusion fed by refusal and acceptance. Her head ached to consider it, and she could not handle that conversation just yet.

Instead, she turned to Jason, allowing confusion to evolve into awe. She saw in him not the terrors of a monstrous existence, but the resiliency of goodness in the face of evil. He could put a stop to the nightmare. She looked around at the faces of her family and knew that they all could.

They were silent.

Jason stood, weighing their silence. He had heard the truth told twice, and the second time deepened it, made it more real. Even here, in the living world, he felt the void, felt the forest, heard it all in his mind like the howl of hurricanes and the whisper of leaves. The Emissary was not just beside him. It and the other dead were as his thoughts, a constant stream of awareness too jumbled to fully understand. But there was something else to the Emissary, something he recognized above the others. He laughed to himself. He liked the Emissary. He had made a friend, and that friend was a ghost.

That realization brought another truth.

He was dangerous. He had some control, but the Emissary had spoken of things within the void—terrible things. Something worse could come through him. He looked at Eleanor and felt another kind of connection, something reserved for the living, something precious. He could not risk destroying that.

He sighed.

"I shouldn't be here," he said. They all looked at him. "I shouldn't...This was my fault. You all almost...I shouldn't be here."

Silence followed. Eleanor stared at Jason, hurt in her eyes. Ian shook his head. The adults looked at one another, and Alexander wondered if perhaps...

"Way I see it," Rosie said, looking at Jason, "your daddy was right: you definitely need to be with us. It's a bigger risk than we thought, that's for damn sure, but it's worth it. We gotta keep you right where we can see you. We gotta keep you safe."

"What if this happens again?" Jason replied.

"Then you better bloody well deal with it, yeah?" Percy said. A hard edge tinged his voice, but there was compassion, too. "You're father's a right bastard for doing this to us. But he was right. You belong here. When the time comes, you'll have our support. I'll see to that myself."

"We're the good guys, right?" Eleanor said.

"That right, Sis," Ian replied. Strange light beat in his eyes. His shadow was perched beside him, watching, and, for a moment, they all swore that they heard it laugh.

Jason sat down on the floor. He looked up at them one last time, expecting them to turn against him. They didn't. His eyes landed on Alexander's. Alexander looked away, cleared his throat, and stood.

"Well, if we're all in agreement, I'd like to get my children home." He gestured to Ian and Eleanor. "Come."

"Nope," Ian replied.

"Sorry, Pop, but you can suck it," Eleanor said.

"Alex, we've got a lot to sort out, mate," Percy said. "We shouldn't go through everything now. I know I can't. But we should...Why don't you go get them some proper clothes. Then we'll discuss what we can. Go on, we'll watch them."

Alexander hesitated. He looked again at Jason. Something accusatory lingered in his gaze, and he seemed at war with himself.

Percy almost sneered.

"Would you rather I go?"

Alexander gave him a flat look. He turned for the door.

"Mr. Demidov," Jason said. Alexander looked at him. "I'm really sorry. I would never want to hurt any of you. Especially...I mean...I swear, I won't let this happen again."

Alexander nodded, and then walked out. He carried his doubts, fears, and frustrations into the hallway where he stopped and stood like a man caught between opposing currents. He collapsed against the wall, pressing his forehead against the cool surface, breathing in bursts. He pounded once with his fist, torn between the relief at knowing his children were alive, and the terror of everything they had been through. That they had suffered at the hands of a crazed ghost. That such a thing were possible, and he powerless to protect them.

He remembered the child he had been forced to kill. Pablo had looked at him one last time, a phantom lost between worlds, waving goodbye to the man who had set him adrift. The forest was supposed to be a place of respite, but what solace there? What solace for any of them?

An apartment door clicked open. Alexander composed himself and hurried to the stairwell, knowing he could not let anyone else see him this way. His children needed clothing. There was a task he could attend, the only one that mattered. But as he walked to the stairs, the shadows of the hallway seemed like deceptive waters, and as he opened the stairwell door, his heart thundered. True horror waited beneath everything. Death was no release. Sweat dripped over his neck, the stairwell was deep and dark, and it was only the love of his children that carried him home.

2

Percy looked up at the Emissary. The ghost seemed to feel his gaze and twisted its head to stare back. Watching the ghost was like looking through an endless mirage. The skull mask steadied, only to stretch and warp and bleed in and out of being. Long black strands dripped from it, coiled, and vanished.

Questions swarmed, but Percy saw them as vague apparitions contorted by the presence of the specter.

They all shared his distaste.

Jason caught their glances, stood, and turned to the Emissary.

"Can you go for a bit?" he said.

The Emissary bowed. Ropes of mist and shadow enfolded it, and it was gone. The room brightened, the ghost taking with it an abscess in reality that distorted all light.

Eleanor sighed without meaning to, heralding relief from the others. Only Ian seemed unfazed, placid and staring inward.

They were silent. Morning brightened the sky, and window shades opened in opposite buildings.

Eleanor sneezed and wiped her nose with her forearm.

"Bless you," Jason and Ian said together. They exchanged a look, and Jason shrugged.

"Thanks," Eleanor replied. She picked at the sleeve of Rosie's sweater. "So...is everyone okay?"

The daylight and her question opened them up. They spoke of Matt. They spoke of ghosts and the impossibilities they had seen, their voices hushed, even as clouds gleamed in the sky. Excitement took hold, as if they were soldiers sharing experiences of a terrible firefight, reflecting from a distance to keep themselves free of the fear in their hearts.

Ian spoke little, and Jason spoke less. The two boys locked eyes, as Rosie explained to Eleanor the depths of Matt's obsession with her. Something passed between the demon and the ghost child, as if for a moment each could see the future in the other. Ian smiled. Jason could not help but smile back, unsure why at first and then understanding that what he saw in Ian's eyes was acceptance. The adults struggled to hide their misgivings, and Eleanor did nothing to hide her concern. He minded neither. The adults would have been foolish to not have doubts, and it was Eleanor's kindness that had given him the strength to balk Matt's illusion. But in Ian he saw an otherness, a living reflection of his own darkness smiling back at him without flinching.

A knock came at the door, and Alexander walked in. His head was bowed, and he cradled coats, jeans, and sweaters in the crook of his arm. A plastic bag held two pairs of sneakers.

"Aw, man," Eleanor said, as clothing was passed to her. "I lost my hoodie. I loved that thing. Not complaining though. We're alive, so, yay."

She grabbed her clothes, dropped them, and went to pick them up. Rosie grabbed them and motioned Eleanor to follow. They made for the bathroom, both limping, grunting.

Eleanor froze by the door.

"Can you come in with me?" she said.

Rosie hesitated, remembering the awful vision in the mirror. How would she adjust to everyday tasks? How..? She pushed the questions aside and took a deep breath. They had always faced the worst.

Though she knew things were different, she also knew they were still the same.

"Sure thing, darling."

They went inside.

Ian was already changed when they returned. Percy spoke in hushed tones, and Alexander absently nodded along. Jason sat on the floor, staring out the window at the slanted shaft of light gleaming over the white bricks of the buildings.

"...think we have to reconsider what we tell the Council about the other night," Percy said. He waited for Alexander to reply. Alexander's eyes were dazed and distant. "Alex?"

"Eh...I'm sorry...I think we should save this for later."

Percy scratched his head.

"Alex..." He sighed, seeing that his friend was not ready. "Right. We could all do with some rest. But soon, yeah?" He turned to Rosie. "There's a lot we have to discuss."

"I know it," Rosie replied.

Alexander was silent.

His children put on their coats, and he waited, warmth shining from his eyes at seeing them alive.

"Well," he said. He looked at Jason and frowned. He saw his best friend in the boy. But he saw death and horror as well. He turned and walked out.

Ian smiled at Jason.

"See you later," he said.

He followed his father. Rosie frowned after him. Eleanor did the same, and both exchanged a look.

"He seems alright," Rosie said. But a question was implied in her tone: how could he be so unfazed?

"...Yeah," Eleanor replied, not wanting to think on it. She went to Rosie and embraced her and did the same to Percy. Percy was taken aback. He jolted as if from reverie, smiled, and hugged her back.

"You're really something, you know that?" he said. She smiled, and then frowned from the aches beating at her muscles and the memory of what they had endured.

"Sleep now, praise later," she replied, kissing his nose.

She went to Jason. He stood. They looked at each other.

"Just so you know," she said. "This wasn't your fault."

"That's not true."

"It is. I'll show you, don't worry." She pointed at herself. "Really stubborn. Hey, uh, thanks for saving us and everything."

"Way I hear, that was mostly you."

"Eh, just did a few magic tricks. No biggie. Ow. I need sleep."

But she lingered. Despite the lightness of her voice, fear was there, ingrained into her by her time in Matt's world, and by the Emissary's story.

"I'm sorry," Jason said.

Eleanor shrugged.

"How's anyone supposed to be ready for something like this? It ain't on you. But no more running. You have friends. Stick with me, kid, I'll take ya places."

They looked at each other, a seed planted between them, a connection rooted into the very air they shared—

She punched him on the shoulder. He cried out in surprise.

Then she waved at Percy and Rosie and followed her father and brother out.

Jason smiled after her, grateful for the way she pulled back the curtains of darkness in his heart to reveal life shining bright and unwavering, an absurd candle burning with laughter in the face of all this madness. She made him wonder if perhaps he and everyone else were more than just prisoners in a dreadful universe.

He turned to Percy and Rosie. They were silent. He shifted from one foot to the other, mussed his hair, and gave a slight twitch.

"Are you sure you don't want me to leave?" he said.

They didn't respond. Rosie looked at both of them.

"Hell of it is," she said, massaging her cheeks. "I ain't even tired anymore."

"I'm starving," Percy replied.

"Hell yes, I can eat."

They turned to Jason.

"Well?" Percy said.

"Huh?' Jason replied.

"You're a famous cook and all that, yeah?"

"I, uh...what? Now?"

Jason thought he would need time to—

Be alone? He realized that was the last thing he wanted. He looked at the kitchen. Sunlight streamed through the window, glistening against the table. To cook a meal seemed like a luxury after all he had been through. He turned back to Percy and Rosie, made to speak again as if in testimony against himself, as if they did not understand the depths of his awfulness. What he found in their eyes was not ignorance, but clear understanding. He was a monster. But so were they. The ghost child stood before the werewolf and the magician, and all of them were hungry.

"We still gotta clean up," he said.

"I took care of most of that," Percy replied. "The rest won't take long."

"The cupboards—"

Rosie waved her fingers in response.

"Magic."

"The living room..."

"I got that, too," Rosie replied.

Jason nodded, took off his black hoodie, draped it carefully over the sofa, and walked into the kitchen.

Percy and Rosie shared a look of uncertainty.

Rosie gestured with her hands, and in that movement was the shared knowledge that they were in this together. Percy nodded. It would always be so.

They held hands and followed after the boy they had taken in as their own.

3

Dreams.

She floated across emptiness twisted by cold and vagrant screams. Pain seared into a place deeper than her physical body, an awareness that permeated everything. Talons of metallic darkness clawed and cut, and she cried out and struggled until the dark itself broke with a great crack. Light spilled forth, and she broke through a crust of dead earth, rising green and shimmering into long forgotten sunlight—

Eleanor awoke.

Late afternoon shadows clung to her room. She clutched Ringo, grateful to feel the softness of the bear in her arms. A roaring ache wrung her muscles into twisted sheets of discomfort. The dream faded, but something of it had been planted deep inside, making the child wonder at the space of missing time ripped from the memory of her ordeal. There had been the bar, and then she had awoken on the canopy bed.

In between...

She hugged Ringo tighter and shivered uncontrollably. Panic stampeded, an overflow of latent terror frothing to the surface in seismic blasts. She breathed through the sensation of coming doom, allowing herself to be afraid, to feel powerless, to be all of the things she knew she couldn't be when faced with terror. She whispered that it could not kill her, would not, and invited fear to do its worst.

It took some time to settle.

Her heart slowed to a steady rhythm, and release brought relief.

She sat up in bed and gazed about her room. The collage of posters, scattered coloring books, and drawings seemed to smile at her from a world of sunshine and jewel encrusted night, a place without ghosts, vampires, and the denizens of dark places. For a moment she wondered how such things could ever matter after everything she had experienced. The fading afternoon sunlight brightened against the wall, illuminating dust that drifted dreamily before the window. A sense of certainty came to her, knowledge that the dark did not diminish the light, but in fact deepened it, made the spectral fires of stars into something holy and luminous. Life shines, not in spite of terror but perhaps for it, as if to guide all those lost in the emptiness to a harbor waiting at the heart of all things.

She hugged Ringo, slipped out of bed, and walked out of her room.

The rising and falling notes of Chopin's "Nocturne No.1 in B Flat Minor" gently sang from the living room like melodic rain drops. Eleanor frowned, both amazed and confused at the sudden precision her brother was showing with the piece. She walked into the living room and found Ian seated at the piano, his eyes dancing across sheet music, his hands fluid over the keys. He was dressed in a pressed shirt, pants, and a pinstripe vest. His hair was sleek and combed, and he looked for all the world like a young gentlemen out of some other time, an adolescent full of grace and intellect.

His shadow was perched on the piano. It twisted its head and looked at Eleanor, and for a moment she swore she could see faint horns inching from atop its head.

Ian stopped playing and smiled at her.

"Hey, Sis."

"Hey..."

She walked over to him, disbelief a cautious mask on her face. She stopped a few feet from the piano, eyeing his shadow. The surface of what passed for its skin roiled in long undulating tendrils, and its eyes flashed red three times in greeting.

"Hungry?" he said. "I can make you a sandwich."

"I guess. Where's Pop?"

"In his room."

"Right. Ian, are—are you okay?"

He closed the sheet music, stood, and pressed his shirt and vest with a downstroke of his hands.

"I'm great," he said. "I can use another sandwich myself."

He made to walk towards the kitchen.

"No, hey," Eleanor replied. "I mean—are you okay?"

His shadow made an airy sound, something between a hiss and a laugh. Ian frowned and darted his eyes at it. The shadow jumped off of the piano and into the floor as if the carpet were water, elongating into the shape of its master spread long and doubled around him.

"We went through a lot," Ian said. "You must be exhausted."

"It's not me I'm worried about."

"I'm fine. Are you really so surprised that ghosts exist? Look at our lives. We should've expected something like this."

"Yeah, but, Matt." She shuddered. "God, I don't even like saying his name. Ian, he hated—he hates you. I gotta believe that he hurt you bad. You seem so fucking calm about it all. You're not freaked out? Even a little?"

Ian was silent. He stared. His pupils swelled by a measure almost imperceptible, the slightest distortion in their perfect circles. Eleanor felt as if she were being weighed and analyzed by an awareness alien to the workings of emotional thought.

He touched her cheek and kissed her forehead.

"I love you, Sis," he said. "And I appreciate your worry, I do. Maybe being what I am has prepared me for something like this. Maybe I'm used to it. But I don't want you to worry about me. Our main concern is Jason. He's going to need friends here. It's incredible, isn't it? There is an afterlife."

"An after—are you fucking kidding me? You heard what it is. Ian—"

"So much to discover. Hm. You know, I already ate, but I am still starving. Jam with your ham and cheddar?"

He walked off before she could answer, leaving her in the dwindling afternoon glow.

She walked past the kitchen and heard him rummaging through the refrigerator. She did not look. She made for her father's room, laid her hand on the knob, and took a deep breath. She inched the door open and peered inside.

A reddish glow hung over everything, as daylight filtered in through the closed curtains. The musk of marijuana smoke lingered in the air, pungent and sweet. Alexander sat on a chair beside the bed, a pipe resting on the bedside table littered with green flakes. Her father still wore his clothes from the previous night, his collar open, his vest rumpled. His eyes were red rimmed and haggard, and he stared off into the distance as if unable to make sense of what he beheld there.

"Pop?" Eleanor said.

He blinked and looked at her. He wiped his nose and did little to hide the heartbreak on his face, the uncontrollable fount of love he felt for her overwhelming everything else. But in his eyes was grief, as if he were already mourning the loss of his children. The horrors of the world had expanded. He had experienced what it would be like to lose his children, and in his daughter he saw what he knew he was powerless to protect.

He forced a smile and beckoned her over with outstretched hands. She went to him, hopped on his lap, and lay against his chest. He held her, and they stayed that way, neither saying anything.

Eleanor took a shuddering breath.

"You okay, Pop?"

"I don't know how to answer that question."

"Yeah. That's okay. Probably the right answer."

He laughed.

"You know," he said, "I'm so proud of you. The way you stood up to that...thing. If only it would have been under different circumstances, we'd be celebrating now."

"I feel like I just lifted a thousand pounds over my head."

"That's natural. I'm almost afraid to say it, but, I haven't seen anything like what you did, since Darius. Don't let that get to your head now."

"I'm awesome, but not that awesome, got it."

He laughed again.

"Wanna talk about it?" she said, sensing in him something she could not bear to have him feel.

He sniffed and cleared his throat.

"All that matters is that you and your brother are safe. I'm sorry that I let this happen."

"You didn't let anything happen."

"I should've not been so eager to take Jason in."

"Wasn't his fault either. Least, I don't think it was."

"Fault or no, I nearly lost the both of you because we allowed him here."

"Hey, you remember what they told us, right?" she said. "Everything about, y'know, what it's like to die, what vampires are doing. We need him. And besides, he saved us."

"I think that was more you."

"Call it teamwork. You forgetting that you helped, too?"

"I suppose. It's—a father is supposed to keep his children safe, and not the other way around."

"Really? Do you know anyone who's ever been able to do that? Pop, I love you. But look at our world. This is as safe as it gets. Why do you think you've been teaching me magic? We're all gonna have to fight."

Alexander dwelled on that. He grimaced, as if swallowing something bitter.

"Maybe we should..." But he couldn't say it. Eleanor looked up at him and shook her head.

"This is home," she said.

"Yes. I suppose it is."

"I'm okay, Pop."

He took a deep breath and buried his nose in her curls.

"Yes you are," he replied. "Thank goodness."

She bit her lip, hesitating.

"Pop...is...is what Matt said true? Was I born a demon?"

Alexander hesitated. He flexed his hands and rubbed them over his face.

"It was so brief," he replied. "Your mother and I thought that, perhaps, it was some kind of mistake, or...I don't know. It's...complicated."

"But I was."

"I...You were very little, but you were showing signs just like your brother. Your shadow...it didn't quite move, but it would...seem off, somehow. And you would know things, just like Ian did. But then you got sick. It got...bad. But you came out of it in a few days, and then you were, well, the way you are now. I didn't believe it. Or maybe...I don't know."

Eleanor let his words wash over her, allowing herself to inhabit this potential new reality. She shrugged.

"I guess it doesn't make a difference."

"No." He held her. "You still are who you are. Nothing changes that."

"Didn't...Darius was a demon, right?"

Alexander nodded. He said nothing more, but the implication was there. Father and daughter both understood. There was something more to Eleanor, something revealed in her fight against the dead. For a moment, heartache lifted from his face, and Eleanor went silent with contemplation, wondering at the fact that she was the same as the first magician.

She bit her lip. She remembered what Matt had shown her, the dead boy and her father's role in it. She looked at her father.

"Pop, did..." But she stopped. He did not seem to hear her, and she saw suffering, saw pain that she did not want him to feel. So she buried her head in his chest, telling herself she would save her questions about the dead boy and so much more for another time.

They stayed that way, silent, together.

A conversation drifted up from Eleanor's memory, a moment with

Rosie that seemed a lifetime ago. She thought of Ian, of the gentle smile on his face, of the strange shape of his pupils. A moment's guilt held her back, but worry overcame shame. She exhaled and again looked up at her father.

"Pop, I think something's wrong with Ian."

"What do you mean?"

"I mean...he's so calm, you know? Like nothing happened. It doesn't seem normal. I don't know if he's pretending or what, but, I mean, I'm freaked the fuck out. He's acting like it was totally normal that we were all kidnapped by a ghost. I didn't want to say anything, but I think you should talk to him, or, I don't know, something..."

After a time, they both came out of the bedroom and went to the kitchen. Ian was spreading jam over sourdough bread. Three plates lay before him on the island, two already fixed with thick folds of ham and squares of white cheddar. He looked up at them and smiled.

"Hey, Pop," he said. "I figured you'd be hungry. Want coffee?"

"Eh, yes," Alexander replied, gazing at his son as if seeing him for the first time. He also replayed a conversation from just a few nights before. Deidre Torres-Olson had been worried about the boy, had warned Alexander that he was too normal.

Ian moved about without a care, humming to himself as he laid the jam laden slice of bread over ham and cheese. In his son Alexander saw many possibilities, all of them pregnant with latent pain and denial, with true demons tearing away at his soul.

Eleanor looked up at her father and felt a moment's relief. She knew that he saw. Ian glanced at both of them, expressionless for just a moment. Then he smiled, opened a drawer, and took out a knife.

"I'll be right back," Alexander said.

Eleanor watched him head towards the living room. She turned back to her brother.

"Need help?" she said.

"Nah, I got this. Just go sit down. I'm making that tea you like."

"Uh. Okay. Thanks."

She turned and walked towards the dining room.

Ian smiled after her. Then he looked down at the knife in his hands. It gleamed sharp and clean. He gripped the handle until his knuckles became pale rocks veined red, and the blade shook. He tapped the blade against his leg, raised the knife, and slowly sliced into the sandwich. From somewhere, his shadow hissed.

Alexander paused before the telephone. He took a deep breath, lifted it from its receiver, and dialed. He walked towards the opposite hallway so his children would not hear. Two and a half rings purred on the other end, and then a click and an answer.

Deirdre was on the other end.

"Hello, doctor," Alexander said. He listened. "Yes. I'm sorry to bother...of course not, I know you meant well. In fact, I was thinking of our conversation...yes. I've reconsidered what you said..."

4

They ate in silence. Percy shoveled forkfuls of Jason's food into his mouth, and Rosie ladled second helpings onto her plate. There had been pancakes mixed with raisins, scrambled eggs that glistened yellow and white like soft clouds, and thick slabs of ham glazed with maple syrup and brown sugar. Jason had watched them eat in the beginning, his focus turned from the revelations of the dead to the satisfaction of the living. When their faces lit with pleasure—when Rosie closed her eyes and savored her first bite, and Percy had immediately forked a second bite into his mouth, the boy had felt a strange release, as if the simple joy of a well made breakfast unburdened him of any doubt that life was worth living. He did not know how long it would last, but the moment was enough. And when he ate, he forgot himself in that timeless ritual of people coming together to eat and give silent thanks for another day's survival.

Morning shadows crept through the windows and stole across the apartment in lacy shawls. Percy finished off the remains of everyone's plates, got up, and made tea thick with milk and honey. The gift of food and the warmth of the tea brought conversation out of their beleaguered hearts. They spoke of ghosts and all they had experienced, Percy white knuckled at Rosie's telling, Rosie tapping her foot to hear Percy's. Both lobbed easy questions at Jason, bringing out of him a scattered history of the haunts he had experienced, interspersed with memories of a brief life with parents who had been his world. They spoke of the Gardens and all the things that awaited Jason in his new home. Jason nodded and smiled at that, but in the brief pauses he caught the faintest doubt in them, glances that radiated dread. They asked questions, but in his heart he wondered if they were for his sake or for theirs.

"Do you got it under control?" Rosie said to Jason.

"I think so."

She nodded, looked towards the window, and sighed.

"I ain't gonna lie to you: I'm scared. We all are. You're carrying something with you that no one should. It's dangerous, hell, beyond words." She shivered and hugged herself. "We see that. We're not blind. But I still am glad that you're here. You're a person first. Understand?"

Jason frowned and didn't respond. Percy leaned forward on his elbows.

"We're taking a risk keeping you here," he said. He looked at Jason, his eyes blue and clear and old. "If it happens again, if another of those things is able to take control of you, I'm not sure what'll happen. Everything we've learned, it's a miracle that what happened to us wasn't much worse. However, we're used to risks. Our whole life is a risk. By all rights, we shouldn't even be in this city. We should've run a long time ago, but we stayed because it was right to stay. We help people. I've lost sight of that. I've been overly concerned. However, you've reminded me of something. Wherever you are, things beyond your control follow. Jason, that means that you have to be honest with us. About anything. You can trust us. Whatever comes, we'll face it. We want you here, understand? I want you here. Whatever else happens, this is your home."

"You're worth it," Rosie said. "You saved our lives. That's something your daddy would've been very proud of."

Jason trembled. Tears came as if freed from wrongful imprisonment, streaming from the boy's eyes in a great torrent of grief. All he had repressed escaped. And he wept. Rosie got up and brought him close, and he buried himself in her hair and was grateful for the strong and sure weight of Percy's hand on his back and for the gift of letting go. It all came out in great tides of feeling that awakened his broken heart to the fact that it was still a heart after all.

Afterwards, Percy carried him asleep into his room, laid him on his bed, and drew the shades. Rosie watched, grateful herself for the moment, seeing in their recent horror a lesson in humility. The darkness waited and was hungry. But there were times like this. There would always be.

They left the door open and lingered in the hallway. Rosie looked to Percy's arm where he had bitten it. Flakes of dried blood lingered black upon his skin, and already the wound was a round welt of scar tissue that would soon vanish. Seeing him bleed, that which he almost never did, brought her to how close they had all been to becoming lost. She took his face in her hands and kissed him and wanted nothing more.

They both sighed with relief.

"What have we gotten ourselves into?" she said.

"Will you believe me now when I say Darius was a complete tosser?"

"You loved him."

Percy was silent. For him, what was obvious did not need to be said, except the thing that needed to be said the most.

"I love you. If I had lost you, I don't know if I could've...I just don't."

"If you lose me," she replied, "then you do what you know I'd want you to do. No matter what happens, that boy is our responsibility. Baby, he's the only hope we got left."

They left it at that. She led them to bed where they slept with the bedside lamp on.

Percy awoke sometime in the afternoon. He sat up and listened to the cadence of Rosie's breath. Then he went into the hallway and looked in on Jason. The boy slept on his stomach, lost to whatever dreams he dreamt. Percy hoped they were good dreams, or perhaps that he did not dream at all, that he rested in the confines of unawareness, warm and safe and absent.

He went into the living room, stood before the windows, and looked out on the Gardens.

Cold and darkness obscured his reflection in the window and crept up his skin. He whipped around, his heart thumping as absence consumed the air.

The Emissary hovered in a veil of shadow, its mask and pieces of its rotting suit peering through the writhing black.

"Beyond the black, beyond the pitch...Percy-Percy-Percy Bowles."

Fear drowned Percy's senses. He watched and waited.

"Forgive the intrusion, Percy-Percy Bowles, but the dead desire to speak with thee. Yes."

"What do you want?"

"Ah, ever the charmer. You are known to us, Percy-Percy Bowles. You have delivered many into our hands. Son of darkness, child of the second born. Another who will not die. Tell us, Percy-Percy Bowles, is it fair that so many suffer, and so few thrive?"

Percy said nothing. The Emissary floated towards him, distorting the air so light and space warped and bent around it.

"We would like an answer, Percy-Percy Bowles."

"It's a foolish question."

"Is it?"

"Of course it isn't fair. Nothing about this is fair."

"Ah. So you understand then, yes-yes-yes. You are part of the problem, you-you and your father. How many years have you walked this earth? Tell us, had you known the cost, what would you have done? What are you willing to sacrifice to right this wrong? Do you understand us, Percy-Percy Bowles?"

He looked away from the ghost. Faintness akin to nausea slithered through his chest. His mind was disjointed, a tangle of thoughts held captive by fear and unease. He closed his eyes and allowed himself respite, a brief space of clarity.

"I understood the moment you finished that ghastly story," he said. He took a long breath. "He's going to have to kill me. I'm no different from the vampires. Isn't that right?"

"Mm. Right and wrong, same old song. Yes, you have to die...in time, Percy-Percy Bowles. But you are no vampire. You did not cause this to happen. The real question is: are you willing to help the boy see his task through, even at the cost of your life? You don't have to. The boy is not immortal. You can walk into his room, crush his skull, and be done with it. You can live all the years of this world, and perhaps all the years of another. You can ask your father to give Ms. St. John eternal life, and the two of you can live, always. What's one more killing, hm, Percy-Percy Bowles, if your reward is eternity with the one you love?"

Percy glared at the Emissary with anger compounded by centuries of struggle, heartache, and violence. A moment's temptation beckoned, filling him with visions of things to come, of a future far stranger than the world he had grown to love. The thought of Rosie sharing in the coming centuries, warmed the part of him that always exclaimed at the sight of her smile. But in the ghost he saw the cost, and for all of his crimes in a life among a family of monsters, he could think of none greater than sacrificing the lives of everyone who had and would ever live, for his own joy.

He clung to anger, allowing it to consume temptation in a furnace of righteous indignation.

"You can stop right there," he said. "I'll not hurt Jason. You have my word, whatever that's worth to you. Now get out."

"Ah. Have we offended thee, Percy Bowles? Good. Then you are the man we seek. You understand what's at stake. It is time for you to lead, Percy Bowles. No more hiding now, no-no-no. Your people look to you, even in death. The boy has much to learn, much to master. He has many battles to fight. Some he must face alone-lone-lone, but others-others, hm, he needs those who are willing to risk everything. Vampires will not die easily, and they have many who serve them. The boy cannot fight this war alone. Will you stand with him, Percy Bowles? Will you give him an army?"

Percy stared at the ghost.

"Who are you?"

The Emissary laughed.

"We will be watching, Percy-Percy Bowles. The dead do not sleep. We have high hopes for thee, yes-yes-yes. Will you disappoint us? We wonder-wonder, wonder-wonder, wonder-wonder..."

The Emissary drifted backwards, disappearing into the darkness, its voice the breath of tombs, the crackling of dead leaves, the ending of all things. The darkness dissipated under daylight released as if from a dam, the living room faded into relief, and the ghost was gone.

Percy stumbled backwards and clutched at the window sill. The Gardens shone behind him, gleaming and still in the winter afternoon, every building filled with those who had come for safety and protection and a new chance at life. They looked to him as the bedrock, a source of perpetual strength in the face of corruption so deep it transcended death. He knew these things and felt their weight. He bent forward and looked towards the hallway that led to Jason's room. There the boy slept, and with him waited the beginning and the end.

He stood between them.

Percy turned and looked out the window once more. Tree branches swayed. Icicles clung to lampposts. Frost caked the meadows surrounding the paths, and teenagers yelped as they sledded down hills. A family walked together, bundled in their coats. Below this shimmering but everyday exterior, the Gardens thrived, filled with magic and people content to be hidden away after so much suffering. He had helped to give them a home. But it was not enough, not so long as countless others suffered so a few could live on as a blight upon the world. Not so long as he held the power to right the ultimate wrong.

The muscles of his jaw tensed with resolve. He was a king before an army, weaving together a plan to action, content to hide no more.

5

Ian pushed the doorbell for Apartment 97.

The door opened after a moment, and Deirdre Torres-Olson appeared in yoga pants, a purple tank top, and a gray cardigan sweater. Her hair was black currents over her shoulders, and Ian was surprised to see her in colorful socks printed with Wile E. Coyote chasing the Road Runner against a desert backdrop.

"Dr. Olson," Ian said, "My father said you wanted to see me."

She looked at him for a moment. Then she smiled a bright smile that Ian had never seen before.

"We're so happy you've come. Please."

She stood aside. Ian took off his shoes, laid them in the vestibule, and entered a wide and clean space that encompassed the living room and kitchen. There was a sofa seated before a flat screen television. There was a kitchen island with a sink, and a square table a few feet from it. A long window took up the entire west wall, and Manhattan towered in the distance like metallic spires drenched in neon flame. The rest was empty space and hardwood floors, minimal and modern. Ian saw no posters or portraits, no works of art. The air was warm and tinted amber, and Chopin played from unseen stereos. Ian recognized the piece.

"I'm learning this on piano," he said.

Dr. Olson closed the door and smiled at him.

"That doesn't surprise me. It's beautiful. Simple, yet complex. Perfect for a young man such as yourself."

"Thank you. If you don't mind me asking, Dr. Olson, I thought you didn't see anyone in your home? Why now?"

"You're an exception. Please."

She touched his shoulder and walked towards a narrow hallway. He followed. There were five doors, three on the left, one on the right, and one at the end of the hall. Again, Ian spied no pictures of Dr. Olson's family, no decorative dressers, nothing but the gleaming wooden floor and cream colored walls.

"Is Janet home, Dr. Olson?"

"You two really like each other."

Ian was silent.

"It's quite alright, Ian. I'm glad my daughter has taken to you."

Ian stopped. Dr. Olson walked to the door at the end of the hall, opened it, and went inside without turning around. He lingered for a moment. His shadow turned to him from the wall. Its eyes flared. A sense of something familiar beat through his awareness, something recognized but still unknown. He looked at the open door ahead of him and wondered why the woman who had always eyed him with such distrust now acted as if he were the son she had always wanted.

He followed after her into the doorway.

The room was painted dark blue. Dr. Olson sat in a chair across from a sofa. A table sat beside her, a dark blue mug on it. A white carpet with red lines forming diamond patterns covered the floor. A window on the right revealed parked cars rising uphill on 31st Avenue, and the shadows of trees splayed over the glass. There were no books or bookcases or desks or cabinets. Dr. Olson curled up in the chair very much like a little girl warming herself on a cold winter's night. She reached for the mug and cupped it in her hands. After a moment, steam billowed from the contents within, and Ian smelled the sweet lure of hot chocolate.

He looked about the room, eyed Dr. Olson for a moment, then

gestured towards the sofa. She smiled and nodded. He took off his coat, laid it over the arm, sat across from her, and watched. Neither spoke. She sipped her chocolate.

"You have a very spacious home, Dr. Olson."

"Are you upset that this is your first time here?"

He shook his head.

"Really?" she said. "Even though I forbade my daughter from bringing you here? I'm sure she's told you."

"It's natural for a mother to be protective of her child. Though, now I'm confused, because you just said—"

"It's even more natural for an adolescent to get angry at things he can't control. Especially when he's a demon."

Ian smoothed his tie with the flat of his hand.

"I suppose I have to earn your trust."

She smiled.

"Suppose? Not guess? You suppose. Well, how very adult of you, Ian. You're always so even-tempered, so well mannered. Many of our children are different. Most are hyper intelligent, or a bit advanced in years. They have to be, given our shared situation. But you are something else entirely. It makes people curious."

Ian shifted on the sofa and once more adjusted his tie. He looked at the doctor and brushed a strand of dark hair from his brow.

"Are you concerned that I'm hiding something, doctor?"

"No."

She smiled and sipped her chocolate. Ian waited. She watched him over the rim of her cup and blew swirls of steam. Ian smiled.

"Okay," he said, speaking slowly, weighing each word. "My father said you wanted to make sure that I was okay, that I knew it was alright to express myself. I tried to tell him that I am very happy. I just understand the danger we're all in. It's given me a certain perspective, makes me appreciate what I have. Of course I get angry, and sad, but I know those are just feelings."

"Yeah...I don't care about any of that."

Ian frowned.

"I'm sorry?"

"This isn't a counseling session, Ian. That's just something I told your father to get you here. Of course, I could've allowed Janet to bring you over, but that would've been viewed as social acceptance. My attitude towards you out there, that's all for show. I wanted you to have a reason to dislike me. I wanted to see how you'd react. Frankly, I'm impressed. You hide it well."

Ian paused, his lips parted, his eyes narrowed. He thought for a moment, trying to glean a pattern out of her sudden shift in attitude.

"Hide what well?" he said.

She laughed, a harsh note of incredulity coating humor. She sipped again at the chocolate and blew steam over the lip of the mug so her eyes took on wavering shapes. She held the mug as if it were a trophy, something she was using to gloat the boy with.

Ian blinked with recognition, almost reeling. The mug had not been steaming when he had entered the room. Watching the steam, he felt a dull throb in his throat, as if he had stumbled on evidence of the impossible. The need for certainty took hold, urging him to be sure, to make no mistakes. He sought backwards through memory to find everything he knew about Deirdre Torres-Olson. He looked away from her, sat up, and affected an air of confusion.

"I think you have the wrong idea about me, doctor. But I get why. I'd be worried, too, if I were like you. It must be strange for you here. There aren't many regular humans in the Gardens. You probably feel...out of place."

She stared at him, and then laughed again.

"When you're beyond our walls, playing the game for real, you're going to have to do much better than that, Ian." She laid the mug down. "You gave yourself away, young man. You stared a little too long at my hot chocolate, and your eyes widened just...so. And then you made that weak segue into my background, which you already brought up the other night. No. No, no, no. You have a lot to learn."

He hesitated for the slightest moment.

"I'm sorry, doctor, but I'm not sure what you mean."

Deidre smiled as if she were toying with a toddler. Then the first tendrils of blood spilled within her eyes, darkening the whites until they were soaked through. Ian's mouth curved into an animal scowl. His shadow climbed over the sofa and leered at her from above his shoulder. His eyes smoldered, unblinking. Deirdre's eyes burned in kind, and she stared at him and smiled her warm smile.

She spoke.

"Of course you're thinking: 'I need to do something about this. I need to escape. I need to tell everyone'. But that's not what's paramount in your mind. What's really bothering you is: how did I escape your notice for all these years. And you're going to want to try and possess me. And you'll fail, because—and listen closely—I am much stronger than you. But, don't worry. I don't want to hurt you. I don't want to hurt anyone here. My intentions are the same as yours: protect our people. At...all...cost."

Ian's lips quivered. His shadow growled. He forced his face into repose, but never let his eyes leave the demon before him.

"Who else knows?" he said.

"Here? No one. Well, my family, of course, but not your father, or anyone else. Abebe Ngombe knows. How are things going with Jason, by the way? Was it strange to see Darius Bardales in the flesh?"

Ian's eyes went wide. Doubt usurped control, leaving him adrift within a storm of uncertainty.

Deidre reached into her cardigan pocket. She pulled out a photo and offered it to him. He hesitated, and then snatched it out of her hand. She leaned forward, knuckling her toes against the blood red lines of the carpet.

Ian looked at the photo. In it, Deirdre was younger, but not much different from the woman seated before him. The same predatory intelligence shone in her eyes as she toasted a glass of wine towards the camera. Phoebe Moore-Demidova was beside her, her hand cradled on Deirdre's shoulder.

"Ian," Deirdre said, her eyes burning and bloody, "you can go and tell everyone. I won't stop you. But you'd be making a very grave mistake. See, I want to teach you the things your mother was supposed to teach you. I know your hatred. I know the hunger that lives inside of you. You hide it well, but not well enough that a skilled demon won't spot it right away. I can help you change that. I've been watching you since you were born. Your calm, your control, is the reason that I'm offering you my tutelage. Janet tells me that you care very deeply for your family, and for our home. Good. I do as well. I've been out there, with the Family, with real monsters. Their time is ending, isn't it? Jason is going to see to that. He will attend to our mutual enemies. And then we have to think about the future. What rises from the rubble, so to speak. The Gardens must take control. Tell me, do you agree that, sometimes, to protect the innocent, and those you love, you need to do certain things, commit certain acts, for the greater good?"

Tears welled in Ian's eyes, not of grief, but of awe. Before him was a door that hid many treasures. A thousand questions burned that he had only now realized had been begging for answers. And something more: a deep seeded loneliness revealed itself. His shadow ceased it's growling and hissed with anticipation.

"Yes," Ian replied, not bothering to wipe away tears that left crimson trails over his cheeks. "To protect the people you love from monsters, you have to be willing to do anything."

"Good. That's exactly what Phoebe would've wanted to hear. So then, you'll let me teach you how to be a demon?"

"Yes. Yes. Yes."

She smiled and stood up.

"Come with me."

They entered the master bedroom. Shadows layered the bed. A bookshelf, file cabinets, two closet doors. Deirdre led them to the closet on the right. She opened it and spread apart the clothing hanging there.

Then she stepped inside and walked through the wall.

Ian hesitated for a moment. He could run. He could go and tell his father. His shadow-self laughed. He walked through the wall after her.

Guns and knives lined the brick walls of a single room. A lamp hung above, shining harsh light upon Janet and Elisha. They stood before a table, Janet wide eyed, a bore brush in one hand pushed into the barrel of Glock 17. The disassembled pieces lay before her on a red square of cloth, oiled and shimming. Elisha glanced up at Ian, distrust in her eyes. She loaded a bullet into the chamber of a silver revolver and flicked the barrel closed.

Hank smiled from behind them, shirtless, a Celtic cross tattooed at the center of his chest. Three bullet wounds scarred his abdomen above his navel. Deirdre went around the table, letting her fingers drift over Janet's shoulder. She laid a hand on Hank. Hank beamed at her.

"Looks like you were right," he said.

"He has a lot to learn. But he's ready."

"Ian," Hank said.

He emerged out of the shade and stood before the boy. Ian took in the weapons hanging on the walls, hunger in his eyes. Hank extended his hand. Ian took it. Janet watched, breathless, waiting.

"I'm so glad you're here," Hank said. "This is a big step for you. You must have so many questions, but I promise this is all quite uncomplicated. You see, there are many threats to our way of life, son, many people who want to do us harm. We can only hide for so long before the time comes to do something about that. And now, with Jason here...There are many, many bad things coming, Ian. We have to be prepared. We must strike first. Because the Family is evil. They have to be destroyed. Deidre and I think that you can help us with that. Can you?"

Ian nodded, his shoulders rising and falling with anticipation. Hank smiled. He reached out a hand, and a knife floated from off of the wall and landed into his palm. He flipped the knife, caught it by the blade, and offered the hilt to Ian.

Ian took it.

Hank nodded towards a boxing dummy against the far wall. Janet and Elisha watched. Ian went to the dummy.

"Deidre says you're in control of your rage," Hank said behind the boy. "Good. But it's still there."

"Oh, it is," Deidre replied. Her eyes burned.

"So we have to focus it, then, don't we? Deidre will teach you how to be a demon. I will teach you how to be...effective."

Ian looked back. Hank's smile was cold and certain. His eyes promised to unveil secrets so well hidden, that no one in the Gardens would ever know. Ian wanted to ask so much.

"In time, young man," Deidre said.

"For now, son," Hank said. "Why don't you show me how you think you'd use this knife on our enemies. Go on."

Ian turned to the dummy. Stab marks and bullet holes riddled its body. A slow smile curdled over his face. Blood bubbled within his eyes. His shadow loomed against the wall and mimicked him as he stabbed the dummy, once, twice, again, forcing the knife deeper, deeper. He growled through his teeth, slashing, stabbing, and his shadow shrieked with the promise of retribution, throwing back its head and spreading its arms wide in frenzied jubilation. The blackness of its skin and the crimson of its eyes were no longer shades of color. They could not be found on any spectrum of light. They were known only to the slaughtered, those legions of helpless souls screaming their last across the geography of time, losing their lives to that ancient and most unholy of arbiters.

6

Alexander sat huddled in a blanket and watched night drain into the pale gray of morning. The shadows of the living room lessened. His throat burned. His wooden pipe was deep brown on the table beside him, still smoking from embers of smoldering marijuana. A mound of shredded green waited in an open mason jar, and before his pipe finished smoking he pinched a bit between his fingers and pressed it into the bowl.

His clothes, the same he had worn for two days, were wrinkled. His hair was a disheveled mess of auburn, and stubble smeared his face. He brought the pipe to his lips, hesitated, and replaced it on the table. He tightened the blanket around himself and shivered. Daylight spread over the edges of rooftops. A few vagrant figures moved below, mostly security or maintenance conducting their rounds.

He envied them their ignorance. They knew of no ghosts. They carried burdens far lesser than the weight of what gnawed at him, that screamed with the mouths of all those he had killed. Pablo's empty gaze waited whenever he blinked, dragging him deeper into a pit that he saw no way out of.

He took the pipe, snapped flame into being, and smoked. The

ease of being high transformed into a greater awareness of exhaustion like metallic threads coursing through his limbs. His neck ached, his throat burned, his eyes begged for succor. But sleep would not come.

The phone rang. He stared at it. On the other end waited the life he had known, a life he doubted he could return to. The ringing stopped. Minutes passed, and the phone rang again. He ignored it.

Daylight filtered through a continent of cloud cover, propelling the hours of morning forward. His children would stir soon—if they were not already awake and dealing with the horror in their own way. He took a shivering breath. That they should know such a thing to exist. That they were born to inhabit a world doomed to fall into the insatiable maw of waking death.

The phone rang again. He almost let it go once more, but his hand seemed to move of its own accord. He snatched it up and answered. Radek was on the other end.

"Boss," he said, his voice exact and crisp. "You okay?"

"Eh, yes, I eh, am not feeling so well. I'm sorry. I should've checked in."

"Percy said. But..." There was a long pause. Alexander could imagine Radek standing rigid and strong, his eyes working with quiet intelligence. "Do you need anything?"

"Just some time. You take care of things. I don't know how long I'll..."

He cleared his throat and fell silent.

"About the other night?" Radek replied. "The warehouse?"

"Discuss that with Percy. I...I have to go now. Thank you."

He hung up before Radek could say another word. He sank deeper in the chair, looked outside, and felt as if every thought was corrupted by an unseen force that leered at him from beyond the fragile veil of their world. Numbness took hold, coating all the things that were supposed to matter in a bitter muck.

Clouds rolled across the sky. Window blinds rolled open in buildings.

A gentle knocking rapped at the front door. Alexander turned his head as if expecting to see death hovering behind him. He stood, let the blanket fall, smoothed his hair, and walked through the hallway to the entrance. He looked through the peephole and froze. Then he took a deep breath and opened it.

Marissa Guiterrez stood on the other side, layered in a thick black winter coat, her hair shimmering with the golden streaks Eleanor had gifted her with days before. A bag of carrots swung from her hand. She smiled at Alexander, but her smile died as she took a good look at him. Her lips formed into coming speech, but she hesitated.

"Bad couple of days," she said. It wasn't a question.

Alexander shrugged.

"You could say so."

"Most def. Haven't seen you in a few. I got worried."

"Right, I was just saying to Radek that I should've...Anyway, I'm under the weather. You probably shouldn't even be here."

She pressed the back of her hand against his forehead, moving swiftly, the gesture intimate, as if there was no doubt in her mind that this was her right.

"You don't feel warm," she said.

"It's, eh, a stomach thing."

Disbelief narrowed her eyes. But she gave a slow nod and took her hand away. They stood in silence. For a brief moment he lost himself in her eyes, a playful intelligence that had, bit by bit, seeped into the back of his thoughts with their every interaction.

He imagined those eyes rotted and saw her face twisted into an agonized scream. He looked away.

"Hey," she said, taking his hand. "What's wrong?"

He pulled away and gestured at the carrots.

"Something different, eh?"

She frowned.

"What's wrong?"

He hung his head and said nothing. She took his hand again, and he clutched at hers, feeling the weight of her fingers like something out of a dream. Then he let go.

"Radek will be handling things now," he said.

"Now? What does that mean?"

"I have to go. Thank you for checking in on me."

He closed the door. She stood uncomprehending, left alone with the sudden loss of the light and playfulness that always filled their interactions, with the weight of despair that bled from him.

He turned around and pressed his back against the door. He opened his eyes and found Eleanor standing before him. She was dressed in jeans, a baggy green hoodie, and a coat. Ringo was cradled under her arm.

"Who was that, Pop?" she said.

"No one," he replied. Marissa's footfalls shuffled away from the door, and he cringed with the certainty that she had heard him refer to her as "No one." He shook it off and nodded at Eleanor. "Where are you going?"

"To the Dungeon."

He frowned.

"So soon?"

"It's not like we have a lot of time. Besides, we weren't really around too much the last few days. I think it's important people see us, or else they might start asking questions."

"I don't know if I want you going off on your own."

"I won't be alone, everyone is gonna be down there."

"I mean—"

"I know what you mean. Pop, you didn't sleep. Again. You...you look bad."

He said nothing. She sighed.

"I'm scared, too," she said. "But you heard what, you know, that— that ghost said. We can stop all of the bad stuff. We can fight back. We can't let it make us sad, or else, I don't know. I figured it's better to just get back to it, practice, you know."

"You will not be doing any magic so soon after...you can't take it right now, you should be resting."

"I know. I just wanna be around people. Why don't you come with me? Ian's waking up. We can grab breakfast before he goes to Dr. Olson's again."

Alexander shook his head.

"I can't."

She hung her head and said nothing else. Then she hugged him. A brief swath of light parted the midnight in his heart. He held her, took a shuddering breath, and did not want to let her go. She let go and went for the door.

"Ellie," he said. She turned. "I don't want you seeing Jason."

"What?"

"Just stay away from him. At least until we understand, or...I just don't want you near him. Please."

She looked at her father as if seeing an imposter with his face standing in his stead. She looked away, heartache in her eyes.

"See you later."

She walked out. He felt her absence like the promise of doom. He almost raced after her. The weight of despair dragged him numb and dazed toward the living room. He gave a furtive glance to Ian's room. A faint red glow shimmered under the door. He almost reached out to look in on his son, but was somehow carried back to his chair where he sat staring out at a world that seemed like nothing more than a cruel lie.

The phone rang again. He took it off of the receiver, pressed the answer button twice, and then dropped it onto the floor. Shadows streaked across the window, the voices of people carried on the wind, and in all things Alexander Demidov felt nothing but the dead.

7

Rosie took a deep breath as she stood before her restaurant. Cauldron Avenue bustled. A group of teenagers emerged from the apartment building to the right of Rosie's, dressed in track jackets and sweat pants and carrying book bags. Some shyly glanced her way, while one openly pulled at his ears, indicating hers. She gave him a flat expression and shook her head not out of anger, but out of a need for normalcy, to return to life after her encounter with those who waited beyond the living world.

She smoothed out her dress and walked past the empty outdoor seats awaiting customers. Two waiters nodded to her as they wiped down tables and adjusted plush chairs. She walked through the open door, parted the curtains, and stepped inside.

Stillness clung to the crimson tinted shadows. The bar was empty, long and black and gleaming. A few figures sat quietly by the windows, eating breakfast sandwiches, or drinking coffee and tea, watching the hum of morning traffic.

She went straight to it—greeting customers, greeting staff, walking through the kitchen just to be seen. Belinda Amaya, the head chef, threw her hands up at her from over a countertop where two silver bowls of eggs whisked themselves by her magic.

"The queen returns," she said.

"Ha-ha," Rosie replied. "Sorry, I needed a few days to get some things done at home."

"That sounds nice. Meanwhile, I'm here, just managing everything else, by the way."

"Oh, hell, you want the day off? I can handle the kitchen."

Belinda laughed, shook her head, looked again at Rosie, and laughed harder.

"Thanks for the vote of confidence," Rosie said. She playfully slapped Belinda across the shoulder and stopped to speak with members of the kitchen staff until she was satisfied that no one had thought her absence a serious matter. Then she moved on.

She unlocked the door to the apothecary, stepped inside, and stood looking at the shelves lined with spells shimmering in their vials. Their labels glowed in near neon lettering, but even without their labels she knew them all, each a piece of her, channeled into existence from the mysterious nether space where magic waited to be molded through a magician. Each spell represented a moment in time where she had lost herself to the inner workings of the mind, where emotion and logic merged into seeds that sprouted potions altered by the deepest parts of her. Here a spell to silence anxious thoughts. Here another that brought hidden truths to the surface. And here an elixir that sent one far into the reaches of some infinite mental space, where one could take time to think, create, and heal.

These and many others all conjured by Rosie St. John. She stood before them like a composer before her music, remembering each note, each change in dynamics. In them she saw at least temporary respite from the nightmares her people had faced. Not cures, but reminders that life was not all bloodshed, torment, and loss.

But she had witnessed the other side—or a part of it. She had seen what happens to the dead. Looking at her spells was a reminder of all that she had done in life, as if the spells were shelter from a storm of howling glass.

She thought of Jason and felt a moment's hope. Or perhaps she imagined it. It made no matter. She held on, reminding herself that in the boy lay an answer, an ending.

And then there was Eleanor. Her power. Her light. She had also saved them, and her strength had been awe inspiring.

There was much to do. Such a secret between her husband and closest loved ones, and somehow they had to manage it. Alexander had not reached out to them, and Rosie worried. She raised her hands and watched her fingers shake until they fell still. There would be time enough to think about these things.

For now...

She went back to the dining area and towards the bar for a cup of coffee, when she saw Martin Gleason, who had come only days before for a spell, clutching the back of a chair, staring at her with a look of disbelief on his face. She stopped and waited a moment, bracing herself.

"Howdy, Marty," she said.

"Rosie. Can I speak with you?"

"Sure thing."

She gestured at the bar.

They sat.

Martin scratched his shoulder through his Sultans of Ping FC t-shirt, watched the waiter standing over a customer, and looked at the bar as if expecting a bartender to emerge from thin air.

Rosie touched his shoulder.

"It's just us," she said.

"This is one of those things that just has to be rationalized before it gets out. Otherwise, I don't know."

Rosie tensed. Her skin erupted into ripples of gooseflesh. She readjusted in her seat and watched Martin, hoping the next words out of his mouth had nothing to do with strange happenings and ghosts.

He looked her in the eyes, unflinching.

"There's no other way to say it, so I'm just going to say it. Rose...I think you've cured me."

A jolt of surprise went through her. Words collided in her mind, and it took her a moment to pick up the pieces.

"I'm sorry, what now?"

"Well, not cure me as such, but...I don't know, like a respite or something."

"Slow down. Let's step back a second."

"It's like this: I haven't turned in almost two months."

Rosie stared at him.

"That ain't possible."

"I'm telling you, it is. I've been overdue for months. At the same time, I've started that new spell of yours for, you know, the trauma and all that. I wasn't sure how to bring it up, until David noticed that I haven't been going all weird as of late. When your husband is wondering why you haven't turned into a fecking werewolf...We figured out that I stopped turning around the time I started with this new series of spells. So, okay, I try an experiment. I skipped the last two days, and last night, no surprise, I start feeling wobbly, like it's time to go to the Den. David was going to take me straight away, but I took your spell instead." He snapped his fingers. "Like that. Gone. I slept in our bed, woke up feeling fine. Okay, so maybe it's not a cure, but I'm telling you, your spell is like some kind of antidote. It's keeping the werewolf at bay."

Rosie leaned her elbow against the bar and pressed her hand over her mouth, piecing together what he just said and what it could possibly mean.

"Hold on, you haven't been down to the Den in two months?" she said.

"I didn't say that now. I've gone. Keeping up appearances and the like. But...nothing's happened."

"And y'all said it was that new trauma spell?" she said.

"I'm telling you, the one so to help me sleep, then the one that so I'm lucid for my dreams, and all that. It was a fucker sleeping the first few nights, I don't mind saying, but it's having the same effect. I don't know, Rose. I just don't know."

Rosie didn't speak. She thought back to the creation of both spells, each variations of the other. Of the clarity she had felt. The sense of understanding that had coursed through her, something she could not now put into words.

She raised her hands before her in a gesture of patience.

"Not a soul," she said. "You can't tell anyone."

"David..."

"That's fine, he's your husband. But just the three of us. No one else, not even...not even Percy. We need to go over this together. Take it day by day, see what happens. If this really is what you say it is, then why haven't I heard about this from anyone else?"

"I don't know. Maybe they don't want to say, or it's specific to me for some reason. But you have my word. We'll keep quiet about all this. But, Rose, if this what I think is—"

"I need a minute. Let me think for a bit, and I can meet y'all tonight at the Frog. I'll see you then."

She patted his hand and hurried off, following the path through the kitchen and beyond the flaps that led to the storage area for drinks and drugs, continuing through the aisle to the door leading to the stairs and down and down until she was aware again.

Rows of cauldrons gleamed black and absolute in the semi-dark.

Martin's story came alive in her mind, branching into a complex network of possibilities. Rosie saw a future where werewolves no longer had to exist, where her spells could reach out to the people of the Gardens and free them from a curse that had ruined so many lives.

"Why just here?" she said to herself. She stared at the empty cauldrons and in them saw a dangerous idea, a weapon nearly greater than any other the Gardens could muster against the Family, against those who tortured people until they turned into monstrosities in need of cages. The cauldrons waited before their magician, hungry to ingest her magic and overflow with bubbling brews that would destroy the foundation of a cruel empire.

They waited for Rosie St. John.

8

Eleanor stood on the top step of her stoop, feeling the cold air roll against her. Trees swayed. A young woman squatted on the left bend of the path, cleaning up after her dog. The sigh of the fountain carried on the wind. Ice glinted over swathes of hidden greenery and on the swinging black chains hanging between fence posts.

Eleanor took it all in, and for a moment forgot that behind it all waited a world of perpetual darkness. She cradled Ringo in the crook of her arm, walked down the steps, and went left on the path, following it towards the nearest gate and transportation to the Gardens-below. But she stopped halfway along, taking Ringo in her hands and staring at the bear as if within the button eyes lingered an accusation. Not against her, but against her father and his fear. Her love for him made her understand. What parent could claim to love their children and not do everything in their power to protect them? But she knew he was wrong. In her heart and bones, through her skin, screaming through her very blood was the knowledge that he had misjudged Jason. She grimaced as if caught between two forces pulling her in opposite directions. She stepped quickly, continuing on the path, but then turned onto a lesser path towards Percy and Rosie's.

The elevator chimed, the door opened with a rush of air, and she stepped into the hallway. She took a deep breath, remembering how the hallway had been distorted into the architecture of nightmares, and then walked to Percy and Rosie's door. She licked her lips and went to ring the bell, but hesitated. Guilt hovered with the haggard visage of her father. She sighed, cursed, and turned to walk away. But she stopped. She could not just leave.

She kissed Ringo on the nose and then sat him against the door. The teddy bear seemed to watch her walk away.

The door opened. Ringo slid backwards against Jason's feet. He blinked in surprise, set down a garbage bag, and bent down to pick up the teddy bear with his free hand.

Eleanor turned to face him. Jason twisted his lips, confused.

"Hey," he said.

"Hi," Eleanor replied.

They stared at each other. Jason hesitated, and then offered Ringo back to Eleanor.

She shook her head.

"I told you before, I want you to have him," she said.

"He's yours. Besides, I don't really need him."

"Yeah you do."

He looked down at the floor and tightened his grip on Ringo. A smile brushed the corner of his mouth.

"I'm too old for stuffed animals."

"Nah, you ain't."

"Thanks," he said. "I'll keep him safe."

She smiled.

"You better."

She turned to walk away.

"You're not coming in?" he said.

She shook her head.

"I can't. I'm...I'm not supposed to be seeing you. My dad doesn't want me to."

Jason went rigid for a moment, his eyes spectrums of hurt. He looked away from her and nodded.

"Okay."

Eleanor sucked at her teeth, her fists clenched, her head bowed. She turned back to Jason.

"It's bullshit," she said.

"Maybe he's right."

"Nah. He's not."

"...Why aren't you afraid of me?"

She shrugged.

"Because you're nice. Right here." She pointed at her chest. "That's where it counts. That's enough for me."

He smiled a true smile, full of the understanding that somehow she saw through him to what was really in his heart, to the yearning for peace that would be with him all of his days. He raised Ringo in his hands and moved the bear's head to mimic speaking.

"'Jason thinks Eleanor's nice, too,'" he said through the bear.

Eleanor giggled.

"He's supposed to have a British accent."

"You hear that a lot in Queens."

"Uh," she said, pointing at Percy and Rosie's door.

Jason shrugged.

"I just met the guy, gimme a break." He cradled Ringo in his hands and played his fingers through the fur. "I think we should share him. He could be there for whoever needs him most. I'll have him for now, but, you know. Whenever you need him, he'll be there."

"I like that."

With that she waved and took a few steps. She stopped again as if debating with herself, and then turned to face him.

"Remember what you said, about how no one tells you that when people die, they're just gone? Well, even if there weren't any ghosts, you'd be wrong. The people you love are never gone. Not even a little bit."

She walked away without another word. He watched her, a girl in a green hoodie and puffy coat, her hair all wild curls. A friend. The elevator door opened, she smiled at him, stepped inside, and was gone.

He went back into the apartment and stood for a moment in the living room. Hip Hop beat from behind Percy's bedroom door in the hallway. Rosie had left earlier, and Jason had expected Percy to be following him like a shadow. But Percy had disappeared into the bedroom after breakfast, leaving the boy to adjust, to become comfortable on his own. Bit by bit the contrast of Percy's computer, wires and gadgets, and Rosie's rocking chair and pictures of horses began to make sense to him. He carried Ringo to the sofa, sat with the bear, and soaked the space in.

Afterwards, he went back to his room—his room—and locked the door. He wondered what adjustments would be made to make it his own. In time, he thought. Maybe.

He thought of his parents.

The call of the otherworld rippled within, and he closed his eyes and let the forest rise out of the ether. The bedroom and the living world faded away, and when he opened his eyes again he stood in the Black Forest.

He looked about, understanding that this, too, was his home, perhaps more so than the other.

The Emissary was a presence in his mind, a string of thoughts about to coalesce into reality. He shook his head.

"Not now, boss," he said.

A hushed sigh came through the trees, and nothing more.

He walked, following a trail through the trees and mist, carrying Ringo through a dead world. He looked from left to right, peering through the deep veil of branches and fog that seemed to stretch into forever. How long had the forest stood? How far did it go? He wondered.

He walked, rising and falling with the trail, climbing small hills, feeling the presence of the dead all about him like frostbitten fingers brushing the back of his neck. Low moaning stopped him. He looked right, towards a warped and guttural cry that carried through the trees with endless sorrow. He knew Matt, felt his grief. For now he knew there was nothing to be done but leave the ghost, hidden away somewhere in the forest. He would see him again. In time.

He walked on, and the yearning in his heart led him to where he had always wanted to be.

He stopped before the clearing. She was there, in her tattered tutu, her hair long, black, and fading into tendrils of smoky mist. She danced, and around her, long vines spun and swayed as if in rhythm with her silent song. She stopped dancing for a moment. She inclined her head his way, her face a profile in ghostly relief. He did not have to see her smile. He did not have to hear her voice. Her love echoed across the realm of never.

She resumed her dance, jumping and spinning over dead earth.

Jason leaned against a tree and watched her. Branches reached out and fell gently on his shoulders and hands, and in them he felt his father, not as the man he had been, but as a presence that lingered beyond the realm of life and dreams.

Jason Escoto, son of life and death, smiled a sad smile and watched her dance and felt the branches against his skin. And the Black Forest swayed and sighed. And Ringo was soft against him. And the boy closed his eyes among ghosts and dreamt of a girl with black curls.

ELEANOR STOOD before the Dungeon entrance on Freeman Way.

All around her was the bustle of morning. Cooks prepared food within the Standing Dragon. Five Security Officers stood before Johnny's, talking over coffee. A few looked Eleanor's way, the question of her father's whereabouts in their eyes. Frank Russo grunted as he and Ray levitated a plate glass window into place in Professor Thirsty's storefront. Carl supervised, gesturing for them to inch the window lower. Glass shards were scattered at their feet, evidence of some drunken accident. Caleb strolled by, his hair disheveled, a dazed look on his face. Carl pointed at him.

"Not now, Caleb," he said.

"It was an accident, man."

"Fuck off."

Caleb groaned and stumbled on.

Aidan Horowitz came running, a red and yellow book bag bouncing on his back. He stopped beside Eleanor, panting.

"Hey, Ellie," he said. "Haven't seen you for a few days."

"Hey, Aidan. Yeah, I was, uh, a little sick."

"Oh no. Want me to tell my dad?"

"Nah, I'm fine."

"Okay. Coming to class?"

"Not today. I–I want to practice some more stuff on my own."

"You're so lucky you get to do that. I'm late. See you later."

He ran to the doors standing in the naked air. They opened, spilling the glow of torchlight onto cobblestones. He descended the stairs and disappeared.

The doors remained open. Eleanor looked within the Dungeon. A chill took her, emanating from the deep shadows. She looked about at all these passing faces—werewolves and magicians, human above all, these bright and lovely nightmares, impossible creatures in an impossible world. They walked about with all the cares of life guiding them on, leading them to one fate or another. She looked again inside the Dungeon and knew that things waited in the dark, knew that life was victim to an ever hungry monster awaiting its end.

Chills rippled through her. All around her, life hummed, and she closed her eyes and let the cavalcade of voices and sound carry her within to where the innermost mysteries of existence waited, to where she felt a presence of light and goodness traversing the prison of death. Perhaps it was magic. Perhaps it was the breath of God. She did not care for its name. She only wanted to stand and fight, to erase the wrongs wrought by the hands of monsters.

To do so, she had to traverse the darkness. She knew this beyond all else.

She opened her eyes, walked through the waiting doors and descended into the Dungeon.

Her footsteps echoed in the dim corridors. She passed a door and heard Ms. Krause's voice in singsong. She passed Mario who smiled at her, though his eyes were red rimmed and his head was killing him.

"You okay, Mr. Gonzalo?" she said.

He grunted and waved her on. She shrugged. Some adults played too hard.

She walked on until she found an open room. She stepped inside, closed the door behind her, and looked about. Bare walls greeted her. The fluorescent light hummed above, blaring against the gentle pulse of the candle flame dancing from its opening at the center of the floor. She stared at it, seeing within a carnival of colors bleeding into its golden skin. She sighed with fear, turned around, and flicked the light switch off. The candle's flame cast a soft aura against the oppressing darkness.

She walked over, sat before it, and let awareness drift into the flame. How many others across time had peered into the depths of fire? What hopes did they find there, in a lone sliver of light against night without end?

So many, she thought, unsure of what the words meant. A feeling bloomed within her, something substantial and pure, weightless. The light was her guide, and she its servant. But she looked about the darkness and knew the answers were there, waiting behind cruel teeth and crazed intentions. Had she never seen a ghost, she still would've known that they were real, right here in this moment. They waited in the invisible places, striking from the dark to fill our minds and hearts with sorrow. For ghosts were those who would not pass, would not let go. She knew this to be true. But even without the events of the past days, she would not have doubted. Not here. Not before the absence of all things.

Fear reached out and coiled itself about her.

She looked at her hands and watched them shake. Let them tremble. Let her be overwhelmed. Let all the fears of night assault her heart, so when the time comes she would stand true. She would wield no magic today. Her muscles ached and her heart could not yet take it. For now it was enough to simply be, to exist among the shadows so she may learn to stoke her inner light. So she would not be corrupted.

These would be the first steps of her quest to stand for the living, and to do so she needed to brave what she feared most.

Eleanor blew a strand of curls from her face. Then she leaned forward and blew out the light.

ACKNOWLEDGMENTS

Nothing worth doing is ever done alone.

During the years I was writing this novel (and many more before them) I had the love, support, and encouragement of many wonderful people.

To Cassandra Chaput for taking the time and effort necessary to comb through every line and tell me what does and does not work. I see bright things in your future.

To James Amoros, for not only reading into the wee hours of the morning (and annoying the hell out of your better half), but also designing a beautiful cover.

To Joyce Stein at JSA Kids Marketing, for your advice and pointing me in the right direction.

To Sandra Gibbons, Mia Manns, Kirk Maile, Katie Commodore, and Irene Elliot for taking the time to read the book and give me your valuable insight.

To Chris Dean, Andrei Dan, Charles Marino, Wendy Wong, Steven LaRosa, Mohammad "Your Uncle Moe" Abdelrahman, Edwina Wilcox, Jay Duran, Adam Marcus, Themis Trilivas, Federico Peña, Ricky Pagan, Robert Apicella, Catherine Apicella, Cheryl LaRosa-Apicella, Miguel Olivio, Juan Pellot, Amy Pellot, Nicole Ford, Gardner Rivera, and Anna Remus for listening to my dumb ideas, acting in some of my horrible short films, and reading my work from time to time. You were more help to me than you could possibly know.

To Anna Badkhen: my constant supporter, my friend, for all of your endless advice. You've made me a better writer.

To Alysoun Roach, and Matthew Risoli, two teachers who made a major impact on me during a rough time. Thank you for caring and being passionate about literature.

To Barbara Beach, for helping us when we needed a break. You're the best.

Lastly, and dearest to my heart, to my wife, Tracy Beach-Diaz: this book would not have been written if it wasn't for you. It's that simple. I love you with all my heart.

Until the next one.

Giovanni Diaz

8/13/2019

ABOUT THE AUTHOR

Giovanni Diaz is the author of These Bright and Lovely Nightmares, Every Breath an Ending, Daryl P. Jenkins Accidentally Blows Up New York City, And Hell Followed With Them, Between the Perfect Lights, and Night Breathes You.

He is from New York City.

a

www.ingramcontent.com/pod-product-compliance
Lightning Source LLC
Chambersburg PA
CBHW020624020726
47494CB00001B/31